Praise for the Martin Preuss Mystery Series

"Levin has a sure hand. The reader can look forward to crisp dialog, fresh and precise descriptive detail . . . and a cast of characters he brings vividly to life."
　　—Rick Bailey, author of *The Enjoy Agenda: At Home and Abroad*, on *Cold Dark Lies*

"This quick-paced and muscular detective novel takes you through the Detroit streets, neighborhoods and alleyways with solid storytelling and a lot of tenderness."
　　—Linda Sienkiewicz, author of *In the Context of Love*, on *Cold Dark Lies*

"There aren't too many mystery writers who can touch us so deeply [or] as beautifully as Levin does in this story."
　　—Reader's Favorite, on *Cold Dark Lies*

"An engaging, emotional thriller that skillfully blends past and present. You'll be rooting for another Martin Preuss novel as soon as you finish!"
　　—Elizabeth Heiter, award-winning author of The Profiler Series, on *The Forgotten Child*

"Great series! With [*Guilt in Hiding*], author Donald Levin has combined his gift for superb storytelling with a complex intertwining of shadowy war crimes tied to contemporary corruptions. . . . This may be both the brightest and darkest tale in this riveting series."
　　—Peter Chiaramonte, author of *No Journey's End*

IN THE HOUSE OF NIGHT

POISON
TOE
PRESS

"MYSTERIES TO DIE FOR"

IN THE HOUSE OF NIGHT

DONALD LEVIN

For John — with best wishes, Donald Levin

A MARTIN PREUSS MYSTERY

Inquiries should be addressed to
Poison Toe Press
PO Box 206
1221 Bowers
Birmingham, Michigan 48012

ISBN: 978-0-9972941-7-0

Cover by Publish Pros
www.publishpros.com

First edition published 2020
Printed in the United States of America

*This book is dedicated in loving memory to Jamie Kril,
the model for "Toby Preuss"
and the guiding spirit of the Martin Preuss series*

Hate is a bottomless cup; I will pour and pour.
–Euripedes, *Medea*

Blessed is the covenant of love, the covenant of mercy, useless light
behind the terror, deathless song in the house of night.
–Leonard Cohen, *Book of Mercy*

Tuesday, February 12, 2013

1

Brittany Fortunato was not happy.

"Has anyone seen Charlie?" she asked.

No one had.

Charlie Bright, the recording secretary of the Woodland Park Improvement Association, had not missed a meeting in ten years. Tonight might be the exception.

The Association met on the second Tuesday of every month in the Media Center at the Roosevelt Elementary School in Ferndale, a city that lay beyond Eight Mile Road north of Detroit. Like many neighborhood associations, it had a small number of officers—a president, vice-president, and treasurer, in addition to the secretary—and a dedicated core of a dozen or so residents who attended every meeting.

Typically, the president would call the meeting to order shortly after seven. They would work through their agenda, and the evening would end with chatting, good-natured ribbing, and the newest gossip over plates of cookies and cups of coffee from the local Biggby Coffee.

Often they invited a guest to speak about issues of interest to the city's residents. Tonight's guest was the police chief of Ferndale, Nick Russo. The topic was local crime statistics.

Ferndale was exceptionally safe, especially considering its proximity to the larger metropolis of Detroit. So Russo saw his primary task tonight as calming nerves and assuring the residents that things were under control. A big, muscular man, he made an impressive sight in his blue full-dress uniform, complete with cap under his arm as he stood talking with attendees.

He seemed unruffled and relaxed.

Not so Brittany, the Association vice-president. The more people who said they didn't know Charlie Bright's whereabouts, the more agitated Brittany became.

"Brittany," the Association president said at last, "what's going on?"

The president's name was Elspeth Cunningham, and she tried but failed to keep the disapproval out of her voice. Brittany was a troublemaker while trying to appear reasonable and friendly.

What's her problem now? Elspeth wondered.

"Charlie isn't here yet," Brittany said. "We can't start without him."

Elspeth shot a look at the clock on the wall. Quarter after seven. "Odd," she agreed. "He's never late."

"Right?" Brittany said. "I talked to him this morning, he said he'd see me here. And we have to get started. I promised the chief we'd be done by nine."

"I'm yours as long as you need me," Russo said.

"But we can't start without Charlie," Brittany said again. "Who's gonna take the minutes?"

"I will," said a man seated at one of the kid-sized library tables, eager for the meeting to begin so he could get home in time to watch Rachel Maddow.

The Association officers looked at each other and shrugged. "Okay," Elspeth said. "Let's get started."

She called the meeting to order.

They adjourned at eight-thirty on the dot. Charlie Bright never showed.

"Now I'm really worried," Brittany said as they stood around the refreshment table. "This is totally unlike him."

"Maybe an emergency called him away," Elspeth offered.

"Charlie never misses a meeting," Brittany said. "Something's not right. I'm sure of it."

They all exchanged worried looks—Brittany's concern was contagious—and everyone's glance settled on Chief Russo.

"If you want," he said, "I can get somebody over to his house, make sure he's okay."

"Would you?" Brittany asked. The others' heads bobbed in agreement.

"Not a problem," said Russo. He pulled out his cell phone and turned away while he called the Ferndale Police Department dispatcher.

"I hope he's all right," someone said.

Russo disconnected and turned back to the group. "A unit'll swing by his house."

With the group slightly calmed, Elspeth unwrapped the tray of cookies and invited them all to dig in.

2

Patrol Officer Paul Vollmer stood on Charlie Bright's front porch in northwest Ferndale and waited.

When nobody answered the doorbell, which Vollmer heard ringing inside the house, he knocked hard on the substantial wooden entrance door.

Still no response.

He shone his flashlight through the dark living room windows. Vollmer couldn't see anyone moving inside.

He came down off the porch and walked around to the back. All the doors and windows were secure. A light shone in the kitchen but he couldn't see anyone there. Behind the house was a garage, but the door was closed and Vollmer couldn't see inside.

He walked around to the front again.

"Yoo-hoo!"

Vollmer turned and saw an older woman peeking around the storm door of a house across the street.

When she saw him looking at her, she waved him over.

He strolled across and she said, "Are you looking for Charlie Bright?"

"I am. Have you seen him?"

"Not today." She must have been in her late seventies or early eighties but her voice was high, almost girlish. She had silver hair set in plump curls and she held a wool coat bunched at her throat against the night's chill.

"Is that unusual?" Vollmer asked.

"Oh yes," the woman said. "I always see him during the day. Usually in the morning before he goes off for his day."

"But not today?"

She shook her head.

He looked back at the dark house. No car in the driveway or the street.

"Maybe he's out of town?" Vollmer suggested.

"He would have told me if he was going away. I always watch his house for him."

She opened her palm and showed a shiny brass key. "I have the key to his house, if you need it."

Vollmer thought for a moment.

On any other night he would let something like this go, but it came directly from the chief, so . . .

Better see it through.

He opened his notebook and said, "Can I get some information from you first?"

He smelled it as soon as he entered the front hall, a sweet scorched odor, like burning paper. There had been a fire in here.

Vollmer switched on his flashlight. The house was larger on the inside than it looked from the street. The front hall opened onto a stairway going up; to the left was a sprawling living room, and to the right was a dining room. The table there overflowed with piles of mail, some opened, some not.

"Hello," he called. "Ferndale Police. Anyone home?"

When there was no reply, he called again. "Ferndale Police. Mr. Bright? Is anybody here?"

Silence.

Vollmer went into the kitchen. No dirty dishes in the sink, the counters clean and tidy, the oven empty and cold. Vegetables in twisted shapes Vollmer had never seen before hung from the ceiling in wire baskets.

A door off the kitchen led to a stairway down to the basement. The burnt odor seemed to originate there.

Vollmer proceeded down the stairs into a basement that was as clean and uncluttered as the kitchen. Very different from mine, he thought; his own cellar was filled with boxes and tools and old chairs and end tables piled high from his wife's antique furniture refinishing sideline.

This one, in contrast, held orderly rows of bookshelves with hundreds of hardcover books. Behind one of the bookcases a cot had been set up.

A light was on in a room in the rear of the basement. The burnt smell was strongest here.

Vollmer looked into the room, which was set up as an office, with a desk and more bookshelves and file cabinets. On the desk, a laptop computer and printer had been smashed to pieces.

In the center of the floor was a large pile of ashes. Vollmer bent down; they were cool. They seemed to be the remnants of sheets of paper, curled and blackened but smashed down so the contents were unrecognizable.

The joists overhead were scorched, but had not caught fire. Fortunately for the house, and for the surrounding neighbors.

Sticking out from a pile of academic journals between the desk and a file cabinet were two running shoes connected to two legs.

A man's body.

Vollmer leaned in and looked into the grey face of an older man.

He felt for a pulse in the man's neck.

Nothing.

The man's skin was cold to the touch. His sweatshirt was dark with blood and seemed to have a dozen slashes through it.

Vollmer knew the detectives and fire inspector would not want him poking around here any longer than he had to. If this was Charlie Bright, he was very dead.

Vollmer called it in and went upstairs to secure the scene and wait for the cavalry.

Monday, February 25, 2013

3

Martin Preuss sighed.

The woman in the visitor's chair on the other side of his desk was interviewing for an associate detective's position in his agency. She had a state-issued investigator's license, but no police experience, no criminal justice training beyond an investigator's certificate program from Wayne County Community College, and a three-year trainee period in a private detective agency that Preuss knew was basically a front for an insurance fraud operation.

And she wouldn't get out of his office.

"If you'd just give me a chance," Angie Sturmer said, for what seemed like the ninth time, "I can show you what I'm capable of."

"I appreciate that, Ms. Sturmer. But I'm only in the interviewing stage right now. I want to see who's—"

"You won't regret it," she interrupted.

"I'm sure I won't."

Not so this interview, he thought.

"I'm a hard worker," Angie said, "and I can handle myself—I teach self-defense for women at the Y. And I can blend into any situation."

Yeah, Preuss thought, if you're undercover in the land of the giants.

She was tall, several inches taller than Preuss, and sturdily built with the wide body of a football lineman and a head of glossy black hair. An attractive woman, but definitely not one to blend into a crowd.

"Please," she said, "I need this job. I'm a single parent. My son is handicapped and his latest medicine is really expensive."

Ordinarily, a plea for pity wouldn't be a wise strategy with him. But this got Preuss's attention.

"Handicapped how?" he asked.

"He's hydrocephalic, with cerebral palsy. He has a shunt in his head to drain the fluid off his brain. But between that and the CP, he's got lots of problems."

Preuss thought of his own son, Toby, and the list of Toby's handicaps, including CP, microcephaly, scoliosis, cognitive impairments, visual limitations, and developmental delays.

To get Preuss's attention, "handicapped" turned out to be the magic word.

"How old is your son?" he asked.

"Fifteen."

Toby would be twenty-one in the fall. As a single parent of a special needs child, Preuss knew what she was dealing with.

"Okay," he said. "Look, thanks for coming in. Let me talk with my associate, and I'll be in touch."

"Do you know when? You'll be in touch, I mean?"

"Next week at the latest. Mr. Greene is having some medical issues, so we have to work around those, unfortunately."

"Oh no," she said, "I'm so sorry. I hope he'll be okay."

"So do we."

Preuss's partner in the firm, Manny Greene, was undergoing a course of chemotherapy for the throat cancer that had been diagnosed a few months ago. Preuss managed the firm by himself temporarily (at least he hoped it was temporary) but he was finding he needed more help than Rhonda Citron, the firm's administrative manager, could give him.

He had asked Rhonda to go into the field a few times on cases where they needed someone to conduct interviews for background checks, and to determine if the agency would take on a case or two. Rhonda performed like an ace.

Still, she had told him she wasn't interested in continuing field work; she wanted the stability of a desk job. Because the agency's reputation was growing and more people were coming to them than ever before, Preuss needed another investigator he could trust in the field as well as someone to answer the phones.

So he was looking for an associate to take over some projects for a few hours a week until Manny came back. None of his contacts wanted to work as long as he needed them to, since they were all employed as full-time investigators or police officers.

The woman he was speaking with now was loud, but something about her attitude impressed him. She made him feel as though she could be useful. Maybe it was even the assertive abrasiveness that so annoyed him.

And then there was her son . . . parents of handicapped kids need to stick together, he thought to himself.

"You have references on your resume?" he asked.

"Yessir. People I've done work for, and a couple attorneys who'll vouch for my character."

"You'll have no problem if we call them?"

"No sir."

He stood and she stood with him. "I'm available any time," she said. "My schedule's wide open."

He wanted to ask who watched her son while she was working, but he was pretty sure he wasn't allowed to do that. Toby lived in a group home, but Angie talked as if her son lived at home with her.

He walked her to the door. Her handshake was bone-crushing.

When she was gone, Rhonda said, "Well?"

"I thought she'd never leave."

"She seemed like a character."

"She was that."

Rhonda was a bit of a character herself. She was small and thin and wore an oversized black turtleneck and black leggings, her standard outfit no matter the season. Her hair was piled high in an arrangement of curlicues and waves bleached almost white.

"Sorry, Martin," Rhonda said. "That was my fault. I saw her resume, but she called up and talked her way into an interview."

"That might be a good sign. She's persistent."

He handed her Angie's resume. "Why don't you call a couple of her references?"

"Seriously?"

"I want to get an objective take on her."

"Martin . . ."

"Call?"

She shrugged. "Okay."

"Anybody else for today?"

"No interviews," she said, "but you have an appointment at four. A new client."

"Good. Have we heard from Manny?"

"We won't. This is his chemo day. He's not always at his best afterwards."

He had thought to stop in to see Manny at his home for a few minutes, but he forgot it was a treatment day. His wife Lila wouldn't want him disturbed.

"Let me know if you do hear," he said. "I'm going out to grab some lunch before the appointment."

"It's good to eat lunch once in a while," Rhonda said. "Even if it is almost dinner time."

"Glad you approve."

He often skipped eating when he was working. With only the two of them in the office, she made it her project to improve his diet.

"Just saying. I know you."

"Bring you back a sandwich?"

"I'm good. Enjoy your lunch."

"Going to try."

"Do or don't do," Rhonda said. "There is no try."

She gave him an overly sweet smile.

He raised a hand of surrender and went to lunch.

4

The schedule Rhonda prepared for him contained one name, but two men came for the meeting.

One was short and squat in a dark grey suit, with a round face and full salt-and-pepper beard. He wore a blue and white knit yarmulke on the crown of his head. Rhonda introduced him as Rabbi Shmuel Rifkin—"Sam," he said as he shook Preuss's hand.

The other man she introduced as Father Lloyd Corrigan. "Lloyd," he said. He was taller and more florid than the rabbi, and wore a tweed sportscoat over an open-neck shirt with no clerical collar. Neither man had overcoats in the unseasonably mild February weather.

"Can we get you a coffee or something to drink?" Preuss asked.

Both men shook their heads and Preuss ushered them into his office with a nod to Rhonda, who gave him a wink in return. Good luck with this, her wink told him.

He closed the office door and took his seat behind the desk. The two men sat in the visitors' chairs facing him.

"Bet you didn't know you were going to have such an ecumenical crew," Corrigan said.

"No," Preuss said. "In fact, I was expecting one client today."

"We thought it would be okay if we both came," Rifkin said.

"Not a problem," Preuss said. "What brings you in?"

"Before we get started," the rabbi said, "let me ask, how is Manny?"

"He seems to be holding his own," Preuss said.

"We go way back, Manny and I," Rifkin said.

"Terrible thing, cancer," the priest said, "I'm praying for him."

"I'm sure he appreciates that," Preuss said.

"It's one God, after all," the rabbi replied, "regardless how we're dressed when we talk to him."

"Amen," said Corrigan.

Preuss stifled the urge to smile at these two, but instead directed the conversation back to the business at hand.

"How can I help?"

Suddenly reticent, Rifkin and Corrigan looked at each other. They were trying to decide who should talk first.

"Rabbi," Preuss said, "you made the appointment, so maybe you can start?"

"Sure. I called Manny when I wanted some guidance," Rifkin said, "and he told me I should speak with you."

"Okay."

"It's about a mutual friend. A friend of all of ours—Lloyd, Manny, myself. We all take part in an Interfaith Colloquium once a month."

"We talk about subjects that cut across our religious boundaries," Corrigan said. "We have priests, rabbis, pastors, imams, Buddhists, lay people, atheists if they want to come. We're open to everyone."

"Our friend is Charles Bright," Rifkin said, "may his memory be a blessing. He died a few weeks ago. He was found in his home in Ferndale. Suspicious circumstances, as they say. Manny told us you're from Ferndale, maybe you heard about it?"

"Of course," Preuss said. Charles Bright's death in his basement shocked the quiet community. Preuss had been the senior officer in the Ferndale PD Detective Bureau. Had he not retired from the force, he would have led the investigation.

"Very sorry to hear," he said.

"Yes, thanks," Rifkin said. "No one seems to know what happened."

"I assume the police are investigating?"

"The Ferndale police and the Oakland County Sheriff's Office," Corrigan said. "But they haven't gotten anywhere. We were hoping you'd have more luck if you looked into it."

"We don't like to get involved in active police investigations," Preuss said. "The police especially don't like it."

"No," Rifkin said, "that I can understand."

"The thing is," Corrigan said, "they all seem to be convinced this is a domestic-type situation. A sexual encounter gone bad."

"And you're not?"

"We're not. But they say they have to go where the evidence takes them."

"Who told you that?"

"The woman from the Sheriff's Office."

Oh, don't say it, Preuss silently pleaded.

Please don't say it.

"A detective named Emma Blalock," Corrigan said.

Damn.

He said it.

"I see." He tried to keep a poker face.

Not very well, apparently. "Do you know her?" the rabbi asked. "You look like you might know her."

"I do," Preuss said. "We've worked together a few times."

"Manny told us you used to be a detective in Ferndale."

Emma and Preuss had a history, which Preuss preferred not to go into at the moment.

Instead, he said, "She's very good."

"Well," Corrigan continued, "Manny said you are, too."

Preuss inclined his head at the compliment.

"Sam and I both think it's more complicated than the police do," Corrigan said.

"How so?"

"Charles was a widower," Corrigan said, "who still loved his wife. He certainly wasn't in the habit of bringing home strangers for assignations."

"That's what they think happened?"

"Yes," Rifkin said. "They said there was no sign of a break-in, so they think Charlie let in whoever killed him. Also the extent of his injuries—the police say he was killed in a fury that points to a domestic crime."

"Who's on the case for Ferndale?"

"A detective named Trombley," Corrigan said.

"I know him, too," Preuss said. "Quite well, as a matter of fact. Look, these are two excellent investigators. If they say this looks like a domestic, I'd be inclined to believe them."

"But we both think there's more to this than meets the eye," Corrigan said. "And they won't move on what we're telling them."

"So we're hoping you will," Rifkin said.

Manny's two friends sat looking at him, silent and plaintive.

"I can look into the corners," Preuss said, "as long as I don't interfere with the main investigation."

"That's all we're asking," Rifkin said.

"All right then, why don't you fill me in on the background. And then I'll turn you over to Rhonda for the financial arrangements."

"Wonderful," Corrigan said.

"I hope you don't have dinner plans, Mr. Preuss," Rifkin said. "Filling in the background is going to take a while."

It was past six when Preuss gave them to Rhonda to sign the client's agreement and pay the retainer.

After they left, Preuss sat on the sofa in Rhonda's reception area. "Thanks for staying," he told her.

"No problem," she said. "Those guys were like a comedy team."

"Or the start of a joke. A priest and a rabbi walk into a private detective's office . . ."

He gave her a summary of the case and said, "This can wait till the morning, but I'd like you to get some information for me to start with."

"No prob."

"Everything you can find about the crime. Newspaper articles, police reports if you can lay your hands on them—whatever's out there."

"Piece of cake. I'll do it as soon as I get in."

"The other thing is, this has to be on the QT. It would be especially nice if it didn't get back to the Ferndale PD."

"I hear you. Anything else?"

"That's it. Why don't you take off?"

"Yeah, I'm done in for the day," she said.

"Feeling okay?"

"Oh yeah. Just tired." She straightened the papers on her desk, logged off her computer, and waved goodbye.

He remained where he sat. He let his head loll back and basked in the quiet. Everyone else in the office building seemed to have gone. The place was silent—no voices, no footsteps, no elevator sounds.

On any other night, he would have roused himself to visit Toby. But tonight his son was off on one of his monthly outings with his housemates. They were going bowling, and Preuss (who liked going with Toby on his outings) had begged off because he didn't know what time he would finish with his appointment. He didn't want to disappoint Toby by not being able to make it.

He made himself a cup of Rhonda's everyday Maxwell House and took it into his office. He opened a new case file on his desktop and began entering his notes from Rifkin and Corrigan.

According to his two friends, Bright was Dr. Charles Bright, professor emeritus of history at Wayne State University in Detroit. Rifkin said Bright was a specialist in labor history who had met Jimmy Hoffa not long before the labor leader disappeared in the mid-1970s.

As well as taking part in the monthly Interfaith Colloquium, Bright was also involved in local peace and social justice movements. He belonged to the Michigan Peace Fellowship Center, and took part in peace demonstrations around the area.

Rifkin said Bright was a *landsman*—a fellow Jew—who was also a practicing Buddhist.

Bright's wife, Dorothy, died six years ago from cancer.

"When he lost her, it devastated him," Rifkin had said. "I don't think he ever came to terms with it."

"They were inseparable," said Corrigan.

"Children?" Preuss had asked.

Corrigan said, "There's a son, but Charlie hardly ever talked about him."

"Any reason why?"

"Well," Rifkin said, "Charlie was a very private person, and evidently the boy hasn't been doing well for a while."

"You say 'boy' . . ."

"Of course, he's no boy. He's in his thirties or forties, right, Lloyd?"

Corrigan nodded.

"In what way isn't he doing well?" Preuss asked.

"All Charlie would say was, 'Larry's got some problems,'" Corrigan said. "He'd never go into any more detail."

"The son's name is Larry?" Preuss asked. "Same last name?"

"Yes," Corrigan said.

"Do you know how to get hold of him?"

"Charlie would make veiled references to Larry being homeless," Rifkin said, "but he'd never go into any detail. He'd always wave it away."

Rifkin imitated the gesture, a hand sweeping away any questions. "You could tell it ate him up inside."

"So you don't know if Larry even knows about his father?" Preuss asked.

Both men shook their heads.

Neither one could think of anyone who would want to harm their friend. Neither man had ever heard him talk about picking up strangers, men or women, and taking them home.

"Though he did have a big heart," Rifkin said. "He often talked about the temptation he felt when he saw a poor soul begging at the side of the road. He always wanted to bring them home for a good meal or a soft bed. But we always talked about the problems it might cause, and he always seemed to understand."

"The investigators think he brought somebody home and it turned nasty?"

"Yes," Rifkin said. "But Charlie had a clear understanding of the dangers in doing that. And he wouldn't do it."

"Sometimes danger is its own reward," Preuss said.

"Very true," Rifkin said. "But Charlie wasn't that kind of guy."

"Did he have any vices you know of? Gambling, drugs, drink?"

"Inconceivable," Corrigan said. "He took better care of himself than anyone I know. He was a vegan, he exercised, he never drank or took drugs."

"Clean liver," Preuss said, remembering this was what he heard the year before about another man whom a client wanted investigated. He turned out to have had a secret life nobody knew about. Few things were inconceivable about anyone.

"Anybody else I should speak with?" Preuss asked. "Other friends? Any other family?"

"Not that I know of," Corrigan said. Rifkin agreed, and said, "Charlie knew hundreds of people. I couldn't begin to tell you everybody he knew, or who knew him."

"But nobody he was especially close to?"

"He was a very private man," Rifkin said. "Except . . ."

He and Corrigan shared another look.

"What?" Preuss asked.

"There was a woman in the picture," Rifkin said. "Charlie would mention her every so often. But neither Lloyd nor I knew her."

"What would he say about her?"

"Oh," Rifkin said, "that he saw her or talked with her. Nothing intimate. But he never used to talk about women other than his wife, you see."

"Do you have a name?"

"Ruth Anne Krider," Rifkin said. "She was one of his graduate students at Wayne."

"And you think Charles and she were involved?"

"I don't see him falling for a young woman like this one," Rifkin said.

"I, on the other hand," Corrigan said, "am convinced they were more than professor and grad student."

"You think they were intimate?"

"I do."

"Why?"

"The way he talked about her. I could tell."

You with your vast experience with women, Preuss thought.

But he said, "Has anyone been in touch with her?"

"I gave the police her name," Corrigan said. "I'm assuming they've followed up on it. We haven't contacted her."

Preuss said nothing, but resolved to talk to Trombley about the woman to see if the police had learned more about the nature of Bright's relationship with her.

When he finished writing up his notes from the meeting with the two clergymen, he reread what he had written. And knew where his first call should go.

5

Sandra Trombley welcomed him into their home in the Dales, the quiet group of streets (Farmdale, Flowerdale, Gardendale, and Meadowdale) just south of Nine Mile Road in Ferndale. The two Trombley girls were screaming bloody murder upstairs.

Sandy shook her head as he entered. "Whatever you do, Martin," she said, "don't ever have girls."

"No immediate plans," Preuss said.

"They've been going at each other like this all day."

"And you've been playing referee?"

Before she could answer, the screaming upstairs rose another decibel.

Trombley came up from the basement. "What's going on up there?" he asked.

"Scuse me," she told Preuss. "I've got two heads that need knocking together." And she zipped up the stairs.

"My brother," Trombley said. They embraced in a tight hug. "Get you anything?"

"I'm good, thanks."

"Some peace and quiet, maybe?"

"What is going on up there?"

"Just those two. Even when there's no drama, they'll do whatever they can to add some. Sandy'll take care of it. Let's go downstairs."

Preuss followed him down to the basement, where he kept an office.

"Sit," Trombley said. A pair of chairs faced each other beside Trombley's desk, and they each took one.

"How's things?" Preuss asked.

Trombley rubbed a hand across his face. He was model-handsome, with fine features and perfect taut caramel skin over crisply-sculpted cheekbones.

"Same old same old," he said.

Preuss retired from the Ferndale PD Detective Bureau when the then-head of the Bureau, Nick Russo, was promoted to chief of police and he hand-picked the next chief of detectives, Stanley Chrysler. Russo had tried to get Preuss fired when he ran the Detective Bureau, but the then-chief of police, William Warnock, saved him. When Warnock retired, Preuss lost his protector and he knew no one would save him from Russo's wrath projected through Chrysler.

So he left before he could be cashiered.

Trombley was managing under the new leadership, but it was stressful adjusting to the new Bureau chief, who was—Trombley had told Preuss—a total micromanager.

"How's my man Toby?" Trombley asked.

"Doing well. I'm going to see him when we're through here."

"Give him a hug for me."

"Will do."

"So what's up?"

"I had a visit today from a couple of new clients," Preuss said. "Friends of Charles Bright."

Trombley said nothing.

"They told me you caught the case."

"Right."

"They want me to look a little deeper into what happened. I told them it's an active police investigation, so I can't step into it."

Trombley nodded approval. But Preuss could tell he was waiting for the other shoe to drop.

Preuss dropped it. "I told them what I could do was take a look around the edges as long as I stayed out of your way."

"Uh-huh."

"I wanted to give you a head's up. And maybe ask you some questions about where you are with it."

"The investigation?"

"Yeah."

Trombley moved a stapler from one side of his desk to the other.

"Man," he said, "this puts me in an awkward position."

"I know. That's why I wanted to talk to you about it."

"Don't suppose I could get you to reconsider?"

"Taking the case?"

"Yeah."

Before Preuss could reply, Sandy's voice came from the top of the basement landing. "Reg?"

She came the rest of the way down the stairs, peeking around a column to where they were sitting.

"You guys need anything down here?"

Trombley looked at Preuss with raised brows, but Preuss shook his head.

"No, we're good, baby. Thanks."

"Thanks, Sandy," Preuss said.

"Sorry I had to run upstairs, Martin," she said. "I know that was rude."

"Not a problem."

"You want anything, give me a shout."

"Will do," Preuss said.

"Kids settled down?" Trombley asked.

"For now."

"You the best."

She scoffed and went back upstairs.

"She really is," Preuss said.

"Got that right."

Then, after a moment of pained silence, Trombley said, "So, Martin . . . Chrysler told me not to share any information with you. Not only about this case. About anything."

"Okay."

"He told me if it ever got back to him I gave you anything at all—especially about an open investigation—he'd bring me up on charges."

"What kind of charges?"

Trombley ticked them off on his fingers. "Insubordination. Discreditable conduct. Disobedience to orders. Neglect of duty. Any other bullshit charge he can think of."

"He's not going to punish the best detective in the Bureau. And the only black one."

"Maybe you think he won't," Trombley said, "but he assured me he'd do it if it ever got back to him I was feeding you information. He's not playing. You know I love you, man, but I can't take the risk."

"No, I get it."

"He clamped down on whatever gets out from the Bureau in general. He wants to be the conduit for everything."

"Sure. And I get it, I won't ask. I'm letting you know, so you won't be surprised if we cross paths."

"All right," Trombley said. "I appreciate it."

"Sorry, man. I don't want to make it hard for you."

"Is what it is. I were you, Martin, I'd make sure we don't cross paths."

It wasn't a threat but a reminder Preuss would be on shaky ground in this case.

"Matter of fact," Trombley went on, "I were you, I'd tell your clients you changed your mind, and give them their money back."

"Well, that's not going to happen."

"I know."

"I'll let you get back to your family," Preuss said, and stood.

Trombley stood, too, and led Preuss to the stairway.

Trombley paused at the bottom step. "You know I'd help you if I could."

"I know that."

"But seriously, man, what I can tell you is this. You got to stay out of the way here. You don't want Chrysler finding out you're anywhere near this. He's not just going to go after me. He's going to come after you, too. And hard."

6

Everybody was yelling in Toby's house—the residents, the staff, even the visitors.

Toby lived in his group home with five other young men and women who were handicapped and considered to be "technologically dependent"—who, like Toby, depended on some function of technology for their survival. Tonight's bowling adventure had been one of the monthly outings for all the residents who weren't tethered to ventilators.

Now all the bowlers were over-stimulated from the trip, so they were yelling and growling and carrying on happily. The staff and visitors weren't as loud, but they were shouting to each other to be heard over the din.

Toby was particularly excited. He lay on his bath chair in the full whirlpool tub in the bathroom, vocalizing at the top of his lungs.

Preuss stuck his head into the room and said, "Man, are you noisy!"

Recognizing his father's voice set Toby off on an even louder outburst. He couldn't articulate words, but he could say syllables and verbalize sounds, and that's what he was doing now.

"Toby had a great time at the bowling alley," his aide, Melissa, said.

"So I hear."

"I thought a bath might calm him down, but not so much."

Preuss leaned over the bathtub. Toby looked at him out of the corner of his eye, which is where he could see best. He had limited vision because of his deteriorating optic nerve, but his other senses were good, especially his hearing.

Preuss planted a kiss on the side of Toby's face, warm, wet, and soapy. Toby wagged his head back and forth happily. He was microcephalic so his head was smaller than normal, a perfect oval setting off his deep brown, almond-shaped eyes. His nose had a slight Brandoesque bump on the bridge.

To Preuss he was beautiful beyond description.

"Did you have fun tonight?" Preuss asked.

Toby vocalized something that sounded very much like, "Yeah!" As a student of his son's communications skills, Preuss could usually figure out his son's mood by the inflections of his vocalizations, his facial expressions, and his general body language. Sometimes it was easy, like now.

"We're almost done here," Melissa said. "Just need to rinse off."

"I'll go lay out his pajamas," Preuss said.

Preuss went into Toby's room and discovered Melissa had already laid out his son's PJs. So he straightened up the room—setting Toby's CDs in order, folding Toby's clean clothes in his bureau drawers—and then picked up the $40 garage sale acoustic guitar he kept in the corner and began to play. It was way out of tune, so he gave it a quick tuning by ear and started picking Dylan's "Don't Think Twice."

As always, playing music calmed him. Preuss had left Trombley's house worried that the case might bring him into conflict—again—with the Ferndale PD. Preuss was still upset at the way he felt he had to separate from the department, and he had suspected that the Bright case would dredge up all his bad feelings.

Toby, too, had quieted down by the time Melissa got him into his wheelchair and rode him back into his room, but as soon as he heard his father's guitar he took a deep snorting breath and began screaming again.

Melissa and Preuss both gave a shout of laughter.

"Toby, you're so funny," she said. "You're never gonna sleep tonight."

Toby squealed in joy, opening his mouth in a crooked smile showing the goofy, charming gap between his front teeth. His laugh was the sweetest sound in the world.

"How was school?" Preuss asked, and found the notebook in Toby's school bag with his teacher's daily note.

"'Toby had a great day,'" Preuss read aloud from Ms. Rice's note. "'We learned about plants, and Toby got 100 on the quiz!'"

Toby had a computerized communications device called a Dynavox. It would replay previously recorded messages Toby could hear whispered in his ear; when the message he wanted to say came around, he hit a switch with his forearm and the device would speak out the message he requested. He used it to communicate in class during their activities, like the test.

"A hundred," Preuss said.

Toby laughed again. He was in a great mood.

"Are you gonna ruin the class average? Be careful, your friends won't like you anymore."

"I never had that problem," Melissa said. "You're way smarter than me, Toby."

Preuss leaned down to wrap his son in a hug. He could smell the apple fragrance in Toby's hair from his shampoo.

"Hey—know what?" Preuss said. "I love you very much!"

Toby hummed his happy reply, which Preuss interpreted to mean: I love you, too, Dad.

The perfect ending to a day, Preuss thought.

There were times when he wished he could stay with his son forever. This was one of them. And today wasn't even one of the worst days. But watching his son's broad grin brought back to Preuss how *present* his son was, how in the moment. It was a skill Preuss wished he could learn from the boy.

As soon as Preuss put on Toby's Judy Collins CDs, Toby calmed down. It was the music he listened to each night. The routine as much as the singer's gorgeous voice was relaxing.

Preuss stayed with his son until Toby fell asleep, then he took himself home and played blues on his red Les Paul fed into his head through a pair of earphones, drowning out all the thoughts, all the worries, all the voices.

The memories.

The demons.

When he grew tired, he turned off the amp, put the guitar back in its case, and went upstairs to bed.

But sleep wouldn't come.

His thoughts kept circling back to his new case, which, he had to admit, he found interesting. Though all he knew about the man was what he had learned today, Preuss already felt a connection with Charles Bright. Both he and Preuss were widowers whose wives had died around the same number of years ago, both were retired from their main careers, both were private men, both had problematic relationships with lost sons—Preuss's older son Jason was long and angrily out of touch . . . would these synchronicities mean Preuss would be able to get inside Bright's head?

He hoped so.

Beyond the details of the case, which would emerge in the course of his investigation, there was also the *fact* of it. He put aside his concerns over possible clashes with his former department and concentrated on the feeling he got at the beginning of every case. There was always an excitement, an eagerness to proceed, to unpack the secrets and realign the separate pieces into an understandable pattern.

To be challenged.

To be tested.

It was almost like the exciting sense of possibility that existed in the beginning of a relationship.

Except in Preuss's experience, his investigations came to much more satisfying conclusions.

Which—he told himself as he slid into sleep—wouldn't be hard.

Tuesday, February 26, 2013

7

Rhonda was already in the office the next morning when Preuss arrived. He had stopped to kiss Toby good morning and help get him ready for school, then took Eleven Mile west toward Telegraph where the agency's offices were.

Rhonda had made a pot of Manny's premium Ethiopian coffee. Its rich, chocolatey perfume filled the area where her desk was.

Coffee never tasted as good as it smelled, Preuss thought.

Nothing was ever as good as it promised. Though Manny would give him an argument about his coffee. Manny was, as he himself would be the first to admit, a terrible coffee snob.

"Manny coming in?" he asked.

"He called a little while ago," Rhonda said. "Said he's going to try and stop in later."

"Did you tell him, 'Do or don't do, there is no try'?"

"No. I save that wisdom for you."

Manny Greene was Rhonda's uncle. She had been a promising law student until a series of nervous breakdowns forced her out of school. Manny gave her what he thought was going to be a temporary job in his office until she got herself together. To his dismay, she found she enjoyed the work so much she abandoned plans to return to law school.

"He must be feeling better. He say when he'd be here?"

"Later this afternoon, depending how things go."

"Great. Soon as I get organized, I'm going out to do some interviews. I'll see him when I get back."

"Before you go off detecting," Rhonda said, "we got a call from Seymour Hersch. He said he needs somebody for a surveillance job tonight."

Hersch was the attorney Manny did exclusive work for before Preuss joined Greene Investigations and the agency became Greene & Preuss. The cases had been mostly Social Security and accident investigations. After Preuss joined him, Manny expanded the services they could offer, and their client base expanded as well.

"Except the guy Manny always uses isn't available," Rhonda said.

"Anybody else free?"

"Everybody on the list's either busy or not interested. Shall I call Hersch back and let him know we have to take a pass?"

"I'd prefer not to turn down a job."

"Maybe we can throw it to one of the people we've been interviewing? Test them out?"

"There's a thought."

"It's a local job," she said, "suspected insurance fraud. This guy hired Hersch to appeal a disability turndown, but Hersch thinks the guy's a fake. Wants somebody to sit on him, see what he does."

"You know what," Preuss said, "call the woman who was here yesterday."

Rhonda looked stricken. "*Angie?*"

"Yeah."

"Does she even have a PI license?"

"Of course. She showed it to me. Give her first refusal, anyway. Be a good way to see what kind of work she does. Overnight surveillance, all she has to do is stay awake."

"Even that might be too much for her," Rhonda said.

"Call her, please?"

"Seriously?"

When he didn't answer, Rhonda sighed theatrically.

"What's the matter?"

"I was not impressed by her."

"And yet you hide it so well," Preuss said. "Let's give her a chance." He knew Rhonda was right, but he couldn't stop thinking about Angie's son.

"Did you have a chance to check her references?"

"Not yet. I will now," she said.

In his office, Preuss returned a few calls, follow-ups on cases he had finished: a home health aide who was suspected of stealing from her charge, a 98-year-old man (Preuss found proof she was stealing), and an owner of a chain of jewelry stores who wanted a background investigation to see if a potential manager he wanted to hire had any skeletons in his closet (he didn't).

When he was caught up, Preuss turned his attention to a call he wasn't looking forward to.

He had her business card in his drawer.

The last time he had spoken with her, Inspector Emma Blalock had been promoted to head the Oakland County Sheriff's Office Special Investigations Unit. He stared at the raised printing on the card, remembering how she had pursued him for a relationship he wasn't interested in a few years ago, before he knew she was still married. Her husband was one of Reg Trombley's best friends. Trombley thought Preuss was the pursuer instead of the other way around, and it turned into a source of friction between them.

They worked through it eventually, but Emma had never forgiven Preuss for spurning her.

In the years since, when investigations had brought them together, she was always frosty. He would have preferred not to make the call, but he did need to speak with her about Charles Bright. She might not tell him any more than Reg could, but still (he told himself) business was business.

He was relieved when his call went straight to voicemail and he heard her deep, silky voice inviting him to leave a message.

"Emma," he said, "Martin Preuss. I need to speak with you about a case I'm working on. Give me a call when you have a minute?"

Before disconnecting, he left his number for her—hoping the formality of the message would enforce the distance between them.

Rhonda appeared in his doorway. "Okay," she said, "so I called three of Angie's references."

"And?"

"One said, and I quote, 'What you see is what you get.'"

"What's that mean?"

"He said she's not very polished, a little uncouth, but she's a decent investigator."

"Promising."

"Another one said she's smart and resourceful, but again he said she's got some rough edges. Last one said be careful. Said she's 'a magnet for trouble.' Exact quote."

"Two out of three. Give her a call. See what she says."

Charles Bright's home was in northwest Ferndale, not far from the Kaufmans. They were the family whose little girl Madison had gone missing five or so years before. It had been a huge case for Preuss and catastrophic for the family.

Bright's house was a large forest green Dutch colonial with a porch the width of the front. If there had been yellow police tape across the door at one time, it was gone, either ripped down or blown away. The two towering white pines on either side of the front of the house gave the setting a damp, cottage-like feel.

A typical middle-class home in a section of Ferndale that had grown more upper-middle-class over the years.

On a whim, he knocked on the door. Of course no one answered.

Nor did any of the neighbors respond to his knocks. The police would have canvassed the area already, he knew. If anybody could tell them anything, they would have already jumped on the information.

Just as well, he thought. In case the police followed up, there wouldn't be anyone to tell them a snoopy private investigator named Preuss was prowling the neighborhood.

What Preuss did see were two lawn signs in front of Bright's home. On one was a stylized drawing of Martin Luther King, Jr., along with his quote, "Injustice anywhere is a threat to justice everywhere." On the other sign was a photograph of Gandhi with a quote from him: "I have always held that social justice, even to the least and the lowliest, is impossible of attainment by force."

Preuss looked closer on each sign and saw both were from the Michigan Peace Fellowship Center and Gallery. He remembered Rifkin and Corrigan talking about how involved Bright was with them.

As good a place to start as any, he thought.

8

The Michigan Peace Fellowship Center occupied a former storefront on Grand Circus Park in downtown Detroit, between the new baseball stadium on one side and the Central United Methodist Church on the Woodward side. He parked in the lot behind the church and walked around to the front.

Inside the Center was an art gallery displaying an exhibit, "Guns: Artists Respond." Paintings and drawings of the many woes wrought by guns filled the walls, with an emphasis on pointless bloodshed.

"Hello."

A woman stood behind a desk at the rear of the gallery. She raised a hand when he looked her way. "Welcome to our Peace Center."

He approached her and introduced himself. "I'm a private investigator. Can I speak with you for a minute about Charles Bright?"

"Of course."

"I understand he was a member?"

"One of our founding members."

"Did you know him?"

"Quite well. What a tragedy, what happened. Such a lovely man."

"Sorry, what is your name?"

"Annie Anderson." She reached out a hand and they shook. She was small, grey-haired, and thin as a nail.

"I'm assisting the police," he said. "I'm looking to speak with someone who knew him."

"I'm your girl," she said. "Let's sit back here."

She led him back to her desk.

"So," she said when they were seated. "What can I tell you?" She had a soft, comforting voice, perfect for a Peace Center.

"Have the Ferndale police spoken with you?" he asked.

"No," she said. "Nobody's talked to me."

"When was the last time you saw Charles?"

She thought for a moment, then said, "At the opening of this show. About a month and a half ago."

She opened her desk drawer and pulled out a postcard and handed it to him. "January 11th," she said. "This was the reception. It was the last time I saw him."

"Did you talk to him?"

"For a minute. Just to say hi, how are you, like that."

"How did he seem? Did he say anything was bothering him?"

"No, but he wouldn't. He wasn't a complainer. He was always cheerful, always optimistic."

"Did he say if he was having a problem with anybody?"

She thought again, and shook her head. "He was his usual self, like I said. Oh, it was horrible, when we heard about it."

"It was," he agreed. "Is there anyone else he was close to here?"

"We all knew him. Some better than others, I suppose. But he was well-liked and well-respected. I'm the only one here right now, but I can give you some names of other people who knew him."

"That would be helpful."

She started writing a list. She looked up phone numbers in a Center membership directory on her desk. "I'd give you my directory," she said, "but it's my only copy."

"No worries."

It took her a few minutes but she handed it over. "Names and numbers. Can you read my writing?"

"I can," he said.

He skimmed through her tiny, cramped handwriting. The names were mostly women, with a handful of men. Peace was women's work, to judge from the membership of this Center.

"Annie," he said, "you told me you knew him well. Do you know if he was seeing anyone, on this list or not?"

"Seeing romantically?" She gave an easy chuckle. "You didn't know Charles, did you?"

"I didn't."

"Well, he was still in love with his late wife. I don't think he'd ever consider seeing another woman."

The buzzer on the front door sounded and a young couple walked in and began chattering about the exhibit.

"I should see if they need help," Annie said. "Anything else I can tell you?"

"No, this is great. Thanks a million. If you think of anything else, could you give me a call?"

He handed her a business card and she held it up. "I've got your number," she said.

Instead of going back to his office to make the calls, he left the Explorer parked in the lot behind the church and walked the two long blocks down Woodward to Campus Martius Park. Might as well enjoy the day. The temperature was in the mid-50s.

Because of the mild weather, the ice-skating rink was a large oval puddle. He bought an overpriced coffee from the snack bar and settled into a chair at a wrought-iron table with his phone and notebook.

First he sat for a few minutes. He could almost smell spring in the air, feel the mellowing of the light as the season began to change.

He thought about his conversation with Annie. He envied men like Charles Bright, whose love for their departed wives could survive even death.

Then Preuss thought of his own dead wife, Jeanette. He had never been with another woman either, since her death. He came close to considering it twice: once with his former colleague from the Ferndale PD, Janie Cahill, the Department's youth officer, and before that with Shelley Larkin, a young reporter he met on the Kaufman case.

Neither relationship went anywhere, though Janey was the more serious possibility. Both felt the strong attraction between them, but they tacitly decided not to act on it because she was married.

And because Preuss was, well, Preuss.

Once she separated from her husband—even though he still lived in their basement—they talked about letting their mutual attraction loose and getting more involved. But she reconciled with her husband before anything could happen between them.

Otherwise, Preuss had been alone, except for Toby, since Jeanette died. Jason was still alive—he supposed—but the boy had been away and out of touch since Jeanette's death. Jason blamed Preuss for the accident that killed her, though he was nowhere near the highway where the drunk driver hit the car carrying Jeanette, Jason, and Toby.

As soon as he was released from the hospital, Jason left and never came back.

Jeanette had been gone almost seven years, now . . . the same amount of time since Preuss stopped drinking. He knew if he had stopped drinking before she died instead of after, she would still be alive; the argument that drove her out of the house with the boys would never have happened.

But as his former chief William Warnock used to say, if things were different, they wouldn't be the same.

Preuss had never gone with another woman not because he was still devoted to Jeanette (they weren't doing well as a couple; if she had lived they would probably have divorced), but because he had lost the urge for seeing other women.

No, he corrected himself, that's not correct. He didn't lose the urge, he lost the expectation that any good would come from it. It left him facing a long and lonely life, but he thought he was at peace with the prospect.

A noisy motorcyclist getting a jump on the season roared by. Preuss turned to Annie Anderson's list and started his calls.

He contacted everyone. Most of the people were retired, and the majority were either at home or reachable through their cell phones.

His initial plan was to set up meetings because he liked talking in person. But everyone he spoke with was happy to talk right then, so he did his interviews over the phone.

Through the conversations, Preuss found out more about Charles Bright:

He was one of the top bridge players in the state; he was an avid golfer; his peace activism went way back—he had been arrested protesting the Viet Nam, Iraq, and Afghanistan wars; he had been a tenured full professor of history at Wayne, as well as an active member of the University Senate and the local chapter of the American Association of University Professors, the professional union for college professors; he won the University Distinguished Teaching Award several times during his career; he retired as an emeritus professor of history four years ago; he was a dedicated vegan; and he had been faithful to the memory of his wife since she died.

One of the people he talked with expanded on something Rifkin and Corrigan had mentioned. Bright was a practicing Buddhist, who spent more time at the Zen temple than he did with the people whom Preuss had spent the afternoon tracking down.

"The temple in Troy?" Preuss asked.

"No, Charlie went to the one in Hamtramck. He tried the one in Troy, but he liked Hamtramck better. He liked the grittier feel. If you want to know about Charlie Bright," the man said, "seek ye no further than the Metropolitan Zen Center."

9

"It wasn't simply the setting that attracted Charles, of course," the Buddhist said.

He was portly in his grey robes, with a round, bald head and a full white goatee that hung down and fanned out about a foot below his chin. He introduced himself as Roshi John Ross, the abbot of the center.

They sat cross-legged on cushions on the floor in his office, a sparse room off the large meditation area formed by shoji screens. It was empty now, but the rough-hewn planks of the floor were laid out with meditation cushions in orderly rows, waiting for the participants in the afternoon sitting.

Roshi Ross sipped from a small cup of tea. He had offered a cup to Preuss, who declined.

"One of his friends told me understanding his connection to the center was central to understanding him," Preuss said.

Roshi Ross took this in. "Perhaps. But we're all composed of multiple personas, aren't we? Multiple masks," he added, for the benefit of what he perceived to be Preuss's limited vocabulary.

"You've heard what happened to him, I assume?" Preuss asked.

"Oh, yes."

"What can you tell me about him?"

"What do you want to know?"

"What kind of man he was. What your impression of him is. If, in fact, understanding his connection here is important to understanding the man. Whatever might help me find out what happened to him."

"That's what you're doing?"

"Yes."

Roshi Ross made a show of taking a thoughtful sip from his teacup.

"He was a searcher," the abbot said at last, "as we all are here."

"Meaning what?"

"What does 'searcher' mean?" He cocked an eyebrow.

I'm not sure I like this guy, Preuss thought.

"I mean what do you think he was searching for?" Preuss tried to keep his voice neutral.

"I suppose what we're all searching for here. Enlightenment. Understanding. How to deal with the suffering that's so much a part of life."

Roshi Ross thought some more.

"Above all, Charles was seeking for a way to be a good man," Roshi Ross said. "The moral precepts of Buddhism appealed to him because he saw in those precepts guideposts for living a good life. But the thing about Charles was, he wanted a good life not only for himself, but for everyone he came in contact with. He practiced the two foundations of Buddhism, *karuna*—compassion—and *metta*—loving kindness—with everyone he met.

"The cornerstone of our practice is to extinguish 'I' and 'me' and act in harmony with 'we.' This is what Charles found attractive here."

"The police are working on the theory he met someone and brought him or her back to his house," Preuss said. "And whomever he met is the one who killed him. If that's correct, from what you're telling me about him, he might well have opened his home out of a sense of compassion and loving kindness, as you say."

"Yes," Roshi Ross said. "I do see it as a possibility. Even a likelihood. Charles was open-hearted. He would always help anyone who needed assistance. Even beggars on street corners."

"Was he in the habit of helping people that way?"

Roshi savored another sip of his tea.

"Yes. He would even bring homeless people here to get warm and share a cup of tea. And perhaps to sit in meditation with us."

"Who would he bring home?" Preuss asked.

"People he knew or saw who needed a good meal and a place to stay for a night."

"But you don't know any specific people?"

Roshi Ross pursed his lips and shook his head. "I don't know specific people. We'd talk after our sittings, but he never mentioned names. There are so many people in this city whose needs are overwhelming. If he could do something for even one of them, he told me he would. Sometimes that meant bringing someone home for a hot meal."

"Or a place to sleep for the night?"

"Yes. A foundation of our practice is what we call the three poisons—ignorance, attachment, and aversion. What we might also call delusion, desire, and hate."

"Those are strong poisons."

"Indeed," Roshi Ross said. "There are antidotes to those poisons. The antidote to delusion is wisdom. The antidote to desire is generosity. And the antidote to hatred is loving kindness. Charles practiced those with dedication."

Preuss considered that. Practicing wisdom, compassion, and loving kindness by picking up strangers and bringing them home . . .

Rifkin and Corrigan both denied he would ever do it. Yet here is Roshi, saying he did.

The police theory of the case seemed to be that he brought someone home for an intimate encounter that went bad. That checked with what Roshi said, except for the intimate encounter. As a good Buddhist and a husband faithful beyond the grave, Charles would have battled against the poison of desire.

Hard to imagine he would have given into it.

Though, as the abbot said, it was a strong poison.

And perhaps he brought home someone who misinterpreted loving kindness as something else, something dangerous, and responded accordingly?

"So you don't know if there's anyone in particular—maybe a member of this community—who Charles might have taken home for a night?" Preuss asked. "To show that kindness to?"

"No."

Roshi Ross sat stiffly, like a statue of the Buddha.

"In your conversations," Preuss said, "did he ever mention any problems he might have been having with anyone? Anybody giving him a hard time? Maybe someone here? Or a student with a grudge?"

"No. But he did miss some sittings at the end of last year. He said he wasn't feeling well, but when I next saw him he was battered and bruised. As if someone had beaten him."

"He never talked about it?"

"No," Roshi Ross said. "I didn't ask, he didn't tell. Now is there anything else? I have to prepare for our afternoon sitting."

"One more question," Preuss said. "Was he close to anyone here?"

"We are a community. We are all connected to each other. Separateness, individuality, are illusions. Ignorance."

"One of the poisons."

"Yes."

"But did he have particular friends here that you know of?"

Roshi Ross thought for a moment. "I can give you the names of three."

"Thank you."

"First, may I say one other thing?"

"Of course," Preuss said.

"This—what you're doing for Charles?" Roshi said. "You should know: this is a good deed."

Preuss was prepared for a snarky remark, but Roshi had surprised him. "Okay," he said.

"Not just for the justice you're trying to provide. But because what you're doing in his name will help him with his next rebirth."

Preuss flashed on "the Grateful Dead," a medieval folktale the band took its name from. A member of the living performs a good deed for the dead, then the dead rise up to help him when he gets into a jam.

Roshi Ross stared at Preuss for another few moments.

"A good thing to do," Roshi said. "On behalf of Charles, I thank you."

Preuss didn't know how to respond.

So he tipped his head in what he hoped would appear as humble appreciation.

Any time you're ready, Charlie, he thought, I could use the help.

10

"I spoke with Angie about the job for tonight," Rhonda said back at the office.

"And?"

"She jumped at it. Said she has a special expertise in insurance fraud."

"There you go," Preuss said.

"That's what you'll be saying to the payment for the job when she screws it up."

"Won't you be surprised when she comes through."

"Surprised? I'll be frickin' amazed."

He went into his office. We shall see, he thought.

This might be a terrible mistake. Or it might be inspired.

He spent the first part of the afternoon adding his interview notes to the case file.

Manny and Lila Greene stopped in after two. Manny was his usual natty self, even though he was not dressed in the suit he typically wore to the office. Instead, he had on a crisp white cotton shirt open at the neck and dark khaki pants with a tweed sportscoat.

He carried his stylish black fedora, even though his silver hair was thinning from his treatments. The former proprietor of a hat store, Manny the Hatter in the Fox Theatre Building in downtown Detroit, Manny was incensed by men who wore their hats indoors.

When Preuss came out to Rhonda's area, the two men shook hands and then hugged.

Manny's wife Lila also gave Preuss a hug. As lean and elegant as her husband, she drove Manny most places now. He insisted he could drive himself, but she didn't want him to take the chance, considering how weak he was from the chemo.

In fact, Manny looked much frailer than Preuss had ever seen him. Before his diagnosis, he had been a hale eighty-four-year-old who had come to the business of private detection late in life but had flourished in it. Now he had lost weight; the lines on his face were lengthened and his nose more prominent.

He had also been having problems with his legs, whether from the chemo or old age Preuss didn't know. But he walked with difficulty, dragging one foot.

A lump protruded on his chest under his shirt from the chemo port the doctors had inserted.

"Let's sit down," Lila said.

Manny led the way to his office. He walked like a man trying to keep his balance without seeming to struggle.

He lowered himself into his desk chair as if every bone hurt.

Lila and Preuss sat in the visitors' chairs across the desk from Manny. Rhonda stood in the doorway.

"Manny," Preuss said, "how are you feeling?"

"Never better," Manny said with a wink. He was hoarse and cleared his throat every few seconds.

"He's lying," Lila said. "Don't believe him."

"How are the treatments going?"

"Fine," Manny said.

"They're hard on him," Lila countered. "Hard on both of us. Tell them the truth," she scolded her husband.

Manny gave Preuss a mournful look and a comical shrug.

"What I'm sorriest about," Manny said, "is how hard this is on this one." He indicated Lila with a tip of his head. "She takes such good care of me."

"You bet I do," Lila said. "And you don't make it easy!"

They gave each other gentle smiles full of the tolerance Preuss suspected they had built up over their years of marriage.

"How are things going around here?" Manny asked.

Rhonda had left a pile of mail on his desk. He gazed at it, unable to hide his mixed feelings: missing the day-to-day routine of the office, but not wanting to be back.

"So far so good," Preuss said. "We've gotten a few new clients since the last time we spoke."

"Sammy and Lloyd got to you about Charlie Bright?"

"They did. I've been spending a lot of time on it."

"Good." Manny shook his head. "I knew him. A good man."

"I'm threading the needle with it," Preuss said. "I need to stay out of the way of the police."

"Smart," Manny said. "I told them it would be tricky."

"And we've taken on a new associate," Rhonda said with a sly glance at Preuss. "The famous Angie."

"She's not an associate," Preuss said. "More like we're giving her a try-out as a stringer."

"Rhonda was telling me about her. She seems . . ."

When he couldn't find the precise word, Rhonda supplied it. "Colorful?"

"Well," Manny said, "sometimes colorful can work in your favor."

"We'll see how she does," Preuss said. "Meantime, we're holding down the fort till you get back."

Manny and Lila exchanged a freighted glance. Preuss wondered what that was about.

He decided to ask "What?"

Lila stared at her husband. She flashed her eyes, silently demanding he speak.

Manny cleared his throat. "We've been talking," he said, "Lila and I. About the future of the agency."

Both Preuss and Rhonda waited. Preuss didn't like the feeling he was having about what was going to come next.

"And we've decided it's time for me to retire."

"Uncle Manny, no," Rhonda said in an involuntary whisper.

Manny paused, letting the news penetrate for a few moments.

"With this cancer, and what the treatments are doing to me," he added, "I'm just not the man I used to be."

Lila turned to Rhonda and Preuss. "It's time."

Manny didn't reply, which was how Preuss knew Lila was right. Any other time and Manny would have kept bantering good-naturedly with her.

Then Manny said, "I've been thinking a lot about what's going to happen. I can't keep this up forever. And when I leave, I want you to take it over, Martin."

This was not news to Preuss. He and Manny had talked about the future of the agency, and Manny hinted he wanted Preuss to take it over when the older man retired. But they both assumed it would happen in some indeterminate future, when there would be time to figure out how to make the change work.

But here they were, talking about it happening soon.

"Manny," Preuss began, but didn't know how to finish. Did he want to ask Manny to reconsider? To delay his retirement? Preuss couldn't possibly ask him to do that, under the circumstances.

No, Preuss knew the truth was as Lila had said: it was time for Manny to bow out. But it was also true that Preuss was still uncertain if he wanted to take over the agency, now or ever.

As if picking up on his thoughts, Manny said, "I know you don't want to do this."

"It's not that," Preuss said.

Manny raised a hand. For the first time, Preuss noticed no fragrant smell of coffee in Manny's office, no white mug of his favorite brew. All Manny had in front of him now was a bottle of water.

"It's not going to happen today," Manny said. "But it's going to happen sooner rather than later. The truth is, I don't know if I'm going to be up to running the place again. Once my course of therapy ends, Lila and I were talking about my working two or three days a week so we can make a smooth transition."

Preuss still didn't know what to say. So he kept silent.

"But even this is still in the future. I don't know when the doctors are going to tell me I'm ready to come back to work, even part-time."

Lila shook her head. "Not going to happen."

"For the time being," Preuss said, "let's everybody remember the main thing is for you to get back on your feet again. Then we can talk about what's next. You shouldn't be worrying about the agency. We have it under control."

Preuss could tell by the sad look on Manny's face that as far as he was concerned, it was a done deal.

Manny pushed some envelopes around on his desk. The paperwork Rhonda and Preuss had been generating while Manny was on leave—contracts, purchase orders, preliminary and final reports—now all went to Preuss.

Manny was right, he wasn't the man he used to be; at his age, the cancer treatments must have been harder on him than he was willing to admit.

Maybe he knew it was time to let go of this business he'd built. And if he trusted Preuss enough to take it over, saying no, or even hesitating, was not an option.

As if the four of them all decided this at once, an awkward silence settled over the office.

Rhonda broke it.

"Well," she said, "I'm going to get back to work. Nice to see you guys."

"You too, honey," Lila said.

When Rhonda left the office, Manny looked at Preuss and gave a "so-there's-where-we-are" shrug.

"Seems like things are going well," Manny said. "See? You don't even need me."

"Manny," Preuss said, "don't ever say that. Or even think it."

Lila gave Manny a significant look, and Manny said, "Well, we're going to go. I wanted to get out of the house and say hello. See how you both were doing."

"Glad you did," Preuss said.

Lila helped her husband up. His legs were shaky and Preuss jumped up to help but Manny waved him away. Preuss was surprised by how weak Manny seemed. His hands shook as Lila held out the sleeves of his overcoat so he could shrug it onto his shoulders.

"Walk us out?" Lila asked Preuss.

11

Preuss followed them out of the office and down the corridor to the main door of the building.

There they paused. Lila hooked a hand through Preuss's arm and leaned forward. "Martin," she said in a low voice, "I didn't want to say this in front of Rhonda because I didn't want to upset her. But Manny's much closer to retirement than he let on."

Preuss said nothing.

"His cancer has spread," she said.

"Oh no."

"It's in his lungs and his bones."

"Oh Jesus. I'm so sorry to hear that."

"Thank you, my friend," Manny said. He held a hand out and Preuss took it.

"He won't be coming back to work," Lila said. "Not full-time, not part-time."

The older man nodded. "Much as I hate to admit it, I'm through."

"He might be coming in for a little while every so often," Lila said, "to help with the transfer. Once he's feeling better, of course. But don't count on him coming back on any kind of regular basis."

Lila raised her eyebrows and inclined her head. *Got it?* her face asked.

She was almost as good at nonverbal communication as Toby, he thought.

"Understood," Preuss said.

Lila patted his arm and guided her husband out of the building.

Preuss processed this as he walked them to Manny's Audi. Preuss helped Manny into the passenger seat and Lila went around to get behind the wheel.

"Don't tell Rhonda," Manny said to Preuss. "I don't want to worry her. And she'll run right to her mother, and . . ." He let his voice trail off and waved away the rest of the sentence with a disgusted hand.

"All right," Preuss said. He took Manny's hand again and held it for a moment. It was dry and bony, like the rest of the man. "See you soon, my friend."

Preuss closed the passenger-side door and Lila started up the car and backed out of the parking spot. Preuss watched the tail lights flash as the car pulled away into Telegraph Road traffic.

Preuss walked back into the building. Rhonda was sitting up straight behind her desk and staring at him when he entered her outer office.

What to tell her?

"Well?" she asked. "What else did they say they didn't want me to hear?"

He shook his head. "He's not doing well."

"I could see that."

"She's very worried about him."

"Looks like he's lost about forty pounds."

Preuss agreed. Manny had always been slim, but the loss of all the weight over the past few months since his diagnosis and treatment was striking.

"Plus," she said, "he didn't want his coffee, which I made especially for him. Said he can't drink coffee anymore. That's how I know he's really sick. The old Uncle Manny would never turn down his Ethiopian."

"All we can do is keep it together for now," Preuss offered.

"Honestly, I'll be amazed if he ever comes back."

"Same here. But as long as he's vertical, he's going to want to come in, even for an hour a week. It's not up to us, in any event."

"No. But still. I can't imagine this place without him."

"Let's worry about it when it happens."

She agreed with a sigh.

He returned to his office and pulled his attention away from Manny to his case notes.

He read through them and stopped at a name: Ruth Anne Krider.

It was time to start looking for her.

Corrigan and Rifkin had said she was a grad student at Wayne State University. Preuss put a call in to the Wayne State Department of History.

He told the secretary who answered the phone what he was looking for, and she transferred him to the graduate office.

There the administrative assistant told him she had never heard of a student named Ruth Anne Krider in their department.

"But that doesn't mean she isn't here," the woman cautioned him. "We have an unusually large class this year and I'm new. Let me transfer you to the graduate program coordinator."

"Before you do," Preuss cut in, "if it helps, she was a student of Dr. Bright."

"Oh, Dr. Bright," the woman said, her voice suddenly full of sadness. "Such a sweetheart. I can't believe what happened to him. Are you a friend of his?"

"I never got the chance to meet him."

"Because if you were, I was going to let you know there's going to be a memorial service for him tomorrow morning on campus. Ten o'clock. If you're interested, I can give you the information."

"Please do."

She told him when and where the memorial would be, and he jotted it in his notebook. The entire university community would be involved, she said. It was to be held in the Hilberry Theatre, on Cass Avenue in Midtown.

"I hope you can make it," she said. "It's going to be our way of saying goodbye to him. Hang on, I'll transfer you to the graduate program advisor."

The number she transferred him to went right to a voice mailbox.

"This is Dr. Joseph Palmer," a broad northern England voice said. "I'm either in class or on another call. Please leave a message and I'll be in touch with you as soon as I can."

At the tone, Preuss left his name and phone number, and said he was trying to connect with Ruth Anne Krider, whom he understood to be a graduate student in the Department of History.

And would Dr. Palmer get back to him at his first opportunity?

He disconnected and started his calls to the names Roshi had given him.

One he had already spoken with, the man who told him about Bright's connection to the Zen Center. The call to another, David Baker, went right to voicemail.

The third answered. "Dr. Kapleau."

Preuss explained who he was and what he wanted. Dr. Kapleau said he and Charles had gotten to know each other well through the Zen Center.

"We're both professors," Kapleau said. "I teach biology at Henry Ford Community College, and he taught history at Wayne State. We saw each other at the Zen Center, and we also played snooker every Saturday afternoon. Usually we went out for a drink or a bite to eat afterward."

"So you've gotten friendly?"

"I'd say so."

"Did you hear what happened to him?"

"I did," Kapleau said. "Horrible and unthinkable."

"Do you know any reason why someone would want to hurt him?"

"I can't imagine. He was the nicest, most generous man you'd ever want to meet."

Exactly what others said about Charles Bright.

"Have you talked to his kids?" Kapleau asked.

Kids plural?

"His kids?"

"Yeah," Kapleau said. "Charlie has two sons."

This was the first Preuss had heard about two sons. He knew about one—Larry—from Corrigan and Rifkin. But there was another one?

"Do you know their names?" Preuss asked.

"Sure. One boy is Larry. The other is Kenny."

"You wouldn't know how I could get in touch with them, by any chance?"

"Well, not Larry. I wouldn't know where to find him. But Kenny works at a private school. I remember because he's in education, like Charlie and me. Except he's not a teacher. I think he's an administrator."

"Do you know where he works?"

"I do, as a matter of fact," Dr. Kapleau said.

12

Kapleau turned out not to know the exact name of the school, but said it was a private girls' school in Bloomfield Hills. Preuss knew of three: Academy of the Sacred Heart, St. Mary's High School, and the Woodbrooke Academy. The other private schools in Bloomfield Hills were co-ed.

First he tried the Academy of the Sacred Heart, but the administrative assistant he spoke with told him there was nobody named Ken (or Kenneth or Kenny) Bright, either on the faculty or the administration. In fact, there was nobody named Ken on staff at all, the woman told him, and she had been there for twenty years so she would know.

Next he called St. Mary's. The woman who answered the phone told him they had no one named Kenneth Bright on staff either, nor anybody named Ken.

The operator who answered the phone at the Woodbrooke Academy likewise told him there was no one named Kenneth Bright. But they did have a Kenneth Krempka, who was their development director. He had been there for a number of years, she told him, and she knew he was local.

He decided to try. Maybe Krempka changed his name from Bright for some reason.

Woodbrooke Academy sprawled over a large campus off Woodward Avenue in the affluent northern suburb of Bloomfield Hills. On the way to the front office to inquire, Preuss passed a display case filled with trophies from every sport, from baseball to soccer and tennis, water polo to equestrian. These are the most privileged girls in the universe, he thought. Whatever they want is available at the snap of their fingers.

The secretary behind the counter in the office pointed Preuss toward a long hallway. A tall man in a white shirt and tie walked out to greet him. He carried a handkerchief in one hand. Late forties. Short blond hair, with a head that seemed too large for his body, as if it had been photoshopped on him from a man twice as large.

"Are you looking for me?" he asked Preuss.

"Kenneth Krempka?"

"Yes."

"Charles Bright's son?"

"Well," the man said, "that's a subject of some dispute."

Close-up, Preuss noticed his forehead was sweating profusely. Krempka mopped it with the handkerchief.

Preuss waited. If the guy had expected the joke to go over, he was mistaken.

After a few awkward moments, the man extended his hand to shake. "Ken Krempka," he said.

"I want to be clear: you are Dr. Bright's son?"

"Stepson, yes."

Preuss shook his hand (fortunately not the one holding the soggy handkerchief) and Krempka said, "What can I do for you?"

"I'd like to speak with you about your stepfather."

Krempka mopped his brow again. "I've got a few minutes before my next appointment. Can we do this in a few minutes?"

"Sure."

"Great. Let's talk back here."

Krempka held out his arm to shepherd Preuss down another corridor into a suite of offices. A young woman looked up from her desk when Krempka walked in. She gave Preuss a once-over and said, "Don't forget, you have a 3:30."

"We're good," Krempka said. He led Preuss into an overheated and messy small office. His desk was piled high with papers and folders and reports in no apparent order. His bookshelves bowed under the weight of bound documents.

Krempka removed a stack of papers from his guest chair and invited Preuss to sit.

"What can I tell you?" Krempka asked.

Preuss handed him a business card. "I'm a private investigator. I assume you're aware of your stepfather's death?"

Krempka nodded.

"I'm sorry for your loss," Preuss said.

When Krempka responded with a stone face, Preuss continued. "I've been hired to look into the circumstances surrounding his death."

"Hired by whom?"

"It's confidential, I'm afraid," Preuss said. "I'm trying to gather information about Dr. Bright to see if I can help validate what the police are doing. Have they spoken with you, Mr. Krempka?"

"Call me Ken, please. They have. A black detective."

"Detective Trombley."

"I think so. Look, I'm afraid I can't be any more helpful to you than I was to him. Charlie and I have been—I believe the polite word is 'estranged.' We haven't spoken in years."

He mopped his brow.

"When was the last time you talked to him?" Preuss asked.

"I can't even remember."

"But not recently?"

Krempka shook his big head and mopped his brow again. In order for his body to grow into that head, he would have to be another foot taller and a hundred pounds heavier.

"We never got along," he said. "I was the proverbial red-headed stepchild. I left home as soon as I could. I've never felt the need to be in touch since."

"So you wouldn't know if anybody had a grudge against him?"

"Besides me, you mean? No."

Krempka turned up the corner of his mouth in an attempt at a smile.

"What about your brother Larry?" Preuss asked.

"What about him?"

"When was the last time you were in touch?"

"Not for years, either."

"So you don't know where he is?"

"I couldn't begin to guess."

Preuss was silent, inviting Krempka to speak further.

And he did. "I don't know anything about them or their lives. I don't know who Charlie's friends are, I don't know if anybody has a grudge against him . . . I don't even know where Larry is right now. They live their lives, I live mine. Never the twain shall meet. So . . ." Krempka raised his hands palms-out in a gesture of submission.

"You weren't ever close with your stepfather?"

Krempka looked around as if he might find the correct answer somewhere in the disorder of the room. "Let's just say he disapproved of my lifestyle and leave it there."

Everyone Preuss had spoken with so far had described Charles Bright as a gentle and accepting man. What about Krempka's lifestyle wouldn't he approve of? If Krempka were gay,

Bright wouldn't have objected to that . . . not if what everybody had said about him were true. What else could it have been?

"So you never visited him at his home?" Preuss went on.

Krempka huffed. "I don't know how else to say this any differently but louder, sir. My stepfather and I were not in touch. So the answer to any question about him is: I. Don't. Know. And may I also say, I don't care."

Krempka picked up the cell phone on his desk and glanced at the screen. "If you don't have any more questions? I need to get going."

"Fine," Preuss said. "I won't keep you."

Krempka jumped up and came around to shake Preuss's hand again.

"I've got a meeting with an alumna who's been very generous to the school. I don't want to keep her waiting."

"Of course."

"Sorry to rush off like this."

"No worries."

"If you want to speak some more," Krempka said, "maybe you could call my office first. Save you a trip out here. My assistant'll put you through as fast as possible. Leave your information with her. Though I don't know why we'd need to talk again."

Before Preuss could reply, Krempka rushed off, his long legs carrying him out of his office and down the hallway.

Leaving Preuss standing there by himself.

Krempka's assistant appeared in the doorway. "If you'd like to leave a number where you can be reached . . . ?"

Translation: Time to go, pal.

13

The day was still mild when he got to Toby's. Toby was alone in his room, sitting up in his reclining chair, dozing. His television was showing the original black and white version of *Invasion of the Body Snatchers.*

Preuss gave his son a soft kiss on the side of his face, which woke Toby up at once. Even though he had stopped by earlier in the morning, Preuss felt like he hadn't seen his son for a long time.

"Hey, Toby," he said, "would you like to go for a walk? Perfect weather for it."

Toby gave him a broad, crooked grin.

"I'll take that as a yes," Preuss said.

He bundled Toby up in his puffy winter coat and a knit hat and scarf despite the mild weather and got him settled in his wheelchair. With his Red Wings poncho covering him, they set out down his street in Berkley toward Twelve Mile Road.

The sidewalks were clear of snow from the mild temperatures, so they had no problem rolling past the neat modest homes of the Detroit suburb. Even though Obama had been inaugurated for his second term a little over a month ago, Romney/Ryan signs still stuck stubbornly out of front lawns of diehard Republicans.

They cut over on a side street toward Coolidge. There they turned right and Preuss pushed Toby down to the library, a one-story glass and brick building surrounded on two sides by a parking apron.

The staff greeted Toby, whom they all knew, and Toby returned the greetings with loud squeals, which made them laugh. In the quiet realm of the library, nobody shushed him. A few patrons turned to see where the commotion was coming from, but made no comments. Toby's joy was infectious.

Preuss pushed him down to the CD section and picked out two books on disk for him to listen to: a Sue Grafton book and a Linda Fairstein book. Toby loved listening to stories, and he particularly enjoyed the voices of the women who narrated those two series, one light and cocky, the other deep and mellow.

When they finished in the library, Preuss pushed his son up to Twelve Mile and they made a big circuit around the neighborhood back to Toby's group home.

The bathtub was free, so Preuss used the overhead electric lift in Toby's room to get him on his bed and went to fill up the tub while tonight's aide, Maria, undressed him. The aides were supposed to take care of Toby's needs like his bath, but they all knew Preuss loved to do this for his son so they let him help.

When the tub was full, Preuss got Toby back into his wheelchair and draped a bathrobe over his chubby naked tummy and slender legs. He pushed his son into the bathroom, where another lift suspended from the ceiling lowered Toby into the tub. Humming and chortling, Toby floated in the tub while Preuss again marveled at how much his son loved his bath and his life. His damp face shone with pure joy.

This gift was surely a compensation for all his disabilities. And Toby himself was a compensation, too, a light in the darkness Preuss often moved through, in his days and in his nights.

When Toby's fingers began to prune up, Preuss let the water out and raised his son out of the tub and got him back into his wheelchair and back in bed. Maria was waiting with his pajamas so Preuss let her finish up with him while he filled the three slots of Toby's CD player with the Linda Fairstein disks.

With Toby in his pajamas, Preuss sat with his arm around his son on the side of Toby's bed and they listened to Barbara Rosenblatt's rich, warm voice narrating the story. Preuss felt the sharp bones of his son's shoulders, fragile and thin, as he propped Toby up.

Toby started rubbing and snuffling his nose on Preuss's arm, the cue he was getting sleepy.

When Toby's head drooped, Preuss laid him down on his bed and tucked him under the sheet and blankets. He stopped the book in the CD player and put on a Judy Collins album. Toby's favorite music helped ease him into sleep. Another woman's lovely voice.

Preuss turned the overhead light off, and lit the floor lamp beside Toby's recliner. With a weak bulb, it cast a faint glow over Toby's bed, illuminating the curves and hollows of his gorgeous face.

Preuss sat in the recliner watching his child, his heart filled with love for his boy, the only family he had left. Toby's older brother Jason was still alive—as far as Preuss knew—but Preuss had no idea where he was or how he was living.

Missing and homeless. Like Larry Bright.

He thought about his interview with Ken Krempka, also isolated from his family.

Not that Preuss was any different. Preuss's mother and father were dead, his father from alcoholism and his mother from cervical cancer. His brother was dead after a life of drug use. Any other family members Preuss had were either dead or lost or unknown to him.

Only he remained. And now only Preuss and Toby (and, somewhere, Jason) remained from the family he had tried to create.

He sat reflecting on his fractured family, their voices like hollow echoes in an empty room, until his phone rang.

He stopped the ringer before it woke Toby up, but the caller's name appeared on the screen.

Emma Blalock.

He had the familiar feeling whenever he saw her name on his phone: to answer or not to answer.

But he had called her, so . . .

He took the phone into the hallway and went back to one of the lounges. Nobody was sitting there because the residents were all in their beds and the staff were attending to night medications and other needs.

He sat on the sofa, took a deep breath, and punched Answer.

"Emma," he said.

"Hey, Martin. How you doing?"

"Doing well."

"Not calling too late?"

"Not at all."

"So what's up?"

"I'm working on a case that dovetails with one of yours. I thought I could ask you where you are with it."

"Uh-huh."

Frosty, as always.

"What's the case?" she asked.

"Charles Bright."

"The Ferndale killing?"

"Right."

"And what's your interest?"

"I have a client who wants me to look into the corners of it. But I don't—"

"Okay, Martin," she cut in, "I'm gonna stop you right there. I don't know what you're gonna ask me, but if it's connected to the Bright case in any way, it's an active investigation and I can't say a word about it."

"I understand—"

"Then you also know you're not an active-duty officer anymore. You don't have the ins you once had. And you don't have access to the information you once had or the people you once knew, either. And that includes me."

"I know, Emma. I'm calling as a courtesy to let you know. I was hired to look into some aspects of the case the official investigation isn't concerned about. In case our paths cross. I wanted to give you a heads up."

"All I can say is, our paths better not cross."

The same thing Reg Trombley told him.

"If I find you've been poking around where you're not supposed to, I'm not gonna have any choice but to come down hard on you," she said. "And I'm not gonna hesitate, Martin."

He paused for a moment to keep himself under control. Nothing worthwhile was going to come of this. All it did was give her a chance to push back at him.

Still, he had to make the call.

"Okay," he said.

"We clear?"

"Clear."

"Fine." She disconnected before he could say goodbye.

And that was that.

It went as poorly as he thought it might. He had some small hope of getting information from her before everything went south, but it was not to be.

Back in Toby's room, his son was sound asleep. Judy Collins was singing about sending in the clowns.

Don't bother, Preuss silently sang along. They're here.

The call upset him more than he thought it would. He felt badly Emma was still so angry with him, but he was annoyed, too. When she had pursued him, he considered getting involved with her. They even went out a few times, but it wasn't clicking for him so he called it off.

Of course, he hadn't felt anything for anyone except Toby since his wife died. And he wasn't even sure what he felt for her, either, when she died, though his guilt over the accident was profound.

Watching his son sleep, he wondered if this was what the rest of his life was going to be like—joyful hours with Toby followed by a lonely vigil over the sleeping young man, followed by long hours alone.

If this was to be his future, he would manage it. He would embrace it, even. Toby was worth every moment.

Some people looked at Toby as one of nature's mistakes. Even one mother of a handicapped girl in Toby's class called her daughter a potted plant. But for Preuss, his son was his most precious gift, to be cherished and protected.

Preuss also knew he was coming to the point in his life where he would have to make the decision either to spend it only with Toby, or make a change that would pierce through his loneliness somehow.

Pushing against this thought was his conviction that any attempt to find someone would be futile.

A stalemate.

He continued thinking like this until he, too, dozed off.

When the night respiratory therapist woke him, it was after two a.m. He roused himself, kissed his son good night—good morning, actually—and drove home.

Wednesday, February 27, 2013

14

At 9:30 the next morning he left his office for the Wayne State University campus in Detroit.

Parking on the street was impossible, so he left the Explorer in a parking structure and walked down Cass Avenue to the theatre where the memorial service was being held.

By the time he got inside, the auditorium was already full. He had to stand with the overflow crowd in the lobby, where a closed-circuit camera broadcast the event on the stage inside.

The dean of the College of Liberal Arts and Sciences was the emcee. Preuss watched and listened as speaker after speaker—administrators, faculty members, staff, and students—eulogized Charles Bright for his kindness, his intellect, his concern for students, his social consciousness, and his sense of humor.

At the end of the first hour, one speaker took the stage with the stereotypical look of an aging male professor (shaggy grey beard, long unruly grey hair, rumpled outdated suit). He spoke with a northern British accent, and told a long anecdote about Bright. Preuss couldn't follow it all, but it seemed to be connected with a tour of Detroit that Bright took his students on every semester.

They would go past famous Detroit landmarks (the Scott Fountain on Belle Isle, the Birwood Wall separating black residents from the whites who wanted to move in with FHA loans, the spot on

12th Street where the blind pig stood that was the flashpoint for the 1967 riot, and so on).

The point of the story was that the tour would always stop at a strip club on Dix Street near the sprawling Ford River Rouge Plant in Dearborn. The name of the club was Chix on Dix.

This prompted a ripple of subdued laughter from the crowd in the auditorium.

The hubbub in the lobby kept Preuss from hearing the speaker's name, but he recognized the voice.

He leaned toward the woman standing next to him who was also trying to watch the CCTV. "Excuse me," he said. "Do you know who this speaker is? I missed his name."

"Joe Palmer," she said. "From the History Department."

"That's who I thought."

"Know him?"

"No," he said. "But I've been trying to get in touch with him and he sounds like the voice on his answering machine."

"I don't know how you could hear anything over the noise out here."

He turned to look at her. Mid-forties or early fifties, dark hair in shaggy curls, large pale eyeglasses. Deep-set blue eyes enlarged by the lenses. Dressed in professor-chic, all black: jersey, blazer, Levis, long peacoat.

They sized each other up, then she looked back at the television.

"Did you know Professor Bright?" he asked.

"I did," the woman said. "Lots of people on campus knew him. Obviously." She held out a hand, offering this well-attended event as proof.

"Pretty well-liked guy," Preuss observed.

"Everybody loved him. He'd been around forever. Really a foundation of campus life. How did you know him?"

"I didn't."

"What brought you here?"

"I wanted to pay my respects," Preuss said. "We have mutual friends."

The woman said nothing in reply, and both turned their attention back to the television.

When the service ended—an hour and fifteen minutes later—the lobby cleared out quickly, followed by people streaming noisily out of the auditorium.

The woman beside him said, "Nice talking to you," and held out her hand. He shook it and she said, "I'm Grace."

"Martin."

She gave his hand a quick squeeze before letting go.

She blended in with the crowd of people on their way out. Preuss elbowed his way to a wall where he could watch the doors leading from the theatre.

He didn't see Palmer pass by. When the last stragglers had left, he peeked inside the auditorium and saw a small group talking together down front, beside the stage. Among them was the man he now knew as Joseph Palmer.

Preuss walked halfway down the aisle to stop a few rows from Palmer. He didn't want to lose Palmer in case the group went another way from where Preuss was standing.

This turned out to be a good idea because the Englishman's friends exited through one of the side doors.

Preuss caught up with Palmer before he disappeared.

"Professor Palmer," Preuss said.

"Yes?"

"My name is Martin Preuss." He gave the older man a business card. "I'm a private investigator. Do you have a minute to talk about Dr. Bright?"

Palmer looked after his departing friends. "I really don't. Look, why don't you make an appointment with my secretary and we'll talk then?"

"This'll only take five minutes."

Palmer gave him a superior, how-dare-you-challenge-a-tenured-full-professor glower.

Preuss gave him a hard cop-glare in return.

Dueling stares.

Palmer's friends paused by the door and glanced back at him. "Joe," one said, "you coming?"

"You go on," Palmer told them. "I'll catch up."

Suspicious, they threw Preuss a look that made him feel like he had cheated on a final exam.

They left and Palmer turned to Preuss.

"What do you want to know, then?" he demanded. "Quickly, please."

"I'm investigating the death of Professor Bright."

Palmer looked at him in confusion, then at the business card he held. "I thought the police were looking into this. You're handling a *private* enquiry?"

"Yes. Going along a parallel track to the one the police are taking."

A nice way of saying I'm not working with them, Preuss thought.

"Well," Palmer said, "I don't know what I can tell you."

"Have the investigating officers spoken with you about Dr. Bright?"

"Yes. I couldn't tell them much, either."

"You were close with Dr. Bright?"

The professor gave an exasperated huff and said, "Oh look, sorry, I don't have time for this."

He turned to leave and Preuss said, "Do you know a grad student named Ruth Anne Krider?"

That stopped him.

15

Palmer turned back to Preuss and reappraised him. "You're the one who left the message for me."

"I am."

"Right." Palmer looked down the aisle, toward the door his friends had left from, as though bidding them a silent goodbye.

"Yes," he said, "I do know her."

"What was her relationship with Dr. Bright?"

Palmer sighed. "We should go somewhere and talk."

He led Preuss out the front door of the theatre and turned right to walk down Cass Avenue. Preuss noticed the woman who had stood beside him, Grace, talking with a trio of people in puffy quilted coats in front of the theatre. She caught his eye and they raised a hand of greeting to each other.

Palmer said, "I need to get a bite to eat before my afternoon schedule. Let's go sit down someplace where we can talk."

Several blocks down, he led Preuss across the street and into the Cass Café. He greeted people at several tables in the long room before moving to a stairway leading up to a balcony. It was empty of customers but as soon as he sat down a waitress appeared.

"Hey, doc," she said. "Same as always?"

"Please."

"For you?" she asked Preuss.

"I recommend what I always get," Palmer said.

"Which is what?"

"Whatever vegan soup of the day they have and Caesar salad without the cheese, and an herbal iced tea."

"I'll have that, except for the herbal tea," Preuss said. "Make mine the real thing. Unsweetened."

The server nodded and left down the stairs.

"I come here almost every day I'm on campus," Palmer said. "Creature of habit, I suppose."

Gone was the prickly, officious professor. Here Palmer was relaxed and even friendly. His accent modulated to a broader northern England drawl. Preuss thought he might be from Manchester or surroundings.

Preuss's father was also a history professor, specializing in Colonial American history. But Joseph Palmer seemed a good deal more—oh, what's the word, Preuss asked himself—*undrunk?*—than the great Professor Preuss.

"Poor Charlie," Palmer said. "Terrible way for a good man to go out."

"It was," Preuss agreed. "But you were going to tell me about Ruth Anne Krider. I understand you're her graduate advisor."

"Was. She's no longer in the program, you see."

"Let's back up," Preuss said, then paused as the server brought over their drinks.

"Thanks, LaDonna," Palmer said. LaDonna smiled in return.

"You and Dr. Bright both knew her, correct?" Preuss asked.

"Yes. As you said, I was her advisor. Charles had her in a few of his courses. Very bright young woman."

"Was he involved with her?"

"Personally, you mean?"

"Yes."

Palmer scoffed. "Not hardly." The officious academic surfaced.

"It wouldn't be the first time a professor and student were involved," Preuss said. "I needed to ask."

"Yes, of course. You're right." Palmer took his back down. "But no, there was nothing untoward about Charles's relationship with Ruth Anne. That wasn't the problem with her."

"What was?"

Palmer stretched out his fingers on the table. "In our institution," he said, "there are a great many students of color. African Americans, Asians, students of Middle Eastern origin. People come to America to study with us, and we also draw from those communities locally. But Ruth Anne . . ."

He stopped as LaDonna, a person of color herself, returned with their meal. The soup was roasted curry lentil and the salad was a large bowl of romaine lettuce and croutons bathed in a creamy dressing.

Palmer started right in on his soup. "Sorry," he said. "Don't mean to be rude. But I need to eat up before my class."

"No worries."

"I was saying," Palmer continued, "Ruth Anne turned out to have a major problem with our student body."

"Which was?"

"If I can speak frankly?"

"Please."

"Though she seemed like a promising addition to the department when she arrived last January, Ruth Anne Krider turned out to be a rather unpleasant racist."

"That's unfortunate."

Palmer nodded. "Very. Try the soup," he insisted.

Preuss tasted a spoonful.

"How is it?"

"Delicious."

"Good. Salad dressing's vegan, too."

Palmer concentrated on his own soup for a minute.

He wiped the facial hair around his mouth with his napkin. "Yes," he said at last, "Ruth Anne couldn't handle being in class with our cohort of students. She was not only disrespectful to them—and to our faculty who are people of color—but she began distributing white nationalist literature around the department and the university."

Preuss took out his notebook and said, "I'm going to make some notes. Do you mind?"

"Not at all."

Preuss scratched a few lines in his notebook while Palmer worked on his salad.

"So. She passed around white power literature," Preuss said.

"Yes. Vile, repellent trash. She put flyers up on bulletin boards, taped posters to walls in the Grad Student Lounge. Real Third Reich stuff."

"And you're sure it came from her?"

"People caught her doing it. They told the department chair. And the department chair told me. I confronted her about it. She freely admitted doing it. Said it was her first amendment right. I told her it met the university handbook's definition of hate speech and was therefore prohibited."

"Did she stop?"

"She did not. Not when I talked to her, at any rate."

"Did Dr. Bright know about this?"

"Of course. Everyone in the department knew."

"What was his response?"

Palmer shook his head, more in admiration and chagrin than in anger. "Charlie didn't have a mean bone in his body. I wanted to throttle her. His response? He wanted to *talk* to her."

"To make her see the error of her ways?"

"Yes. As if that would work with those people. Poor Charlie. The eternal optimist, always relying on people's goodness. Last fall, this was. And I have to say, after talking with him, she did stop. But then she finished out last semester, and never showed up for classes last month. Just disappeared. Saved us the trouble of dropping her. Awful stuff, that. Viciously racist anti-Obama flyers, anti-Semitic posters. 'America First,' 'Jews Will Not Replace Us,' and so forth. Adverts for Klan meetings. Disgusting."

"Do you remember which groups held the meetings?"

"It was one group organizing most of it, an outfit called the American Identity Brigade."

The name sounded familiar. After 9/11, Preuss had taken some terrorism training sessions and he recalled the name. It was associated with a homegrown terrorist organization.

"They're rabid haters," Palmer said. "I ran into them when I volunteered with the ADL."

"The Anti-Defamation League?"

Palmer nodded. "I give talks for them in schools when I can. This is very close to my heart, you see. I'm Jewish. My family name was originally Polyakov. My father changed it in England during the Second World War to try to avoid the English anti-Semites. Of which there were, and are, multitudes. Turns out you can't escape them anywhere, even in the New World. Maybe *especially* in the New World. So the trash she was posting I took personally, as you might expect."

"Do you know Emmanuel Greene? He's also active in the ADL."

"Manny Greene? Of course. Wait."

Palmer looked at Preuss's business card, "He's the Greene in Greene & Preuss?"

"He's the one."

"Sure. He's on the Michigan ADL board. How is he? I heard he was sick."

"He has been. We're all hoping he's on the mend."

"Such a small world. Give him my best."

"Will do."

Palmer gulped down the rest of his soup. "What else can I tell you?"

"You said Ruth Anne Krider disappeared from the program?"

"She dropped out. Bright young woman. But terribly misguided."

"Do you have a contact number for her?"

"In my files, not with me. My administrative assistant should have one, too. Hang on."

Palmer punched in a number on his cell phone and had a brief conversation.

"She's going to check my office," he said to Preuss.

After another minute, he held out a hand for Preuss's note pad and wrote a number on it.

"Thanks," Palmer said, and ended his call. He handed Preuss the notepad.

"Here's what we have for her. I can't say how up-to-date it is."

The phone number was a 734 area code, with an address in Westland, a town about the size of Ferndale but sixteen miles due west of where they were sitting.

"Is there any reason you can think of for someone to harm Charles Bright?" Preuss asked.

Palmer gave him a look of immense sadness.

"You know," Palmer said, "when I heard what happened to him, I wondered about that. I went back over former students and so forth, anyone who might have harbored a grudge. Students today aren't what they used to be, I'll tell you that. Especially American students, funnily enough. The foreign students still show respect toward their faculty. And I don't know if you've heard, but somebody roughed him up last fall."

"I'd heard about that."

"I asked him about it, but he wouldn't tell me."

"Is it connected with what happened to him?"

"Couldn't say. For the life of me, I can't think of any bloody reason someone would want to hurt that sweet, gentle man."

Back at the offices of Greene & Preuss, Investigations, Preuss didn't have to be a detective to know all wasn't right.

One look at Rhonda's face told him.

16

"I hope you're happy," she said.

Before he could ask why, she said, "I've been on the phone all morning with Seymour Hersch, and let me tell you, *he's* not happy."

He sank onto the sofa in her reception area. "Tell me."

"Your new detective? Angie?"

"She's not our new detective, but go ahead."

"She never showed last night. Seymour called me after you left this morning and bawled me out like it was *my* fault."

"How does he know?"

"One of his other investigators had the day shift yesterday. He was supposed to leave when Angie checked in, but she never did."

"Did you talk to her?"

"I called her right after I got off the phone with Seymour."

"And?"

"She told me she got in an accident on the way to the job."

"Is she all right?"

"Oh, she's fine. But her car is totaled."

"And she didn't try to call us?"

"No, because her phone was out of juice. And she couldn't use the phone of the guy who hit her because he took off. And the police wouldn't let her use their phone. Remember what one of her references said? She's a magnet for trouble? So, yeah. By the way, she wants to talk to you. And Hersch *really* wants to talk with you."

"I'll bet he does."

This is exactly why I don't want to be in charge, Preuss told himself. When you're the boss, everybody else's problems become *your* problems.

"I told him you'd call," Rhonda said.

Preuss boosted himself up from the sofa. "I'll do it now."

"What are you going to tell Angie?"

"Her first assignment with us isn't off to a great start."

"Ya think?"

He went into his office and called Seymour Hersch first. This was the more important call. A long and important connection existed between the two agencies, and Preuss didn't want to jeopardize the relationship.

He phoned Hersch's private number and got the answering service. He left his name and phone number and reason for the call, and then punched in the number for Angie Sturmer.

Hersch called him back right then and he disconnected Angie's call and connected with the attorney.

"Seymour," Preuss said.

"Martin," Hersch began, and Preuss held the phone away from his ear as Hersch yelled about how disappointed he was.

When Hersch paused for a breath, Preuss said, "Seymour, I'm sorry about this. You know this isn't how we operate. We're short-handed with Manny out, so I had to call in somebody we haven't used before. Can you give us another chance at this? I'll get an experienced agent on it. This one's gratis. Okay?"

Hersch grumbled for a while but finally agreed. He was somewhat mollified by the time they disconnected, but he wasn't finished ragging on Angie Sturmer, even though he didn't know who she was.

"Rhonda," Preuss called.

She appeared in the doorway.

"Can you please see if we can find somebody else for this job?"

"Somebody besides the one who was supposed to do it last night?"

"If we can't find anyone else, I'll do it myself."

"You shouldn't have to, you know."

"It's not like there's much of a choice. I got Hersch to agree to give us another chance. We need to make sure it's done right."

Rhonda went back to her desk to check the stringers folder on her computer.

Preuss dialed Angie again.

She picked up on the first ring, and before he could say a word, she started.

"Mr. Preuss, I am *so* sorry," she said. "This isn't like me *at all!*"

"Angie," he began, but she cut him off.

"I am so sorry," she said again. "As I told Ronna—"

"That's Rhonda."

"—I dropped my son off at my mom's so she could watch him for the night and my car got hit on the way to the job site and it got totaled and I couldn't drive it and there wasn't any way for me to get in touch with you because the guy who hit me kept going and it was a hit-and-run and—"

"Angie," he said, "stop."

She went quiet.

"These things happen. I get it. But you left us in the lurch last night and now the client's furious."

"Please, let me make this up to you. I'll do the job for nothing. I wanna show you—"

"Angie."

"—what I can do. I wanna do a good job—"

"Angie."

"—for you guys—"

"Angie, *stop!*"

She went silent.

"I'll give you another chance—"

"Oh, *thank* you, *thank* you!"

"But not with this client. He's our biggest one. I can't take—"

"Nothing will happen! I promise!"

"Angie, you have to let me finish a sentence."

"Sorry, Mr. Preuss," she said, and fell silent again. He waited a few seconds to make sure she wasn't going to start up again.

Then he said, "I'll give you a call when we have another job for you, okay?"

When he got off the phone with her, he sat with his head in his hands for a few minutes. Maybe Rhonda was right; Angie was a mistake. He was taken in by her story about her handicapped son. Anybody can have a cascading series of problems, but maybe she was a magnet for trouble.

Whatever she was, he couldn't worry about it right now. The first priority was finding someone for the Hersch job—which Rhonda was taking care of—and the next was to keep moving the Bright investigation along.

He typed up notes for today's interview with Joseph Palmer, and Ken Krempka from the day before, then called the number the professor gave him for Ruth Anne Krider.

No longer in service.

He googled her, but found only older hits from when she was still in Palmer's graduate program. No photo beside her name on the grad student page, and two or three mentions in the department newsletter for conference papers she had presented.

He would get Rhonda to work her sources and see what they came up with.

Next he searched for the American Identity Brigade. He couldn't find a website, which was not surprising. As these groups became more and more extreme, they protected their sites from public view by encrypting them in the dark web, or else hiding them behind nondescript names.

He did find multiple references to them, though. They were listed as a hate group by the Southern Poverty Law Center, as well as by the ADL and the FBI.

He found news reports of their members being arrested on charges of assault, conspiracy to commit murder, arson, and multiple reports of painting swastikas on the walls of synagogues and mosques. Mug shots of group members who were arrested showed white men in their twenties and thirties, bearded and surly and sneering into the camera with dead eyes.

This case was already taking an unpleasant turn . . . a peace activist killed in his own home, and now the investigation brushing up against a violent group of white nationalists.

It was too soon to form any theories of the crime, but these bits of information were already starting to circle each other.

Manny Greene might know about this group if he was on the executive board of the Anti-Defamation League. He would be aware of local neo-Nazi groups.

Preuss called the Greene home, hoping Manny felt well enough to talk.

Lila answered. He asked if he could come and talk to Manny about a case. She wasn't wild about the idea, but she said okay.

Rhonda appeared in the doorway. "Bad news," she said. "I called all our regulars. Carlos Guevara, Jack Pennington, Sharon Burkhardt . . . Nobody's available."

"Okay," Preuss said. There went his night. "I'll do it. Get me the address. Meantime, could you see if you can track down this woman?"

He handed her the sheet of paper from his notebook. "This number's disconnected. Not sure about the address."

"Ruth Anne Krider? On it."

17

Lila Greene opened the door to their arts and crafts bungalow in Birmingham. Though "bungalow" was too modest a term for the home, which was as sprawling and well-appointed as a classic California arts and crafts beauty, all polished oak and square-cornered, Gustav Stickley-style Craftsman furniture.

They hugged and she held Preuss at arm's length. "*Don't wear him out,*" she commanded.

"I won't."

She narrowed her eyes at him with mock strictness.

"What kind of day is he having?" he asked.

"He's been good today, but I don't want him overdoing it. You know how he gets."

"I won't keep him long."

"Ten minutes. Tops."

She led him through the living room into a sitting room at the back of the house. Manny sat in a leather chair with a book in his lap. He made to get up but Preuss waved him down, saying, "Sit."

Manny half-rose anyway and Preuss wrapped him in a hug and helped him back into his seat.

"This is a pleasant surprise," Manny said.

"I gave him permission," Lila said from the doorway. "As long as he doesn't tire you out." She gave Preuss a look and then left the two men alone.

"Before you get started with what you came for," Manny said, "now that you're here—I heard from Sy this morning."

Seymour Hersch.

"Not happy," Manny said. His voice was gravelly from the throat cancer, and softer than usual.

"I talked to him, too," Preuss said. "I calmed him, I hope."

"What happened?"

"None of our guys was available, so I tapped the woman we interviewed the other day."

"The 'colorful' one?"

"Angie. Figured I'd give her a try. It was just a surveillance job."

"Seems like she was a little too colorful for it."

"Yeah," Preuss admitted. "She no-showed. It was a bit of a comedy of errors, to hear her tell it. A perfect storm of bad luck."

"A comedy of errors, except it wasn't so funny. It put Sy's nose out of joint, and jeopardized our relationship with our best client."

"I told him we'd take care of it tonight."

"Who'd you get?"

"Nobody's available. I'm going to do it myself."

"Oh, Martin. You can't do everything at once."

"Manny, there's literally nobody else to ask for this. I didn't want to turn the job down."

Manny raised a hand. "Do what you think is best."

The gesture was ambivalent, part *You're in charge now* and part *I don't want to be bothered with this anymore.*

Preuss noticed again how bony Manny's hand was. Manny always had long, slender fingers, but with all the weight he'd lost with the cancer his hand was skeletal.

"Lila's got me on the clock here," Preuss said. "I met an acquaintance of yours today. Joseph Palmer."

"Yeah, Joe, sure. How is he?"

"Seemed well. I saw him at a memorial service for Charles Bright."

"Sorry I couldn't be there."

"We talked for a bit afterwards. I wanted to ask him about a woman who's come up in connection with Bright."

"And?"

"He knew her, too. An ex-grad student in their program at Wayne."

Manny was silent, waiting for Preuss to explain the reason for his visit.

"She seems to be associated with a group of neo-Nazis called the American Identity Brigade," Preuss said. "They might be involved with what happened to Charles Bright."

Manny pursed his lips. "A bad bunch."

"That's what Palmer said. I thought you might be able to tell me something about them."

"You're not planning to pay them a visit, I hope?"

"Right now I'm gathering information."

"Then here's some information for you: These are vicious, dangerous people. They justify their extremism by pointing to the threats to white supremacy around the world. All orchestrated by the Jews, of course. They're not to be trifled with."

"Could you tell me anything you have on the leaders and membership?"

"You're playing with fire here, Martin. Please be careful."

"I will."

Manny considered it for a few moments, then said, "I'll talk to the ADL director. She'll make sure you get what you need."

"Thanks, my friend."

Preuss reached out and took Manny's hand in his own.

Lila pecked her head around the corner of the sitting room. "Time's up," she said with a grim smile.

When he returned to his Explorer, a text came through from Rhonda with the name and address of his surveillance job for the night. He searched for the address on his phone and found it in Sterling Heights, on the northeast side of the city.

He called her.

"Hey," he said, "thanks for the information for tonight."

"No problem."

"Anything going on?"

"You got a call from Rabbi Rifkin."

"Everything okay?"

"Yeah. He just wants to know how it's going."

"But it wasn't urgent?"

"Not that he said. Get back to him when you can. Otherwise all is quiet. I have my boys running down the name you gave me."

She maintained a few contacts from her days as a law student that she refused to divulge—her "boys"—and in addition to her organizational skills, Preuss had begun to rely on those contacts to get information not otherwise available.

Neither Preuss nor Manny asked about those contacts, or worried overmuch about whether the information she obtained was legally gotten. This request, though, should be easy.

"Oh," she said, "and the police report is here."

"Good," Preuss said. "I was going to head home for a couple of hours and see if I can fit in a nap if I'm going to be up all night. But I'd rather take a look at the report."

"It'll still be here in the morning."

"I know. I want to see what it says."

"Up to you. It's on a disk on your desk."

18

He slipped the disk into the CD slot on his desktop and sat back to study the Ferndale PD report on Charles Bright.

Waiting for the file to open, he wondered again about Rhonda's sources.

Preuss suspected they had something to do with her former fiancée being a detective in the West Bloomfield Police Department. The fiancée jilted her at the altar (which prompted one of her breakdowns), but they subsequently reconciled as friends and now Preuss wondered if she played on his guilt to find information for the agency.

Like this file, which came from the Ferndale PD . . . it was an open investigation, and if they knew Martin Preuss was reading it, a series of heads would explode throughout the department, starting with the police chief Nick Russo and continuing down through the chief of the Detective Bureau, Stanley Chrysler.

And the shit would flow downhill to Reg Trombley, who had no part in this at all but whom Chrysler would no doubt blame for it.

Preuss had never served under Chrysler, but when Russo appointed him as chief of detectives, Russo had done a formidable job of poisoning Chrysler against Preuss. Chrysler even put Preuss in the Ferndale PD lockup briefly when he found Preuss at a scene connected with an open case a year or so ago.

Now he saw that Patrolman Paul Vollmer wrote the initial call report for the Bright investigation, and when Reg Trombley took the case over, his case notes were as clear, well-written, and thorough as Preuss would have expected.

The circumstances were much as Corrigan and Rifkin described them. Photos of the scene showed Bright's body underneath a mound of journals. On the desk, a laptop and printer had been destroyed, with pieces of plastic and circuitry scattered everywhere. In the center of the room was a heap of ashes.

The medical examiner thought Charles Bright had been killed between noon and two p.m. on Tuesday, February 12th.

Except the clergymen had omitted one fact. They had said Bright was stabbed numerous times. But according to the Oakland County medical examiner's autopsy, the actual cause of death was blunt object trauma to the head.

There were stab wounds, true, but they were all post-mortem. Somebody had bashed Charles Bright's head in, which killed him, then stabbed him after he was dead.

Stabbed him fourteen times.

And killed his computer.

This was not simply a murder, or a robbery gone bad. Not even a crime of passion. This was a crime of hatred.

Preuss read the statements from the canvas of the neighbors. One woman, Margaret Slater, lived kitty-corner across the street from the Bright home. She told the officer interviewing her she remembered seeing what she assumed to be homeless people coming and going in Bright's house "all the time" (whatever that meant), including the night before Bright was found.

The officer pressed her, and she admitted she thought the people in Bright's house looked "rough and dirty, like people who might be homeless."

She thought they were all men, but she couldn't be sure. She thought somebody might have been staying with Dr. Bright for a few nights at the beginning of the year as well as the night before he was killed.

And she said she saw a man who looked like he was homeless running down the street around the time Bright died. She said she thought it was a man because of the way he ran, but she couldn't tell the race.

Preuss read through the rest of the file. Reg Trombley was the detective of record on the case, and Preuss knew Reg would not have missed this. So he would be focusing on the homeless population around Ferndale.

Preuss wondered if the domestic violence theory came from Reg or from Emma.

Maybe either one assumed there was a personal relationship between Bright and one of the homeless people, and that's why it was looking like a domestic.

Unfortunately, there was no way Preuss could ask Trombley about it. His friend and one-time apprentice had made it clear Preuss was on his own in this one.

And Emma wouldn't even take his call, he was certain.

He reread the report.

He opened the Charles Bright file. He spent the next hour typing up his notes and impressions from the police report. He didn't want to add the report itself, which he wasn't supposed to have. Charles Bright was starting to come into focus, though Preuss couldn't help wondering if there were a dark side to the man so many described as "sweet" and "kind."

When he was finished, he read through his case notes again. Corrigan and Rifkin had said they thought Charles Bright's son Larry was homeless. How did that fit in?

Did Trombley know about it? It wasn't in his case notes.

Could it have been coincidental that Charlie Bright helped the homeless and his son was homeless? Was Charlie trying to expiate whatever guilt he might have felt about his son's situation?

(Preuss knew all about this; it was one of the things that most pained him about his missing son Jason—his own culpability in it.)

Was Charlie Bright trying to find his on? Had he found Larry? Was his son the unknown person who had stayed at his house the night before Charlie died?

And then was seen running down the street on the day of the murder?

Preuss went out to Rhonda's area. "Larry Bright," he said. "Can you start a file on him?"

"Relation to Charles?"

"Son. Try and find out what you can about him, okay?"

"Will do. Larry or Lawrence, right? Still working on the last known for Ruth Anne Krider."

A short while later, Rhonda stuck her head in his doorway. "I have the dossier on Larry Bright."

"That was fast."

She brought in a manila folder and handed it to him. "Not much here," she warned. "I'll keep looking, but . . . he must spend a lot of time off the grid."

He opened the folder and scanned the papers. "Got an address?"

"Not so much an address," she said, "as the absence of an address."

"Meaning?"

"Seems like he's homeless. At least as far as the system is concerned. No current fixed address. A slug of priors, mostly for vagrancy and petty theft, but there's a few drug beefs in there, too."

"Good work. I'll take this with me and have a look at it tonight."

"Speaking of which . . ."

"Yeah," Preuss said. "I'm leaving. Anything happens, give me a call. Otherwise I'll be at home till it's time to check in."

"Rest well."

"Yeah. I wish."

19

Preuss set his phone alarm and laid down on the sofa in his living room, but it was no good; he was too wired to sleep. He made himself a baloney and cheese sandwich and wrapped it in aluminum foil. He took it and a thermos of coffee (just like the old days on stakeouts) and headed out toward Sterling Heights.

The job was located on a cul-de-sac off Utica Road south of Metropolitan Parkway. On one hand, the situation was a tricky one: he couldn't park up the street from the home he was supposed to observe because the home was in a neighborhood where strangers stuck out. Preuss knew some area mafia figures lived around there. Neither they nor the local police would be happy about someone sitting in his car observing them for hours.

On the other hand, because it was a dead end he had some leeway in where he parked. His subject couldn't leave without Preuss noticing him.

He decided to park around the corner from the home he was observing. He still had a clear view of the house, and he could change his observation location so he wouldn't be conspicuous.

When he got into position, he called a number at Hersch's office and told the operator he was relieving the afternoon agent.

"I'll let him know," the operator said.

He settled in to wait.

Seymour Hersch had told him what he was looking for. The resident of the home, a man named Philip Ruhle, had been rejected from a Social Security Disability claim on the grounds that he wasn't disabled from an accident, as he insisted. He signed with Hersch to appeal the decision, and Hersch wanted to make sure he was physically disabled enough so he couldn't work.

Preuss's shift that night was part of an ongoing surveillance of the guy.

An Acura was parked in the driveway, which Hersch had said was the subject's car. A disabled tag hung from the rear-view mirror.

At 8:23, Preuss saw the garage door open. A man came out on crutches, walking awkwardly and robotically, as though he still hadn't gotten the knack of maneuvering. He eased into the front seat of the Acura, grimacing in pain, then sent the garage door down by pressing a button on top of the car's headliner.

He backed the car out of the driveway, and took off down the road.

Preuss followed in his Explorer. The Acura drove up to Garfield Road, then took a left and drove south to Metropolitan Parkway. The car turned west and drove along the Parkway.

Ruhle slowed and entered a parking lot in a strip mall and drove around to a club called The Jay Spot, set in a corner between a Chinese restaurant and an Office Depot. He parked the Acura in a handicapped space and toddled into the club on his crutches.

Preuss sat for a few minutes to make sure Ruhle wasn't coming right out. Then he followed.

He took a seat at the bar where he could see the entire layout of the small club. Onstage in the rear, a loud quintet sounded like they were performing an endless Grateful Dead jam. Except the guitar player was no Jerry Garcia.

In fact, Preuss thought he sounded like Jerry Garcia might sound on the guitar *after* he was dead.

Preuss ordered a Diet Coke and scanned the room. His target sat at a table with a man and three women.

Preuss's phone rang.

He didn't recognize the 313 number, so he let it go to voicemail. When his phone dinged with a message, he listened to it, one finger blocking his other ear to keep out the bar noise.

A woman's voice.

"Hey, Martin. This is Grace Poole. We met at the memorial for Charlie Bright, out in the lobby? I was standing next to you and we chatted? Yeah, so, I got your number from Joseph Palmer. Hope that doesn't freak you out or anything. I'm not a creepy internet stalker, I promise. I just wanted to say hi, see if maybe you might want to meet for a drink sometime. Call me when you get the chance, if you want, okay? If not, no problem. Thanks. Talk soon, I hope."

He disconnected from the voicemail system and laid his phone on the bar.

His first thought was, Okay, Grace's last name is *Poole?*

He remembered from his English minor in college that "Grace Poole" was the name of the woman who guarded Mr. Rochester's insane first wife in *Jane Eyre*. Preuss supposed Grace could be an old family name, but still . . .

And his second thought was, Grace Poole is calling *me?*

He conjured up their brief conversation. She was an attractive woman, he remembered, and remembered too the little squeeze she gave his hand when they shook.

While keeping one eye on the table where his surveillance subject was holding forth, Preuss googled Grace Poole on his phone. It took a while to work through the Jane Eyre references, but he found an entry for Grace C. Poole, Ph.D., associate professor in the

WSU Department of Education. He went to her department page and confirmed it was the woman he had spoken with by her photo on the faculty page.

He clicked on her individual page and read through her information, while making sure not to lose his subject (who continued sitting at his table). Dr. Grace C. Poole taught master's and doctoral courses in English education and in reading, language, and literature.

She coordinated the Reading, Language, and Literature Program. Her research interests were adolescent literacies, gender and literacy, sociocultural theories of literacy and identity, and twenty-first century literacies.

There followed a lengthy list of her publications. The titles included multiple uses of words like *discourse, disclosure, agency, politics, constructing and (re)constructing race and gender in the classroom,* and *critical narrative inquiry.* He found some of her articles on the internet, and began to read them until all the terms with prefixes in parenthesis made him give up.

He got it: she was smart.

He had learned enough about her for now.

It was time to change his location, so he signaled the barman and paid his tab, then wandered over to the other side of the restaurant. There he planted himself against a wall, and while appearing to listen to the music, he continued watching Phil Ruhle.

Who was, Preuss saw, having a good time, even though he kept squirming on his seat and every so often had to stand and stretch and hobble around his table.

He's having a much better time than I'm having, Preuss thought. It wasn't so much that he was tied up in a bar after having been sober for seven years. That didn't bother him. But he had forgotten how tedious stakeouts were; whenever he and Manny needed one now, they tapped one of their associates.

Besides which, this one was making him miss his evening with Toby.

And he told Seymour Hersch he would do it for free.

Bad deal all around.

Preuss got up and wandered around the bar, keeping to the corners and shadows. When he was tired of doing that, he went outside and stayed near the front door until the smokers drove him away.

He strolled around the back to see if there was a rear entrance. There was, so he climbed into his car and moved it to where he could see Phil Ruhle's Acura and both front and rear entrances.

While waiting, he thought more about Dr. Grace C. Poole.

One of the problems with stakeouts: too much time to think.

And brood.

He went back to her faculty page on his phone. She was a good-looking woman, no question. In her photo she had a big, wide smile. A great smile, if he were being honest.

But no.

Nothing here for me, Preuss told himself.

Or for you, he informed her.

Whatever she wanted, he had no intention of calling her back. Sorry, Grace. It's not in the cards.

Until he listened to her message again.

Heard the sound of her voice. Low and soft, inviting, grainy but not raw like a smoker's.

Thought about being courteous. And sociable.

And found himself punching in redial.

She answered on the third ring.

"This is Grace."

"Hey. It's Martin Preuss, returning your call."

"Martin! So glad you called back. Remember me from the theater?"

"Of course."

"Fantastic. So I was calling to see if you'd be interested in meeting up for a drink sometime."

"Yeah," Preuss heard himself say, "I'd like that."

"Fantastic! You're not free tonight, by any chance?"

"No, sorry, tonight's not good. I'm working."

"Yeah, Joe told me you're a private detective. How exciting! Sort of late to be working, though, isn't it?"

"There aren't any set hours. You go where the cases lead you."

"Are you on a *stakeout?*" He caught the unsubtle irony in her voice. A warning flare went up; was she one of those *wry* professors? He grew up among professor friends of his parents who dripped condescension, and couldn't stand it. He hated wry.

"As a matter of fact, I am," he said, perhaps more icily than he meant to.

"How very cool."

This, at least, seemed serious.

"Yeah, well," he said, "it's cooler to hear about than it is to do, I'm afraid. It's a lot of sitting and watching."

"Like in the movies?"

"If they showed an actual stakeout, you'd ask for your money back," he said. "Unbelievably boring."

She laughed. A good laugh. Genuine, unforced, musical. Unironic.

Unwry.

It went with her smile.

"So you probably can't talk for long," she said.

"I can't. But I wanted to get back to you."

"Yeah, thanks. So when do you want to get together? I can't do it tomorrow. It's my long day and night at school. How's Friday look for you?"

He thought for a moment, then said this weekend wouldn't be good, for no particular reason other than he didn't want to do it so soon. He was already sacrificing time with Toby tonight; he didn't want to give up any more of their time together on the weekend, especially for a woman he didn't know well.

"Monday's better for me," he said. "Will that work?"

"I can do Monday. I get out of class at three-thirty. What's your late afternoon like?"

"Always hard to say ahead of time. Why don't we say four o'clock and we'll connect on Monday, make sure it's still okay?"

"Perfect. We'll pick out a place then, too."

"Great."

"Thanks," she said. "Looking forward to it."

"Me, too."

"Have a good weekend, Martin."

"You do the same."

They disconnected, and sitting there he realized he *was* looking forward to it.

He ate his sandwich and drank the coffee in his thermos, then went back into the bar. Phil Ruhle was still there.

Preuss replayed the conversation with Grace Poole in his head, and googled her image again.

She had a Facebook page with photos of her exotic travels: hanging off an overloaded train in Turkey, standing on a pyramid in Peru, sitting on a camel in Morocco. In all the photos she was looking into the camera with a wide smile under a floppy sunhat.

And she was enjoying herself.

I'll take care of that soon enough, Preuss thought, if this goes anywhere beyond meeting for a drink.

Having already convinced himself it wouldn't work out between them, he made himself forget about her and instead focused on his case.

He had brought Larry Bright's dossier in with him. He sat at the bar going through the file while keeping an eye on Phil Ruhle's table.

As Rhonda said, there wasn't much here. Inside were a few printed pages with information on Larry Bright, plus a photostat of his driver's license. It expired three years ago. Larry would be 33 today.

Even as a thirty-year-old in the photo, he seemed to have lived a rough life. He had a headful of close-cropped stubble and a rectangular face with deep lines around his mouth, like parentheses. His eyes were sleepy and hooded as though he were stoned. His jaw was set at an angle that made him looked pissed-off.

He did not look like any encounter with him would be pleasant. Not particularly dangerous, just disagreeable.

His address was listed on Chicago Boulevard in Detroit. Preuss copied it into his notebook.

The page of information repeated most of what Rhonda had already told Preuss about Larry Bright.

There was, however, a surprising fact: Charles Bright's son Larry had a bachelor's degree from the Sacred Heart Major Seminary in Detroit.

Preuss knew it. An arch-conservative post-secondary training ground for Catholic priests. So what was the son of *landsman* Charlie Bright doing there?

Neither Rifkin nor Corrigan had said much about Charlie's wife—maybe she was Catholic and Larry was following her path instead of his father's?

He googled the seminary on his phone. The address was the same as the address on Larry Bright's driver's license.

Again, Preuss wondered if he was duplicating steps the Ferndale PD had already taken. He wished he could have called Reg Trombley to ask a few simple questions. He knew Trombley would agonize over whether to tell Preuss anything (assuming he knew) before deciding he couldn't, and Preuss didn't want to put his friend through that stress.

For now, he would pursue his own investigation, and try to keep his head down as much as possible.

The information about Larry Bright was pointing to a part of Ferndale that was, for the most part, invisible to most people. Ferndale was a stable community of single-family homes, and there wasn't a large homeless population. But there was a group who were either chronically homeless or homeless by choice. They tended to congregate under the Woodward-Eight Mile overpass. Roughly a dozen regulars panhandled and slept near the intersection.

Trombley has likely been through there already.

But I need to go there myself, Preuss thought.

But I can't do it because I'm *here.*

As though to rub it in, his subject stayed in the bar until shortly after midnight.

The people at his table rose as a group and walked to the door, chatting and laughing. As soon as they were out, Preuss jumped up from the bar and went out the back way.

He watched Ruhle stand chatting with one of the women. Then they exchanged a brief kiss. She walked over to her car, a

Hyundai Sonata that looked sepia under the sodium lights of the parking lot.

Ruhle made his way to his Acura and they pulled out onto Metropolitan Parkway, one after the other. Preuss followed in the Explorer.

Ruhle made a Michigan left to go back toward his house, but the woman continued down the Parkway in the opposite direction.

Preuss followed Ruhle, keeping a safe distance behind.

By the time Ruhle pulled into his driveway, Preuss had caught up with him and driven past the house to turn around in the cul-de-sac down the street. He watched as Ruhle drove into his garage and hobbled into the back door of his home. He closed the garage door from inside the house.

In for the night? Preuss wondered. It was 12:32.

Preuss made a note of the time in his notebook, then decided he would wait for a while. Seymour Hersch had said he didn't need the house watched throughout the night, just until it was clear Ruhle had gone to bed.

Preuss wound up staying another hour. He spoke some notes into his iPhone for transcription later. Nothing he had seen tonight indicated Phil Ruhle was anything other than what he had claimed to be.

He was about to leave when he saw a movement in the darkness by the house. A large, dark shape like a concentrated shadow.

Preuss froze.

20

As he watched, a narrow shaft of light as from a penlight clicked on, and swept over the outside of the garage. The dark figure holding the light tried to lift the garage door, but there was no handle.

The light continued to play over the front of the house—the bushes, the broad darkened picture windows, a gazing ball in the front garden, the front entrance.

Preuss made sure the overhead light of the Explorer was off, and opened the door and eased it closed. He trotted down the road and up the driveway in the chilly air.

Angie Sturmer gasped once and shone the light right into Preuss's eyes.

He put his hand up to block the beam and she turned it off. She gaped at him.

He held a finger to his lips and, as angrily as he could while still not making a sound, he waved her out of the driveway and away from the house. She followed him back to his car and slipped into the passenger seat.

He took several deep breaths to calm himself. Then he said, "What are you doing here?"

"I felt bad about messing up last night. I wanted to do it right this time."

"So when I told you not to come out here, that didn't mean anything? You decided to do it anyway?"

"I didn't see you here," she said. "I thought you couldn't get anybody so I decided to come out and see what I could find out. I didn't see you here!"

Like that was an excuse for disregarding his instruction.

"Staying out of sight is the point of surveillance," he pointed out.

"I know, I know. I'm sorry."

"And what did you think you were doing, trying to get inside his garage?"

"I thought I might find something incriminating."

"Like what?"

"I don't know. Golf clubs, maybe. To show he's being active."

"You think he's going to play golf in his garage in the middle of the night in February?"

"I didn't know," she whined.

He took another few breaths and made himself relax.

"You were lucky there were no motion detector lights. You're lucky the door didn't have a pressure alarm sensor. You're lucky the local cops didn't get called on you. How would that go over?"

"Not good," she admitted.

He watched her in the dim light from the streetlamp down the street. She hung her head in an exaggerated pantomime of shame.

"Angie," he said, and she looked up at him. "Go home, okay? Right now. We'll talk more about this in the morning. Come to the office."

"All right. Mr. Preuss, I'm so sorry—"

He held a hand up to cut her off. "Come in around ten."

She nodded her understanding, and opened the car door.

"How did you get here?" he asked. "I thought your car was totaled."

"I borrowed my mom's Odyssey. I'm parked around the corner."

"Go home, Angie. I'll see you at the office."

"Yessir."

She eased the door closed and disappeared into the darkness.

I'm going to have a problem with her, Preuss thought.

Going to? he corrected himself. How about *having* a problem? She isn't going to work out, he decided. Whatever she has to do to take care of her handicapped child, it's not going to be detective work for this agency.

He waited a little while longer, then started up the Explorer and drove away from Phil Ruhle's darkened home.

Thursday, February 28, 2013

21

"How'd it go last night?"

Preuss filled his cup with everyday office coffee and eased his exhausted body onto the sofa in Rhonda's outer office.

He took a long drink before answering. The coffee was hot and bitter and scalded his throat going down, but he felt its rejuvenating effect at once.

"It was quiet," he said. "As far as the surveillance was concerned," he added.

"That doesn't sound good."

"Angie showed up as I was getting ready to pack it in."

"Yikes."

"Yeah."

"What was she doing there? Wait, don't tell me: she was trying to make up for the screwup the night before."

"You got it."

"What'd you tell her?"

"I told her to go home. And we'd talk this morning."

"Do you think she did?"

He shrugged.

She looked up into the corner of the room and stroked an imaginary beard while pretending to consider what he had said.

"If only someone had warned us about her," she mused.

"This wasn't her screwing up, this was her ignoring what I asked her to do."

"Same difference. If she won't follow directions, what good is she going to be?"

"Fair point."

"What time did you roll out?" she asked.

He told Rhonda about his evening, including the prolonged stay at the bar.

"Did you get any sleep at all?"

"A few hours. I had to skip Toby's last night, which I was annoyed about. And I couldn't drag myself out of bed to see him this morning."

"You can make up for it later on. Should be a slow day. Calendar's clear. We just have to go over expenses at some point so I can cut a few checks."

"Nothing else going on?"

"Nope."

"Angie should stop in around ten. So we can finish our talk from last night."

"I'll look forward to seeing her," Rhonda drawled.

"Aren't you chipper this morning," he said.

She raised her shoulders around her ears, then let them drop.

He imitated the gesture. "What's this mean?"

"Means I had a nice time last night. I met someone."

"Rhonda, that's great."

"Yeah, well. We'll see."

"Any details? Name? Occupation? Net worth?"

"Not yet. I don't want to jinx it."

When he first started working with Manny, Preuss considered there might be something to pursue with Rhonda. She was an attractive woman, and had told Preuss she had a multiply-handicapped sister who had died a few years before. She had first met Toby at a small dinner party at Manny and Lila Greene's, and both she and Toby had fallen in instant like with each other.

She was on the young side, but it didn't keep Preuss from imagining a storyline for them both. After all, he had a known (and futile) attraction to younger women.

Until Manny told him a bit about her background, and how fragile she was. And Preuss rethought the possibility of a relationship with her.

But now he was glad—if, he had to admit, a bit jealous—to hear she might have found someone.

Maybe.

"Well, good luck with it," Preuss said. She accepted his good wishes with an incline of her head. The tower of blonde curls tilted.

He sat for a moment longer, collecting himself, then heaved his tired body off the sofa and trudged into his office. I'm starting to feel my age, he thought.

Or my age plus fifty, he added to himself. He couldn't function after a late night the way he used to.

He checked his phone messages, then spent an hour writing up a report on last night's surveillance for Seymour Hersch. (He left out the part about seeing Angie.) Before he could send it, his cell rang with a number he didn't recognize.

"Mr. Preuss," a woman said, "this is Sylvia Bloom. I'm vice president of the Michigan Regional Anti-Defamation League. I'm calling at the request of Manny Greene."

"Yes," Preuss said, "he said he was going to get in touch with you. Thanks for checking back so fast."

"My pleasure. He said you have questions about the local white supremacist scene?"

"I do. One group in particular: the American Identity Brigade."

"Aha," she said.

"I take it you know them."

"I do indeed."

"Can we meet to talk?"

She was silent.

"Just checking my schedule," she said. "The first available opening I have is on Monday. Unless . . . I have some time later today. How's midafternoon look? I have a couple meetings downtown, but if you don't mind coming down here, we can find someplace to chat in between."

"What time?"

"Around two?"

"Perfect," he said. "Let's plan on it."

They decided to meet at the Cass Café, where he had lunch with Joseph Palmer.

They disconnected and he heard a commotion in Rhonda's outer area. He recognized the voice at once.

Rhonda appeared in his doorway.

"You have a visitor."

Before he could reply, Angie Sturmer loomed large behind the petite administrative assistant. Angie could have picked up Rhonda with one hand and moved her aside, but instead she said, "Excuse me. Mr. Preuss?"

Rhonda stood aside and Angie entered the office. A folded newspaper stuck out from the handbag on her shoulder.

"You told me to come and see you," Angie said. "And I have something really, really important."

"Okay," Preuss said. "Have a seat."

Rhonda threw him a wink and closed the door.

"Did you leave when I asked you to?" Preuss asked.

"Well," Angie said, "not exactly."

"What does 'not exactly' mean?"

"It means I stayed around for a bit longer."

"Why did you do that after I asked you to go?"

"I sorta fell asleep."

Preuss expelled a breath of exasperation. "Can you tell me why you didn't leave when I asked you to?"

"Okay, but wait," Angie said.

"You know what, I don't—"

"Wait, please, Mr. Preuss. Can you hear me out?"

Another sigh. "Okay."

"So it's true, I sat in my car for a few minutes after I left you."

"How much longer?"

"Um," she said, "about twenty minutes."

"Because you thought that would give me enough time to wait for *you* to leave, and then I'd go on my way."

Without responding, she said, "I walked back around the corner to the subject's house. The home was dark, but something about it made me nervous."

Made *you* nervous, Preuss thought. Great.

"I was trying to learn to trust my instincts," she said. "Isn't that what everyone says? A good investigator learns to trust her instincts? Right then my instincts told me all was not right. I thought I'd hang around to check it out."

Preuss was too angry to say anything.

"I thought you were already pretty pissed at me," she said.

"This is true."

"But if I could bring back some worthwhile intel about this subject, I thought you'd get over being annoyed."

Intel?

"Besides," she said, "I arranged for my son to spend the night with his father. So I was free. I figured I might as well stick around for a while longer. Unfortunately, after an hour or so, I fell asleep leaning against a tree."

"Angie . . ."

"But a car woke me up. It pulled into the subject's driveway and a woman got out and went into the house."

Angie pulled the newspaper out of her handbag. She set the morning edition of the *Free Press* on the desk in front of Preuss and tapped a finger on a story on page three.

"Take a look at this," Angie said.

He skimmed the article. It was about the discovery of a woman's body near the Clinton River in Grant Park in Utica.

"Why am I looking at this?" he asked.

"Because I know who did this, Mr. Preuss."

"*This* being . . .?"

"Who killed this lady and dumped her in the river."

Preuss examined her face, which was intent and serious. She's not kidding, he realized.

"Who did it?" he asked.

"The guy we were watching last night."

"Phil Ruhle?"

"Yes."

"You know this how?"

"Because I saw him do it."

"Wait," Preuss said, "you saw Phil Ruhle kill this woman?"

"Well, no," Angie said. "I didn't see him *kill* her. But I saw him dump the body. At this park," she added, pointing to the newspaper on Preuss's desk.

"When?"

"Last night. Or early this morning, to be accurate."

"Let's back up. You're telling me you saw a woman arrive at Phil Ruhle's house, and later watched him dump this woman's body in the Clinton River."

"Yessir. I followed him from his house and watched him do it."

"What time did she get there?"

She pulled a notebook out of her purse and consulted it. "Two-oh-five a.m."

"How did she arrive?"

"A car dropped her off. Might have been an Uber, I don't know. He dropped her off and then drove away."

"You're sure it was this woman?" Preuss tapped the paper.

"Yes. Well, pretty sure."

"Angie?"

"No, see, I thought it was weird, somebody going into his house so late. So I stayed and watched some more. Then"—here she consulted her notes again—"at 3:19, his garage door opened and I see his car pull out and drive away.

"So I go, 'Wow, that's kinda strange, that time of night,' so I run back to my car and follow him. And he drives around and winds up in Grant Park. I stayed a ways behind him and I watched him pull into the park and get out of his car. He walks around to the trunk and takes out a big bundle and dumps her into the river. He weighed the bag down with stones, like, and waded out into the middle of the river and let her go. I saw her go under."

"He wasn't on crutches?"

"No! I'm saying—he was walking as good as you and me!"

"And then what happened?"

"Then he drove home and pulled into the garage. I waited a little while in case he was going to come out again. But when I thought he was done for the night, I left."

Preuss picked up the newspaper article again, and read it more carefully.

"It says here they believe the body'd been in the water for several days," Preuss said.

"That can't be right. I saw him dump her."

"You think you saw him dump a *bundle.* But you can't be positive the woman's body was in it, can you? Or *any* body was in it?"

"Well," she said, "no, not a hundred percent sure. But why else would he have gone out there in his car at three-thirty, four o'clock in the morning, if not to dump a *body*?"

Preuss sighed.

"We don't know anything about this guy. The visitor could have been his wife or his girlfriend. Or a woman he met at the bar that night. Or his cousin who flew in from Kansas. Or an out-call prostitute he hired for the night."

"But why would he go to the river and dump whatever it was in the water?"

"I don't suppose you took any photos of it?"

"I forgot to."

"And because you left, you don't know if the woman is still at Ruhle's house or not?"

"No," she admitted.

"Did you tell anybody about this? Like, the police in Utica?"

"No. I wanted to tell you first. See what you thought we should do."

"*We?*"

"Well, yeah. I was on assignment for you guys."

"Uh, no, you weren't. I told you not to be there. Twice, in fact."

"But still. What should we do about it?"

"*We're* not going to do anything. If I were *you*, I'd go talk to the police in Utica, see what they have to say about it. And don't tell them you were working for us, because you weren't."

She looked crestfallen. I guess I was supposed to jump right up and run out to the river with her, Preuss thought.

"Angie, I have to ask," he said, "you're certain you were awake during this whole time?"

"Yes, I was awake."

Insulted.

"All right," he said, "here's what's going to happen. You're going to write up what you saw. If you did see this guy carrying something—whether it was a body or something else—then it means he's not handicapped, which is what we've been trying to prove. Can you do that? Today?"

He was about to tell her he'd pay her for her time, but then remembered it could then be argued she was in his employ, so he let it pass.

"Thank you, Mr. Preuss. You're the best!"

Angie left and Rhonda appeared in the doorway. "Well?"

"She thnks she saw our guy dumping a body in the river last night."

"Oh pu-leeze."

He shrugged.

Rhonda pursed her lips and twirled her index finger around her temple.

22

Preuss left the Explorer in the same parking structure he had used for Charles Bright's memorial and made the long walk down Cass Avenue to the Cass Cafe. The day was bright, but the temperature had dropped sharply overnight.

His cheeks stung with the cold by the time he walked into the restaurant. A woman at a table by the bar stood and motioned to him. She was small and severe in a grey business suit with a white blouse, but a fierce energy radiated from her.

"Mr. Preuss?" she said.

"Yes. Ms. Bloom?"

"The same."

She held out a hand and they shook. "I ordered coffee. Did you want something?"

"Coffee for me," he told the server who came over with Sylvia's drink.

"I googled you," she said, "so I'd know what you looked like."

"I didn't know I had an online presence."

"Everyone has, these days," she said. "I found you in some of the annual reports for the Ferndale Police Department, and a couple of news articles. And of course on your business website."

Rhonda was in charge of the agency website. He had never thought to check it.

"You've had an interesting career," Sylvia Bloom said.

"It's been a good ride. For the most part," he felt compelled to add.

But he didn't come to talk about himself. "Thanks for meeting me," he said.

"Oh, my pleasure. Any friend of Manny's, and so on. How's he doing?"

"It's hard to tell with him. He's very private."

"He is that. So you two work together?"

"We do. I started with him last year. We're sort of seeing how it goes."

"And?"

"So far, so good."

"I'm sure he appreciates having you there, now."

"His illness caught us all by surprise."

"I've known him a long time," she said. "I knew Lila first, but I met Manny not long after."

His coffee came and he set it to one side. He wanted to get right to business.

"I wanted to talk about the American Identity Brigade," he said.

"What would you like to know?"

"Whatever you can tell me."

"Right." She reached into her purse and withdrew a manila envelope and laid it on the table. "I copied some information for you. Basically, they're a hate group. They believe white people are literally the God-given rulers of every country in the world, most especially this one. The group you're asking about is part of a rising tide of neo-Nazis we're tracking around the country. And the world, for that matter. Every time we have a Democratic president, the agitators on the far right get restless, dress up in their army costumes, and make noises about taking their country back. Remember the upswing in militias during the Clinton years?"

"Who could forget the black helicopters coming to take our guns away."

"Same thing's happening now under Obama. But this is worse, Martin. By a factor of ten. They're violent anti-Semites and racists, and they're getting organized. They're learning how to refine their messages for mass consumption."

"Through the internet?"

"In part," she said. "But it's also because their ideologies of racism and open hatred are becoming more acceptable in more parts of the country. They're getting bolder and more vocal in expressing their beliefs, at the same time as they're learning how to play on people's fears."

"Once this was the fringe of the fringe," Preuss said.

"Not any longer. That's the other thing they're learning—how to package themselves so they have mass appeal. Neo-Nazi, white nationalist cells are forming all across the country. The hate crimes are already ramping up—against Jews, against blacks, against Muslims, Asians, Latinos, LGBTQ populations. And the crimes are becoming more violent. These are violent people, ethno-nationalists who espouse racial and religious hatred.

"We've been following the American Identity Brigade for a while. Sometimes they deface synagogues and churches and mosques and headquarters of LGBTQ organizations. Sometimes they phone in bomb scares, or place bombs in a shul or a church, or attempt to kill their enemies."

"Real heroes."

"These people are always cowards. If they weren't so dangerous, they'd be pathetic."

She pushed the envelope across the table to him. "These come from our file on them. I thought it might be helpful."

He withdrew the folder inside and opened it to a series of photographs.

"Their leadership," Sylvia Bloom said. "Like most of these groups, the faces change, but the attitudes don't. These are the ones we've been able to identify as being at the head of it most recently."

They were not the glowering skinhead menaces he expected. Instead, they were clean-cut and banal-looking, like sales managers at a car dealership, or accountants.

They wore the uniforms of the new Nazis: jackets and ties and polo shirts and khakis.

"Walk me through these guys?" he asked.

She scooted her chair over next to his. "This is the leader."

She tapped a photo of a pudgy, round-faced man in his thirties. "He looks harmless, but don't let that fool you. He's a rabid anti-Semite. Clark Turner. President of the AIB. Lives in Westland."

Another photo revealed a pleasant-looking man in his forties who bore an eerie resemblance to the actor Jeff Daniels, down to the square jaw and shock of straw-colored hair falling over his forehead.

"Kevin Johnson," she said. "How's that for an all-American name? Lives in Helmford. Long police record for hate crimes, battery, domestic abuse, unlawful discharge of a weapon, and assorted other anti-social activities."

Preuss turned another photo over and looked at a perfect Aryan type, cold blue eyes in an oval face with a smarmy smile. Silver hair cut in what used to be called a Princeton. A clean-cut, All-American guy.

"Warren Cattrell," she said. "Also in Westland. He made his bones with extremists on the right years ago . . . Ku Klux Klan, Young Americans for Freedom, Youth for Western Civilization. You name it, if somebody's against liberalism or globalism or diversity, he'll be there fomenting discord."

Next came several pages of bulleted material. "This is what we've been able to glean about the group from the Michigan State Police. What they believe in, what connections they have with other white power groups, and so on."

One sheet contained a detailed genealogy chart linking the different hate groups, leaders, and tenets across the country.

Another sheet showed a map of the United States with pinpoints for the largest hate groups in different parts of every state.

"Damn," he said.

"Scary, isn't it? Every time I see that map, it turns my stomach."

"These aren't isolated whackjobs."

"You're right," she said. "They're widespread, well-armed — and increasingly coordinated — networks of white nationalists, neo-Nazis, and Christian extremists."

He flipped through the rest of the file, which also contained a list of a hundred and fifty names.

"Those are the people we've been able to link with the AIB," she said. "Again, the membership is fluid, but those are the ones we're certain of. The actual membership is in the hundreds, at least. And growing by the year."

The contact for the group was a post office box in Westland.

"They operate out of Clark Turner's house," Sylvia said. "But they have operations across the state. Cells around here and near Grand Rapids, up in Petoskey and Alpena . . . pretty much everywhere you look, you'll find them. Even in the UP."

They talked for another half-hour. By then it was coming up to three o'clock.

She gulped down her coffee. "Sorry to run, but I need to wrap this up. You can hang onto the file. I have copies."

"Thanks a million for this, Sylvia."

"If you need anything else, don't hesitate to give me a call. What's your interest in them, if you don't mind my asking?"

"I'm looking into the death of a man named Charles Bright. He was a history professor here at Wayne, and he was involved with some peace groups around the city. One of his graduate students is connected with this group. I'm looking into whether they might have had any contact with him."

"I read about his murder in the paper. Are these guys involved?"

"Hard to say. I'm trying to find the connection, and it seems to be this student."

"What's the student's name?"

"Ruth Anne Krider."

She took back the file and ran a finger down the list of associates.

She tapped a finger on a line. "Here she is."

She pushed the file back to him. Ruth Anne Krider was listed as an associate of the American Identity Brigade. Her address was also in Westland.

That would be his next stop.

23

She lived in a small house on Harvey Street North, off the intersection of the main arteries of Wayne and Ford Roads. Preuss drove around the block and parked on the next street over and walked back.

It was a brick ranch, tiny and compact, like thousands of homes in the metropolitan area. A "No Solicitors" sign on the storm door warned off unwanted visitors, as did a hand-scrawled note beside it:

This home protected by Smith & Wesson
I dont call 911

He climbed the front steps and rang the bell. After a few moments the door swung open and Preuss stood facing a man in his thirties with a neat silver beard and long silver hair swept back into a pony tail. He was handsome, with regular features and a movie star's straight jaw. He had grown his hair out, but Preuss recognized Warren Cattrell, one of the men in the photos Sylvia Bloom had shared of the leadership of the American Identity Brigade.

He and Preuss gave each other the once over.

"Help you?" the guy said. Pleasant enough, no hint of threat.

"I'm looking for Ruth Anne Krider."

"Yeah? Who's asking?"

Again, not belligerent. More curious.

"Martin Preuss."

"Police?"

"Private investigator." He handed the guy one of his business cards. "You are?"

The guy took Preuss's card, but didn't look at it.

"I don't believe I'm legally obliged to give you my name. Mind telling me what you want with Ruth Anne?" the guy asked instead. Still pleasant, now leaning against the door.

"We keep answering questions with questions, we're not going to get very far," Preuss said. "Is she in?"

The guy kept smiling but his eyes hardened. He stared at Preuss for a few moments, then said, "Sorry, guy. Nobody here by that name." He gave an uplift of his chin—get lost, the gesture said—and closed the door in Preuss's face.

Preuss waited a moment and rang the bell again and Warren Cattrell swung the door open again.

"I guess I didn't make myself clear," Cattrell said. "There's nobody here by that name."

Cattrell stood back so he wasn't visible from the street and lifted his tee shirt up to show the butt of a big gun stuck into his waist. A big .45.

"Now you want to come inside and debate the issue with me?"

Preuss looked at the butt of the gun, then up at the man standing there.

Watching Preuss with a hard smile.

Behind Cattrell, Preuss saw a red, white, and black flag hung on the living room wall. At its center was the trident-shaped "life-rune" that Preuss remembered from his European history courses.

The Nazis had adopted it for the SS leading up to the Second World War.

Preuss considered: Do I want to get into it with this guy?

He had a staring contest with Cattrell, then decided he didn't want to. Not now, anyway. There might be another chance later.

But Preuss kept looking at him. Decided to jerk his chain a bit. Said, "Wait. I know you."

"I don't think so, friend."

"Yeah. Aren't you Warren Cattrell?"

Cattrell blinked. His smile disappeared. "Do I know you?"

"No, but I know you," Preuss said.

"From where?"

"Around."

"Around where?"

Pissed, now.

Mission accomplished. "Ruth Anne comes home," Preuss said, "let her know I'm looking for her? Have a nice day, Warren."

He felt Cattrell's eyes on his back as he walked down the block until he disappeared around the corner to where he left his car.

Really don't feel like being phony-tough today, he told himself.

Especially with a white supremacist standing there with a .45 in his waistband.

He moved the Explorer down the street from Ruth Anne Krider's house, and parked where he could watch it.

He waited.

At a little after 5:30, a grey Ford Escape pulled into the driveway. The driver, a woman, stayed in the car, and in another minute an F250 pickup roared into the driveway behind her.

Three beefy white guys hopped out of the cab looking like they just got back from a deer hunt. One wore a beige Carhartt coat with an American flag sewn on the back, another had a dark hoodie, and the third had on a plaid shirt. All wore camo baseball caps. The hoodie slung an AR-15 across his chest and strutted around in front of the home.

The three guys looked up and down the street, and when they gave her the all-clear, the woman inside the car must have felt safe enough to come out.

Preuss had never seen a photo of Ruth Anne Krider, so he had to assume this was her. He was far enough away to be able to form only an impression: tall and slender, with a mass of dirty-blonde waves and holding a backpack.

The men surrounded her and walked her into the house.

Preuss sat for a while longer. He took a small pair of binoculars from his glove box and trained them on the car. He wrote down the license plate, and checked out the rest of the vehicle.

On the rear bumper was a sticker, "John Glenn High School," with "Staff" in smaller letters.

Also on the bumper was a sticker with the replica of the tri-color flag in the living room of the house.

Preuss examined the pickup and noted its license plate. A Confederate flag sticker and the tricolor flag sticker were on the truck's rear bumper.

He stayed for another hour to see if anybody came in or out of the house.

No movement. With the four men inside, he wasn't going to get to her tonight, so he left.

He needed to see Toby.

He had to get the taste of these people out of his mouth.

24

The flashing lights were visible all the way down the block. Red, white, red, white, alternating in the curious way they had of synchronizing briefly before getting crazily out of sync.

An electric stab of fear went from his throat to his bowels.

A Berkley Fire Rescue truck was parked in front of Toby's group home. A Berkley Public Safety squad car was in the driveway, and a Fire Department supervisor's car behind that.

There were no open spaces, so Preuss veered into the curb, slamming the Explorer's front wheels, and leapt out of the car and ran to the group home's front door.

Inside all was quiet. On the television in the living room, the news played at a low volume. Katy, one of Toby's housemates, reclined in her wheelchair, napping as a clip of President Obama walking around a corner in a gaggle of reporters showed over and over again.

Preuss passed through to the back of the house. Three men stood in the hall talking with Connie, the buxom respiratory therapist with an arc of floral tattoos across her chest and upper arms visible in the low-cut scrubs top she always wore. One of the men was a Berkley police officer, taking down information she was giving him. The other two were from Berkley Fire Rescue.

They looked to be standing outside Toby's room.

When she saw him—and the look on his face—she said, "Martin," but he pushed past her to Toby's room.

Which was empty.

He turned back to Connie. "Where is he?"

That's when he noticed the men were crowded outside of Ginny's room, across the hall from Toby's. Ginny was on a respirator twenty-four hours a day.

Preuss looked into her room and saw two EMTs strapping her onto a gurney along with her respirator.

The head EMT turned toward him. "Are you the father?"

"No," Preuss said.

"The parents are on their way," Connie said.

"They should meet us at the hospital," the EMT said. "We gotta go. 'Scuse us," he said to Preuss.

Preuss stood back and the EMTs rolled the gurney past him. Ginny looked tinier than ever, with her thin arms and skinny body restrained. Her face was grey. Her eyes were half-closed and her ventilator breathed for her, puffing in and out in a gritty wheeze.

Connie finished giving the information to the officer. He folded up his notebook and stuck it in his back pocket. He nodded to Preuss and followed the gurney out to the fire rescue ambulance. One of the aides followed in her car to be with Ginny at the hospital.

Connie looked almost as bad as Ginny. Her face was dead white and she leaned against the wall. Preuss thought she was going to faint.

"You okay?" he said.

She nodded, but still looked like she was going to pass out. He reached out a hand to steady her.

"Want some water?" he asked.

She shook her head.

"What happened?"

"I was walking by her room and peeked in. She was grey and when I nudged her she was unresponsive. I couldn't find any heart sounds, so I started CPR. I had to perform it for over a half-hour before her heart started again."

She closed her eyes. "I'm gonna be sick." Ginny had her own bathroom, so Connie rushed through the room and Preuss heard her retching into the toilet.

The house manager came running into the back of the house. She was a short, solid woman named Deb Hilbert. "They called me," she said, breathless. "What's going on?"

"Ginny had a crisis," Preuss said. "She's on her way to the hospital. I just got here myself."

"Where's Connie?"

He pointed toward the bathroom. They heard the toilet flush, and in a few moments Connie came out to the hallway. She was wiping her damp face with a paper towel and her color was better.

"What happened?" Deb Hilbert asked.

"Before you tell her," Preuss interrupted, "where's Toby?"

"Having his bath," Connie said. "He's been in the tub the whole time."

Preuss nodded his thanks and went further down the hall to the bathroom. Sure enough, his son was floating in the tub while his aide Melissa was rinsing him off with the hand-held shower.

Preuss leaned into his son's line of vision. Toby's eyes were half-closed and he wore his silly crooked grin showing the gap between his two front teeth.

"Well," Preuss said, "I see I didn't need to worry about you!"

After the bath, Preuss sat on the side of Toby's bed with his arm around his son to keep him propped up. With his cerebral palsy,

Toby couldn't sit up by himself, or perform any of the skills of daily living; he needed constant care. Preuss hated having him in a group home, but he had tried keeping him at home and couldn't manage it, even with daily nursing care.

He hugged Toby's fragile shoulders to him and rested his head on top of Toby's sweet-smelling hair. They rocked back and forth, Preuss humming a tuneless song and Toby humming back.

"I was scared when I saw all those cars out front," Preuss told him. "I thought something happened to you. What would I do without you? How would I get through my days without you to come back to?"

Toby hummed a reply.

"I know," Preuss said. "I don't either. I hope Ginny's going to be okay."

In truth, Preuss didn't know if his son ever understood him. But he knew there was nothing to be lost by assuming Toby understood it all without the ability to reply, so Preuss often carried on conversations like this, as if Toby had made an actual comment.

Toby hummed his response. One thing Preuss did know was that this was all so fragile. As Ginny's experience tonight proved again, everything could change in an instant with young people this medically frail.

With all of us, he thought—but especially people like Toby.

So Preuss had to enjoy every second with him. Toby seemed to know this instinctively, and Preuss was trying his hardest to learn it from his wise old soul of a son.

No, the likelier question was what would happen to Toby as he grew older and put on weight and became harder to move around. How would he fare when Preuss died? Would there be anyone to take care of him, or would Toby be cared for by strangers in a setting like this—or worse, an institution—for the rest of his life?

These were questions Preuss couldn't answer.

They were hard enough even to ask.

Well, he thought, tonight let's practice one of Toby's great skills, being present in the moment. Let's not imagine a future that hasn't happened yet.

"Want to hear about my case?" Preuss asked. Toby made the quietest little hum and settled deeper in the crook of Preuss's arm.

"I have this case," Preuss said. "It's taking a while to shape up."

Toby stopped wiggling; he was listening.

Preuss didn't want to upset his son with the details of the crime, so he skipped them.

"The police suspect it's a personal encounter that went bad. From what I've seen, that doesn't sound right. I can't get anybody to tell me anything, but from the viciousness of the attack I can see how they might think so. For me, other lines of inquiry make more sense.

"The first is, everybody says my guy used to bring homeless people to his house for a meal, and one person went crazy on him. I suppose that's closest to the police version, but the police are convinced there was a personal element to it and it was some kind of domestic violence situation. My guy brought home a lot of strangers, and trying to find the one bad one he brought home isn't going to be easy.

"The second is the white nationalist connection through one of his former students. A nonviolent peace activist versus violent white power nationalists? Might be, Toby. I need to talk with this grad student, but she's been hard to get close to.

"The third is my guy's son, Larry. He might connect with the homeless scenario, or he might have his own reasons for hating his father enough to kill him. I have to find this guy and talk to him.

"And the fourth is the one I haven't found yet. What do you think of these, Detective Toby?"

Toby took a deep breath and offered his opinion in a series of murmured vocalizations ending with, "Num num num."

"I agree with your analysis," Preuss said, and kissed the top of his son's head. "Thanks for helping me talk my way through this."

They sat together until Toby's head began to droop. Then Preuss laid him out on the bed and tucked the covers around him. Toby's eyes fluttered, and he drifted into sleep.

While Preuss was searching through Toby's CDs for the Judy Collins disks he listened to at night, Connie peeked her head in the room.

"Just wanted to let you know," she whispered, "Ginny's stable. She was down so long, they don't know what the long-term effects are going to be. But for now she's okay."

"You saved her," Preuss said. "Not a bad night's work."

"For a while there, I wasn't so sure."

She gave Preuss a wan smile, then disappeared down the hall.

He continued searching for Toby's music. He found the disks he was looking for. He sat while his son slept as Judy Collins sang "Farewell to Tarwathie" against the haunting, elegiac chorus of the songs of the humpback whales.

He drove home with the lonely whale calls echoing in his head.

Friday, March 1, 2013

25

John Glenn High School was a sprawling one-story building in Westland. On the left was a glass-enclosed rotunda, and a straight run of classrooms and offices took up the rest of the block. The effect was of a filmstrip spooling out of a reel.

Inside was a clean, well-lighted space, all beige and teal. Preuss stopped at the main office beside the entrance doors and told the clerk who he was looking for.

The clerk, a heavy-set woman with dyed jet black hair, gave him a serious hairy eyeball. "Can I ask what this is about?"

He showed his identification. "I'm a private investigator. Ms. Krider's name came up in connection with a case I'm working on. I need to do a routine interview with her."

"Uh-huh."

Preuss could see her mentally running through all the possibilities for why he *really* wanted to see the woman: he was Ruth Anne's abusive spouse, he was a non-custodial parent looking to snatch a child from the premises, he was an all-round crazy about to whip out the AR-15 hidden under his coat . . . all the possibilities ending with bloodshed.

And all were, he had to admit, eminently plausible.

"One minute," she said.

She turned away and typed something into the computer terminal at her counter.

"Ms. Krider's in class right now," the woman said. "She can't be disturbed."

"When is her next break?" Preuss asked.

"I can't give out that information, sir." She decided she wasn't trusting him after all.

"Fair enough," Preuss said. "I'll catch her another time. When do classes let out for the day?"

"Three-fifteen."

"Great. Thanks for your help."

On his way out of the building, he saw a security guard catching a smoke at the side of the front entrance. The guard locked eyes on him, then raised his chin in a man-to-man greeting and looked away. He took one last long drag on the smoke, then tossed it into the bushes and went back inside.

Preuss would have sworn it was one of the men who came to Ruth Anne Krider's rescue the night before.

The one out front with the assault weapon.

"What's doing?" Preuss asked when he got into his office.

"Couple calls for you," Rhonda said. "Not much else."

She handed him a pair of salmon-colored While You Were Out slips. Though she was computer literate, Manny insisted she use these old-style message slips for phone calls because he wanted to have an actual paper trail for all calls.

"I have a present for you," he said. He handed her a sheet with the license numbers of the two cars he saw last night in the driveway to Ruth Anne Krider's house, Ruth Anne's and the pickup. "Can you get your secret friends to run these down?"

"Sure."

"Thanks. Soon as you can."

"You got it."

"You're the best."

"As good as Angie?"

When he didn't laugh, or even smile, she said, "What a grouch. Mail's on your desk."

He gave her a small smile in reply, hoping this buoyancy didn't mean she was entering into a new manic phase because of the new guy in her life.

It's okay to be happy, he thought. Just don't get too happy.

That could even be my motto, thought Martin Preuss.

The two messages on his desk were from Seymour Hersch's secretary. He called her and she told him Hersch needed another copy of the final reports for two cases Preuss had finished up for Manny. He made a note to ask Rhonda to send these off.

Rhonda had already sorted through the letters on his desk, opening them and stapling the envelopes to their contents. He went through them, initialing invoices and associates' expense reports for payment, then took them and the two messages from Hersch out to Rhonda.

"Here you go," he said.

"Thanks."

He poured himself a cup of everyday coffee, and went back into his office. He opened the Bright case file and added his notes from his encounters the day before. He also added the reflections he had made with Toby.

He thought back through the possible scenarios. He was going to talk with Ruth Anne Krider this afternoon, so that would move one scenario forward. He needed to find Larry Bright and speak with him, and he also needed to check the local homeless population to see if any of them knew or went home with Charles Bright for any reason.

It wouldn't be easy. With his teaching, his peace activism, and his work across Wayne State's academic community, Bright ranged around the entire metropolitan Detroit area—where over two thousand people experienced chronic homelessness.

Easy, tiger, he told himself.

Let's start local.

26

A homeless encampment had formed beneath the overpass to the Woodward and Eight Mile Road interchange. It was there even in the winter. Periodically the police would clear it out when the tents and shopping carts and sleeping bags began to block the broad sidewalk on both sides of Eight Mile. But right now it was down to only a few piles of belongings.

One of the homeless men who hung around the interchange was stretched out on a chaise longue on the sidewalk of southbound Woodward. He was sound asleep despite the traffic sounds around him. If it hadn't been for the mouse-colored parka he wore against the weather—in the teens with light snow—the young man could have been relaxing at the beach.

Beside him was a hand-lettered sign.

WILL WORK FOR FOOD
GOD BLESS YOU

Preuss pulled the Explorer onto the sidewalk beneath the overpass on Eight Mile. He trotted across the road to where the young man was asleep.

Preuss recognized him. He'd been out here for years; close up he didn't look as young as he did when you were sailing past in a car.

His face was lined, puffy, bruised, his head a mass of filthy clumps of matted ginger hair, his lanky frame monkish in the hooded parka. His street name was "Lucky," though nothing about his situation screamed good fortune.

Preuss knelt next to him. The air was foul with gasoline fumes and engine exhaust.

"Lucky," Preuss said, and nudged him.

No response.

On the nod, Preuss thought. The homeless crew on this corner sometimes peddled heroin as a side gig for some of the local pushers, and they liked to sample their own product when they could afford it with contributions from passing motorists.

"Lucky," Preuss said again, this time louder. A firmer shake of Lucky's arm.

Still nothing.

"Lucky!"

Lucky was out cold, but Preuss saw movement in a makeshift hogan of thrown-together blankets and old coats spread over grocery carts. A woman emerged, scowling and primed for a fight.

"Whaddaya want?" she growled. "Whaddaya always bothering us for?"

"You know Lucky?" Preuss asked her. As Lucky looked older than his years, this woman looked younger, with broad cheeks red from the cold and a runny nose. Preuss realized she was pregnant under the long woolen coat she wore, stiff with dirt. She noticed him looking at her belly and wrapped the coat around herself defensively.

"Yeah," she said. "He's my boyfriend. What do you care?"

"Is he doing okay?"

"What's it to you?"

"Maybe I can ask you what I was going to ask him," Preuss said. He came toward her and she backed away.

"Stay away from me," she warned. "I got a knife."

He held his hands up. "I just want to ask you a question. Do you know a homeless guy named Larry Bright?"

"Who?"

"Larry Bright. He might have a street name, but I don't know what it is. Here. This is him."

From his pocket, Preuss withdrew the DMV photo Rhonda had gotten for him and he showed the woman.

She squinted at it, then back up at Preuss. Her eyes were unfocused. She was on something, too.

"Know him?" he asked.

She shook her head.

"Never saw him around?"

"No. I told that to the other cop."

"What other cop?"

"The black guy."

"Detective Trombley?"

"I dunno his name. Is this guy in trouble?" she asked. "Why all you cops looking for him?"

"He's not in any trouble," Preuss said. "And I'm not the cops."

She took a closer look at him, squinting. "You look like a cop. I seen you around."

"Used to be," he admitted. "Not anymore."

"So why you looking for him?"

"His father was killed a couple weeks ago. I want to make sure Larry knows about it. Thought I'd take a chance somebody around here might know him."

"Yeah?" she said. "Oh, I'm sorry to hear that."

"So can you take another look? Maybe you remember him?"

She squinted at the photo again, then said, "No. Sorry."

Preuss folded up the photo and put it back in his pocket. "Thanks. His father's name was Charles Bright. Know him?"

She shook her head. "No, sorry."

"How about a citizen who takes people home to his house, gives them a meal and a bed for the night?"

"I wish, pal. Hey, you wouldn't have a couple bucks on you? Me and Lucky, we could use a hot meal."

He pulled a twenty out of his wallet and gave it to her. "Thanks for your help. Get yourself some good food."

She grabbed it and stuck it in her pocket.

"God bless you."

"Listen," he said, "there's a free clinic called FernCare on Nine Mile. Let them have a look at you, eh? For the baby?"

"Maybe," she said.

He knew she wouldn't.

He trotted back across Eight Mile to the Explorer. At a break in traffic he pulled out and made a quick left onto Woodward going north. There was one more place he wanted to check.

Like most urban libraries, the Ferndale Area District Library was often a refuge for homeless men and women during its operating hours. A foyer outside the library proper with table and chairs offered a respite from walking the streets, and inside the library were comfortable chairs and even a cozy fireplace. As long as they didn't sleep or cause problems, people without a place to live were welcome here.

The library was part of the compact Ferndale civic center on Nine Mile, separated from the Shanahan Law Enforcement Complex by a parking lot and City Hall. Preuss had brought Toby to the library many times, and knew the head of reference and adult services, a man named Pat Ryan. Preuss asked for Ryan at the front desk, and the young woman staffer with purple hair disappeared for a moment and returned with Ryan.

"Martin," he said. "How are you?"

"I'm good, Pat."

They shook hands and Ryan said, "Where's Toby?"

"At school. I'm here on business today."

"What can I do for you?"

Preuss showed him the photo of Larry Bright. "I'm looking for this guy. Larry Bright. His father was found dead over on Oakridge."

"Yeah," Ryan said, "I read about it. I knew the guy."

"Did you?"

"Sure. Nice fellah. Used to be on our community board. Helluva way to end up. Are you on the case? Wait, I heard you retired."

"I did. I'm working private now. The Ferndale PD has the case. But I'm trying to lay hands on the son. Ever seen him around?"

Ryan took the photo again.

"It's a couple years old," Preuss said.

"Yeah," Ryan said. "I've seen him here, sure. Didn't know he was related to Charlie."

"Seen him lately?"

"Not for a while. He looks the worse for wear these days compared to this picture."

"I checked with one of the crew down at the underpass, see if they knew him, but no luck."

"Sorry," Ryan said. "Wish I could help."

"Not a problem. Look, here's my number." Preuss handed him a business card. "Call me if he comes in?"

"Will do. I'll let the others know, too. He comes by, we'll give you a holler. Can I make a copy of this?" He held up the photo.

"Sure."

Ryan took the photo and ran a copy of it in the back. He returned the original to Preuss. "I'll make sure everybody knows about it," he said.

"Good deal. Everything else okay?"

"Yeah," Ryan said, "can't complain. How's your boy?"

"Better than ever."

"Haven't seen him in a while. Bring him around sometime. Love to see him again."

"Will do."

Everybody loves Toby, Preuss thought.

And Toby returns the favor.

27

He rolled to a stop in the parking lot of John Glenn High School as the 3:15 dismissal bell rang inside.

He parked in a corner of the lot where he could see Ruth Anne Krider's grey Escape. When the doors of the school burst open, a sea of teenagers poured out as if they were fleeing an active shooter. Except they wore smiles and not masks of fear.

Most of the cars in the lot belonged to students, so by the time a woman walked out of the building with the security guard, the lot was more than half-empty. She was the same woman he had seen from a distance the afternoon before.

Close up, the mass of blonde curls framed a severe rectangle of a face with a bony jaw.

As Preuss watched, she looked around and gave the security guard a quick kiss on the lips before turning toward her car. The guard watched her go for a few moments and then went back into the school.

Preuss left his Explorer and approached her. "Ruth Anne Krider?"

She stopped, looked up, eyebrows raised, put off by his sudden appearance. She was hugging her backpack to her chest so her arms were full.

"Talk to you for a minute?" Preuss said.

Her eyes narrowed.

"My name's Martin Preuss. I'm a private investigator. I'd like to ask you some questions about a case I'm working on."

She looked around. The guard was nowhere in sight.

"Preuss." She seemed to taste the name and find it unpalatable. "You're the guy came to my house yesterday?"

"I am."

"Yeah, well, I don't have anything to say to you. Excuse me."

She stepped around him and beeped the car unlocked with the set of keys in her hand.

"Won't take a second," Preuss said. "It's about Charles Bright."

She got the rear hatch open and dumped the backpack inside. "I don't know anybody by that name." Her voice was high and nasal, almost a whine.

"That's not what I hear."

"No disrespect, but I don't care what you hear, okay?"

"I'm wondering what you know about Charlie's death."

"I told you. Never heard of the guy."

He waited.

She glared at him, then reached into her purse and brought out a cell phone. She punched a few buttons and said, "Can you come out here? There's a guy bothering me."

She disconnected and said to Preuss, "My boyfriend's coming. I were you, I'd get going while you can still can."

"He the one I met at your house yesterday?"

"No."

"Who was that?"

"My brother. Who also wouldn't want me talking to you, by the way."

Nice, Preuss thought. The family that stays together, preys on minorities together.

Now Ruth Anne turned and pointed toward the security guard trotting toward them, his belly jiggling under his uniform shirt and the change rattling in his pockets. He was the one Preuss had seen that morning.

"Told you," she said. "He's not happy."

Before he could answer, the guard came up to them. His name tag said, "Roger."

"This the guy bothering you?" he asked Ruth Anne. He was breathing hard from his jog. He wouldn't be much use against a fast high school kid trying to outrun him.

He was shorter than Preuss by a couple of inches but twice as wide. He had a bulldog fierceness to him, almost a fury. His voice was comically high, higher even than Ruth Anne's.

Ruth Anne said, "He was just leaving."

"You heard the lady," Roger said. "Get going."

He took a step in between Preuss and Ruth Anne, bumping bellies with Preuss.

Another phony tough guy, Preuss thought.

They're everywhere.

"Go on. Get out of here," Roger said, and nudged Preuss again with his large belly. "Before I make you regret it."

Preuss stepped back from the belly bump but didn't otherwise move.

"I said get lost." Roger brought up his arm to push Preuss away.

Here we go.

Preuss took a side step and grabbed Roger's chubby arm and bent it behind the guard as he used his momentum to turn Roger around and slam him into the side of Ruth Anne's car.

The first move they teach you in cop school, Preuss thought.

He kicked Roger's feet apart and mashed Roger's face into the top of the Escape with a forearm behind his head.

Roger grunted and struggled but he was too off-balance. Preuss held him fast.

"Lemme go!" Roger cried.

"Let him go!" Ruth Anne cried.

Preuss turned toward her.

"I want to know what you know about who killed Charles Bright."

"I told you, I don't know him."

"He was your professor at Wayne, Ruth Anne."

"You're wasting your time. I got nothing to say to you. Let him go!"

"What about your friends?"

He pulled Roger an inch away from the car and pushed him back into it. "The white power squad. They involved?"

"You're making a big mistake, asshole," Roger growled in his high voice into the metal top of the Escape.

Ruth Anne pulled at Preuss's sleeve.

"Hey, look," she said, "I'm not going to tell you anything, and neither is anybody else. So whyn't you get lost, okay? And leave him alone before I call the cops."

Preuss gave her a long look, and released Roger and pushed him a few feet away.

Roger wasn't armed, not even with a billy club, so he couldn't come back at Preuss with anything. And now he knew he wasn't a match for the taller man. He stood and shook with rage and frustration.

"You're dead," Roger said.

His only weapon was a fat pointed finger.

Preuss ignored him.

"We're not finished," he told Ruth Anne.

"And neither are we," Roger piped in his comical voice.

28

Rhonda had gone for the day by the time he returned to the office. She left a note on his desk:

> MP—
> I don't know if you remembered, but I'm taking a personal day on Monday so I won't be in. I'll be in tomorrow for a couple of hours to catch up and get some stuff ready for next week.
>
> I left a few messages on your desk, including some from your new best friend. ☺ Contracts and POs to sign, too.
>   RC

My new best friend. Preuss thought: hah. Rhonda, you wag.

He wrote out a return message for her, acknowledging he remembered her day off.

He set aside the messages from Angie Sturmer and skimmed through the paperwork Rhonda left for him. She had it all organized by job numbers, with little "Sign here" sticky notes.

He didn't know what he would do without her . . . this was one of the many tasks connected with running a business that he hated.

He set the paperwork aside—forms and contracts and purchase orders and final copies of client reports—and sorted through the rest of the phone messages.

Nothing required him to return any calls, so he saved them for Monday.

Then he read Angie's messages.

Just her name and phone number on three message slips. He guessed Angie wanted Rhonda to take down a long message, but she would have declined.

And not politely, either.

He steeled himself to call her back.

It went straight to voicemail.

Such a shame, thought Martin Preuss.

Not.

He left a return message for her and disconnected. He wasn't in the mood for her.

He sat for another hour, updating his notes. He was certain Ruth Anne Krider knew more about Charles Bright's death than she claimed, and he didn't take her word that Roger or the other members of their hate group weren't involved.

He had learned nothing from his conversation with her. She was lying about not knowing Bright, and she knew Preuss knew she was. He'd have to come at her another way. She might be more forthcoming if he could get her away from the thugs who surrounded her, but that would take some doing.

Considering the fury of his attack, whoever killed Charles Bright must have hated him. So who might have carried that kind of hatred?

Would Ruth Anne? Maybe, but he doubted it. Bright was the one who tried to talk sense into her, to keep her in the department. She would have no reason to hate him with such intensity.

He could see Roger and the others mustering mindless hatred for the peace activist, but would they have mutilated the body the way they did?

He could see them ganging up on Bright and beating him to a pulp, since they were cowards trying to wrap themselves in the old mantle of Nazi cruelty.

But would they kill him?

They would more likely leave him alive as a reminder of how dangerous they were.

Like it took a lot of courage to gang-jump an old man.

Even so, what he was lacking was a connection between the group and Charles Bright. Ruth Anne was the obvious choice, but what he knew now wasn't enough.

So who hated Bright enough to bash his head in and stab him over and over again?

Once again he regretted not being able to talk about the case with Reg Trombley. Or even with another of his former colleagues, Janey Cahill.

He had not been in touch with Janey since she got back with her husband the summer before. As far as he was concerned, they could stay out of touch. By now he knew he would have no future with her.

Pull me close, push me away: that was her strategy with him.

At one time, Preuss could have talked over the case with Manny. But Manny had his own problems right now. And Lila would kill Preuss herself if he interrupted Manny's recuperation.

That left Toby . . . dear, sweet, loving Toby. Who would give Preuss all the good advice in the world, if only he were able to.

No matter, Preuss thought. He tries in his own way to make me better, and that's enough.

If Preuss could just learn all Toby had to offer.

By the time he finished, he remembered he hadn't gone through Rhonda's paperwork in any detail, nor signed any of it. He would have to do it another time . . . he was getting too tired to focus.

It was already eight-thirty, so he turned out the light in his office. He wouldn't get to Toby's till nearly nine, and by then his son would have had his bath already and gotten ready for bed.

Preuss was going to see him again in the morning for their weekly Saturday breakfast, and—he realized as a wave of exhaustion overcame him—he was beat.

So he decided to head home, even though the only thing waiting for him was his big empty house.

Later he would think to himself: I wish that *had* been all that awaited me.

Saturday, March 2, 2013

29

The phone brought him out of a dead sleep.

2:35 by the clock on the bedside table.

As always, his first panicky thought was: *Toby!*

But he didn't recognize the number in his groggy state. He knew it wasn't Toby's house.

He connected to hear the voice he most didn't want to hear.

"Mr. Preuss!"

Angie Sturmer.

At 2:35 in the morning.

Sounding frantic.

She said, "Mr. Preuss!" again.

"Angie, do you know what time it is?"

"I know, I know. I'm sorry to call so late . . . but . . . I sort of got arrested."

They were holding her to see a detective later in the morning, she said.

Preuss showered and threw on some clothes and at six o'clock drove out to the Sterling Heights Police Department on Dodge Park Road. He told the officer at the intake desk why he was there, and the officer asked him to wait while he made a call. In

another five minutes, a woman in a Kalamazoo College sweatshirt
and Levis opened the door to the back offices for him.

"Martin?" she said. "Detective Marian Everts."

She held out a hand and he shook it. She motioned him in.
"She's back here."

She led the way through a warren of desks to a small
interview room with cinder block walls and a door with a wide
window. Angie Sturmer was looking woebegone in a plastic chair at
the table inside.

"That's your girl?" Everts asked.

"That's her," Preuss said. "Though she's not my girl. What
happened?"

"A call came in overnight about a suspicious person in a
subdivision off Utica Road and the Parkway. A patrol officer
questioned her and she claimed she was there acting on your orders."

"Completely untrue. In fact, it's the opposite of what I told
her."

"Well," said Everts, "it didn't sound right to us. But your name
was familiar. You used to be on the job, right?"

"I was a detective with the Ferndale PD. I retired a couple
years ago."

"Yeah, that's what one of our guys said. Lou Warranow."

Preuss thought a moment and said, "I don't know him."

"Said you know his brother, Gus?"

"Oh right," Preuss said. Gus Warranow played bass in The
Flynns, the band Preuss sat in with when he had the time. Which he
hadn't had much of lately, with Manny Greene out of action.

"Yeah," Everts said, "Lou told me you were a good guy, so I
wanted to keep Ms. Sturmer out of the system till I spoke with you."

"Thanks. I appreciate that."

"The thing is, Martin, she told us a story about seeing a Sterling Heights resident dumping a body in the river in Utica."

"I heard all about it. Phil Ruhle, right? I'm guessing he was the one she was staking out? Or stalking, as the case may be."

"I can't comment on that, Martin. What troubled the shift supervisor about her, there was a body found in the same spot, except it'd been in the water for a while."

"That's what I read in the paper."

"What you didn't read because we haven't released it—that was the third body of a murdered woman that's been found."

"You're thinking you may have a repeater on your hands?"

"Yes. So when we found Angie loitering in her car, it got our attention."

"Sure. You talked to her?"

"First thing this morning, when I got in. I'm satisfied she has no involvement with the murders of the women. So you can take her home. The thing is, if we pick her up in Sterling Heights again, we'll have to charge her."

"All I can do is let her know."

Detective Everts opened the door to the interview room where Angie Sturmer sat frowning. She jumped up when she saw Preuss and he held up a hand to stop whatever she was going to say.

"Angie," Everts said, "I'm not going to process you this time. I'm going to release you into the custody of Mr. Preuss here."

"Thank you," Angie said, subdued. "Thank you, Mr. Preuss."

"We're doing you a favor here, Angie," Everts said. "In return, we don't want to run into you in this city again. You understand me?"

"I understand."

"She's all yours," Everts told Preuss.

"Outside," he said to Angie.

Preuss thanked the detective one more time, and walked Angie through the department offices and out into the cold morning air.

"Where's your car?" he asked.

"Back at the house."

"Ruhle's house?"

"Yes."

He led the way to his Explorer. "In."

Once they were under way, she turned in her seat and said, "Can I explain?"

"Not interested."

She went silent.

In Phil Ruhle's neighborhood he pulled up beside her car, a dark Honda Odyssey. Of course there was a citation on it.

"I don't know if I'm madder at you for doing this incredibly stupid thing," he said, "or passing yourself off as one of my agents."

"I know."

"What were you thinking?"

He felt like he was talking with his elder son Jason after one of his scrapes . . . he felt the same adolescent annoyance and shame radiating off her.

When she didn't reply, he said, "Well? Angie, I'm asking you. What were you doing here?"

"I wanted to keep an eye on this guy."

"But why? I asked you to drop it."

"I know," she said, wincing as if she were in pain. "But I have a bad feeling about him, Mr. Preuss. I do."

"Based on what?"

"A hunch."

"A hunch? From what, all your years in law enforcement?"

Silence.

"I'm not going to tell you this again," he said. "Stay away from this guy. And I'm not going to come to your rescue again. This happens another time, call somebody else. But most of all, don't let it happen again. Do you understand?"

"Yes sir. But before I get out, can I tell you what my hunch is?"

"Angie," he said, "I'm tired. You woke me up at 2:30 in the morning and I never got back to sleep. If you have something to say to me, put it in the report I asked you to give me, which you never did do."

She paused again, her hand on the door latch. She opened her mouth and seemed like she might be going to say something else, but when she saw the forbidding look on his face she evidently thought better of it.

Instead she opened the door and said, "Thank you again."

"Angie? This better be the last time you tell people you work for me."

She nodded and closed the door—all with a hang-dog dejection—and got into her own car. Preuss waited till she started up and pulled out, and then he got behind her and followed her for another mile before she turned off.

He needed his Toby fix in the worst way.

30

Saturday morning at the Big Boy in Madison Heights.

Preuss's favorite time of the week.

They had been coming here for years, every Saturday whenever Toby was feeling up to it and Preuss wasn't working. Toby had been having a long stretch of good health, and with Preuss's schedule post-retirement, they had become regulars.

As soon as they walked in the door and Toby heard the familiar hubbub of the place—people talking, silverware crashing into busboys' tubs, plates sent spinning out of the kitchen to the shelf under the heat lamps—he perked up.

The servers all knew Toby by now, and whether or not he sat at their stations they stopped by to say hello and wish him well. He loved the attention—as who doesn't, Preuss thought—and was happy and chirping throughout the meal.

Which Toby couldn't share because he couldn't eat by mouth. The risk of pneumonia from aspirated food was too great. He took his nutrition by the g-tube in his tummy. As the timing went, though, he was often between feeds when he came here with Preuss. So they spent their time chatting . . . Preuss would catch Toby up on his latest activity and Toby would make his typical sounds through a mouth and tongue twisted and betrayed by cerebral palsy—ums, hums, occasional chirrups of laughter, and a word that sounded like "onion."

Preuss responded to these as if they were actual language initiatives, weaving them into the conversation and replying to them as though he understood exactly what Toby meant. Most times he thought he did; Preuss was a student of Toby's communications.

Today, however, Toby was particularly vocal, offering up his thoughts on the Charles Bright case. Preuss was always careful about what he shared with his son in public settings, but he loved listening to the boy chatter on as if he had important thoughts he needed to share.

And for all Preuss knew, Toby did. And was happily sharing those thoughts with his father.

Detective Toby, Preuss thought.

And then thought this might be a good main character for a children's book . . . He couldn't remember ever seeing a multiply handicapped character like Toby in the children's books he read to his boys, nor even in the books for grown-ups he read.

When Preuss's breakfast eggs came, Toby began to quiet down, and by the time Preuss sopped up the remnants of the egg yolk with a last piece of toast, Toby was dozing. Too much excitement, Preuss thought.

His phone buzzed with a text.

Rhonda.

Did you sign those contracts yesterday? I need them today.

He texted back: *No, sorry. I'll swing by in a little while and sign them.*

She texted back a thumbs-up.

As he finished his coffee, he watched his son, and Preuss again was overcome by how much he loved the boy. His wife Jeanette had gone into a major depression when the doctors told them soon after his birth that their son would be profoundly handicapped. One doctor recommended they put him right into an institution without even taking him home. It turned out Toby was, indeed, profoundly handicapped, but Jeanette pulled herself together and became Toby's best advocate, the poster woman for engaged parenting.

Though Preuss was drinking heavily by then, they both loved their son fiercely, and Preuss's love had only grown since Jeanette's death.

Toby was sound asleep when Preuss pushed the wheelchair up to the register to pay for breakfast. As he did every Saturday, the manager standing there taking the money reached into a fishbowl filled with Tootsie Pops and offered one to Toby across the counter.

As always, Preuss took the Tootsie Pop and put it in his pocket with a nod of thanks for the man. Preuss had explained about Toby's condition, how he couldn't eat by mouth, but each week the man held out the Tootsie Pop and each week Preuss accepted it with thanks for the gesture.

Outside, the cold breeze woke Toby with a snort. Preuss stopped pushing his wheelchair long enough to get his knit hat pulled down over the boy's ears, then continued to the Explorer.

He got Toby buckled in and they drove out Thirteen Mile to Preuss's office on Telegraph.

Where Rhonda was hard at work, as she said she would be.

"Hey, look who's here!" she cried when Preuss unlocked the front door and backed in with the wheelchair. "My friend Toby!"

At the sound of her voice and then his name, Toby gave a huge crooked smile.

Rhonda came around the side of her desk and wrapped Toby in a hug. Even today, on a weekend, she had her hair worn in her usual high mound of bleached blonde curls; they trembled as she rocked Toby in his wheelchair.

Toby squealed in glee.

Rhonda ended her hug with a noisy kiss on top of the boy's head—"Mmmwah!"—and sat back on her heels to look at him on his level.

"You're stylin', there, Tobias. Where'd you get that cool cap?"

"Grandma made it for you, didn't she," Preuss said, answering for him. Jeanette's mother in Traverse City made it for Toby and gave it to him the last time Preuss took him up there for a visit. It was red with white rings and a heavy knit weave.

Toby hummed his own response.

"What a nice surprise," she told Toby. "I didn't expect to see you today. But I'm so happy you're here! Come on over here and sit next to me."

She pulled his wheelchair around so he was sitting beside her. She patted his leg. "Wanna help me do some work for your dad?"

Preuss left them working together on Rhonda's computer and went into his office to go through the papers he should have signed the day before. Even with Manny on leave, they were busier than they had been since Preuss first joined the firm. He wasn't going to be able to put off hiring an associate for much longer.

He signed the contracts, initialed the purchase orders, and set aside the final copies of client reports for Monday, when he would have more time to read them.

When he went out to Rhonda's area and set the signed papers on the edge of her desk, Toby was sitting on Rhonda's lap. He was gazing sideways into the computer screen where she had found a high-contrast video game for him to play. She tried to hold his bent hands so he could press the keys to play the game, but she couldn't unfold his fingers.

"I'm afraid I'm going to hurt him," she said to Preuss.

"He's pretty tight."

"You sure are," Rhonda said into Toby's ear. Which provoked another squeal of laughter.

"He likes you," Preuss said. "A lot."

"I like him back a lot," Rhonda said, and gave Toby a kiss on his chubby cheek.

She eased Toby back into his wheelchair and made sure he was comfortable on his hips before buckling him in.

"You're so good with him," Preuss said.

"Thanks. He reminds me of my sister. I miss her so much."

She gave Preuss a wan smile. "Sorry."

He put a hand on her shoulder and felt the delicate bones underneath her black sweater. Fragile bird bones, like his son's.

"What else do you have to do today?" he asked.

She shook her head. "I'm done. Waiting for Mike to pick me up."

"Mike?"

"My new friend."

"Ah. Your secret source?"

She gave him a sly smile. "I'll never tell."

"Okay," he said. "Have fun. So I won't see you Monday?"

"Nope. I'll be in Tuesday."

"Right," he said. "Well, Toby, let's you and me get going and leave Rhonda to her weekend."

"Bye-bye, sweetheart," she said, and gave Toby a kiss on the other side of his face.

Preuss drove Toby back to the Ferndale house. They would spend a few hours here, then Preuss would take Toby back to the group home. He would give his son a bath and spend the evening with him, reading aloud and listening to music.

He stretched his son out on the sofa in the living room and changed his diaper and put a clean set of jogging pants on him. Then he turned Toby on his side and tucked a blanket around him and a pillow beside him so he wouldn't roll off.

"Time for a nap, sweetie," Preuss told him. After his busy morning and visit with Rhonda, Toby closed his eyes and dozed.

Preuss put John Prine's *Sweet Revenge* on the CD player and sat in the chair across from the sofa. He also closed his eyes. He was exhausted from his busy night, and felt like he could drift off, too.

He tried, but he couldn't fall asleep.

Instead he sat thinking.

He thought about the Charles Bright case, and then his thoughts went to Grace Poole. He was going to meet her for coffee on Monday—or that was the plan, anyway.

But why?

What could come of this, besides more disappointment, ultimately more sadness, more anger?

Well, because this is what people do, he told himself, trying to be patient with his own stupidity. They interact with other people in social situations. And maybe it's fun and worthwhile and maybe it isn't. But they make an effort.

Sometimes he felt as unfamiliar with human dating rituals as an alien abandoned on planet Earth with no knowledge of planetary customs.

Martin Preuss, phone home.

Strangely enough, though, as he thought about it, he was not regretting having agreed to meet with her. He was looking forward to it. He supposed this was significant of something.

He looked over at his son.

Toby was sleeping. Remember what Toby would do, if he could, he told himself. Be present. Enjoy.

WWTD.

What would Toby do?

His cell phone rang.

Sam Rifkin.

Whom Preuss had forgotten to call back.

He went into the kitchen so he wouldn't disturb Toby.

"Rabbi," he said.

"Martin. Wanted to touch base and see how you were doing."

Preuss gave a quick summary of what he had been up to.

"Sounds like you're making progress," Rifkin said.

"I am. The investigation's opening up beyond the police theory of the crime. I feel like I'm closing in on it."

"Great," Rifkin said. "Do we need to meet for any reason?"

"Not right now. Unless you and Lloyd feel the need."

"Not really. We have confidence in you, Martin. I'll relay this to Lloyd. We'll talk soon."

Preuss had a thought.

"Hey, Sam," he said before the other man hung up. "I do have a question. Do you know anything about the Sacred Heart Seminary?"

"Down on Chicago?"

"Yeah."

"Not much, personally. But if I'm not mistaken, Lloyd was a seminarian there. Should I have him give you a call?"

"That," Preuss said, "would be terrific."

Monday, March 4, 2013

31

Preuss woke to the smell of coffee.

Thinking at first his house was on fire as the odor penetrated his dreams, he scrambled out of bed. He rushed down the stairs to the kitchen.

Nothing was burning. Instead, the carafe on the coffee maker on the counter was full and fragrant with dark coffee. Two empty cups were set out beside it.

The sky outside the kitchen window was still dark. It was 4:27 by the clock on the microwave.

Franklin McShane stood in front of the sink.

Tall and lean, wearing his standard uniform of dirty long raincoat, wrinkled khaki pants, and Keds. He didn't have his ball cap on his head, though; his silver hair was drawn back in a ponytail.

The former FBI agent poured Preuss a cup of coffee as if it had been Preuss and not McShane who was the guest here.

"Here," McShane said, "you look like you need this."

Preuss accepted the cup and said, "What are you doing here at 4:30 in the morning? And how did you get in?"

"You call the things on your doors locks?" McShane said. "Those aren't locks. Those are open invitations to a burglary. You should put a sign on them. 'Please walk in.'"

Preuss took a sip of the coffee. It was scalding hot and stronger than any he or Rhonda ever made. He felt its heat penetrate his body, including his dull morning brain.

"Come on," McShane said. "Let's talk."

He led the way to the table in the dining room.

Preuss stared at him. McShane stared back. From his previous encounters with McShane, Preuss knew it was a mistake to have a staring contest with this man, so he said, "Seriously. Why are you here?"

"Manny called me about you a couple days ago."

"Because?"

"Said you were getting mixed up with some bad actors. Asked me to check it out."

"Anybody in particular?"

"The American Identity Brigade."

Preuss nodded. Figures, he thought. Manny was his surrogate father, and he was afraid Preuss wouldn't heed his warnings about them. Which of course he wasn't. So he got McShane on the case.

Dangerous, crazy, paranoid McShane.

"He asked me to keep an eye on you," McShane said.

"So you've been watching me?"

"Sure. Not so you could notice."

"No, I didn't. But then being under surveillance wasn't on my list of concerns."

"Doesn't matter. That's the point of surveillance. What's the good of it if you know you're being watched?"

Preuss raised his cup in recognition of McShane's point. Preuss had said the same thing to Angie Sturmer.

"For example, most people have no idea the government's watching their every move," McShane said. "So they don't modulate their behaviors. And the watchers pay close attention, believe me."

Wow, a full minute went by before talking about government surveillance, Preuss thought; McShane must have something truly important on his mind.

Preuss took another sip of the coffee. He could feel the hit from the strong drink start to perk him up. But this isn't my coffee, he realized. It must have twice the caffeine content. Did McShane bring his own coffee?

"Okay," Preuss said. "What do you know about these guys?"

"For starters, they're on every watch list of domestic terrorists. The Bureau's had their eye on them for a long time. They even have a UC embedded."

"The FBI has an informer in place?"

"Yeah. Dunno who. Everybody's keeping an eye on them. The Southern Poverty Law Center, Hatewatch, the Anti-Defamation League, ProPublica, even the damn TSA's got them on their watch list. These aren't a bunch of drunk fat guys playing wannabe soldier-boy in the woods," McShane said. "They're a danger to the democratic way of life. And they're only getting stronger."

McShane had a tendency toward hyperbole, but he still had good sources in the government. Preuss knew he was reliable, once you got beyond the overt paranoia.

And what he was saying matched what Preuss had heard from Sylvia Bloom.

"They're committed to achieving a white, Christian America," McShane went on. "They're changing the entire face of conservative politics in this country. They're not just ideologues. They don't hesitate to back up their words with actions. I'm talking about kidnapping, murder, torture . . . these guys don't play. And what's worse, this group is part of a whole connected network of people who've been chugging along under the radar for years and now they're getting active, all of them all at once. There's going to be a dramatic change in the next four years with the Republican shift to the hard right and the Democratic lack of a spine. If Republicans take the White House in 2016, these guys are going mainstream. Mark my words."

"You think it'll come to that?"

"I don't think, I know. You may think we're moving toward the sunny liberal utopia you dream about," McShane said, "but we're going backwards. We're not headed into the sun, Preuss. We're retreating further into the dark of the night."

He took a gulp of his coffee.

"These groups are infiltrating the infrastructure of the nation. They're seeding themselves in law enforcement, in the military, and with right-wing politicians at every level, all based on the poisonous ideology of a white ethno-state. They live and die by the sacred slogan of the white nationalist movement: 'We must secure the existence of our people and a future for White Children.' The sacred fourteen words. Manny knows it, which is why he asked me to keep an eye on you. Make sure these animals aren't getting too close. And you're not getting too close to them," he added.

"So you were watching me last week, at the high school in Westland?"

"I was," McShane said. "For a minute there, I thought you were going to get into it with that security guard. But you handled him."

"And you were watching me when I went to the house in Westland the day before."

"Of course. If the balloon'd gone up, I'd been there for you."

"I appreciate that. But I'm taking it easy with these guys. So far, anyway. I'm not sure how they're involved in my case yet. Until I know for certain how they're connected, I'll leave them alone."

"Yeah, that would work if they were leaving you alone."

"What do you mean?"

McShane withdrew a pair of photos from a pocket of his raincoat and passed them to Preuss across the dining room table.

One photo was a night shot showing a dark Impala with heavily tinted windows. It was parked down the street from Preuss's house in Ferndale. He couldn't make out who the driver was because it was night and the windows were dark.

Preuss's immediate thought was that Jake Aklawi, the local head of the Chaldean mafia, was behind this. A party store in Warren was his base of operations for controlling a large portion of the drug traffic in and out of the metropolitan area. He looked like a shopkeeper, but Preuss knew not to underestimate him. He was a dangerous man, and Preuss had a run-in with him the year before that left Aklawi's nephew dead and a target on Preuss's back.

But Preuss knew Aklawi was out of the picture, at least for now. He was on trial for ordering a shooting that went bad and killed an innocent bystander. All his energy would be going into holding his operation together while he tried to keep himself out of jail.

The other photo showed the driver clearly. He was getting out of the car. White, in his late thirties, slender in a black sweatshirt under a bulky canvas jacket. His head was shaved and he had a bushy Taliban-style beard.

"You know this guy?" Preuss asked McShane.

"No."

"Neither do I."

The Impala was parked in front of the Westland house Ruth Anne Krider shared with her brother, Warren Cattrell.

Preuss looked at McShane, who was rolling his coffee cup between his hands.

"This guy's watching me?"

McShane nodded.

"You know who lives in this house?" Preuss asked.

"I do," McShane said. "The head Nazi. There's something else you need to see."

He handed Preuss another photo from his raincoat. This one showed the same Impala, only this time parked in a different location on another suburban street.

One Preuss recognized.

Toby's group home was in the background.

"Jesus Christ," Preuss said.

"Thought you should know."

"I'm going to kill him."

"No, you're not. Don't do anything stupid. For now they're just watching you."

"And my son," Preuss said. "They're watching Toby. How do they know about Toby?"

"They've been watching you. Tracking your movements. They've seen you go there. Seen you with him. I told you, these guys are dangerous."

"Thanks for letting me know about this."

"Don't tip your hand, Preuss. I'm the last guy in the world to tell anybody to cool it. Right now you want to tear their heads off."

"I do."

"I get that. But they don't know you know they're watching you. You have the upper hand. I'm going to keep an eye on you and them," McShane said, "but I can't watch your boy, too. You want, I can arrange somebody for that."

"No," Preuss said. "I'll take care of it."

"Good. Meantime, let me know if you need my help with anything."

"I will," Preuss said. "I most definitely will."

32

Once McShane left, Preuss went back upstairs for a shower. He turned the water on as hot as he could stand it and stood under the plumes of steam with his mouth open in a wrenching silent scream.

They were watching Toby.

He wanted the water to exorcise him of the fury he felt; he wanted his rage to melt away in the sting of it on his skin.

But of course it didn't.

When he turned the shower off, he stood, dripping and chilled in the sudden cessation of hot water. He took deep breaths to calm himself; otherwise he would have dried off, dressed, and gone out to the tiny house in Westland and killed Warren Cattrell with his bare hands.

Toby was exactly the kind of person neo-Nazis would go after: somebody they considered "defective," somebody they might feel they could hurt because he couldn't put up a defense.

Calmer now, more clear-minded, he dried off, dressed, and went downstairs to call one of the agency's associates. Carlos Guevara was a good man, dependable and tough, who had done protective work for Preuss and Manny in the past.

Carlos picked up on the first ring.

"*Martín*," Carlos said.

"How are you, my friend?"

"Never better. *Qué esta pasando, 'mano?*"

"Carlos," Preuss said, "are you busy today?"

"You got a job?"

"I do. An important one."

Carlos agreed to guard Toby for the rest of the day, at school and later at home. He said he would hire someone to take over the evening shift, too, and make up a schedule so Toby would be protected around the clock for the next few days. Preuss would deal with Cattrell himself later.

By the time Preuss got to Toby's, Carlos was already there, sitting in his grey Jeep in the street in front of the group home. Preuss took him inside to introduce him to the staff. He didn't want to worry them, but he also wanted to make sure they paid attention to any strangers who might be hanging around the house.

So he decided on the truth.

He told them he didn't have any specific information about threats, but he was worried about Toby's safety. So for his sake, and the sake of everyone else in the house, he was putting it under a twenty-four-hour watch.

As he suspected, they were antsy but understanding. The house manager said she appreciated the concern.

When Toby's bus took him off to his school program—followed by Carlos—Preuss relaxed, knowing Carlos wouldn't let anything happen to his son. He turned his attention back to his case.

He drove south on Woodward through Highland Park and into Detroit. A light snow had started to fall, which slowed traffic. He wanted to check out the Sacred Heart Major Seminary on Chicago Boulevard. Larry Bright had used it as his mailing address and Preuss wanted to satisfy himself Bright wasn't still staying there.

The spires of the gothic revival seminary soared above the street, where the snow had begun to accumulate. Lloyd Corrigan had told him where to go once he got to the campus. He stopped at the security kiosk in the main entrance off Linwood, and told the officer on duty what he wanted.

The security guard directed him toward the seminarian residences. Inside, another guard gave him a day pass and told him how to access the residential manager.

The residential manager didn't recognize Bright's name.

"He would have been a student roughly twelve or thirteen years ago," Preuss said.

"So around 2000, 2001," the manager said. A seminarian himself, he had the doughy, smug look Preuss had seen on Lloyd Corrigan. "That narrows it down. Way before my time, though. All the records have been computerized, so if he was a student, he'll be in here."

He clicked through his screens for a minute, then said, "Yup. Got him."

On the other side of the counter from the seminarian, Preuss said, "Can I take a look at his records?"

"No, sorry. Student educational records are confidential. FERPA rules prohibit it."

Family Educational Rights and Privacy Act. Toby's teachers talked about it in his Individualized Education Program meetings.

"Fair enough," Preuss said. "Can you tell me when he was here? Dates of attendance are considered 'directory information,' which is allowed to be given out."

The residential manager gave him a look. "You a lawyer?"

"No. Just know about this."

The manager shrugged and consulted his screen again. "Lawrence Bright, there he is. Here from 1998 through 2001."

"Can you tell me an address?"

The young seminarian consulted another screen. "I guess it would be okay. Addresses are allowed," he said. "Looks like he lived here in the residence hall while he was a student. No information about where he went after he left."

"On his last driver's license, which was three years ago, he listed the seminary as his address," Preuss said.

"Oh, no, he shouldn't have done that. Only seminarians are allowed to stay in the residences. He wasn't a student three years ago, so he couldn't have used the place as his mailing address."

"Could somebody else have received his mail for him?"

"Nope. No way. Couldn't happen."

33

Rhonda was taking her personal day, so when he got back to the office he made himself a pot of everyday coffee and sat at her desk to listen to the phone messages. There were eight: four about cases already under way, and three from people wanting to make appointments.

Another three potential new clients. And one of them was an attorney, who might throw even more work their way. Preuss was going to have to move on hiring another associate.

He remembered again why he hadn't wanted to take over the agency. He hated these kinds of decisions.

It might serve him—and the agency—better if he could put Rhonda back out on the street as an investigator and hire somebody else to take her place. He wondered if she had reconsidered staying at her desk. He wrote a note to remind himself to sit down with her the next day and talk about this. Remembering what Manny had told him about her fragile mental state, he didn't want to put any more pressure on her.

He saved the new client callbacks for Rhonda to make the next day. The eighth call was from someone named David Baker. Preuss thought for a moment, then remembered it was one of the names Roshi Ross had given him, someone close to Charles Bright.

He returned the call and Baker answered right away.

"This is Martin Preuss. Thanks for returning my call."

"Oh, sure," Baker said. "Sorry it took so long."

"No worries. This a good time to talk?"

"Sure."

"Roshi at the Buddhist Center gave me your name. He said you and Charles Bright were friends."

"We were."

"I'm investigating the circumstances of his death," Preuss said. "Can you shed any light on it?"

"I sure can't," Baker said. "It was a total shock when I heard about it."

"Did he have any enemies you know of? Anybody have it in for him?"

"None I can think of. He was the kindest man you'd ever want to meet. Really lived the precepts of Buddhism. Wouldn't hurt a fly. Except for maybe one time . . ."

Preuss heard the hesitation. "Dave, is there something you want to say?"

"Well, I'm not sure how important this is."

"Tell me anyway."

"It's just . . . Charlie and I were at a demonstration a few months ago. A Women in Black demo. Do you know about them?"

"I do," Preuss said. They were a movement of women demonstrating for peace and justice and against war. Detroit had a chapter that held events around the area. Preuss had seen them when they brought their protest marches to Ferndale—silent, peaceful, and grave. They were joined by anybody who supported them, which apparently included Charles Bright.

"Yeah, so, the demo was in Flint," Baker said, "and Charlie and I were there. A carload of white nationalists showed up and started pushing everyone around. Armed to the teeth, of course.

Charlie wouldn't back down, and he got into a fight with one of them. The guy was roughing him up and Charlie knocked him right on his ass. And the rest of the gang jumped Charlie and kicked the shit out of him. I tried to help, but there were too many of them. And they were too vicious."

"When was this?"

"Back in November."

This would explain how Charlie Bright got beaten up at the end of last year, Preuss thought. Roshi Ross talked about Charlie being black and blue and missing sittings at the Zen temple. And Charlie's Wayne State colleague Joseph Palmer mentioned it, too.

"Did Charlie ever hear from this guy again?"

"Couldn't tell you."

"You never got his name? Or who he was with?"

"No, sorry."

"Okay, Dave," Preuss said, "that's helpful. Anything else you can think of?"

"Don't think so."

"Give me a call if you do remember anything else?"

"Will do."

They disconnected and Preuss entered notes from the conversation into the Bright file.

Pieces were starting to align. Charles Bright was active in the local peace movement, Ruth Anne Krider was a white nationalist, Bright tried to talk her out of her beliefs, then Bright ran afoul of a group of white nationalists at a demonstration . . . was there a connection between Ruth Anne Krider and this incident in Flint?

Who were the white power guys? The same group threatening Toby?

And how does Larry Bright fit in here? He had trained for the priesthood at one time; some yearning for the spiritual from his father the Jewish Buddhist must have rubbed off. But now he's homeless and lost.

What happened to him?

A text came through from Grace Poole: *Hi. Still on for today?*

In his distress over Toby's threat, he had forgotten about meeting Grace.

He texted back: *Sure. Looking forward to it.*

She replied: *Great. Where do you want to meet? My suggestion: Traffic Jam on Canfield.*

He texted: *Sounds good to me. See you at 4.*

She texted back a smiley face emoji.

The phone rang at Rhonda's desk. He was going to let it go to voicemail when he glanced at the caller ID on his own extension.

The Royal Oak Library.

He picked up the receiver and said his name.

"Mr. Preuss," a woman said. "This is Mary Cassidy. I'm the Adult Services Librarian at the Royal Oak Public Library. I hear you're looking for Larry Bright."

"I am," he said, "but how do you know that?"

"I saw a post about it on the Michigan Library listserve. You talked to Pat Ryan in Ferndale?"

"I did."

"Well, he put out a notice about it. Your man Larry is a fixture in our library. And as luck would have it, he's here right now."

34

"Is he still in the building?"

Preuss stood at the Information desk where Mary Cassidy sat. He scanned the library tables behind her. They were full of young people with books and laptops open in front of them. The Royal Oak branch of Oakland Community College was a few blocks away from the library and many students came here to study.

"He was over here," Mary Anne said, and led him across the main floor to another wing with more tables and shelves of videos and books on disk and a wall of magazines.

"Don't see him," she said.

"No," Preuss agreed. He walked around the shelves but didn't see Larry Bright, just a handful of other men sitting in armchairs or at tables reading books and newspapers.

"Okay if I take a quick look around?" Preuss asked.

"Be my guest."

The library had two floors. He walked around the main floor, and peeked inside the Men's Room, which was empty, and the quiet study rooms and conference rooms. Larry Bright was nowhere.

He went downstairs to the lower level, which was the children's section. A group of young mothers sat in a circle with their infants as a storyteller held up a picture book and read from it in different characters' voices.

All the heads turned toward Preuss.

He made a circuit of the room and again didn't see Larry. He went back upstairs and made another circuit, then returned to the Adult Services counter where Mary Cassidy was seated.

"No?" she asked.

He shook his head. "I don't see him anywhere."

"Sorry. He must have left right after I called you."

"No," he said, "I appreciate the call."

"A lot of shelter folks hang out here during the day. We don't mind it as long as they don't sleep and don't bother anyone. Most of them keep to themselves. Larry, though."

She shook her head.

"He's a talker. Always comes up and tries to engage me in some conversation or other. I always let him talk."

Preuss showed her the DMV photo. "This is the guy we're talking about, right?"

"That's him. Is this an old picture? He looks much the worse for wear now."

"It's an old driver's license photo. Know anything about him? Where he goes when he's not here?"

"No, sorry. You might ask some of the fellas over there, though."

She pointed across the main floor to the other section.

"When he comes in, he sometimes sits over there. I've seen a couple of the guys talking to him."

"He comes in again, let me know?"

"Absolutely. I have your number."

Preuss showed Larry Bright's photo to the men sitting in the other section, but none of them said they recognized him.

He was about to leave when another man wandered in. A light-skinned African American in an army coat, he seemed to carry all his belongings with him. Like many people without a place to live. He had a guitar gig bag hanging across his back, along with a backpack and the plastic bags that were the luggage of convenience for people without a home.

He and Preuss shared a glance, and then he unloaded his bags and guitar case and dropped into one of the armchairs.

Preuss went over to him. "Excuse me. Do you know this guy?" He showed him the photo of Larry Bright.

"What'd he do?"

"He's not in any trouble. I just need to talk with him."

"Po-lice?"

"No, private investigator. I need his help on a case."

"Yeah," the man admitted, "I know him."

"Have you seen him today?"

He shook his head. "Just got here myself."

"When was the last time you saw him?"

"Last night. At the warming center."

"You stay in the same place?"

"Last night, yeah. Not every night. They fill up fast this time of year."

Preuss dragged a chair over from a library table to sit beside the man.

"Martin Preuss," he said. He held out a hand and the man shook it.

"People call me Rabbit," the man said.

"Good to meet you, Rabbit. When he's not at the shelter or here, do you know where he hangs?"

"Couple places around town."

"Can you show me?"

"Aw man. I been walking all day. My feet killing me."

"I'll make it worth your while," Preuss said. "I'll drive you around. No walking, I promise."

Rabbit sighed.

"It's important," Preuss said. "I wouldn't ask if it wasn't. I need to find this guy."

Rabbit sighed again, then heaved himself to his feet and got his bundles together.

"I'll give you a hand," Preuss said, but Rabbit said, "*Uh*-uh," and Preuss backed right off. Rabbit had it all down, *this is my stuff,* what to pick up and how to hold it, and didn't want interference.

Rabbit stowed his bundles in the back of the Explorer, and they set off around Royal Oak. Rabbit directed him past the parks where he had seen Larry Bright.

"Got to leave the shelter in the morning, see," Rabbit said as Preuss drove, "so we find someplace to stay during the day. Weather good, no problem." He looked at Preuss. "Weather go cold, start to snow, like today, different story. Only so many places we can go."

"The library seems like a good place."

"Yeah," Rabbit said, "they good to us, don't give us no trouble. Not every place that good."

He first directed Preuss up Troy Street beside the library, where there was a pocket park behind the theatre complex and next to a high-rise senior residence. Preuss got out of the car to take a quick look around on the benches and inside the gazebo in the center of the park, but there was no sign of Larry Bright.

Next Rabbit directed him up Main Street to a larger park. Preuss drove around the perimeter, but didn't see anyone. "He stay here during the day," Rabbit said, "usually he on one of them." He pointed to the benches along the sides of the park.

"He stay anyplace besides Royal Oak?" Preuss asked.

"Oh yeah. All over. I do, too."

"Yeah," Preuss said, "I thought I recognized you. I used to see you walking around Ferndale, going up and down Woodward. Carrying the guitar case."

"Yeah, I go all over."

"What's in the gig bag?"

"Clothes, anymore," Rabbit said.

"No guitar?"

"Nah. Used to have one, but it got stole. Can't keep nothing when you homeless. Now I steady carry clothes in it."

"What kind of guitar was it?"

"Stratocaster."

"Nice."

"Yeah. Good guitar. Seen me through some good times, once. Who know who got it now. Can't give up the case, though. Remind me what I used to have."

Preuss gave him a sideways look. Rabbit's hair was thick and black but he kept it short and shaved to the skin on the sides and around the back, which gave him a monk-like appearance. He could have been anywhere from thirty to seventy.

"What kind of music you play?" Preuss asked.

"You name it, I play it. Used to make my living with it."

"Seriously?"

"Yeah, man. Play jazz, funk, blues, rock. All that."

"Where'd you play?"

"All around. Session player. Know what that is?"

"I do."

"Ever hear of Jiff Riddler?"

"Sure." Riddler was a local jazz songwriter and producer, a keyboardist whose specialty was funk and electronica. "You played with him?"

"Yeah, man. I play with him when he start out."

Preuss had heard Riddler at Baker's Keyboard Lounge and other spots. As a guitar player himself, he always paid attention to who was on guitar, but he couldn't remember seeing Rabbit.

"What name did you play under?"

Rabbit gave a bitter chuckle. "Don't matter. Old news."

"What happened, brother?" Preuss asked.

Rabbit scoffed. "What always happen," he murmured, and looked away. Preuss didn't push it.

Rabbit was silent for the rest of the trip except for directing them to four other locations where he thought Larry Bright might be in Royal Oak and Ferndale. Bright wasn't anywhere.

"All I can think of around here," Rabbit said.

"Okay," Preuss said. "I can check these places again later. Or tomorrow. Where will you stay tonight?"

"Never know," Rabbit said. "Depend how early I get to the shelter. I steady stay at four. Larry stay at them, too."

"Can you take me past them?"

"Sure. But they don't let nobody in till six."

Rabbit sent them past three churches in Royal Oak and one in Ferndale. The South Oakland Shelter had arrangements with them to rotate offering beds for a night. There were churches all over the county, but Preuss concentrated on these three because they were the closest to Ferndale, and because Rabbit said these were the ones where Larry Bright stayed most often.

Preuss drove him back to the library. "Thanks," he said.

"No problem. Sorry we couldn't find him."

"I will, sooner or later," Preuss said.

He reached into his pocket and withdrew a fifty-dollar bill. "Here," he said. "Get yourself some hot meals, okay?"

"Awright," Rabbit said, and smiled for the first time. Preuss saw gaps in his mouth where teeth were missing. "You awright" He gave Preuss a fist bump.

"I'll see you again."

"No doubt," Rabbit said, and climbed out of the Explorer and loaded himself up with his belongings, all in the right order and proper place.

He strolled up to the automatic front doors and disappeared inside the library.

By then it was time to meet Grace Poole.

35

The Traffic Jam was an older restaurant that had gone through several incarnations and now fashioned itself as an artisanal microbrewery and bakery in Midtown (a name the city made up to differentiate it from the grungier Cass Corridor, as the area used to be known).

He got there a few minutes after four. After taking a walk through the restaurant to see if she was here yet, he sat on one of the banquettes in the foyer for a while. When the host asked if he wanted to get a table, Preuss let himself be led to a secluded booth in a corner where he could keep an eye on the front door.

A half-hour passed.

At close to five o'clock, he was gathering himself to leave when a text came through from her: *Sorry! Held up with a student conference. Still have time to meet?*

He texted back: *Yup. Still at TJs. I'll wait till you get here.*

She replied: *TY!*

In another twenty minutes, she strode into his secluded corner of the restaurant in a sweep of cold and snow and the light floral scent of her perfume. He stood up and they shook hands and she shrugged out of her cloak (black, of course) and tossed it in the corner of the booth. She slid in after it.

"I'm *so* sorry," she said. She looked at him and smiled. It brightened her face. And the booth. And the rest of the room.

And a good portion of the darkness in the corners of his life.

She shook the dusting of snow from her hair and said, "How long have you been here?"

"Not long."

"I think you're not telling the truth," she said with a sideways look at him. She glanced at her phone, which she set down face up on the table. "I'm over an hour late."

"Hadn't noticed."

Another smile. It was broad and genuine.

"Are you hungry? Do you want to eat anything?" he asked.

"No," she said. "I just have time for a cup of coffee. I didn't want to completely stand you up, but I have another class tonight I have to get ready for. As I was walking out of my afternoon seminar, one of my students caught me. She's been gone for a couple of weeks so I had to talk with her and listen to her story. She lost her home in a fire a couple weeks ago so she had to find someplace for herself and her kids to live, and then her car died, and then her children's father started to give her a hard time . . . I tell you, what some of these students go through to get to school is amazing."

He was content to sit back and listen to her talk in her post-teaching high. In fact, he was content just to sit there and look at her. Again, she was all in black except for a colorful silk scarf tied in a complicated knot around her neck.

The server came over and Grace ordered a latte. He ordered regular coffee. Is this my tenth cup of the day? he wondered.

"So," she said. "The famous Detective Preuss."

"Famous? Don't think so."

"You're way too modest. I googled you."

"You're the second person in a week to do that. I'll have to see what the internet says about me."

"Who else did it?"

"Somebody I met last week from the Anti-Defamation League. She said she googled me to see what I looked like before we met. So she could recognize me."

"I did research on you because that's what I do for a living. Matter of fact, I hired my own detective. He's going to give me his report on you next week." She gave him a wink. "Did you do me?"

"Of course," he said. "Because that's what *I* do for a living."

They both laughed.

Attractive, easy to talk to, easy to laugh with . . . what's going on here? he wondered.

"I bet you didn't find anything as interesting as I found," she said.

"You're the author of lots of books and publications," he said. "You give papers at conferences all over the world. There are words in your titles I suspect you make up."

"Those papers aren't supposed to be read, you know. Or understood. In higher ed, the point is to never have an unpublished thought. They don't have to be good thoughts, you understand, they just have to appear someplace where they were refereed."

"As long as *somebody* thought they were good thoughts."

"Or good enough to publish. Not quite the same thing."

"According to my own background check of you," he said, "you're an associate professor. So you have tenure, right? Can you start to ease off?"

"Not really. There's still one more rank to scratch and claw my way to. And how do you know about the arcane hierarchy of academia?"

"My parents were professors."

"Where?"

"Eastern Michigan."

"What did they teach?"

"Father history, mother English."

"A woman after my own heart. I started out as an English major in college. How'd they feel when you became a policeman?"

"Yet another in the series of constant disappointments that was my life as their son."

She smiled.

"How'd you end up in the Department of Education?" he asked.

"I taught high school English for eight years," she said, "then I burned out. I decided to go back and get my Ph.D. so I could teach college."

"Where'd you go?"

"State University of New York at Buffalo. When I was thinking about going back to school, I went up to the English Department because they had some heavy hitters on the faculty. Leslie Fiedler, Susan Howe, and so on. But I got bad vibes as soon as I got off the elevator. I thought: nope, nope, nope. So I went over to the School of Education and found it much more to my liking."

"What were you doing in Buffalo?"

"I was married to a lawyer there."

"Married as in past tense?"

"I haven't been married for a while."

The server brought his coffee and her latte.

"You?" she asked. "Ever married?"

"Widower."

"Oh, sorry. I'm a widow."

"Sorry."

"Yeah. Members of a club nobody ever wants to join."

"The lawyer?"

She nodded. "Any kids?"

"Two boys," he said.

"Nice. We never had any. I wanted them, but it wasn't to be. Just as well, now. I moved here when I got this job at Wayne. Would have been harder with kids."

"Did your husband come, too?"

"He died while we were in Buffalo. I stayed there long enough to finish my degree and then left."

"How'd he die?"

"Leukemia. Yours?"

"Car accident."

"So it goes," she said, and they were quiet for a moment.

"So how did you know Charles Bright?" he asked. (Speaking of dead people, he thought.)

"Originally, we served on the University Senate together," she said. "We were on a subcommittee and got on. No surprise there. Everybody got on with Charlie."

"So you said at the memorial."

"Does your case have anything to do with how he died?"

"It does."

"Are you trying to find out who killed him?"

"Officially, that's the police's job. I'm working the margins."

"Very post-modern." She watched him for a few moments. "You're the real deal, aren't you? Not just a keyhole-peeper."

"Can't remember the last time I peeped through a keyhole."

"Oh shit," she said, "I didn't mean it as an insult."

He waved it away. "Don't worry about it."

"No. As soon as I said it, I knew it sounded like an insult. Sorry. I don't mean to disparage what you do."

"I've been called a lot worse, trust me."

She kept watching him. "How's it coming? The case?"

"It's complicated. Couple of different avenues to follow, all while making sure I don't step on any police toes."

"But you like it," she said. "The business, I mean."

"I do."

"I can tell. Your face sort of lights up when you talk about it."

He shrugged.

She held up her cup in a toast. "Here's to crime-fighting."

"And to education."

They clinked and each took a sip from their cups.

As though some alarm had gone off somewhere—Danger, danger: Martin Preuss is getting too close to enjoying himself—his phone rang.

"Sorry," he said.

He looked at the screen. A call from Toby's group home.

"I have to get this."

"Please do."

He connected and eased out of the booth and into the restaurant foyer.

"Martin. Deb Hilbert."

"Deb. What's the matter?"

"Toby's fine," she said, "but he had a little trouble with his g-tube today. One of the aides hooked him up for his four o'clock feeding and he must have grabbed the tube because he pulled his button right out of his tummy."

Preuss's stomach sank.

"He's fine—he even surprised himself when he did it—but we ran him over to Beaumont to have him looked at anyway and get it reinserted. The stoma looked a little raw. We thought it was best. So that's where he is now. Melissa's with him."

"I'm on my way."

He hurried back to the table where Grace Poole was waiting. She looked up and saw the look on his face. "What's wrong?"

"It's my son. He had a small medical emergency in his group home. They took him to the hospital. I have to leave, Grace. Sorry."

"Of course. Don't apologize. Go."

He leaned in to grab his coat. She slid out of the booth and gave him a quick hug, ending with a pat on the back.

"Go," she said. "I'll get the check."

"Thanks. I'll get the next one."

"Call me later, let me know how he is."

"I will."

He raised a hand in farewell and rushed out of the restaurant and across the street to the parking lot.

36

Beaumont Hospital in Royal Oak wasn't far from Toby's group home. He left his car in the Emergency lot and trotted up to the registration desk. Carlos Guevara was sitting in the lobby, keeping watch. He must have followed them over.

Good man.

"Toby Preuss was brought in a little while ago," Preuss told the registration clerk. "I'm his father."

The clerk buzzed him back into the Emergency Department and he got the attention of a nurse behind the main station. She directed him to a cubicle around the corner.

The door was closed but he opened it and earned a quick harsh look from the young physician who was leaning over Toby's gurney. Toby was lying flat on his back. A cover was over his tummy with an opening for the spot where his g-tube used to be. On the side of his belly was a ragged opening in his skin about the size of a dime.

His aide Melissa sat beside him, holding his hand.

"Who are you?" the doc asked.

"Toby's father," Preuss said.

"Come in and close the door, please. I'm Dr. Prakash."

"Martin Preuss."

The doctor with his dark good looks seemed only a few years older than Toby himself. Melissa scooted out of the way so Preuss could get next to his son.

"Hey, Toby," he said. He held Toby's hand, which was warm and damp from Melissa's. "What's going on?" His son looked up at him out of the corner of his eye and forced a wan, crooked smile and a tiny "Hmm."

"He was getting his feed when he got home today," Melissa said, "and all of a sudden, quick as a wink, he grabbed the tube and pulled it. His button came completely out."

Dr. Prakash was dabbing at the raw area around the stoma with a sponge. "Cleaning up the site a little, and then we'll pop the new button back in and inflate it and you'll be good to go."

"We can put the button back in ourselves," Melissa said to Preuss, "but this time there was some blood, and the area around it looked inflamed. Deb thought somebody should take a look at him."

"Better safe than sorry," the young doctor said. "Nothing to worry about here, but I'll put some antibiotic ointment around the stoma. I'll cover it with a gauze pad. Leave it on for the night, and it can come off in the morning," he told Preuss.

Preuss looked at Melissa and she nodded her understanding.

Prakash finished cleaning the stoma and then unwrapped a new gastrostomy tube package. He filled a small syringe with water and inserted it into the inflating port. He injected water into the port to swell the balloon at the end of the tube to the size of a quarter. Then he withdrew the water, put lubricant around the end of the g-tube, and replaced it in the stoma.

Toby began to whine. "This is a little uncomfortable for him," Dr. Prakash said. "If he's still agitated when he gets home, give him some Tylenol."

The physician reinserted water through the inflation port to inflate the balloon again, then wiped off the area around the stoma and gave a gentle tug on the tube to make sure it was seated properly.

He took a bolus feed syringe out of the g-tube kit and attached it to the button. He ran some water through it and examined the site. "No leakage," he said. "Looks good."

He removed the bolus tube and added some antibiotic ointment around the site and covered it with a gauze pad.

"All set, young man," he told Toby. "Good as new."

He pulled off his gloves and patted Toby on the shoulder.

"I'll write up the discharge and you'll be all set."

"Thanks, doctor," Preuss said.

"My pleasure."

"Can he have his bath tonight?" Melissa asked.

"No reason why not," Prakash said. "I'll get you some more ointment to put on the site afterwards, when he's all dried off."

Toby screwed up his face the way he did when he was in discomfort. "I have some Tylenol in his bag," Melissa said. "I'll give him a squirt while we're waiting for his discharge papers. In your *new button*, Toby!"

At the group home, Carlos Guevara turned over the night shift duty to another guard, a woman named Nancy Fields. "I thought a woman might be best for the night shift," he told Preuss, "seeing as there are kids involved."

"Good idea," Preuss said. Nancy Fields was sitting in a car in front of the group home. She was an off-duty police officer in Hazel Park, and Preuss had worked with her before. She seemed serious and thoughtful.

Preuss asked her to come inside where he introduced her to the night duty aides. He asked if she could sit in the living room instead of outside in the cold, and the aides readily agreed. It would be good to have her in the house.

When she was settled, Preuss walked back to the bathroom. Toby was already lounging in the bathtub. By then the Tylenol had kicked in and he was nice and relaxed, rubber-limbed and ruddy-faced and happy in the suds.

After his bath, Melissa got him dried off, then gloved up and applied the antibiotic ointment to his button site and covered it with a gauze pad. She got him into his pajamas and left him to commune with his father.

Preuss pulled the chair over till he was right next to the bed. He rubbed Toby's back as Judy Collins sang him into sleep.

Preuss stayed with him for a while longer, then leaned over to give him a soft kiss on the side of his head.

As medical emergencies went with Toby, this was relatively benign. An easy problem, easily fixed. There were no broken bones, no gushing blood, no cyanosis, no fevers, no pneumonia, no life-threatening paralytic ileus—all of which had sent Toby to the hospital in past episodes, sometimes repeatedly.

It was still early enough to do what he had planned to do after meeting with Grace Poole—look for Larry Bright. The Royal Oak churches Rabbit had taken him by were closest to Toby's house, so he would start there.

On the way into Royal Oak, he punched in Grace Poole's number on his phone.

She picked it up right away. "Martin," she said. "How is your son?"

"He's fine," Preuss said. "Not calling too late?"

"Not at all. What happened?"

He explained what the problem was. "They were concerned at his house because there was some blood around the stoma. But it wasn't serious."

"I'm so glad. Thanks for letting me know."

"I appreciate your concern."

"Sure. Why is your son in a group home?"

"He's multiply-handicapped," Preuss said. "Cerebral palsy, cognitive delays, seizures, what they call 'profoundly involved.'"

"Aw."

"He needs around-the-clock care, and with my schedule I couldn't take care of him at home by myself after my wife died."

"No, of course."

"He's in a great place. It's nearby, the people are excellent. I visit him every morning and every night . . . I spend as much time as I can with him. He seems to like it there. I wish he could be home with me, but . . ."

"I can tell you love him."

"I do. He's my best friend."

"That's so sweet."

Preuss said nothing. For him, it wasn't sweet or not sweet; it just was.

"You said you have two boys?"

"I have another son, Jason," Preuss said. "He's older."

"What does he do?"

"Hard to say. He's disappeared somewhere in America. He's been out of touch for a while. That's another whole long story," he said.

"I have time."

"Let's take a rain check, okay?"

"Sure. You sound like you're in the car."

"I am. On my way to an interview."

"This late?"

"Detectives doze, but we never close."

"I'll let you go, then," she said. "Thanks for calling. I was worried."

"Sure thing. Continue this another time?"

"I'd like to."

"So would I."

37

The Royal Oak churches weren't hosting the overnight shelter program this week. The Renaissance Vineyard Church in Ferndale was, and that's where Preuss found Larry Bright.

A volunteer with a warm smile met Preuss at the door of the church on Pinecrest near Nine Mile.

The smile vanished as soon as Preuss explained who he was and who he was looking for.

"I'm really sorry," the volunteer said. He was a heavy-set young man with a full shaggy brown beard and a tan toque. He had on checkered Bermuda shorts despite the weather. "This is a safe place for our guests. We can't have law enforcement coming in to make arrests."

"No," Preuss said, "in the first place, I'm not law enforcement. I'm a private investigator. I don't have anything to do with the police. And in the second place, I'm not here to make an arrest. I'm here to talk with Larry. It's about the death of his father."

"Larry's father died?"

"Under suspicious circumstances. And I need to find out if he knows about it. I have no intention of rousting him out of here, I promise you."

The volunteer gave Preuss a wary sideways glance. Then he said, "He's not in any trouble?"

"None I know of."

"And you're not going to disturb him? Or any of the other guests?"

"I'll try not to."

"Wait here then."

The volunteer turned and disappeared down some stairs to a lower level. In a few minutes, he returned, but not with Larry. He came up with Rabbit.

"Hey man," Rabbit said, and gave Preuss a hand pound.

"Rabbit," Preuss said. "Glad you have a warm place tonight."

"Yeah. Yo, I heard Brandon talking to Larry. You still looking for him?"

"I am. He's downstairs?"

"Brandon axe him if he want to see you. But Larry, he—he not doing so good tonight. Wasn't gettin' through."

"How about if I try?"

"If you want."

"I do."

"A'ight."

Rabbit led Preuss down the stairway at the side of the entry foyer. The volunteer Brandon stayed to keep up his doorman duties.

The staircase ended in a large open area lit by overhead fluorescents. A small altar stood on a stage at the far end of what would have been the room for church functions. Now, roughly thirty men of multiple races lay bundled in bedding scattered around on the floor. Some were snoring, some were murmuring to their neighbors, and some were silent, watching Preuss and Rabbit with angry, suspicious eyes.

A line went through his head: *Make me down a pallet on your floor.*

Everybody had a version. Mississippi John Hurt. Jim Kweskin. Gillian Welch.

I'm tired, lonesome weary
And I can't work no more
Make me a pallet on your floor.

Rabbit led the way through the sleeping pallets to where Larry Bright lay under a blanket by the stage. Rabbit's belongings, including his gig bag, were on the floor beside Larry's pallet.

"Larry," Rabbit said. "Somebody here to see you, man."

Larry lay on his side with his knees drawn up close to his body. Preuss saw he was rocking under his blanket. He did not look at or respond to Rabbit.

Preuss sat cross-legged on Rabbit's pallet beside Larry. "Hey Larry," he said. "You're a hard man to find."

More rocking. No eye contact with Preuss.

"Larry," Preuss said, "I came to talk to you about your father."

Larry closed his eyes and buried his head in his pillow.

"You know what happened to him, don't you?" Still no sound from Larry. "He passed away a couple weeks ago."

"Oh man, seriously?" Rabbit asked.

Preuss nodded.

"Oh no, man, sorry to hear that, Larry. I pray for your father."

For his part, Larry murmured, "My father," into his pillow.

"That's right," Preuss said. "I'm sorry to say, somebody killed him, Larry. Somebody killed your father."

For the first time, Larry looked straight at Preuss. Larry's eyes were wide open, but his pupils were pinpoints. He's flying, Preuss realized.

A mixture of smells was hanging in the room—the stale smell of sweat on unwashed bodies, a deeper, more animal smell coming off some of the ones who had been on the street for longer, and, under it all, the skunky-sweet smell of marijuana.

It was coming off Larry, and off Rabbit, too. Rabbit's eyes were sleepier than they were this afternoon, and not because he was tired. He was stoned, too.

"Larry," Preuss said, "how about we talk for a second, okay? In private. Away from all this." He waved his hands around, at the stench, the sleeping men, and those craning to hear.

Preuss stood. "Let's go back there for a minute." He pointed toward the back of the rec room, near the stairwell.

Larry looked to Rabbit for a clue on how to respond. Rabbit came through; he nodded, said, "Go on, man. He just want to talk."

Preuss leaned down and reached out to take Larry's arm to help him up, but Larry pulled his arm away as if a snake had bitten him.

Preuss stood back, hands up, let Larry disentangle himself from his covers. He stood on his wobbly legs, then followed Preuss through the people on their sleeping pallets.

In the back of the room beside the stairway was an inglenook that gave them some small privacy. Preuss took his phone out and placed it on a shelf beside them. He opened the Notes app and hit Record; whatever Larry wound up telling him, he wanted to have saved.

"Larry," Preuss said, "do you know what happened to your father?"

"My father?"

"Yes."

"My father," Larry said, glancing around, "is not of this earth."

The look in Larry's eye—not totally crazy, but not sane either—was alarming. Preuss had seen it before, on men in custody who were seconds away from decompensating.

"My father is a heavenly father," Larry insisted. He spoke fast, as though reciting rote phrases. "He is slow to anger, and abundant in loving kindness."

"But your earthly father. What about Charles, your earthly father?"

"Will you judge the abominations of the father?" Larry hissed.

"Larry," Preuss said, and grabbed Larry by the arms to get him to focus. Larry struggled but Preuss held him firm. "Do you remember when your father died? Do you remember where you were?"

"Oh come, the seas will bother and stress her," Larry said—or Preuss thought he said. He repeated it two more times, then said, "God will forgive me."

He was spouting gibberish, and getting more agitated.

"Did you hurt your father, Larry? Did you make your father die for his sins?"

"They shall *all* die for their sins! Those that are under sin held low shall die, and those that are subject to its power and control shall die!"

"Larry, listen to me. Did you hurt your father?"

Larry closed his eyes and swayed in a circle, as though his head were swimming. As it may well be, Preuss thought, with this jumble of ideas pulsing through it. Larry began muttering, but Preuss couldn't catch it. The words were too low.

Then, as if a high-speed switch had been thrown, Larry began shouting. "They are displeasing to God," he cried, "and they are the enemies of all mankind. Hated by everyone! Finish the job! For our people! For a future for our children!"

"Larry! Larry!"

Larry covered his ears with his hands, whether to keep the voices out or the jumble of words in, Preuss couldn't tell.

"Okay," Preuss said. This wasn't working. "Calm down. Calm down. Let's go back."

He retrieved his phone and with his arm around Larry—now allowing himself to be touched, as though his outburst had drained the last of his energy—they walked back through the bodies stretched out in their bedding on the floor. A bank of overhead lights had been turned off, and the buzz of noise was lower as men began sliding into sleep to a chorus of sighs, snores, and occasional sobs.

Rabbit was sitting up on his pallet. He watched Preuss guide Larry back to his place.

"Get what you needed?" Rabbit asked.

"No. I got a lot of Bible gibberish, but nothing helpful."

"Yeah," Rabbit said, "that sound like him. He go on like that. Specially when he stoned." He gave a short laugh.

"Did you get him stoned?"

"No," Rabbit said, but his own gaze was unfocused and Preuss half-expected him to start talking about Jesus, too. "Weed ain't hard to find up in here."

"Looks like you might have found some for yourself, too."

"Whatever get you through the night and day, know what I'm sayin'?"

Preuss got Larry settled under the blankets on his pallet and sat next to Rabbit.

"You're close with him?" Preuss asked Rabbit.

Rabbit shrugged.

"Do you know if you were with him on a night almost a month ago? It would be January 8th. A Monday night."

Even as he said it, Preuss realized the absurdity of the question.

Rabbit knew it, too. The question even made him smile. "Yeah, well, I got to axe my social secretary where I was in my busy schedule."

"I take it that's a no."

"I don't know, man. You lose track of the days."

"Fair enough. Are you with him every night?"

"Lotta nights. But every night? Uh-uh. Sometime we get in different warming sites. We tight, you know, but . . ."

He let the rest of the thought fade away. In the chaos of surviving on the streets, it was hard to maintain close contact.

"Do you remember where you stayed in the beginning of January?"

"Probably here. It's when they open for the year. Right after New Year."

"Do they keep records of who stays here?"

"They sposed to axe, but nobody give his real name."

"No, right."

"You think Larry killed his old man?"

"I don't know," Preuss said. "He ever mention it to you?"

Rabbit thought for a moment, then said, "Larry don't have it in him, man. He crazy sometime, but he harmless. But you know, pretty sure a few days after the first of the year, I didn't see him around anywhere."

"How sure is pretty sure?"

"Ain't a hundred percent. And not sure about the time. But yeah, he disappear for a while around the turn of the year. Didn't see him at the library or any our other places. I thought something happened to him. But then he turn up looking and talking like always."

Preuss considered it. If he hadn't been seen around the streets and warming centers, there was a chance Larry was the one who stayed at his father's house in Ferndale. At least according to Margaret Slater, who lived across the street from Charles Bright. In her police statement, she had said she thought she saw a rough-looking man hanging around Bright's house in the days before he died.

As well as running down the street on the day of Charles Bright's death.

She didn't know if they were the same man, but she assumed whoever it was, was homeless.

Another bank of lights blinked off overhead.

"Getting ready to turn off for the night," Rabbit said.

Before he lost all the light, Preuss took out his iPhone and snapped a few photos of Larry Bright. His eyes were closed and there was a scowl on his face, as though he were having some kind of serious internal argument with himself. The Larry Bright of today was older, heavier, and in worse shape than in his DMV photo—but Preuss might be able to get some identifications off the snaps he was taking.

"All right, Rabbit," he said, "I'll let you go. Thanks for your help, man. Take care of yourself, all right?"

"All right, Mr. Detective. Hope you catch your man."

"So do I."

They fist-bumped and Rabbit lay down and burrowed into his bedding with a satisfied groan.

Before burrowing into his own bed, Preuss called Nancy Fields, the security agent at Toby's house. She told him all was quiet at the group home. Toby and the rest of the residents were sleeping, and the night staff were catching up on their notes.

The street outside was quiet.

He thanked her, and reminded her to stay alert.

He thought about calling Grace Poole again.

No. The hour was late, and talking three times in one day might be pushing it.

He lay on his bed and tried to sleep after such an exhausting day. But he couldn't. He was too wired.

Instead he listened to *Highway 61 Revisited* on his iPod. It was one of his all-time favorite albums, not solely for the music but for the ways Dylan's songs spoke to him as they skittered along the edge of chaos, hopelessness, despair, cynicism, and—occasionally—redemption.

All of which captured the current essence of Martin Preuss's complicated, often incomprehensible world.

Tuesday, March 5, 2013

38

Carlos Guevara was already at Toby's house when Preuss came by in the morning. Toby was recovered from his ordeal of the day before and was happy and chirping as his aide got him ready for school.

At the office, he told Rhonda about the calls from the day before, which she already knew about because she had listened to her messages.

"So what do you want to do?" she asked.

"We'll have to hire somebody else temporarily. Not Angie," he added before she could object.

"Any possibilities in the group you interviewed?"

"No. Thought any more about going back into the field?"

"No."

"You were a natural—"

"I don't mean I haven't thought any more about it. I mean no, I don't want to do it."

"But you're so good—"

"No."

"It'll be easier to hire someone for inside—"

"No," she said. "No. No. No."

"So that's a maybe?"

"Martin!"

"Okay. I'll check with Carlos, see what's going on with him. Maybe he knows somebody. I talked to him this morning. I'll see him later and feel him out."

"You talked this morning? What about?"

"Personal job. I'm seeing some threatening behavior around Toby. I asked Carlos to keep an eye on him for a while."

"Not Toby!"

He explained about the white nationalists.

"You shouldn't have to pay for that yourself," Rhonda said. "Let's run it through the business. I'm sure Manny would agree."

"Let me think about it."

"Nope," she said. "Nothing to think about. I'm doing it."

She turned to her desk and began the paperwork right then.

"Thanks," he said, and took his coffee into his office. He opened the Charles Bright file and spent the first hour writing up his interviews and visits with McShane, the Sacred Heart Seminary, David Baker, the Royal Oak Library, Rabbit, and Larry Bright.

No wonder I'm so tired, he thought. Yesterday was a killer day and he had been too wired to sleep when he got home. This morning he was logy and exhausted.

He might have tended to write off Larry's comments as the ravings of someone with mental problems, but he resisted the impulse. Instead, he played his recording of their conversation and transcribed it to get down, as exactly as he could, what Larry had said. He couldn't catch some of the words because Larry spat them out too low and fast, but he got most of it.

A knock came on his doorframe.

"I could have been doing this for you," Rhonda said. She indicated his phone and the transcribing he was doing.

"I know," he said. "But some of this was hard to catch. I wanted to get my take on it first. Then I'll ask you to go through it to double check everything. Okay?"

"Sure."

He printed out his transcription and brought it out to her along with his phone. "I tried to get it all down, but maybe another set of ears can catch things I didn't get. Can you go through this for me and check if I got everything?"

"Absolutely," she said.

He returned a few calls and heard her clicking through the recording. Then he reread his own transcription, and the notes from the previous day. As with many homeless people Preuss had known, it was unclear if Larry Bright had lost his way because of mental illness, or if the mental illness came on as a result of his becoming homeless. The Sacred Heart seminary was a conservative place, and maybe being so immersed in religion and religious study there encouraged his tendencies toward extremism.

Preuss was sure of one thing: he had not gotten through to him last night. He didn't know if bringing him in and getting him calmed down with a solid meal would make a difference, but it might be worth a try. Of course, this meant finding him again.

Rhonda appeared in his doorway, holding his phone and his transcript.

"Okay," she said, "I listened to it a few times, and I got some things you might have missed, or misheard."

"Good."

"There was one thing I found that sounded kind of interesting," she said. She laid the transcript on his desk. She had crossed out some passages and filled them back in with her miniscule handwriting.

"It's here," She flipped through to the end of the conversation. "Here, you said 'inaudible,' but to me it sounds like he said: 'Will my brother? Will my sister? Who shall pass judgment on their manifold sins?'"

"Yeah, it sounded like he might have said something about his brother and sister, but I couldn't understand it."

"At first I thought he was using those as general terms," Rhonda said. "You know, like my brother and sister in Christ kind of thing. But look here, right afterwards, he says something else you might have misheard."

She pointed to a line on the transcript. "You thought he said, 'Come, the seas will bother and stress her.'"

"Which didn't make sense to me. But that's what I thought I heard."

"Right, because the recording was fuzzy. But what if he said, 'Ken and Cecille, my brother and sister'?"

He thought about it for a moment, then said, "Let's listen again."

She played the section of the recording.

"Could be," he allowed. "We know his brother—or his stepbrother—is named Ken. So who's Cecille?"

"The name hasn't come up in the investigation so far, has it?

"No. Play it again."

They listened to the line another five times. Each time, it seemed plainer Larry Bright was saying what Rhonda heard: *Oh, Ken and Cecille, my brother and sister.*

"So who's Cecille?" he asked. "If she's part of the family, it's odd nobody's mentioned it."

"Exactly."

"Could you see if you can track down anyone named Cecille Bright? Or Cecille Krempka," he added. "If Larry's crying out to them as his brother and sister, we need to know what that's about."

"Do you want me to start by asking Ken Krempka?"

"Not yet. Let's keep him as a last resort. Start with their mother. Dorothy Bright. Her maiden name was Krempka—the name Ken Krempka assumed when he made his split from the Brights."

He tried to remember what he had found out about her. His clients, Father Corrigan and Rabbi Rifkin, didn't seem to know much about her . . . who else had he spoken with who did?

One person in particular had said she knew Dorothy well.

39

Margaret Slater was the older woman who lived across the street from the Bright home in Ferndale. Her statement was in the police report.

She opened the door as soon as he knocked. She must have been waiting for him after he had called and asked if they could speak.

She invited him in and had a white china teapot and cups ready on a table in the living room. It was an older woman's house, with dark, heavy furniture and little light sneaking in through the curtains.

"Thank you for seeing me on such short notice," he told her. He could have done this over the telephone, but he felt like he was closing in on something important in this case and wanted to do as much as he could in person.

"I don't know how I can help, but I'm always willing to try," she said.

She looked to be in her eighties, a slender woman with quick, bird-like movements as she poured them both a cup of tea.

"You knew Dr. Bright and his family?" Preuss asked.

"Yes. I wasn't so much friendly with him, as with Dottie."

"So you told the police. I heard they were very devoted to each other."

"They were. So much. You could tell just by looking at them."

"Did they have children?"

"Oh yes. Two boys."

"Ken and Larry?"

"Yes."

"And you knew them, too?"

"I did. This was a long time ago," Margaret said. "Right after they first moved in, both boys lived with them. But it wasn't long before the older boy moved out. The younger boy finished high school, and then he left, too."

"Did Dottie ever mention if there was a third child? A girl?"

Margaret scowled in thought. "A girl . . ." Her eyes were lost behind her glasses as she tried to look back into the past.

"A sister of Ken and Larry," he said.

"I don't remember hearing Dottie ever say anything about having a daughter."

"Did she ever mention anyone named Cecille? Or maybe Cissy?"

He let her think back some more.

"No," she said, "I can't remember another child. As far as I know, there were just the two boys."

"Okay," Preuss said. "That's helpful."

"Now," Margaret said, holding up a finger knotted with arthritis, "*Dottie* had a sister."

"Dottie had a sister? Her name wasn't Cecille, by any chance?"

"No. It was . . . let me see . . . oh, my mind is such a sieve these days . . . no, Dottie's sister was Carol. Don't recall her last name. And Carol, *she* had a daughter."

"You don't remember the girl's name?"

"No, sorry."

"Did Carol's daughter ever live with the Brights?"

"No, she just visited. And not all that often, either, if I remember right."

"Is Carol from around here?"

"Don't think so. Carol would stay with Dottie when she came, which I always thought meant she lived out of town. Dottie may have told me where they lived, but if I ever knew I've forgotten."

She laughed at her own frailty, a girlish tinkle.

"Okay," Preuss said. "Before I go, can I ask you one more question?"

"Of course, dear."

"You told the police you used to see people you thought were homeless going in and out of Dr. Bright's home."

"Yes."

"And you said you remembered seeing somebody go in with him the night before he was killed. Somebody you thought looked homeless?"

"Yes."

"But you couldn't remember any description. Have you thought any more about it?"

"No, dear. I can't bear to think about that poor man. I'm sorry."

"No worries, Mrs. Slater. You've been great."

Sitting in the car in front of Margaret Slater's home, Preuss called Rhonda.

"Hey," she said, "how'd you do?"

"The neighbor here says there was no daughter. She does remember Dorothy Bright had a sister, named Carol. Can you do some quick checking? See if you can find Dorothy's obituary. She died six years ago. And see if you can find any mention of her sister."

He remembered Ken Krempka saying he took his mother's last name. "Carol's last name might be Krempka," he said. "Try it, anyway. If we're lucky, there'll also be a mention of a niece to Dorothy, whose name Margaret here can't remember."

"Are you thinking Larry Bright mixed up his cousin with his sister?"

"Could be. He was pretty out of it. If there's a mention of Carol Krempka, see if you can track her down, too. She might live out of town."

"Will do. Where are you?"

"Still in Ferndale. Going to grab some lunch and then I'll be back. Want anything?"

"Nope, thanks. But *bon appetit.*"

He was standing at the counter in his kitchen finishing a cheese and tomato sandwich when his phone rang.

Rhonda, with news.

40

"Okay," she said, "two things. First, I found an obituary for Dorothy Bright. It was in the *Free Press*. And it did list a sister, Carol Krempka. But here's the rub: Carol Krempka pre-deceased Dorothy."

"Damn."

"Yeah, she's been dead ten years. Scratch her off the list."

"Anything about a niece named Cecille?"

"Not in the article I saw. But—and here's maybe the good news—it also listed as a survivor an uncle named Chester Krempka."

"Good."

"Chester was listed as living in Grand Rapids, which is where Dorothy and her sister came from."

"Did you check the Grand Rapids directory?"

"I did."

"Of course you did."

"And there's a listing for one Chester Krempka. Want the number?"

"Hang onto it. I'm coming in."

His enthusiasm soon flagged.

He tried the number Rhonda gave him for Chester Krempka and found it had been disconnected.

There were three other relatives mentioned in Dorothy Bright's obituary: an aunt, Ida Pulaski, and two nephews, Randolph Pulaski and Frederick Pulaski.

Rhonda had found the numbers for them, too. When he called the number for Ida, a man answered the phone.

"I'm calling for Ida Pulaski," he told the man.

"Yeah? Who's this?"

A rough voice, raspy like sandpaper.

"Martin Preuss. I'm a private investigator looking to speak with Ida."

"Yeah, well good luck with that," the man said. "She's in a nursing home."

"Do you have her phone number?"

"Phone number's not gonna do no good, pal. She's out of it. She don't even know what day it is."

"Who am I speaking with?"

"This is Ida's son."

"Randolph?"

"No, Fred. Who did you say you were?"

"A private investigator. I have you on my list to call, too, Fred. Did you know Dorothy Krempka?"

"Aunt Dorothy? Sure."

"I'm trying to verify some information, Fred. Dorothy had two sons, Kenneth and Larry?"

"Yeah."

"Were there any other children?"

"Nope."

"Do you know anyone named Cecille? Possibly Cecille Krempka."

Fred thought for a moment and said, "Could that be Cissy?"

"Is she one of Dorothy's relations?"

"Sure. Dorothy's sister's girl."

"Carol's girl?"

"Yup."

"Do you know how to get in touch with her?"

"No," Fred Pulaski said. "I haven't seen or heard from her in years. Don't even know if she's still alive."

The sucking sound of Fred taking a large drag off a cigarette.

"Where was she when you last heard from her?" Preuss asked.

"Might be here in Grand Rapids. You know who'd know for sure? My brother Randy. He's got the memory in the family. Like an elephant: never forgets."

Randy Pulaski sounded like he had one foot in the grave and the other on a fast train to nowhere. He had a high, weak old-man's voice that quavered when he spoke. He whistled when he breathed.

His brother Fred said Randy was also in a nursing home and suffered from emphysema, but he was sharper than he sounded.

Preuss hoped so. He explained what he wanted. He decided to do this over the phone rather than spend three hours traveling out to the west side of the state to Grand Rapids, then another three coming back, all for what might be a dead end.

"Dottie?" the old man said. "Dottie's long gone."

"I know that," Preuss said. "But I'm investigating a case connected with her. The death of her husband, Charles."

A sharp intake of breath.

"Charles is dead?"

"Yessir. Afraid so."

"Oh, I'm so sorry to hear it."

More whistling.

"Was it sudden?"

"Pretty sudden," Preuss said. "And unexpected."

"Such a shame," Randolph said. He tsk-tsked.

"Your brother told me Dottie's sister Carol had a daughter named Cecille. People called her Cissy."

"Right. Cissy. Born . . . let's see . . . 1970. In November, if I'm not mistaken."

"Fred said you had a good memory."

"Well," Randy said with a chuckle, "on top of everything else, my eyesight isn't very good anymore. Got this macular degeneration, you know. Have to rely more and more on my memory."

"So Cissie is Carol's daughter?"

Randy hesitated. Preuss heard his whistling breath.

"Randy?" Preuss said.

Another hesitation.

"Can I let you in on a little family secret?" Randy said at last.

"Please do."

"Most people thought Cissie was Carol's daughter. Carol even said so. Truth was, Carol only raised her as her own. Cissie wasn't really Carol's."

"Whose was she?"

"Dottie's."

"I want to make sure I'm understanding this," Preuss said. "Cissie was Dottie's daughter, not Carol's?"

"Yup."

There was a third child named Cecille in this family after all.

"Can you say more about the circumstances?" Preuss asked.

More whistling breath. "It's complicated," Randy warned.

"It always is."

"Well, Dottie, she was a wild one when she was young, see. Sort of a hippie in her time."

"So I understand."

"And she lived in a, I guess you'd call it a sort of commune-type arrangement up north back in the sixties and early seventies. She had a baby with a guy who was part of the scene back then. A little boy named Kenny."

"I've met him," Preuss said.

"Dottie never married the father. And then one day a few years later she went and got herself pregnant again by the same character. And not only didn't he marry her, but he run off entirely."

"So much for free love."

"So there she was, Dottie with two littles ones and no husband or father to her children, and no way to make a living. And after a while, no place to live because the commune was starting to go to pieces."

"They never lasted long."

"No sir, they didn't," Randy said. "So she moved back to Grand Rapids, lived in a little hole-in-the-wall apartment downtown. She didn't feel like she could raise another child by herself. Her parents didn't want anything to do with her on account of how she was living, see. So Dottie and Carol decided Carol and her husband at the time would raise the child. Might have started out as temporary, but Carol fell in love with the little girl, and the two sisters decided they'd make it permanent."

"Why didn't they tell anybody what they'd done?"

"Wasn't nobody else's business. Both sisters were rebels, in their way, and the family pretty much disowned them. So they said screw you and did what they wanted to do, and told the family what they wanted them to hear."

Randy paused to take a few wheezing breaths.

"Quite a tale," Preuss said.

"Yeah. Like I always say, family life."

"You wouldn't happen to know where Cecille is now?"

"I do indeed."

"Randy, you are an amazing man."

"Ah," he said, and laughed off the compliment. "Guy my age, what else is there to do, except remember the past? You want to wait a second, I'll try to find the address for you."

"Cecille Krempka?" Preuss asked into the phone.

A small hesitation on the other end.

"I haven't heard that name in years," the woman said. Deep, throaty voice. A life-long smoker's voice.

Randolph didn't know if Cecille had married or changed her name, so Krempka was the only name Preuss had for her.

"Am I speaking with Cecille Krempka?" Preuss asked.

"Yeah," the woman said, "that'd be me. Or used to be, anyway."

"My name is Martin Preuss. I'm a private investigator down near Detroit, and I'm calling because one of my cases is connected with Dottie Krempka. Or Dottie Bright."

"Another name I haven't heard in a while."

"I'd like to ask you some questions, if you don't mind."

41

She lived on a dairy farm outside North Lakeport, Michigan, above Port Huron on Lake Huron. It was an hour-and-a-half trip, but Preuss thought it would be worth speaking to her face-to-face.

"If you get into the city, you've gone too far," she had told him. He turned off at the sign directing him to the Zimmer Dairy Farm, with the cartoon logo of a laughing cow, and drove down a long, frozen road toward a picture-book farm: red barn, silo, neat Victorian farmhouse.

She must have been watching for him because as soon as he pulled onto the apron between the barn and the house, she came outside.

She was a weathered woman in her forties, with blonde hair escaping from a watch cap, and wearing a baggy pair of camo pants tucked into work boots and several layers of hoodies under an outer layer with a mustard-colored check pattern.

"Mr. Preuss?"

"Yes."

She came forward with an outstretched hand. "Gloria Krempka," she said. Her wide mouth was smiling.

When he shook her hand, he felt the strength of her; her grip was hard as a brick.

"Good to meet you," she said.

"Likewise."

A man came out of the barn wearing a red plaid jacket and knee-high rubber boots. He was a big guy with a watch cap pulled low over his forehead. "Thought I heard voices," he said.

"That's my partner, Hugo," the woman said. "He's the Zimmer who runs the place. Hugo," she said, "this guy knew my mother."

Preuss was about to correct her—he never met Dorothy—but Hugo nodded and raised a hand in greeting. Preuss returned it.

"Come on inside," she said. "We'll talk."

She led him through the back door into the kitchen with countrified decorations (roosters, pigs, "Jesus Bless Our Home" framed needlepoints, red and white gingham curtains) and the ubiquitous damp farmhouse smell from the cellar. She had coffee brewing on the counter.

"How do you take it?" she asked.

"Just as it comes."

"My kinda guy."

She poured them both a cup and they sat across the kitchen table from each other. "Sorry I don't have any cookies or cake to offer you. I don't keep any sweets in the house. That's all Hugo would eat if I did. Man loves him his sweets."

"Not a problem. Sorry," he said, "but did you introduce yourself as Gloria?"

"Yeah."

"I was under the impression your name was Cecille."

"It was. I always hated the name Cecille. I changed it to Gloria when Carol died. So," she said, settling back in her chair, "you want to talk about Dottie Bright."

"Right. I'm looking into the death of her husband."

"Charles is dead?"

"He is."

"What happened?"

"Somebody killed him."

She didn't bat an eye. She took a sip of her coffee.

"Some questions have come up about Dottie," he said. "I'm hoping you can help answer them for me."

"Well, she didn't kill him, I'll tell you that for free. How'd you find me?"

"Your uncle Randy told me."

"Oh." She laughed, sounding like a bag of gravel shifting in her chest. "That old woman."

She put a pack of Marlboro Ultra Lights on the table. "Do you mind?" she asked.

"Your house, your rules."

She shook a cigarette out and lit it. She held the pack out to him but he shook his head. She got up and retrieved a glass ashtray off the counter and returned to her seat.

"So what else did randy old Randy tell you?" she asked, with the cigarette dangling from the side of her mouth. She squinted an eye against the smoke.

"He told me Dottie Bright was your mother."

She took a long drag, turned her head to blow the smoke away from Preuss, and washed it down with a drink of coffee.

"He's worse than an old woman," she muttered.

"Is it true?"

She gave a grudging nod. "It's true."

"But everybody thought her sister Carol was your real mother."

"Right again. Ain't life a bitch?"

Another wheezy laugh.

"I'm interested in how that arrangement came about," Preuss said.

"You are, eh."

She sized him up. "And for what reason, if you don't mind my asking."

"I thought there were two kids in the Bright family, and when I discovered there might have been three, it piqued my interest."

"Filling out our family tree, are you?"

"In a way."

"Why's that?"

"I want to find out what happened to your stepfather. I'm trying to figure out the dynamics."

"You think *I* killed him?"

"Did you?"

Another phlegmy laugh.

"Might have wanted to at times, but no, I didn't."

"I didn't think you did, Gloria. But I am wondering about the family relationships here."

She took another long drag and tapped the ash off the cigarette. With care she shaped the glowing end on the side of the ashtray.

"Kenny and I are brother and sister, that's true. Larry's our half-brother. Same mother, different fathers. That enough for you?"

"I talked with Kenny," he said, "and he didn't say a word about you."

"We're not in the habit of talking to strangers about our personal life."

Yet here you are, he thought, telling me all about it.

"Dorothy was your biological mother," he said. "Charlie Bright was your stepfather. Who was your biological father?"

"Nobody worth talking about. Just some Jew musician back in the day."

The casual vitriol behind the way she spit out "Jew" took him by surprise.

"Okay," he said.

"Yeah, I barely remember him. One thing I do remember, he wanted to be a rock star. He wasn't living in the commune Dottie made us live in back then. Those people weren't welcome."

"Those people?"

"Jews. But he and Dottie, they connected somehow. I dunno how. He knocked her up with Kenny, and a few years later after he'd knocked her up with me, he disappeared. I guess one kid was okay, but two was too much. We never heard from him again. And I never heard *about* him, either, so I guess he never made much of himself."

"Did you know him, or did he leave before you were born?"

"Oh, I knew him. He took off when I was about five. So I knew him. I don't remember much about him anymore."

Except that he was Jewish, Preuss thought.

"It was around then when the commune went all to hell, and everybody scattered," she went on. "My mother didn't have any money, and my father wouldn't do nothing to help us out, of course. He was long gone by then, and we couldn't pry a nickel out of his family. Cheap kikes. We lived in a dump with rats in the bathroom in Grand Rapids. My mother had a bit of a nervous breakdown around then and made an arrangement with her sister Carol to take care of me. Then when Dottie moved downstate to start up at Wayne State University, I just stayed with Carol and her husband in Grand Rapids. Dottie took up with Charlie—he was one of her professors— she wound up marrying him."

She took a long drag on her smoke.

"Horny bastard," she said. "Saw a young woman who needed help and moved right in on her. Typical of those people."

"So you never lived in Ferndale?"

"Never."

"You never wanted to live with your real mother?"

"If it would have been just her, I'd been happy as a clam. But once she was well-off enough to take care of me after she got married, I just stayed with Carol. I'd never live in the same house as another Jew as long as I lived."

Again she spat out the word. She watched him to see what kind of reaction he would have. But he was used to keeping a poker face, so he didn't respond. Didn't even blink.

"These Jews, they're pushy and greedy. They run the whole fucking world. All the banks. Own all the politicians, all the media. They pull the strings behind all the governments in the world, too. Did you know that? George Soros? That name ring a bell? Goddamn Christ killers. I say too bad Hitler never finished the job."

He was always surprised the way all these centuries-old anti-Semitic tropes were not only still alive, but were held to so fervently. How old would she have been when her mother married Charlie Bright? Ten? To be instilled with such hate at such a young age—especially with a Jewish father and stepfather—she must have been taught it young, by others in the commune who didn't let Jews in.

"Them and the blacks," she said. "Mud people, all of them. Country'd be better off without them all. And someday it will be."

She ground out her cigarette and reached for another.

"Still wondering about my family?" she asked with a ghost of a smile.

"The neighbor across the street told me Carol stayed at the Bright house when she visited Dottie."

"The old Slater lady? Another busybody. She's right, though. Carol stayed there with Dottie, but I never did. I wouldn't stay under the same roof as him, I stayed with cousins in Dearborn."

"And did you see Ken during those times?"

"Sure. By then he was old enough to drive, and he'd come out to get me."

"Did you ever hear of the American Identity Brigade?" Preuss asked.

"The which?"

He repeated it and she said, "Never heard of them."

"Did your brother Ken share your beliefs?"

"About Jews? You bet your life he did. That's why he left home as soon as he could."

Gloria Krempka stood up to get the carafe of coffee to fill up Preuss's cup. But he held his hand over it; he didn't want to stay here any longer than necessary.

"If anything," she said, "Ken's even worse."

The present tense caught him up. "You've seen Ken recently?"

She gave him a bitter, hard-edged smile. "Sorry, pal. You've used up all your questions."

42

"He's in a meeting," the young woman sitting outside Ken Krempka's office said. She was a different woman than the one Preuss had spoken with the other day. This one was a lovely young Latina with long black hair and an overbite.

"I have an appointment with him."

She made a show of checking Krempka's online calendar. "Mr. . . . . Pree-us?"

"Preuss," he said. "Rhymes with juice."

After he left Gloria's farm, Preuss had called Krempka's office at the Woodbrooke Academy and made an appointment to see him at 4:30. He must have made the appointment with another secretary.

"Okay," the young woman said, "so, he got a last-minute call to go into a meeting with the headmistress?"

"Did he say when he'll be free?"

She shook her head and gave an apologetic shrug.

"Mind if I wait?"

She held out a hand to him, inviting him to sit in the small sofa in her waiting area.

While waiting, he called Rhonda. All was quiet at the office, she said. He checked his emails and his texts, and found a text from Grace Poole that had come in while he was at the Zimmer farm.

Hey. How's your day going?

He decided to wait to respond.

At five minutes to five, the secretary began to pack up for the day. She turned her workstation off and unlocked the bottom drawer of her desk to get her purse.

"Quitting time," she told Preuss. "Are you going to stay?"

"If that's all right with you."

"Oh, it's fine. If you decide you don't want to wait any more, could you just close the door when you leave? It'll lock automatically."

"Will do."

"Thanks. Bye-ee!"

And she was gone.

At a quarter to six, Preuss heard shoefalls coming down the hall. Ken Krempka turned into his office suite and stopped cold.

He mimed being surprised at seeing Preuss there. "You!"

"I made an appointment with your secretary for 4:30."

He gave an exaggerated grimace. "Sorry. When the head gal wants to see you . . ." He let the sentence trail off with a shrug. When you're as important as I am, his tone and gesture said, you're in constant demand from the best people.

"Still have time to see me?" Preuss asked.

"Sure. Come in."

Krempka unlocked his office door and went inside. He threw a folder on top of the other folders on the mess on his desk and sat in one of the visitor's chairs. He held a hand out to Preuss to sit in the other one. This time Preuss had to move the papers on his chair himself. He put them on the ground, careful to maintain the disorder.

Krempka sat back in his chair. He mopped his sweating brow and crossed his hands together behind his head. "So what's up?"

"The last time we spoke," Preuss said, "you told me you didn't know of anybody who had a grudge against your stepfather, except yourself. Tell me more about that."

"It was my failed attempt at a joke."

"But say more about the grudge, would you?"

Krempka lifted the side of his mouth in what could have been a smile but looked more like a sneer.

"I don't know who your client is," he said, "but you must be billing them by the minute."

Preuss ignored the comment (another failed joke) and waited.

Krempka sighed. He wiped his face. "Okay," he said. "Fine."

He got up and went around the other side of his desk. He opened a drawer and withdrew an eight-by-ten photo in a silver metal frame. He handed it across to Preuss.

It was a color photo of two tow-headed, tanned boys, one taller and older than the other. They were squinting into the camera.

Behind them stood a woman with a hand on each boy's head. In the background was an expanse of water and, on the side, a dock where boats were moored.

"Your family?" Preuss asked.

Krempka nodded. "The woman is my mother. Dorothy. I'm on the left."

"Larry's the kid on the right?"

"Yeah. It's from 1983. I was three. He was sixteen. Daddy Charlie is behind the camera. His happy little family," Krempka said, his voice sharp-edged with resentment.

"Larry is Charlie's biological son," he continued. "I'm the bastard stepson from a previous relationship my mother had before they met."

Preuss examined the boys' expressions. Larry had a slight smile as he squinted into the sun, but Krempka's expression was a sneer, angry and unpleasant. Frown lines in his forehead weren't from the sun, but from what he had been forced to endure through his role in the family.

"And where's your sister?" Preuss asked.

"My sister? Well, you have been busy. I guess you really are a detective."

Krempka took the photo back and returned it to the bottom drawer. He sat in his chair behind his desk and kicked the drawer shut with his foot.

"I didn't see her in that happy little group," Preuss said.

"Congratulations," Krempka said. "You've discovered our family's dirty little secret. My cousin is my sister. Nice work, Mr. Gittes."

Preuss let the allusion to *Chinatown* pass.

"She never lived with us," Krempka said. "She had her reasons."

"I just came from her farm," Preuss said. "She told me all about those reasons."

"People are what they are," Krempka said.

"She told me you share her views of Jews and blacks."

He waited for Krempka to respond.

Instead of denying it, Krempka said, "How is that relevant?"

"Did you ever hear of the American Identity Brigade?"

"Never."

"When was the last time you saw your sister?"

"Years. I can't even remember."

Preuss watched for a tell that Krempka was lying. Krempka returned his gaze evenly.

"Not much of a family man?" Preuss asked.

"You might say that."

Krempka wiped his brow. Was that his tell? Did the lies ooze out of him like sweat?

"I'm sure you've heard people talk about what a wonderful man my stepfather was," Krempka said.

"Something like that."

"He was. To my stepbrother."

"But not to you?"

"Old story, right? The 'real' son is the fair-haired boy, and the stepson is the ne'er-do-well? Us in a nutshell. To the rest of the world, my stepfather was a great guy. Wonderful professor. Kind, patient, loving, even. He wasn't any of that to me. My sister tell you we lived in a commune?"

Preuss nodded.

"My biological father—Gloria's and mine—deserted us after Gloria came along. The other men in the commune had no interest in being a surrogate father . . . they were too stoned most of the time to even notice us. But I needed help. I was always a troubled kid. I had trouble in school, trouble with the law . . . Nothing big, you know. Minor-league stuff. I broke into cars, but I never stole them. Your basic JD wannabe."

Krempka paused to see what effect his monologue was having on Preuss. Which made Preuss wonder if this were all for show. If any of it were true.

"But Charlie never had anything for me," Krempka continued. "No time, no patience, no sympathy . . . nothing. Whatever he had, he gave to Larry, when he came along. *Heaped* on Larry. His *real* son."

Listening, Preuss thought back to his own father, an unavailable alcoholic, and the mess of his own family with his ne'er-do-well brother whose drug problems sucked out of the family whatever oxygen was left after the toll of his father's alcoholism. Krempka's experience was the flip side of Preuss's, whose troubled brother got all the attention, leaving Preuss to gasp for air. A fish flopping on the dock, suffocating.

Of course, this was Krempka's version, Preuss understood. Who knew where the truth lay?

"I got out of the house as soon as I could," Krempka said. "I even changed my name back to my mother's maiden name because I didn't want to be associated with him."

Krempka sat back in his chair, with his arms raised and crossed over his head again.

"Enough of a grudge for you?" he asked.

"If your family was so unhappy, why save the photo?"

"So I can remember it," Krempka said, "if I ever start to forget."

"Where were you when your stepfather was killed?"

For a moment, Krempka gaped at Preuss.

Then he threw his head back and laughed.

"You're kidding, right?" he asked.

"Did the police check your alibi?"

"I have no idea."

"So where were you when he was killed?"

"Remind me again when it was?"

"Tuesday, January 8th."

With merriment in his eyes, Krempka said, "I was at an event here, at school. It was a luncheon for alums and guests. We spent three months planning it. We're starting a project to upgrade the gymnasium, and we gave a presentation on the athletic program. About a hundred and fifty people saw me. The program started at eleven and lasted till three. I was here from seven in the morning through six at night."

He searched through a pile on his desk and pulled out a brochure.

"See? I not only organized it, I was the emcee."

The brochure was a program for the luncheon. Prominently featured in the schedule was Krempka's name as emcee, introducing the event and each of the speakers.

"I can give you about a hundred photos proving it," Krempka said. "There's also a video of the whole thing."

He searched through the mess on his desk and pulled out a DVD in a jewel case. He handed it across to Preuss. "With my compliments," Krempka said. "In case you have any spare cash lying around you'd like to donate to a good cause."

Preuss didn't say anything and Krempka said, "Did I hate Charlie enough to kill him? Yeah. Did I kill him?"

He shook his big head.

"No way. Afraid you'll have to keep looking for somebody to pin this on."

"When was the last time you saw Larry?" Preuss asked.

Krempka held his hands up in a *Hey, don't ask me* gesture. "Don't know. Don't care."

43

Before he left Woodbrooke Academy, he texted Grace Poole: *Hey. Got time to meet for coffee?*

She texted back: *Now? Sure.*

She lived in Hamtramck, so she suggested they meet at Suzy's Bar. It was a tiny place on Evaline. The wall behind the bar was cluttered with bottles and memorabilia—greeting cards going back years, photos of the pope and local nuns, snaps of customers old and new.

It wasn't crowded on this Wednesday night but it was loud, the handful of regulars shouting booze-fueled mock insults at each other.

Grace was already there when Preuss arrived, and she was obviously part of the usual crowd. She was giving as good as she got.

She was seated on a stool on the wall opposite the bar, near the entrance. When she saw him she stood and hugged him.

"Hi," she said.

"How are you?"

"Better now."

He sat on a stool beside her and shrugged off his jacket. He folded it up and laid it on the shelf beside him.

An older man with thinning hair came over and set a tall glass of dark beer on the counter where they were sitting. "Hey Joe," she said, "this is my friend, Martin."

"Hiya, Martin," Joe said. He and Preuss shook hands and Joe said, "What can I get you?"

"Just coffee, thanks."

"Cream and sugar?"

"Black."

"You got it."

"Wait," Grace said, "you don't drink." It was a statement of insight more than a question.

"No. Seven years sober."

"That's why you said meet for coffee and not for a drink. And I brought you to a bar. I'm so sorry. Look, let's go someplace else."

"No worries," he said. "I'm good."

"You're sure?"

He assured her he was and Joe brought his coffee.

"Are you in AA?" she asked.

"I tried when I first stopped. Wasn't for me. Giving it up was easier on my own."

"One of my ex-husbands was in AA. Did him a world of good."

"If it works, it's great. If it doesn't . . ." He shrugged.

"Yeah."

"Biggest obstacle for me was the whole higher power concept," he said. "They say you can understand it in any way that works for you. My problem was there wasn't any way to interpret it that made sense."

"Not religious?"

"No. You?"

"I was brought up Catholic. I don't believe in God anymore, after what I've seen. And I sure don't have much use for the church."

"How many ex-husbands do you have?"

She laughed. He remembered she had a good laugh.

"Two," she said. "I divorced the first one. Second one died."

"The lawyer in Buffalo."

"Yeah. I told you about it. Leukemia. Horrible death."

She shook her head at the memory and took a sip of her beer.

"How's your son?" she asked.

"Yeah, good, thanks. As medical emergencies go, this wasn't bad. He went to his school program today, and I'll see him later on."

He pulled out his phone and showed her Toby's photo on his wallpaper. It was one of Toby's school photos. He was wearing his red Halloween tee shirt with bats on it and he was looking off to the side with his gorgeous brown eyes. His mouth hung slightly open in a crooked little smile. His arms were folded in front of him on the tray of his wheelchair, and his wrists were bent from contractures from the cerebral palsy.

"Photo's a couple years old," he said, "but it's one of my favorites of him.

"He's adorable," she said. "I love the way you look at him."

"He's my best friend."

"I can tell."

She raised her beer glass. "To Toby and a chaotic, Godless universe," she said, "full of sound and fury."

"Signifying nothing," he added, and clinked his coffee cup against her glass.

"My goodness," she said, "Shakespeare."

"Told you, English minor. Speaking of which," he said. "Grace Poole. That's a very literary name. What do you hear from crazy Mrs. Rochester?"

"Oh, the poor dear died in a fire, haven't you heard? Tragic."

She grinned. She had a good smile. Genuine. Wide. Toothy. Not at all wry.

"Poole is my second husband's name. After he died, I decided to keep it. I couldn't deal with changing it. It would have been like losing him all over again."

"Got it."

"I'm originally a Murphy. From the old country," she said, in a reasonable approximation of a brogue.

"Aren't we all."

"Where are your people from?"

"Refugees from the Prussian Empire on the paternal side," he said. "On the maternal side, Scots by way of Canada."

"Of course," she said. "Preuss, derived from 'Pruzzen.' The people indigenous to the region."

"Are you making that up, like the titles of your articles?"

"Nope. I'm a bit of a polymath."

"Okay," he said. "Just for your information, I know exactly what that means."

"I'm sure you do."

They smiled at each other, and sipped their drinks.

"So I'm glad you texted," she said.

"Thanks. I am, too."

"You look like you've had a day."

"I've had a couple of days. I needed to speak with a normal person."

"So you called *me*?" She snorted.

"Leap of faith."

"Good luck with that."

"In the last twenty-four hours, I've been trailed by neo-Nazis, visited the Sacred Heart Seminary downtown, gone on a tour of

Oakland County homeless hangouts and shelters, interviewed a crazy homeless guy who spoke in garbled Bible verses, and had a conversation with a good, old-fashioned, Old World anti-Semite up near the thumb. Is this a great country, or what?"

"And you're still clean and sober? I salute you." She raised her glass and he clinked it again with his coffee cup.

"Usually I end the day with a visit to my son. Which I still will do. But I wanted to see you first."

"Oh," she said, "what a nice thing to say. And do."

"It's very unlike me," he said. "If you knew me, you'd be even more impressed."

"Do you let many people get to know you?"

"A few."

"Are you seeing anyone now?"

He shook his head. "You?"

She paused before answering.

"Depends on what the definition of 'seeing' is. There's this guy in my department. We've been out a few times. Nothing serious. He reminds me too much of my first husband."

"Bad thing?"

"Very. We got married when we were both twenty-one. Too young. Didn't last long. He was a serious graduate student. He was looking for his manic pixie dream girl and he mistook me for one of those."

"What's a manic pixie dream girl?"

"Oh, she's like a stock character in the movies. I'm sure you've seen a hundred versions. You know, a quirky, vivacious fantasy girl. The kind whose life's mission is teaching a dour, serious young man how to enjoy life."

"Like Jeanne Moreau in *Jules et Jim*."

"*Jules et Jim*? In French, yet? *Est-ce que tu parle français?*"

"*Un petit peu.*"

"*Merveilleux.*"

"I'm not just a dumb flatfoot."

"I can see that."

They regarded each other in companionable silence.

"Well," she said at last, "judging by your day, you win today's misery sweepstakes. Your day has mine beat. All I did was teach a course on research methods in education, attend a faculty meeting, go to a dissertation defense on the history of writing instruction in Canada, and teach a class on how to use computers in teaching writing. Tonight I have miles of essays to grade before I sleep."

"Sounds very academic."

"I am the very model of a modern academical."

"And very well acquainted, too, with matters mathematical?"

"Wait, Gilbert and Sullivan, too?"

"Music is my life."

"I have a feeling you're going to be a constant surprise, Detective Preuss."

They talked for another hour, enough for one more beer for her and another coffee for him. Outside Suzy's he said, "Where are you parked?"

"I walked. I live around the corner."

"Want a ride? I'm in the lot over here."

"I wouldn't turn it down."

She told him to turn left out of the parking lot, and take a quick right. Three houses down she said, "There's me, on the left."

"You weren't kidding you're close."

"Nope."

He pulled over in front of a wooden three-decker. "I'm in the upper flat," she said. "I'd invite you up, but I really do have to grade papers tonight."

"Another time."

"For sure."

Before getting out, she leaned over and gave him a quick kiss on his cheek. She ended it with a warm palm on the side of his face, as though sealing in the kiss.

"Bye," she said, and flashed her smile. She hopped out of the car. He watched her go up the front steps and unlock the downstairs door. Before going inside, she turned and gave him a wave.

He waved back and when the door closed he drove on down the street.

Wait'll Toby hears about this, he thought.

Toby was in bed with the light out by the time Preuss got to the group home. Judy Collins was singing "Sisters of Mercy" on the CD player.

Preuss leaned over the bed. Toby was lying on his sleep side and resting with his eyes open. "Hey," Preuss said.

Toby said, "Hmm," and gave his father a sweet smile but he didn't raise his head. He was tired.

"Glad I caught you before you fell asleep. Were you waiting for me?"

"Mmm."

Preuss bent down to kiss Toby on the side of his face, on the same spot where Grace Poole had kissed him.

"This was a busy day," Preuss said. "And you know what else? I had a date tonight."

"Mmm."

"I know. First one your old man's been on since Mom."

It was hard to tell what Toby was thinking because he was nonverbal, but Preuss was a connoisseur of the boy's body language. At the mention of his mother, Toby grew focused and knit his brows.

Preuss knew Toby missed her terribly even though he couldn't put it into words.

"We'll see what happens, Toby," Preuss said. "Nobody will ever replace your mother."

Toby gave a small grunt, not a hum but a little sound of agreement.

"Not anything I was expecting," Preuss said. "I guess you never do, right?

Then he summarized his busy day for his son. Toby attended closely.

When he finished, Preuss sat for a while longer until Toby closed his eyes and was out for the night. Preuss gave him a gentle kiss on the forehead and tiptoed out of the room.

He was calm and at peace as he drove home to Ferndale, his thoughts split between his son, his case, and Grace Poole.

The white nationalists caught up with him a few blocks from home.

44

Turning off Woodward down the street to his house, he saw the lights from a car following him. Alarm bells went off in his head when the pickup roared past him and cut him off.

He jammed on the brakes.

Before he could throw it into reverse, they burst out of the truck. Three of them, straight from Central Casting—shaved heads, shaggy beards, camo hoodies. Two went right for Preuss, pulling open the driver's side door and yanking him out. The third man leapt atop the Explorer's hood and smashed the front windshield with a baseball bat.

The two who pulled Preuss out of the car threw him to the pavement. One aimed a kick at his head but Preuss rolled away from it. The second man in a camo cap pounced on him and lifted him up for the first one—a big, furious, Grizzly Adams-type—to punch him in the stomach hard enough with a ham-sized fist to double Preuss over.

He couldn't catch his breath. He felt like he was going to suffocate right then and there.

The man behind him straightened him for another blow.

Before Grizzly could take a swing, Preuss—still breathless—leaned against the man behind him and kicked up into Grizzly's chin with the toe of his running shoe. It snapped Grizzly's head back and rocked him for few moments.

Enough time for Preuss to stomp down hard on Camo Cap's instep. It loosened the grip that held him and Preuss pivoted with an elbow into Camo Cap's nose. Blood burst over his face.

Preuss followed with a side kick to the man's groin and he went down.

Grizzly came at him and Preuss swept the big man's feet out from under him. Grizzly went down hard but scrambled right to his feet.

Before he could come at Preuss again, a second car screeched to a stop behind the Explorer and Franklin McShane was out the door before the car settled into park. He came out with his own baseball bat and broke it over Grizzly's head before the big man could react.

The guy on top of the Explorer jumped onto Preuss but Preuss caught him and threw him over and into the street. The baseball bat he was using on the Explorer clattered away.

He jumped up and came at Preuss with a growl. Preuss picked up the bat the guy had dropped and took a mighty swing that caught the guy flush on the forearm that he threw up to defend himself.

The arm broke with a sharp "crack" and he cried out in pain.

Preuss swung for the fences again and broke the guy's collarbone.

He yelped, backpedaled fast, and ran to the pickup truck and clambered behind the wheel. Still clutching his groin, Camo Cap got to his feet and hobbled toward the pickup, too. He threw himself into the front seat.

They had left the motor running so the driver wrestled it into gear with his left hand and went forward over somebody's lawn and burned rubber down the street.

With the passenger door swinging open and Camo Cap hanging on for dear life.

Preuss turned to where McShane was standing, watching him.

"Nice moves," McShane said. "You didn't even need me."

Preuss grabbed up the other half of the broken bat and held it out.

"Get out of here," he said. "Now."

Without a word, McShane grabbed the broken piece of his bat and dove into his car and made a fast U-turn and headed back toward Woodward. He pulled out into traffic and disappeared.

Preuss stood over Grizzly, motionless on the pavement. The big man was still breathing. That cut down on some of the complications, at least.

He called 911.

And thought: I'm going to have some 'splaining to do.

The responding officer, a woman new to the force whom Preuss didn't know—her name badge said Lewis—told him her shift commander gave her orders to bring him in.

"What am I being charged with?" he asked. "I was the one who was attacked."

"They'll explain when we get to the station, sir."

"Am I under arrest?"

"No, sir. My orders are to bring you in."

"For what reason?"

She didn't reply.

They stood by her squad car while the ambulance crew loaded up Grizzly Adams. The responding EMTs did a double take when they saw Preuss standing there, and when they got their patient loaded into the bus they came over to say hello to him.

Which was not lost on Patrol Officer Lewis.

"I used to be in the Detective Bureau," Preuss explained.

"I know," she said. "I've heard of you."

"As a bad example, I'm guessing."

"No sir. People say you were one of the best."

"You must not have heard what some of the other people have to say. They're why you're bringing me in."

"Following the shift commander's orders, Mr. Preuss."

Preuss nodded. As handed down from Chief Nick Russo through Chief of Detectives Stanley Chrysler, no doubt.

Still, he wasn't about to give her a hard time. She was doing her job, as he had done time and again over the years. Until he couldn't bring himself to do it anymore.

She brought him in through the sally port behind the Eugene Shanahan Law Enforcement Complex on Nine Mile in Ferndale.

"You again," said the intake officer, whose name was Keegan. "What you do this time, Preuss?"

"You tell me," Preuss said. "I was attacked and now I'm the one being detained."

"Life being inherently unfair," Keegan said.

"Sarge said don't process him," Officer Lewis put in. "Sit him in Interrogation 1."

"Follow me, then," Keegan said. "Your accommodations are ready."

Preuss nodded at Lewis, who again said, "Sorry," with a shrug before she went off to write up her report.

Keegan didn't put him in a holding cell, as they did the last time Preuss was brought to the station. Instead, Keegan opened the smaller of the two interview rooms, a six-by six cement block box with a table in the middle.

It was cold in the room, so Preuss kept his jacket on. He knew they were just giving him a hard time—he had given Officer Lewis all the information about what happened, so there was no need to bring him here. He tried to make himself comfortable in the plastic molded chair and waited.

And waited.

Rather than allow himself to get annoyed, he let his head fall forward and tried to sleep. It wasn't easy. The little room was filled with echoes of his interviews here with victims and perpetrators of crime in his twenty-year tenure with the Ferndale Police, first as a patrol officer and then as a member of the Detective Bureau. He was glad to get away when he retired, but the circumstances of his retirement left him bitter for almost the entire first year.

Like everyone else in the entire department, Russo had known Preuss was his best detective. But Russo was the father of Preuss's late wife Jeanette, and blamed Preuss for her death. Once he became chief of police, nothing would have prevented him from bringing Preuss up on more trumped-up charges and forcing Preuss to resign in exchange for dropping the charges.

Preuss knew what was coming, so he acted first and put in his papers.

Now they're still playing games, he thought as he watched the minutes tick off on the clock on the wall.

Finally—two-and-a-half-hours after Officer Lewis brought him in—the door to the interrogation room opened and Reg Trombley walked in.

Looking very unhappy.

Trombley sat across the table from him. They didn't shake hands.

"Martin," Trombley said.

"Reg."

Preuss could tell Trombley knew they were going through the motions, so he played along.

Trombley opened a file on the table and made a show of reading the report Officer Lewis had filed.

"They got you out of bed for this?" Preuss asked.

Trombley ignored the question.

"Want to walk me through what happened?" he said.

Preuss took him through the attack, leaving out Franklin McShane's role.

"Did you know these men?"

"Never saw them before," Preuss said. It was the truth.

"Why do you suppose they did this?"

Preuss considered playing dumb, and would have if anybody other than Trombley were sitting across from him. That's why they brought Trombley in for this, he thought . . . Preuss could finagle any of the other detectives, but he wouldn't do it with Trombley. Under ordinary circumstances, they would be right; Preuss would be straight with his friend.

But they were holding him to give him a hard time, and Trombley acted like they weren't close friends. Preuss could playact, too.

"You'd have to ask them," he said.

"We will," Trombley said, and wrote something on the legal pad in the file in front of him. "If the gorilla you brained ever wakes up. Which for your sake, I hope he does. Otherwise you're really in the shit."

Preuss was silent.

"So there were three of them, correct?" Trombley asked.

"Yes."

"And two got away."

"Yes. I gave you a description of their truck."

Trombley made another show of looking through the initial police report from Officer Lewis.

"They did a job on your Explorer," he said.

Preuss didn't think this warranted a response. Now we're just killing time, he thought.

"You took on three guys by yourself?" Trombley asked.

Challenging me to tell the truth, Preuss thought. Or lie.

He had thought about this during the time they kept him cooling his heels. He had decided to tell as much of the truth as he could, while still keeping McShane's name out of it.

"Pretty much," Preuss said. "Except a passing motorist saw what was happening and stopped to help."

"A passing motorist."

"Uh-huh."

"Lucky you."

"I already had the situation in hand."

"What happened to him?" Trombley asked. "The 'passing motorist'?"

"He left before the police showed up."

"Also lucky, Martin, because a witness who lives on the street said you weren't alone out there fighting these guys."

"I wasn't."

If Trombley wanted to challenge him, he'd tell him the truth, but not here. Not in the station.

But Trombley must have known this because he didn't push it.

"Okay," Trombley said instead, "Martin, I have to ask you this. Does this altercation have to do with the Bright case?"

The $64 question, Preuss thought.

"Why would it have to do with the Bright case?" he asked.

"Please answer the question."

"If I don't know who they were, or why they did this, how can I know the answer?"

"Is that your way of telling me you're still on the case?" Trombley asked.

Trombley stared at Preuss. And waited.

When Preuss didn't respond, Trombley said, "Think about your answer, Martin. You were warned off this investigation."

"Is this why you're keeping me here? And why they brought you in? So you could ask me that?"

Trombley said nothing.

Preuss leaned forward. "And also to push me around a little bit, too, I think, right?"

"We want to make sure you're staying away from the Bright investigation. As you were asked to."

Preuss caught the use of the plural and the passive. Trombley's way of letting him know this wasn't his idea.

Still, it was late, Preuss was tired, he was sore, his body where Grizzly clobbered him throbbed, and he was annoyed. He couldn't stop himself from saying something he knew would irritate his friend and whoever else might be listening in.

"*Is* there still a Bright investigation?" Preuss asked.

"What do you mean by that?"

"It doesn't seem like it's going anywhere."

"Like you would know," Trombley snapped.

Preuss saw he got up Trombley's sleeve. Maybe even nudged him a bit too far.

"What, Martin," Trombley said, "you think you're the only one knows how to investigate a crime?"

"Certainly not."

"Then don't talk shit about it, all right?"

Preuss raised his hands in surrender. "Sorry I said anything."

"You better be." Trombley slammed the file shut and stood. "You can be a phenomenal pain in the ass, you know that?"

"So I've been told. Reg, am I under arrest?"

"No."

"Then I'm leaving."

"Good. I expect you remember how to find your way out?"

Trombley left the room in a huff.

Preuss sat, regretting having pushed his friend's buttons. But it accomplished the purpose of ending this sham.

Then he stood and he, too, left the small concrete room.

I'm guessing I'm not going to get a ride back to my car, he thought.

The shift commander stood in the doorway to his office and watched Preuss pass. Preuss raised his chin at him, who turned away without an acknowledgement.

Preuss continued through the station and walked out the front. He nodded to the information officer in the window in the outer lobby, and continued out the door.

He would walk home. Ferndale wasn't that big a city; it would take him just a few minutes. He'd get his car in a few hours, after the sun came up.

He started walking down Nine Mile, deserted at this hour, when a Taurus stopped short next to him.

The passenger window came down.

"Get in."

45

Preuss got in and Trombley peeled off down Nine Mile.

"What the hell was that all about?!" Trombley demanded.

"What was what all about?"

"'A passing motorist'? Seriously? I look like a gaping asshole to you?"

"It's the truth."

"I'm already gonna be in the shit because we were supposed to hold you till the morning. I'm trying to get you out and you're giving me bullshit? What am I supposed to tell Chrysler when he sees I let you go and reads my report and thinks you took me for a fool?"

"I'll tell you who it was," Preuss said, "but you have to keep his name out of the report."

They crossed Woodward and Trombley veered into a parking space at the side of Nine Mile.

"Now you're telling me what I can put in my report?" Trombley demanded.

"I'm saying, after that little intimidation charade in there, I'll decide what you should know."

"I should bring you back in for obstructing justice."

"Knock yourself out," Preuss said.

They glared at each other, then both men backed off before this got too far out of hand.

"I was trying to get you out of there before Chrysler came in," Trombley said, calmer now. "He gave the command to hold you till he got there."

"Won't you get in trouble?"

"We didn't have any reason to keep you. He was just going to be an asshole about it."

They sat in silence for another half-minute, then Preuss said, "It was McShane," hoping to lower the volume.

"That crazy-ass ex-FBI agent?"

"Yeah."

"Since when is he your fairy godfather?"

"He's been keeping an eye on me since a group of neo-Nazis started following me."

"Wait, are you telling me you *do* know who these guys are?"

"Not by name."

"What are you doing mixed up with neo-Nazis?"

Preuss considered how to answer. He opted to be honest with Trombley.

"That's where the Bright case is pointing," he said.

"The Bright case. Even though I asked you to keep your nose out of the Bright case?"

"You asked me to stay out of the way," Preuss corrected him. "You asked me not to cross your path. And I've stayed as far out of the way as I could. I never asked you about the case, I never called you for information after you told me the first time you wouldn't give it to me . . . I've done what you asked me to do. So don't pull your aggrieved betrayed friend act on me, okay?"

Trombley thought about that. "Fair enough," he admitted. "So this wasn't planned?"

"What wasn't planned?"

"You didn't draw these guys into a fight?"

"Why would I do that?"

"So you could put one of them in the hospital? Send a message to the rest of them?"

"Reg, I didn't even know these guys. You think I roam the streets at night trying to bait white nationalists into a three-on-one fight?"

"Then what's the connection between these guys and Charles Bright?"

"I'm supposed to tell you everything and you won't tell me anything?"

"Yeah," Trombley said, "that's how this works. Or did you forget already? Besides, I don't know where this stands now. Emma Blalock has the case. She's shutting us out completely."

"I heard she was part of the investigation."

"Yeah, well, now she's running the show."

"What happened?"

"Chrysler pulled it. Asked Emma to run it."

"Why?"

"He's on a new kick. Decided he doesn't want us to pursue cases we can't close in seven days. If we can't close them within that time, he foists them off on the Oakland County Sheriff or the State Police. He says they both have more resources so they're better suited for the complicated cases."

"So instead of fighting for more resources, he's cutting back the Bureau's remit."

"Welcome to my world."

Both men were silent.

"Anyway," Preuss said, "I'm not sure what the connection is between Charles Bright and the American Identity Brigade."

"That's their name?"

"Yeah. But the case is trending in that direction. You never had an inkling of it?"

Trombley shook his head.

"You do know that Charles Bright was a peace activist?" Preuss asked.

"Of course."

"Last November, Charles Bright was in a Women in Black demo in Flint. A group of white nationalists tried to break it up. Bright got into it with one of them and laid the guy out."

"Nothing says peace activist like a good old-fashioned punch in the mouth," Trombley said.

"The rest of them jumped him and beat the crap out of him."

"So why would they come back and kill him?"

"I'm still working on it."

"We never got that far," Trombley admitted.

He threw the car into gear and drove on in angry silence. Though this time the anger didn't seem to be directed at Preuss sitting next to him, but rather at the situation he was caught in.

In a few minutes, Trombley pulled over in front of Preuss's car on the street where the fight took place.

"I don't suppose you want to come back for a coffee," Preuss said.

"I don't. I want to go home to my wife in my own bed and get some sleep in what's left of this night."

Preuss eased himself out of the car. He was starting to stiffen up from being thrown around. His stomach was killing him where Grizzly Adams hit him.

He paused before closing the door. "Reg. I didn't want to argue with you. I know you're under pressure. I hope I didn't make it worse."

Trombley sighed. "Don't worry about it. Sorry I went off on you."

"No worries."

"Take care of yourself, okay?"

Preuss nodded and closed the car door. Trombley and Preuss both looked around, and when they didn't see anyone lurking in the deserted street they nodded at each other and Trombley drove off.

The car was littered with pebbles of safety glass from his smashed windshield. He brushed them off the front seat as well as he could and navigated home with cold air blasting him in the face. It helped keep him awake.

When he got back to his house, he called Nancy Fields at Toby's. She was working the overnight shift.

All was quiet.

He took a shower and tended to his scrapes from the fight. A purplish bruise like a dark storm cloud was forming in the center of his stomach.

He laid his aching body on his bed. His cell phone rang as soon as his head hit the pillow.

Franklin McShane.

"Can't leave you alone for a minute," McShane said before Preuss could say hello. "What happened when the cops showed up?"

"They took me in for questioning. And intimidation."

"What did you tell them?"

"I didn't mention you by name. I said a good Samaritan saw what was happening and stopped to help."

"Why'd you even say that much?"

"There were witnesses. They already knew someone stopped to help me. I couldn't deny it."

"They bought that lame-ass story?"

"McShane, I'm tired. What do you want?"

"I got something to do later on today besides babysit you. Can you keep out of trouble for a couple hours?"

"I'll try my best."

"Yeah," McShane said, "good luck with that. How's it working out for you so far?"

Without saying goodbye, he disconnected.

Preuss set his cell phone beside him on the bed and closed his eyes. He wanted only to put this day behind him.

Wednesday, March 6, 2013

46

He stopped at Toby's to say good morning and check in with Carlos Guevara, who was starting the day shift. All was well, Carlos assured him.

Then he took the Explorer to an auto glass shop on Woodward to get his windshield repaired. Baseball Bat Guy had also smashed in his headlights, he had discovered on the way home the night before, so he got those repaired, too. The dents on the hood would have to wait.

When he got to the office, he found a visitor.

Poised on the edge of the sofa in Rhonda's outer area was Angie Sturmer.

With a newspaper in her hand.

Again.

Exactly who I don't want to see, Preuss thought.

Déjà vu all over again.

"Mr. Preuss!" she said. She jumped up when he walked through the door.

Rhonda was behind her desk, swiveling back and forth in her chair, ready to dig on the show.

"Angie," Preuss said. "This is a surprise."

"Did you see the paper this morning?"

"Not yet."

"Well, I brought you a copy. You better take a look at this."

"I don't have time right now. Why don't you make an appointment and we'll talk another time?"

"But you really need to see this."

"I really don't. I'm jammed this morning. Leave it with Rhonda and I'll look at it when I can, okay?"

It came out sharper than he meant it to.

Rhonda said, "Martin, maybe you should take a look."

"What's so urgent?"

"They found a body right where Angie said it would be. In the Clinton River."

"Are they thinking it's the same body you say you saw?" he asked Angie.

"Timing looks right."

He went into his office and dropped into his chair. Angie followed and handed him the paper.

He scanned the article. Sure enough, another body of a woman was discovered in the Clinton River in Utica. In a black plastic bag.

"See?" Angie said.

"I see. Did you go to the Utica police?"

"No, sir. I didn't."

"Why not?"

"I didn't think they'd listen to me if I was by myself. I was hoping you'd come with me."

He kept his temper in check.

"Okay," he said, instead of exploding. "How about you do this. Go up to the Utica police station and ask for Detective Juhasz."

"But they told me not to come back."

"No, that was Sterling Heights. Go to Utica. Ask for Juhasz." He spelled it for her. "Tell him I sent you, and then tell him your story. I promise he'll listen."

"Okay," she said. He could hear the dejection in her voice. "Can I tell him I'm working for you?"

"You can tell him you're one of our associates."

That perked her up a bit. "Thank you," she said. "I'll go there now."

She paused at the door to his office. "Thank you, Mr. Preuss." And she was gone.

"Meanie," Rhonda called from the other room.

He picked up the newspaper article Angie had left and read it, carefully this time.

Angie might have stumbled onto the serial killer operating in Macomb County that the Sterling Heights detective had mentioned.

That would be droll, he thought . . . not that there was a serial killer in their midst, but that Angie Sturmer of all people might be the one who nailed him.

He set the paper aside and tried to clear his head. There was too much ping-ponging around in there at one time: Larry Bright, Charlie Bright, Angie, Grace, Toby, Jason, the American Identity Brigade . . .

He leaned forward with his elbows on his desk and laid his head in his hands. The world is too much with me, he thought. He read that line once in a poem in a college English class. He couldn't remember who wrote it, but it was certainly accurate.

He turned to his computer and began entering notes from yesterday. He hoped it would help him focus.

When he finished, he sat rereading what he entered until Rhonda appeared in his doorway.

"Wow," she said. "Testy today."

"I had a long night. Including an unexpected stay at the Ferndale police station."

"Again? Man, they have it in for you. What for this time?"

She sat in one of his visitor chairs.

"Some guys stopped me on my way home from Toby's. Tried to rough me up."

"Jesus, are you okay? I don't see any damage."

He touched his stomach where the big man had walloped him. "I'm mostly okay. Little sore. My car got the worst of it. Frank McShane was following me and helped me fight them off. The cops brought me to the station to give me a hard time about the Bright case. They got Reg Trombley out of bed to talk to me."

"Poor Reg."

"He wasn't happy with me about it, either. He wanted to know if I'm still on the Bright case."

"And you said?"

"I told him the truth."

He covered a yawn with the back of his hand. "Sorry."

"Whyn't you take the morning off?"

"Too much to do."

"At least have some coffee. I'll bring you some."

She fetched a cup of her everyday coffee. It was nice and hot, but he'd been drinking so much coffee in the last few days it lay sour and grainy on his stomach.

He finished rereading what he had entered into the Bright case file, then went back to the material Sylvia Bloom had given him.

There was a connection here he was missing.

He turned past the photographs of the leaders of the American Identity Brigade to the membership list.

Another page in the file contained a list of white nationalist websites. He opened a few and surfed through them.

They ranged from pseudo-intellectualized rationales for refusing immigrants, to holocaust denials, to virulently anti-Semitic pornography showing Jewish caricatures raping Aryan girls, to insane conspiracy theories that Jews were shape-shifting reptiles, to appeals to historical anti-Semitism ("All Intelligent People in History Have Hated Jews," one headline read)—to calls for the extermination of Jews, blacks, and all brown people, en masse and individually, with instructions for volunteering for the effort and step-by-step lessons in how to appropriate their properties after their owners were dead.

As disgusting and hate-filled as these sites were, he kept going. He searched for photos of the three men who attacked him last night, looking for names—but also to delve deeper into the pathology of these groups.

He never found the three from last night. They were most likely low-level thugs. But he did find several sites managed by Ruth Anne Krider's brother, Warren Cattrell. He searched through the index of one site, *VolksGuard*, where he discovered an article titled, "Finishing the Job the Fuhrer Started." It was about exterminating the Jewish population of America. Preuss remembered Gloria Krempka using the exact phrase. Not unusual, since it was a familiar trope among anti-Semites.

But what drew Preuss's attention were several paragraphs:

The Führer proved mass extermination could solve the Jewish problem. Until a state-sanctioned program of compulsory extermination allows Amerika to return to its white Christian roots, I propose formation of groups of American Identity Warriors *whose function is undertaking guerrilla operations against enemies whose racial, ethnic, religious, and sexual orientation differences put them in conflict with the White Christian values that founded this nation.*

Operations will include individual assassinations of high-value targets. These may be either one-man operations or small cadres of soldiers undertaking dramatic, terror-inducing acts targeting those members of the lower races: Jews, blacks, Catholics, and homosexuals.

As a further act of patriotic warfare, whenever possible responsibility for these acts of heroism should not be claimed by the heroic American Identity Warriors themselves, but should point to unwitting members of the sub-races.

To inflict the maximum amount of indignity on victims, and as a warning to others, the targets' bodies should be bludgeoned once, symbolizing the might of united White People, and stabbed exactly fourteen times, once for each one of the sacred Fourteen Words. Thus showing how little these abominations before God matter to the glorious white Christian nation that is even now coming into being.

The author of the piece was listed as "Hans Goring," which the article noted was "a *nom de guerre* for a Minister in the Christianity United Movement and a Citizen of the United White States of America."

Preuss reread the paragraph. It described the murder of Charles Bright, the Jewish professor found bludgeoned and stabbed fourteen times in his basement in Ferndale.

Preuss searched among the *VolksGuard* back issues and found several editorials written by "Hans Goring." All were fueled by the same degree of racial hatred.

He searched for articles that might have been written by Gloria Krempka in the *VolksGuard*, but found nothing.

He began searching through other white nationalist websites, and discovered some also featured articles by "Hans Goring," all with themes similar to his article in *VolksGuard*.

Preuss continued searching for Gloria Krempka, and discovered a few pieces with her byline. They all carried the standard tropes, themes, and names: railing against the Globalist-Soros-Rothschild-Israeli conspiracy to corrupt and control the American news media, calling out the Black Lives Matter movement for perpetuating hoaxes of blacks being killed by police at the same time as the articles used black deaths at the hands of police as proof of the inherent lawlessness of African Americans . . .

On another website, the *Aryan Heritage Alliance*, Preuss found a photo of Gloria Krempka standing next to Kevin Johnson, one of the leaders of the American Identity Brigade. They were among a group of others at an event the caption identified as the Aryan Heritage Alliance Annual Convention in Dallas in 2010.

The caption also identified one of the subjects standing beside Gloria as Hans Goring.

In the photo, Gloria Krempka was standing next to her brother, Ken Krempka.

Smiling, with their arms around each other.

There was no mistaking him. His height and his freakishly large head gave him away.

Ken Krempka was "Hans Goring"?

So the "lifestyle" that Krempka said his father didn't approve of wasn't his sexuality after all . . . it was his white supremacy.

The Dallas convention was three years ago. Ken Krempka had been in touch with his sister Gloria recently. Could Ken have killed his father? Not if his alibi held up and he was at the school event, as he claimed.

But if Ken was connected with the American Identity Brigade, he could have gotten someone else to do it.

Like any of the neo-Nazis in the organization.

Or someone like his half-brother Larry.

The gibberish Larry Bright muttered when Preuss tried to speak with him mirrored the language in the editorial about finishing the job Hitler started. Along with bits of the fourteen words that he remembered McShane telling him: "our people . . . our future . . . our children . . ."

Did these represent Larry's beliefs? Or was he voicing his half-brother?

If so, then, as his claim to not seeing his sister was a lie, Krempka's claim he hadn't seen his half-brother recently was also a lie.

Could Larry have killed his father? The Larry Bright whom Preuss talked to could not by himself have mustered the intention—or the ability—to inflict the kind of violence Charles suffered.

Unless he was put up to it by Ken Krempka. Was Krempka doing a dry run of his terror squads by manipulating his brother?

His Jewish mentally-ill half-brother, at that.

Preuss glanced at the time. Already after six. He had spent the entire afternoon looking through the venom spewed on these websites.

"Rhonda?" he called.

No, Rhonda was gone.

Now he remembered . . . she stuck her head in his office to let him know she was leaving. He had raised a hand, but realized now he hadn't listened to her. He was too immersed in the hate-filled websites he was investigating.

If Gloria Krempka and her brother Ken Krempka were in touch, then Preuss was certain she would have let him know about her conversation with Preuss.

From there, Ken Krempka would realize Preuss would work out the connection that also existed between himself and Larry Bright.

And maybe how Ken had manipulated his brother, and what he might have manipulated Larry into doing, with or without the aid of another neo-Nazi.

If Larry killed Charles Bright, Ken Krempka would not want Preuss to find him.

Which meant Preuss had to find him before Krempka did.

He locked up the office and ran out to the Explorer.

47

Traffic was heavy on 696 as he made his way into Ferndale. Things were moving, so it would still be faster than taking surface roads—but he was conscious of every minute ticking past.

He exited at Woodward and sped south toward Nine Mile. He took a right on one of the side streets and floored it till he got to Pinecrest. The Renaissance Vineyard Church was near Nine.

He roared into the parking lot.

And found the church locked up.

A sign on the back entrance read, "SOS Warming Shelter is now at the Good Shepherd Presbyterian Church, Lafayette Street in Royal Oak."

He rattled the door handle in frustration and ran back to the Explorer. The church was a few miles away, but this was rush hour and there was no way he could get to it quickly.

He sped up Pinecrest into Pleasant Ridge, then turned right on Oakdale, where there was a traffic light where he could make a Michigan left and continue north into Royal Oak. He got caught at the light and punched in the number for Franklin McShane.

Of course McShane didn't answer. McShane never answered. If he felt like calling back, he would. And if he didn't feel like it, he wouldn't.

"McShane," Preuss said into the phone, "I'm headed into Royal Oak, to the Good Shepherd Presbyterian Church on Lafayette. I'm trying to get to Larry Bright before his brother does. Get over here as fast as you can."

He disconnected and when traffic made the slow turn onto Woodward he cut around the dawdling cars onto the service drive.

There were fewer cars on Washington, so he took a side street to Lafayette and got to the church in another few minutes. He left the Explorer in the lot and rushed up to the front entrance.

An attendant was sitting at a desk by the inner door. Preuss showed his ID and said, "I'm a private investigator. I'm looking for someone I suspect might be spending the night here."

The young man rose behind his desk. He was a clone of the attendant at the Ferndale church . . . pudgy, bearded, a toque on his head, a tatty grey sweater with a collar keeping him warm but with plaid Bermuda shorts.

"Wait a second," he said.

"Sorry," Preuss said, "this is an emergency. I need to find Larry Bright. Is he here?"

The attendant checked on the attendance roster. "I don't see his name on the list. Does he have another name he might use?"

"If he does, I don't know what it is. How about a guy called Rabbit? Again, I don't know his real name."

The attendant checked. "No, sorry. Not here either."

"Can I take a walk through your warming center? I might be able to spot him."

The young man was suspicious of that idea.

"Look," Preuss said. "I don't have time to explain, okay? Larry might be in a lot of trouble if I don't find him."

"Okay then," the young man decided. "Down that corridor, in the activities room." He pointed around a corner from where they stood.

"Thanks."

Trotting down the hall, he could smell the activities room before he found the door—a heavy fug of body odors, old clothes, and despair.

It was still early enough for the lights to be on, and before the spaces were filled up with bedding. Preuss walked through the ragged rows of people spending the night. No Larry Bright.

And no Rabbit, either. More couples were here than he had seen at the Ferndale church, young, most down on their luck and in thrall to a drug habit that kept their lives from moving forward.

He asked a few people if they knew Larry Bright or Rabbit, but nobody was willing to talk to him.

Back out front, the young attendant was checking in another man for the night.

"Any luck?" he asked Preuss.

"No. Neither one of the guys I'm looking for was here."

"Sorry," the young guy said. "Hey Bill," he said to the older man who just entered and was now trudging down to the activities room, "you don't know—what was his name?"

"Larry Bright," Preuss said.

Bill stopped. He looked all around in awe as if God himself were talking to him.

The attendant repeated the question.

"Never heard of him," Bill said.

"How about a guy named Rabbit?"

Bill thought for a moment, as if he had to process the question from one language to another.

"Yeah," he said at last, "Rabbit I know."

"Yeah?" Preuss said. "Have you seen him tonight?"

"Sure. I just passed him. Outside Starbucks."

"On Main Street? Just now?"

"Yeah."

Preuss said, "Thanks," and trotted out the door and down the street towards Main. It was a few blocks away, and when he got to Starbucks, he saw Rabbit sitting on the curb out front with his belongings arrayed around him, hands wrapped around a steaming cardboard Starbucks cup.

"Rabbit," Preuss said.

"Hey, man."

"Have you seen Larry? I looked for him at the church just now, but he wasn't there."

"No," Rabbit said, "he wouldn't be."

"Why? Where is he?"

"He took off with somebody."

"When was this?"

"Little while ago. We both heading to the church for the night when a car pull up and somebody tell him to get in."

"Did you see the guy in the car?"

"Yeah, man. Larry, he didn't wanna get in, but the guy sort of forced him. Gimme a dub to look the other way, too. So I came here and bought me one of these." Rabbit held up the paper cup. "Better'n that shit they give out at the shelters."

"What did this guy look like?"

Rabbit thought for a few moments. "White guy," he said at last.

Preuss waited but nothing more came.

"Anything else you can tell me about him?" Preuss asked. "Distinguishing features?"

"Happened kind of fast. But yeah, he was, um, blond guy. Big head."

Ken Krempke.

"What kind of car?"

"Big."

"Big like luxury, or big like SUV?"

"Man, don't be asking me. I don't know nothing about cars. Ain't driven one in years, don't pay attention to them."

"You know an SUV when you see one, right?"

"Yeah."

"So was this an SUV?"

"Yeah. Mighta coulda been."

"But you're sure Larry didn't want to get in with him?"

"Well," Rabbit said, "he didn't scream or run away or nothing. He said no at first and started to get hinky about it. Then the guy got out and starting to pull him into the car, and Larry, he got pretty mellow right away. Got in, sweet as pie."

Rabbit thought some more, then said, "Oh wait. I remember. He did say something."

"The guy?"

"No, Larry. Called the guy by a name. Benny, maybe?"

"Not Kenny?"

"Yeah! That was it. Kenny. Was all I could make out, man."

"Okay," Preuss said. "That's helpful. Thanks, Rabbit."

"Fixin' to go over to the Warming Center, soon's I finish here. Should I hold a bed for him?"

"I'm thinking he's not going to need it tonight."

Ken Krempka's phone number was unlisted, but Preuss found his address through one of his enhanced search engines. Krempka had an address in Birmingham, off the downtown core.

Preuss shot up Woodward Avenue. He was there in fourteen minutes.

One minute for every one of the fourteen white power words.

Krempka's house was a tidy two-story Tudor in one of Birmingham's upscale neighborhoods. A neat, very upper-middle class setting.

Preuss trotted up the front steps between two artfully sculpted juniper bushes. He rang the doorbell and banged on the door, but there was no response.

He couldn't see into the garage because there was no window in the door, but he walked around to the back of the house. The place was closed up and he could see no one inside.

His phone rang.

McShane.

"Preuss, where the hell are you? You called me to come help you and you're not even here."

"I'm out in Birmingham."

Preuss could feel McShane's anger radiate all the way through the phone.

"*Birmingham?*" McShane barked. "You asked me to meet you in Royal Oak. I get here, you're gone."

"Somebody there saw Larry Bright get into a car with a guy who matches the description of his half-brother, Ken Krempka. My witness even said he called him Kenny. I thought Krempka would take him back to his house, which is where I am now. But neither one seems to be here. And he's not answering his cell."

"So he took him someplace else. Duh."

"Meet me at my house in Ferndale in fifteen minutes."

48

When Preuss arrived home, McShane was sitting at the dining room table, drinking a cup of coffee he made in Preuss's coffeemaker.

"Comfy?" Preuss asked.

McShane ignored the question and Preuss sat across the table from him.

"When we talked before, you told me you thought there was a UC in the American Identity Brigade," Preuss said.

"Yeah. All these groups are infiltrated."

"Is the UC still in place?"

"Pretty sure. These guys don't bail unless they're made."

"Can you find out who it is?"

"I could," McShane said. "But what will that tell us?"

"By itself, maybe nothing. But if we can get to whoever it is, we might be able to find out where Krempka took his brother."

"What makes you think Larry Bright isn't at the bottom of the Detroit River by now?"

"He could be. And if he's not now, there's a good chance he'll end up there. But he's been missing for less than an hour. Krempka isn't the kind of guy who dirties his own hands. I think he got Larry to kill their father, and because I'm getting close to him he's going to get somebody else to kill Larry. My money's on one of the Nazis."

"That'd be my bet, too."

"But until it happens, Larry Bright is going to be stashed someplace where nobody can find him."

"And you're hoping the UC can tell us where?"

McShane thought about it, said, "Let me make some calls."

He went out onto the back deck. Through the doorwall, Preuss saw him talking on his cell phone, cupping the bottom of the handset. McShane was wearing his Tiger ballcap and thin raincoat, not much use against the cold. But he didn't seem to mind.

He made several calls in quick succession, not staying on the phone more than five seconds for each one. At one point, he put the phone in his pocket and leaned against the deck railing. He hugged himself against the cold. Preuss expected him to come back inside, but McShane stayed out for another twenty minutes.

McShane's cell phone rang and he connected the call and listened for a few moments. Then he disconnected and came back inside where Preuss was waiting.

"Well?" Preuss said.

"We have to wait. It'll take a while for the word to get through, and then it'll take him a while to get back to us."

"We might not have a while."

"We have what we have. You said you thought nothing's going to happen to this guy."

"Not right away."

"So we have time."

McShane poured himself another cup of coffee and took it out onto the deck. Through the doorwall, Preuss saw him lean against the railing and sip from the cup that steamed in the cold evening air.

Preuss's phone buzzed with a text.

Grace Poole. *Hey. It's me. What are you up to?*

He replied: *Waiting on a call from an informant. You?*

Working on an article. Thinking about you.
Got a minute to talk?
In five seconds his phone rang.
"Hey," he said.
"Hey. Waiting on an informant, eh? Wow. Cop talk. Love it."
"It's how I roll."
"Do you have to keep the line clear?"
"No. Somebody else is here. The call'll come through to him."
"And then what?"
"Depends what the caller says. I'm starting to zero in on a suspect, but I don't know where he is."
"That's what the informant's going to tell you?"
"It is to be hoped."
"What happens when you find out?"
"We go after him."
"We?"
"My associate and I."
"What an exciting life! It's like you live in a television series. 'The Martin Preuss Mysteries.'"
"It's not always this exciting. But the case is starting to break. Things tend to move fast."
"It's a lot more exciting than academia. Although sometimes the academic battles are every bit as fierce as in your line of work. Know why academic fights are so bitter?"
"No."
"Because the stakes are so low."
He gave a soft laugh. "Too true."
"Right?" she said. "You grew up in an academic family. You should know that."
"Sounds right to me."
"The academic world is apropos of nothing," she said.

"I'm not sure many academics would agree with you."

"Most would, if they were being honest."

She made a little squeak, as if she were stretching. "I'm not sure I care what other academics think at this particular moment in time."

"What's your article about?" he asked.

"Transformational critical narrative inquiry in the history of the English writing classroom."

"Okay then."

"Yeah, you're jealous as hell, I can tell. Only thing you're doing is waiting around for a secret informant to call so you can go out and chase down the villain and solve a major crime. Ho-hum."

Through the doorwall he saw McShane take a call on his cell phone.

"Looks like my call's coming through," he said. "Gotta go."

"Okay, baby. Good luck. Talk to you later."

They hung up.

When was the last time anybody called him *baby*? Even Jeanette never called him *baby*.

A line from *The Producers* popped into his head.

"Why does he say this 'baby'? The Fuhrer has never said 'baby.'"

How apropos.

McShane slid the doorwall open.

"UC doesn't know. He's going to find out and get back to me. But it's not going to be tonight."

Preuss sighed.

"Won't be until at least tomorrow," McShane said. "This is coming through three separate blind levels."

"You're sure the message came through intact?"

"Of course I'm sure."

McShane put his empty coffee cup in the sink.

"I'm going to take off," he said. "We're not going to know anything else tonight. I'll call you as soon as I hear something."

"Right. How'd you get here? Need a ride?"

"My car's around the corner. Think you can stay out of trouble while I'm gone?"

"I'll try."

McShane paused at the door and looked back. He straightened the ball cap on his head. "Preuss," he said. "I know you can handle yourself. I've seen you. But these guys . . . they're vicious."

"I know."

"I told you, they're not fat losers playing soldier in the woods anymore. Those assault rifles they carry aren't for show."

"Okay."

"Call me if anybody shows up tonight. I mean it, Preuss. Call me, not the cops."

It was too late to go to Toby's. He called the protection number and Nancy Fields answered. All was quiet.

He felt like calling Grace back to hear her voice again. He thought he heard a trace of the south in it. She had said she lived in Buffalo, but he knew the Buffalo accent was more midwestern. She didn't mention where she originated from, only that she moved to Michigan when she began teaching at Wayne.

He took another cup of coffee into the living room. He turned his CD player on and slipped in the new Joe Bonamassa disk, *Driving Towards the Daylight*. The first song, "Dislocated Boy," started up with an easy organ and then slid into the power groove Bonamassa was so good at.

Preuss listened for a while, then Grace Poole called him.

"Hey," she said. "Wanted to hear your voice again."

"Hey. I was just thinking about you."

"Great minds, et cetera."

"Are you from the south?"

The question took her by surprise. "Well, yeah. I lived in Virginia for the first ten years of my life. Then we moved to New York. Why?"

"Just curious. I thought I heard a little bit of the south in your voice."

"Wow," she said, "are you like a detective or something?"

"No," he said, "but I play one on . . . oh wait, I am a detective."

"Did you get your call?"

"Yeah. It's all on pause for the night."

"So no middle-of-the-night raids? Kicking doors down, rousting gangsters and their naked molls out of bed, and so on?"

"Not tonight."

"Seriously, you do have an interesting life."

"It might seem that way from the outside. But my life revolves almost entirely around my son. I spend my time with him when I'm not working."

"Friends? Hobbies?"

"Music."

"Close friends?"

"Not many."

She was silent for a few moments.

"Can I ask a question?" she said. "Before we go too much further with this?"

"Sure."

"Is there room in your life for anything else besides work and your son?"

"Good question, professor."

"What's the answer?"

He thought about it.

"Honestly," he said, "I don't know."

"Don't you think maybe it's time to start finding out?"

Thursday, March 7, 2013

49

He awoke at 4:06 by the red numbers on the clock on the nightstand, before the sun had begun to lighten the sky.

The woman next to him gave a small moan when he rolled out of bed. She resettled herself and stayed asleep. He made sure the covers were up over her bare shoulders.

It was chilly in the room. No, it was *cold.* She had said she couldn't sleep in a warm room, but she never mentioned sleeping in a meat locker.

He padded into the bathroom to pee, then stood in the doorway to her bedroom watching her sleep.

It had been years since he'd shared a bed with anyone. Even before his wife died, they had slept in separate rooms.

Preuss was out of practice for this in so many ways.

The woman he'd just spent the night with purred, tousled hair across her face.

In the two minutes he had been gone, she had wrapped herself in the covers and lay diagonally across the bed. To crawl beside her, he would have to move her and steal the covers back. He preferred to let her keep sleeping, so he collected his t-shirt, Levis, shoes, and socks and eased out into the hall.

He dressed in the cold hall and went through to the kitchen.

Where it was also freezing.

His mouth was cottony, so he searched for a glass and downed a full glass of water.

When he got to Grace's the night before, she suggested they walk to Suzy's around the corner for a nightcap. "Coffee only," she said, for his benefit.

"Late for coffee," he offered.

"Caffeine has no effect on me," she said. "I can drink gallons of it and sleep like a baby."

On the way to the bar, she linked her arm in his and leaned into him without speaking. Before going in, she stopped at the entrance and wrapped him in her arms and pulled him toward her. They kissed, and again without speaking of their intentions they put their arms around each other and walked straight back to her apartment.

Now, standing in her kitchen, remembering the night before in the frigid home of this woman he hadn't even known a week and a half ago, he felt as though he had entered an alternative reality where he could be happy and things would—*could*, he corrected himself—start looking up.

In other words, another life than the one he had been living.

Better enjoy it, he cautioned himself with his usual fatalism. This will disappear soon enough.

Melted into air, into thin air.

The kitchen was old-fashioned, with an ancient sink made of chipped and stained porcelain and a narrow counter topped with what appeared to be linoleum. She made up for the lack of storage space with two utility carts, one for coffee fixings and the other set up as a bar.

Which, he noted with something like distress, was stocked with an array of bottles of booze and liqueurs. Grace was a drinker; he didn't know how that was going to work.

He made a pot of coffee and stood against the counter with a steaming cup in his hand. The temperature outside had dropped overnight and she had said she kept the house at a steady 58 degrees in the winter. The window in the kitchen was a drafty double-hung so it was even colder standing beside it.

She lived on the top floor of a three-decker house from the early twentieth century. The window looked out onto the darkened windows of another house across a narrow walkway—no driveways for any house on this old block. Light flurries drifted down in the rectangle of light from the kitchen.

Preuss took his coffee with him into the living room. His shirt was still out here, along with her University of Buffalo sweatshirt and white cotton bra. He picked up her clothes and folded them on a chair. Once the clothes had started coming off last night, they had run back to her bedroom, both giggling in the cold, and hit her bed with gratitude for the warmth of the sheet and blankets as well as for the sudden welcome heat of their unfamiliar bodies holding each other under the covers.

She was warm and supple and strange. Afterwards they lay in each other's arms until they fell asleep.

Lost in the remembrance of the feel of her skin, he sat on the sofa with his cup of coffee on his lap.

He closed his eyes.

He dozed.

He awoke when the cushion next to him sagged with Grace Poole's weight. She took the cup from him and kissed him on the lips. She had found her sweatshirt and put it on.

Saying, "G'morning," she wrapped them both in the blanket she had brought with her.

"What are you doing out here?" she said.

"Drinking coffee. Didn't want to disturb you."

"You made it?"

"Yeah."

"Settling right In, are we?"

"Can we open some windows? Getting kinda warm in here."

She smiled and nestled against him in the crook of his arm, and they breathed together for several minutes.

Then she said, "This is nice."

He hummed agreement. He reminded himself of Toby, humming his responses.

Be present, he instructed himself. Savor the moment.

She took in a deep breath, let it out slowly. "I feel like I've been waiting for you," she murmured. "At the same time as I've been dreading your arrival. Does that make any sense?"

"It does," he said. "I feel much the same way."

She pulled back to examine his face, and as she did he examined hers. Her most striking features at this close range were her eyes, deep-set and intense, blue, with the beginnings of wrinkles and dark smudges from lack of sleep underneath and at the corners.

She looked back at him with the same intensity, then put a hand behind his head and drew his face toward hers for another kiss.

Who are you? he thought.

And how did this happen?

Likely she was asking herself the same questions.

They lay in each other's arms under the blanket, withdrawing again to the solitude of their own bodies, their own thoughts.

His phone rang.

The world intrudes.

She stirred. "Do you have to get that?"

"I better."

They disentangled their limbs and he crossed the room to where he had left his leather jacket. He could feel her eyes on him as he stood sorting through the pockets for his cell phone.

She raised her head to peer at the time on the clock on top of the television in the corner. "Who's calling you at this hour?"

"Whenever the phone rings like this, I always think it's about Toby."

"He can't call you, can he?"

"No, it would be his caretakers. Which would mean there's a problem. Even if it's not about Toby, a phone call at quarter to five in the morning is never good news."

He saw from the caller ID it was McShane.

"Work," he said.

He took the phone into the kitchen.

"McShane," he said.

"Preuss. I got something."

None of the niceties one might expect after calling at quarter to five. Are you up? Did I wake you? Good morning?

"Go," Preuss said.

"I heard from the UC. He wants to meet. Doesn't trust the phone. He says the group's got all the phones bugged."

"A man after your own heart. When?"

"This morning. Pick you up in half an hour."

"Make it an hour and a half."

"Why?"

"I'm not home."

A long pause.

"An hour and a half then," McShane said, and disconnected.

Back in the living room, Grace Poole was huddled under the blanket.

"What was that about?" she asked.

"My case." He sat back beside her and burrowed into the blanket she held up for him. He welcomed her warmth.

"I have to go," he said.

"So early?"

"Yeah. Sorry."

"Time for a quick shower first?"

The sky was still dark with a half-moon casting a cold light on the one-way cramped street in front of her house. Parked cars were jammed in on both sides. It had snowed overnight. He walked to his car through a cold caramel fog. Despite the haze, the world had a heightened, almost hallucinatory clarity.

How odd, nothing had changed out here, because in his heart everything was different.

He was surprised how sorry he was to leave her. He felt alone, even abandoned though he was the one leaving, not her.

They had showered together, or more accurately held each other while the water poured over their heads and down their backs, and decided they should talk about this but now wasn't the moment. They needed to have more time than he had. And they both needed to think more about whether this was a carefree roll in the hay or the start of something more, something with the potential to change their lives.

When they toweled off, she asked if he had time for breakfast, but he said he didn't; he needed to get home and change. She gave him a lingering kiss before he slipped away.

They promised to be in touch during the day, which he knew was going to be long and hard. He told her he would text her and call if he had the chance, but if he didn't she shouldn't think he was avoiding her.

He drove home. The first thing he did when he got there was change his clothes. He no longer wore suits, but he wanted to get into clean clothes so he put on a pair of black Levis and a black cotton sweater.

By the time he was ready, he heard Franklin McShane calling him from downstairs.

He thought for a second about getting the locks changed, but he knew McShane could still get into his house faster than Preuss could with a key. It wasn't worth the effort.

50

McShane didn't talk to the UC directly, but the message came to him through the layers. The meet would be in the parking lot of a Big Boy restaurant on Ford Road near the Ikea in Canton. They were to park at the rear of the lot.

McShane pulled his Lexus into a slot at the far corner, facing out so he could keep an eye on the restaurant.

They waited for half an hour, then McShane got a call on his cell phone. He listened for a few seconds and disconnected.

"What?" Preuss asked.

"Bus shelter on Ford Road."

He pulled out and made a Michigan left to start driving in the opposite direction. He drove west on Ford Road for another mile, past Beck Road. On the right side of the street was a bus shelter.

McShane pulled over and as soon as he stopped a man darted out of the shelter and jumped into the back seat. He ducked down and said, "Drive."

Preuss in the passenger seat turned to look at him. Like the rest of the white nationalists, he had a full ragged beard and a camo baseball cap. He was slender in a blue and mustard-colored checked padded flannel shirt and baggy Levis.

He smelled like he hadn't washed in a week.

"Alright?" Preuss asked.

"Yeah," the guy said.

McShane said, "Where to?"

"There's a cemetery up on the left. Pull in there."

"That's appropriate," McShane muttered.

But he did as directed. He turned left into the Sunset Ridge Cemetery.

"What now?" McShane asked.

"Drive along and pull over someplace."

McShane parked in a lay-by near a broad section of headstones.

"We're clear," McShane said. "Nobody's around."

The guy sat up. Preuss turned around to shake his hand. "Preuss," he said.

"Douglas. So here's the deal. I tried to ask around discreetly, and this guy you're looking for?"

"Larry Bright," Preuss said.

"Somebody's got him, for sure. I dunno where yet. I'll try to find out today and let you know. I have to be careful about how I press it. I'm not in the inner circle."

"Sure. I'll give you my cell number," Preuss said.

"Don't want it. The less I have or know, the better. I know how to get in touch with this guy," he said, pointing his chin at McShane, "so that's how we'll keep it."

"Good," Preuss said.

"I can't promise anything," Douglas said. "I'm not going to jeopardize my own investigation. Or my life, for that matter."

"Sure," Preuss said. "No worries." To McShane, he said, "Work for you?"

McShane nodded.

"Good deal," Douglas said.

"Anything else?" Preuss asked.

"Yeah," Douglas said. "You guys hear anything about a death list?"

That got McShane's attention. With narrowed eyes he watched Douglas in the rear-view mirror.

"No," Preuss said. "What is it?"

"I've heard it batted around. Supposedly they're putting together an assassination crew. They drew up a list of targets."

"Who's on the list?"

"Couldn't tell you. Just thought you might have heard about it."

"Not so far," Preuss said. To McShane: "You?"

McShane nodded. "Rumors about it. Always rumors, even back in my day."

"I'm hearing more than rumors right now," Douglas said. "It's a thing."

"Every once in a blue moon a judge'd get killed, or a reporter," McShane said. "But it always turned out to be lone wolves. Used to be, these morons couldn't organize a bread fight in a bakery."

"Not anymore," Douglas said. "They're coordinating and connecting. And now these guys are putting together hit squads."

"You pass that up the chain?" McShane asked.

"Of course. I haven't heard what they're doing with the information."

"Neither have I," McShane said.

"You're McShane, huh?" Douglas asked.

McShane just watched him on in the rear-view.

"Heard a lot about you," Douglas said.

McShane was silent. Then he said, "Watch yourself with these guys."

"Always do," Douglas said. "Now how about taking me back to the bus stop?"

"I wonder if Charles Bright was on that list," Preuss said.

McShane shook his head with his eyes on the road back to Ferndale. "Why would he be?"

"Socially active guy. Make an example out of him?"

"Take a lot more than that. There's a thousand socially active people around this town. Why him?"

"Maybe his son Larry can tell us."

"Maybe," McShane allowed without much enthusiasm.

"Soon as we find out where Larry Bright is, we can go ask him," Preuss said.

"There's a better way."

"Which is?"

"We grab one of these Nazis and ask him. Hard."

Preuss saw a dozen ways this wouldn't be a good idea. "That would only work if he knew."

"We can lay some pain on him in the meantime. So it wouldn't be a total loss."

"Look," Preuss said, "this is in the works. Let's give this guy a day. If we don't hear from him by tonight, we'll do it another way."

McShane grumbled, but was silent for the rest of the trip.

"I'll be in touch," McShane said. He had driven once around the block and asked Preuss if anything looked out of order.

"No," Preuss said, and started to say he'd be in his office if McShane needed him but McShane had already roared off in the Lexus.

Preuss went inside his house, which seemed bigger and emptier and colder than ever after his night with Grace. He realized he was hungry—he hadn't eaten since the night before—so he made coffee and toasted an English muffin, which he slathered with peanut butter and ate standing at his kitchen counter.

Through the kitchen window he saw the few inches of snow that had fallen overnight were molded over the bushes in his backyard. The scene was all shades of brown and grey, from the dull ivory of the snow to the dark brown of the dormant bushes.

He glanced at the time. Too late to say good morning to Toby. So he missed his son twice, last night and this morning. He would have to see him tonight, or at least this afternoon when Toby got off the bus from his school program.

A death list, Douglas had said. McShane was right: Why would a retired professor be on the kill list of a gang of white power thugs?

Unless he wasn't. Unless somebody else killed Charlie Bright for another reason altogether.

He rinsed the dishes and stacked them in the dishwasher, then got ready to go in to work.

On the way, he got a call from Reg Trombley.

He punched the Bluetooth button on the steering wheel. "Reg," he said.

"Hey Martin. How you doing?"

"Good. What's up?"

"I wanted to give you the courtesy of a call. I heard from Emma Blalock last night. They caught the guy who killed Charles Bright."

51

Preuss pulled into a 7-Eleven lot and transferred the call from Bluetooth to his hand-held.

"What do you mean, they caught him?"

"They arrested him. He's in custody. He's no longer at large."

"Who is he?"

"Martin," Trombley began.

"Come on, Reg. If he's the guy, the case is over and it's going to be public in about ten minutes. Who is he?"

"Some doofus who works at the Wendy's down there. Name's Devonté. He cleans up, wipes the tables, mops the floor. Apparently, Bright went there for breakfast a lot and got friendly with the guy. Had him over to his house and so forth. Devonté developed a sick obsession with him. He admitted to breaking into his house a few times. He did it one day when he thought Bright wasn't home, discovered Bright there, and went nuts on him."

"How do you know this?"

"Emma told me. He confessed."

Preuss processed that.

"What did he do," he said, "just walk in and confess?"

"An anonymous tip came into the station pointing at this guy. So they tracked him down. It's called police work. Maybe you remember it?"

Preuss ignored the snark.

"Case closed," Trombley said.

"Do you believe this is the guy?"

"What can I tell you, Martin? Emma told me this is the guy. She faxed me the confession and I read it. You really think she'd bring in the wrong guy?"

With an edge to his voice.

"Charles Bright was a vegan," Preuss said, "who was careful about what he ate. Why would he go to Wendy's every morning for breakfast?"

"I'm not saying he went every morning. Look, this is all out of our hands. And none of your business, I might add. I'm giving you the courtesy of a heads-up because I know you're working the case."

Trombley left unspoken the rest of the sentence . . . *in spite of everyone warning you off.*

Trombley said, "Well, now you're not. It's done. Take it easy, Martin." He disconnected the call.

Preuss sat in the parking lot for a while longer. This guy no more killed Charles Bright than I did, Preuss thought. Not only because of Bright's eating habits, but also because the evidence is leading in another direction entirely.

It wasn't unusual for people to confess to crimes they didn't commit. But Trombley was a good investigator; if he read the confession, he wouldn't be fooled unless it was backed up with evidence.

Neither would Emma Blalock.

So where did that leave Preuss's investigation?

Larry Bright was still missing, and as far as Preuss knew still in danger. And still in the frame for his father's murder, regardless of what Emma Blalock had found.

No, this didn't sound right.

He turned around and went back to Ferndale.

The Wendy's on Woodward was open for breakfast. Preuss parked in the lot and went inside.

A young woman stood behind the counter. Her name badge said "Kiki." "Welcome to Wendy's," she said. "How can I help you?"

Preuss handed her a business card and introduced himself. "There's a guy working here who cleans up, buses the tables, named Devonté?"

She nodded. "We call him Dee. If you're looking for him, he's not here. The cops came and hauled him away yesterday."

"I need to ask a little bit about him. Did you know him?"

"I guess."

"Can you tell me what he was like?"

The woman behind the counter shrugged a shoulder. "He's okay, I guess."

"I understand he spent some time talking with this man." He showed her a photo of Charles Bright.

"Yeah," she said, "he's been in."

"I heard he comes in sometimes for breakfast?"

"I don't work every morning. But yeah, I see him come in occasionally. Not every day. But he never eats. Just has a cup of coffee and chats with people."

"You mean like with Devonté?"

"Yeah. Other people, too."

"Do you remember who?"

One question too many.

"Um," Kiki said, "I think you better talk to my manager."

She raised a slim finger and slipped off behind the food prep area. She returned followed by a dark-skinned man whose name badge said, "James."

"You're asking about Devonté Richards?" he said. "Let's go over here and talk."

James came through a side door behind the counter and led Preuss to a table by the windows on the Woodward side.

"I'm not happy one of my employees got arrested in my store," James said.

"I wouldn't think so. What happened?"

"Sheriff's deputies walked in and scooped him up. Hauled him right out in about ten seconds. You want to know about him?"

"I was just asking Kiki what he was like."

"You never met him?"

Preuss shook his head.

James took a deep breath and seemed to search for words to describe Devonté. He settled on, "He's a good man. Hard worker. But very troubled."

"In what way?"

"Devonté, he's slow, you know what I'm saying? And he hears voices sometimes. I try to get him to take his medication, and most times he does, but whenever he starts feeling better he goes off the meds. That's what gets him in trouble."

"Happens to a lot of people."

"Yeah. When he's on his meds, he's fine."

"Sounds like you know him well."

"He's my brother-in-law. I've been trying to help him out. I figured if I gave him steady work, he'd have a regular life. Schedules help him, keep him on an even keel. And like I say, he's a good worker, he is. The problems start when he stops taking his meds."

"When he's off his meds, is he ever violent?"

"Never. He's just . . . off. He can be scary, but I've never seen him get violent."

"Has he seemed that way lately? In the last couple of weeks?"

"Not that I've noticed."

"Nothing different about him? How he looks, what he does?"

"Not so I'd notice."

"So as far as you know, he's still on his meds?"

"Far as I know."

"The Sheriff's investigators believe he killed a man named Charles Bright," Preuss said.

James shook his head. "I don't believe that in a million years."

"They say he confessed."

"Devonté, sometimes he's like a little kid, he wants to be helpful. He'd say whatever they wanted him to say."

"Did you know Charles Bright?"

"I'd seen him. He came in with a homeless guy every so often, and he started talking with Devonté. I guess they got friendly."

"Do you know the homeless guy?"

"No. Sorry."

Preuss showed him the photo of Larry Bright. "This guy?"

James looked, said, "It kinda looks like him, but I can't say yes or no for sure."

"Charles Bright was killed in a gruesome way. The body was mutilated. Is Devonté's capable of that?"

"If there's one thing I've learned in life, it's hard to know what anybody's capable of at any given time. But I have to say no. I don't believe Devonté would ever hurt a fly."

Preuss was heading out to the Explorer when Kiki came out the side door of the restaurant.

"Sir?" she called.

He stopped and she caught up with him.

"Sorry, but I overheard you talking with my manager. And you asked if there was something different about Dee?"

"Right."

"Well, this might not be important, but he gave me this."

She pulled a necklace out from under her uniform. A small pear-shaped emerald hung from a silver chain.

"That's beautiful," he said.

"Yeah. He gave it to me day before yesterday. I told him I couldn't accept it, but he said he bought it specially for me."

"He likes you?"

"He does. I told him I like him but not as a boyfriend, but he said it didn't matter. He wanted me to have it. He wouldn't let me give it back."

"How could he afford that on what he makes here?"

"That's what I'm saying! Dee, he doesn't have that kind of money. He said he came into some bank and wanted to give me something nice."

"Did he say how he came into some bank?"

"No. I didn't ask him."

The gem caught the morning sunlight.

"Seemed pretty odd to me," Kiki said. "I thought it might be something you'd want to know about."

52

"Martin," Rhonda said, "are you okay?"

"Sure," he said. "Why?"

"You look . . . I dunno. Strange."

"I'm fine," he said. He sat on the sofa in her outer area with a cup of her everyday coffee. "This has been a busy couple of days. The Bright case is taking some very odd turns."

As is my life in general, he thought.

He explained what Trombley told him.

"But that's good, isn't it?" she asked.

"If this guy did it, yeah."

"You don't think he did?"

"I didn't at first. But I talked with a young woman who told me the guy they arrested just found a lot of money. Now I'm wondering if he stole it from Bright's house when he killed him. And maybe he is the right guy after all. I don't know what evidence they have, beyond the confession."

"They must have something or they wouldn't hold him, right?"

"Right."

"Well, I can't help you. I broke up with my secret informant."

"Oh, Rhonda, no. So sorry to hear that."

"Yeah. Whatever."

He was silent while he thought through a few alternatives in the case.

"Or it might also be," he said, "this guy could have stolen the money another time when he broke into the house, which he's also confessed to doing."

As he thought, he remembered a phrase from the *VolksGuard* website article proposing American Identity Warriors.

Responsibility for their acts of "heroism"—murder and terrorism—should point to "unwitting members of the sub-races."

In other words, they should frame somebody else.

Somebody like Devonté.

Such brave warriors these guys are.

"There's another possibility," Preuss said. "Somebody might have paid that poor guy to confess to the murder, which he didn't commit."

That would explain where he got the money for Kiki's necklace, he thought. And also explain why someone like Devonté would confess to a crime he didn't—and by all accounts couldn't—commit.

So did that put Larry Bright back in the picture? Did Larry kill his father (at Ken's direction, maybe) while Ken or someone else got Devonté to take the blame for it?

"You know," Rhonda said, breaking into his thoughts, "we almost have enough to do around here without you having to worry about this."

"I know," he admitted.

His cell phone rang.

Unknown number.

Bet I know who this is, he thought.

"Preuss," McShane barked. "I got the address where your boy's being held. How soon can you pick me up?"

53

McShane was standing by the air pump at the side of Vern's Minimart on Mack Avenue and Cadillac Boulevard on the east side of Detroit. Vern's was a tiny Shell station, convenience store, and snack bar, and for some reason McShane had picked this spot for their rendezvous the last few times. Preuss had learned better than to question him about it.

McShane wouldn't divulge where he lived, and Preuss had no idea if it was near this Shell station or not.

McShane wore his beige raincoat over a green Wayne State University sweatshirt, soiled khakis, and filthy Keds, with a Tiger cap on top of his long silver hair.

He heaved a tote bag into the rear seat of the Explorer and jumped in after it. The bag made a heavy metallic clunk. Preuss knew what was in it—McShane's portable arsenal. They could fight a small war with what was in this bag.

McShane directed him onto the I-94 expressway for a few miles, and then exited and hopscotched around on roads until Preuss was on Ford Road heading west.

According to Douglas, the house where Larry Bright was being held was near Central City Park in the city of Westland, close by John Glenn High School where Ruth Anne Krider taught. It was a small one-story red brick duplex at the corner of Bock and Arthur

Streets, the last house on the street with woods directly across from it on Bock as well as on the opposite corner of Arthur. An entrance door with a tiny porch was on each side of the front of the duplex.

"Stop here," McShane said as they approached from Wayne Road. The entire street was filled with small one-story homes that looked prefab.

"I don't like this," McShane said.

"I'll check it out," Preuss said. "You can hang back if you want."

"No way. We do this, we're gonna go in fast and hard. But we're not going to walk up to the front door and ring the bell like Jehovah's Witnesses. Turn around."

Preuss made a U-turn and drove back down to Wayne Road. He took a left and made another left on the next side street, Donnelly. He drove down Donnelly to midway in the last block before Arthur.

McShane unbuckled his seat belt and turned in his seat. He unzipped the tote bag and withdrew an AK-47 and two 30-round magazines, which he stuffed in his pockets.

"Want some heat?" he asked Preuss.

"No."

"You're sure? You're not going to be able to talk these guys out of whatever they have in mind. This is what they understand." He held up the weapon.

Preuss considered it for a few moments. He hated guns; he was convinced they caused more problems than they solved, and ramped up the violence in any situation. His refusal to carry a gun was one of the sticking points when he was a detective in Ferndale.

But McShane had a point about the people they were dealing with.

"Yeah, okay," Preuss said.

"Now you're being sensible."

McShane took another assault rifle out of his bag, but Preuss said, "No. Handgun."

McShane came up with a sleek two-tone, silver-and-grey pistol.

"Kimber Rapide Black Ice 9 mm 1911," he said, and handed it to Preuss.

"Only as a last resort," Preuss said.

"Just don't lose it. That gun's top of the line. Cost a fortune."

They stepped out of the car and Preuss stuck the pistol in his back waistband under his leather jacket. He had no plans to use it, but they didn't know what they were walking into.

McShane hid the assault rifle under his raincoat and they walked down the road.

They stopped at the corner of Arthur and Donnelly and McShane scoped out the scene behind the little duplex on the next street.

Trees behind the garage blocked the rear sightlines from inside the house. But because they were bare of leaves it was possible to see somebody walking back there.

Using the tree trunks as cover, Preuss and McShane approached from the rear. They tramped through the snow between the trees and the garage.

McShane peeked around the corner of the garage, then pulled his head back. "Small patio, two rear entrance doors," he whispered. Preuss gestured that he would take the right door and McShane should take the left.

McShane nodded, and after glancing out one more time to make sure no one was looking out the back windows, the two men ran from the garage up to the house.

They went silent for a full minute as each listened for movement, voices, any sound from either half of the duplex.

McShane shook his head, but Preuss thought he picked up voices inside his side of the building. He tapped his ear and pointed inside.

Definitely voices.

Men.

At least two.

From outside all he could hear were murmurs so he couldn't tell what they were saying.

McShane came over to the back door on Preuss's side and tried the storm door.

Unlocked.

He opened it and, ducking down beside the window in the inside back door, turned the knob. He pushed the inside door open as quietly as he could.

The voices inside went silent.

McShane pulled the assault rifle from under his coat and set himself to rush inside.

Before he could move, a blast from inside splintered the door frame and threw McShane onto his back on the patio.

Two men came barreling down the back stairs from inside the house, blasting away with big handguns.

From where he was lying on his back, McShane opened up with the assault rifle and blew one of the men back inside with a ragged wound that exploded in his stomach.

Preuss launched himself into the guy who came out of the house on his side, knocking him to the ground. While on top of him, Preuss pulled the gun from his waistband and brought the butt down hard on the side of the guy's head.

The man's handgun went clattering away on the concrete patio and he went limp.

Preuss jumped up and raced inside the house, gun up, with McShane at his back.

The kitchen and the living room were empty.

McShane raced into the back of the home and together they breezed through the bedrooms and the basement, but they were alone.

"No Bright?" McShane said.

"Not here," Preuss said.

"Come on!"

They ran out of the house and McShane blasted the locks off the back door of the other home in the duplex. They searched every room inside. It was a mirror image of the home on the right, but it was empty—not even any furniture.

Back outside, panting, McShane said, "This was a damn trap."

The man Preuss had clocked was lying on the ground, still out cold. Preuss checked the one McShane had shot. He was on the back landing with his top half on the stairs down to the basement. He was breathing through groans.

"Let's get out of here," McShane said. He stuffed the rifle back under his coat and led the way down the side street to where they had left Preuss's Explorer. Preuss expected to hear sirens any moment, but none came.

Inside the Explorer, Preuss said, "Let's go back."

"No! We have to get out of here."

"This'll take a second."

Preuss drove back to the house on Bock. The guy he clobbered was still out on the patio.

"Give me a hand," Preuss said.

Together they lifted the unconscious man into the back of the Explorer.

"Now," McShane said, "you're talking my language."

As they sped away, McShane called 911 and told the dispatcher about the wounded man at the duplex, but hung up without giving his name. He removed the battery and broke the cell phone into pieces and tossed them out the window when Preuss turned onto Wayne Road.

"This was a setup," McShane said. "They were waiting for us."

"They must suspect they have an informer," Preuss said.

"All these groups are compromised. If they didn't know they had an informer before, they do now. I'll have to get word through to Douglas. Let him know he might be blown."

He looked at the man in the back seat.

"Good idea, grabbing this mook," McShane said. He looked at Preuss. "He and I, we're going to have ourselves a talk."

54

McShane directed them to a warehouse in Corktown in downtown Detroit. Preuss drove the Explorer into an alley and McShane got out and opened a set of old wooden garage doors. Preuss pulled into a large empty space and McShane closed the doors behind him.

"What is this," Preuss asked, "your bat cave?"

"I come here when I need to get away from the prying eyes of the surveillance state," McShane said.

The garage was empty except for a worktable on one side. Sound-proofed walls, stained concrete floor. A door at the back of the space.

"Where does that go?" Preuss asked.

"Noplace to do with you."

Their passenger was groggy but had still not regained consciousness. Preuss and McShane hauled him out of the Explorer and dragged him over to a wall. They leaned him against it but his legs gave out and he slid down. He was wearing the uniform: full ragged beard, camo pants, a blue and yellow checkered padded flannel shirt.

"Jesus," McShane said. "It's like these guys are all from Central Casting."

He went over to the worktable and returned with a bottle of water. He poured it over their hostage's head. The guy sputtered and snorted.

McShane knelt down in front of him. "What's your name?"

The guy closed his eyes and didn't say anything.

McShane slapped him across the face. "What's your name!"

Still no response.

McShane flipped him over and pulled the guy's wallet out of his back pocket. He looked through the contents and tossed the wallet away.

"Eddy," McShane said. "Well, Eddy, we're going to have a talk, you and me."

"Yeah?"

"Yeah."

"I don't think so."

"Oh, I do."

"I ain't telling you shit," Eddy said.

McShane's punch, short and lightning fast, caught Eddy full on the nose. His head bounced off the brick wall behind him and his nose spurted blood down his front.

Preuss handed McShane a towel from the work table, and McShane gave it to Eddy, who held it up to his face to stanch the bleeding.

"Maybe you can tell me this, Eddy," McShane said, "and save us all some time. Where's Larry Bright?"

Whether out of confusion from his head injury or stupidity or defiance, Eddy only stared at McShane.

To Preuss, McShane said, "Still got the Kimber?"

"Of course."

"Give."

"What are you going to do with it?"

"I find gentle persuasion to be over-rated and unhelpful with people like Eddy. So I'm not going to be gentle."

Preuss handed the weapon to him and said, "Don't kill him."

"I won't. Unless I have to. Hold him up."

Preuss held Eddy upright and braced against the wall. Before Preuss could react, McShane took Eddy's right wrist, held his arm out, and shot him through the palm.

Eddy howled.

"McShane!" Preuss said.

But McShane dropped Eddy's right hand and held up his left hand, which clutched the bloody towel. McShane grabbed the towel and threw it behind him.

Eddy cradled his wounded hand against his chest and whimpered.

"Are you going to tell me where Larry Bright is?" McShane said.

Eddy sobbed in reply.

"Now I'm going to count to *two*," McShane said, "and if you don't tell me where Larry Bright is, I'm going to shoot you through your other hand. And if you still don't tell me, I'm going to count to two again and I'm going to shoot you in the head. And trust me on this one, Eddy, nobody'll ever find you."

This got Eddy to pull himself together, though his sobs had turned to messy blubbering. He looked at McShane in wide-eyed terror.

"Not so brave now, are you, tough guy," McShane said, "without your Nazi pals and your assault weapons."

McShane was hard-eyed and cold and Preuss had no doubt he would kill Eddy right there.

McShane said, "*One.*"

"Don't kill me," Eddy managed.

"A decision entirely up to you. *Two.*"

He shot Eddy through the palm of his left hand.

Eddy screamed.

McShane stepped back and held the gun at arm's length but pressing against Eddy's forehead. "I don't want to get your brains all over me," McShane said. "Preuss, you can stand back, too."

Eddy began to wail. His legs went out from under him and he slid down the wall.

"*One!*"

"No," Eddy yelled through tears. "Wait!"

McShane came up close to Eddy's face with the gun now pressed under his chin.

"Tell me, tough guy!" McShane shouted in his face. "Where's Larry Bright?"

Eddy said something unintelligible.

"I can't hear you!"

"Kevin's," Eddy said, careful this time to articulate the words as well as he could through his sobs.

"You sure?" McShane said. "Your life depends on this, you disgusting scum."

"I swear. I swear it's the truth. He's at Kevin's."

"You know this Kevin?" McShane asked Preuss.

Preuss recalled Sylvia Bloom mentioning the name, and he remembered seeing it in the file she had given him.

"Kevin Johnson?" Preuss asked.

Eddy nodded rapidly, gratefully.

"Yeah," Preuss said. "He lives up in Helmford."

McShane pulled the gun barrel away from Eddy's chin. "Good answer," he said.

He held the pistol next to Eddy's ear pointed up. He fired into the ceiling, a painful explosion in the enclosed space.

Eddy grabbed his ear with a bloody hand and collapsed in a heap on the stained concrete floor.

Preuss thought he was starting to understand how the floor got stained.

"Rhonda," Preuss said into his cell phone.

"Martin," she said. He heard the exasperation in her voice. "Where *are* you?"

"I've been in the field all day. What's going on?"

"I just get nervous when I don't hear from you."

"Sorry. It's been a day. Listen, can you do me a favor? On my desk is a blue file from Sylvia Bloom. It should say American Identity Brigade on the front. I need you to find an address for me."

55

Helmford was a small town in Michigan farming country past Howell on I-96 west on the way to Lansing, an hour away from Detroit. In rush-hour traffic it took them almost two hours to get there. Preuss drove.

McShane sat in the back seat of the Explorer with Eddy. McShane had bandaged Eddy's hands before they left his bat cave and given him a Vicodin for the pain. But Eddy would still need medical attention.

"Not surprised we're going to Helmford," McShane said. "The Michigan Grand Dragon of the KKK lived there. Used to have meetings on his farm. Turned the whole place into a hotbed of white nationalism."

McShane turned to Eddy beside him. "You ever been up here?"

Eddy said, "What?"

"Ear still bothering you?" McShane asked.

"What? I can't hear nothing out of it."

"Yeah, sorry about that. Hearing'll be gone in that ear."

"What?"

Preuss took the Michigan Avenue exit off 96 and drove north. They passed a carved wooden sign reading, "Welcome to Historic Helmford—Established 1834." It was picture-book

Americana, a thriving small town with neat two-story red brick Victorian shops, pubs, and restaurants.

Preuss's GPS directed them past the downtown to a compact bungalow on several acres of land near Thompson Lake. A long driveway led up to the house from the side street. Two pickup trucks were parked in front of the house.

Preuss recognized one of the trucks with the Confederate battle flag and the tricolor trident bumper stickers.

Preuss stopped the Explorer in a crunch of gravel. He punched in a number on his cell.

The call sounded over Bluetooth.

"Yeah?"

"Calling for Kevin Johnson," Preuss said.

"Who wants him?"

"Martin Preuss."

"Who's Martin Preuss?"

"Is he there?"

"What do you want him for, Martin Preuss?"

"Is this Kevin?"

"Maybe."

"Look," Preuss said, "I don't have time for this. How about you go get Kevin for me?"

"Not till you tell me what you want him for."

"Larry Bright," Preuss said.

A pause. "Who's Larry Bright?"

"I want to make a trade."

"What kind of trade?"

"Say hello, Eddy," Preuss broke in.

He held the phone up so Eddy could say, "Hey Billy, it's me."

Billy said, "Eddy? What—"

Preuss took the phone back. "Billy, how about you go get Kevin, okay?"

After a minute another voice came on the line. "Yeah?"

"Kevin?"

"Who's this?"

"Martin Preuss. I'm a private investigator. I'm sitting at the end of your driveway with Eddy—" He turned around and said, "What's your last name?"

"Slovenic," Eddy said.

Preuss got back on the phone. "Eddy Slovenic."

"Yeah? So?"

"So I'm interested in a little trade. I'll turn over Eddy and you give me Larry Bright."

"What makes you think I got Larry Bright? Or I want Eddy back?"

"Eddy told me he's there."

"He did, eh? What would you want with him, if he was here?"

"I want to talk with him about a case I'm working on."

"Yeah? What case?"

"The murder of Charles Bright. Larry's father."

"You think Larry killed his old man?"

"I do. That's why you're holding him here, right?"

"You think we made a citizen's arrest? I'm not holding him. He's free to leave anytime."

"Then send him out."

Preuss heard Johnson hold the phone away from his ear and say, "Larry. Some guy wants you out there. You wanna go with him?" After a silent pause, Johnson said, "Yeah, he says no, he don't wanna."

Preuss heard guffaws in the background.

"If you'd rather," he said, "I'll come back with the state police and we'll see what they have to say about it."

"Yeah? You think that's a threat?" Johnson said.

The front door of the bungalow opened and Kevin Johnson came out with a cell phone to his ear. Preuss recognized him from his clean-cut, All-American good looks. He fits right in with this town, Preuss thought.

He gave Preuss a smarmy smile. He moved up to the top wooden step leading to the front walkway. Preuss saw a pistol holstered on each side of his belt.

Behind him, three white men squeezed out of the front door and arranged themselves on the porch behind Johnson. They were outfitted with assault rifles, holstered sidearms, and tactical vests loaded with ammo.

"Knock yourself out," Kevin Johnson said. "See what they do."

Preuss heard him both through the phone and from the porch. He was standing in front of his posse, sneering. "Maybe they won't be as helpful as you think, especially when I tell them you're trespassing. Now, look, Martin Preuss—this is private property, and you're trespassing. I'm going to ask you to leave. I won't ask twice."

Preuss disconnected from the call and eased out of his Explorer. "Preuss," McShane said, but Preuss ignored him.

He walked past the pickups in the driveway toward the house with his hands out. Johnson put his phone in his pocket and stayed where he was. The three men behind him held their weapons at the ready.

"Far enough," Johnson said.

Preuss stopped. "I figured as long as I came all the way up here, we should talk face-to-face."

"We got nothing to say to each other. Matter fact, I were you? I'd get back in your car and go back where you came from."

"Thing is, Kevin, besides wanting to talk to Larry, I have some questions about something you bought and paid for."

Johnson scoffed and turned to the three men behind him, who were now part of his audience. "You got Eddy? Keep him."

"I'm not talking about Eddy. I'm talking about Devonté Richards's confession."

"Who's Devonté Richards?"

"The guy you paid to say he killed Charles Bright."

Johnson turned around again, playing to his posse. "Sounds like a spook name to me. I'm afraid I'm not familiar with that individual."

"We'll keep him safe with the other guy who carried out your little ambush today, along with Eddy."

Johnson turned back to Preuss, the smile still on his face.

"My partner shot him," Preuss said. "He might be alive, I dunno. Still . . . gut shot, close range . . . I'm not hopeful. If he's still alive, he'll be in custody, talking his head off."

"You know what? Get lost."

Preuss took a few seconds to take the measure of this scene. Standing in front of him, four heavily armed men. Behind him, McShane in the car, a one-man army, true, but by the time McShane could get out of the car, Preuss would be dead three times over.

He heard the Explorer door open and close. He glanced back and saw McShane on the other side of the pickups with his own weaponry.

Now things were a bit less one-sided.

"I'm not leaving without Larry," Preuss told Johnson.

He continued walking toward Johnson and the porch.

"Then you may not be leaving at all," Johnson said.

He turned to his boys on the porch and gave them a nod.

56

In the space of thirty seconds, this happened:

One of the men on the porch behind Johnson lifted his assault rifle and aimed at Martin Preuss.

He squeezed out four quick shots.

Bang bang bang bang.

Preuss pulled the Kimber from his waistband and dove behind the nearest pickup.

The shots from the porch missed Preuss and slammed into the pickup he was hiding behind.

Preuss fired at the men on the porch.

McShane leaned around the front of a pickup with his own weapon aimed at the man shooting the rifle on the porch.

McShane shot him.

Then McShane turned his fire on the other two on the porch.

Who had never been in an actual firefight, so they lacked the presence of mind to be effective. Shots from their weapons went everywhere: into the pickups, into the dirt, into the trees on either side of the driveway.

Eddy Slovenic chose that moment to leap out of Preuss's Explorer. He was hit by the wild gunfire from the porch and fell to the ground.

McShane fired with pinpoint accuracy and shot each of the other two men on the porch. They fell one after the other.

Kevin Johnson was nowhere to be seen.

When the shooting stopped, Preuss jumped out from behind the pickup and he and McShane rushed the house.

Preuss leapt over the three men writhing on the porch and went through the front door with McShane close behind.

A commotion and gunfire came from upstairs. Preuss moved to the stairway in time to see Larry Bright somersaulting down the steps from the second floor. He flopped at Preuss's feet.

Preuss registered the blood on Bright when Kevin Johnson appeared on the landing at the top of the stairs.

He aimed his two handguns at Preuss.

Preuss fired first.

Even though Preuss was shaking with adrenaline and fear, one of his shots caught Johnson in the stomach.

Johnson went over backwards.

McShane came around Preuss ready to shoot Johnson again but the neo-Nazi remained down.

"Anybody else here?" Preuss asked. He could barely see from the pressure behind his eyes. He hadn't been in a gunfight for years.

As though in answer to Preuss's question, a woman came through an archway behind them and fired a handgun at them.

She missed but McShane raised his weapon and shot her in the shoulder.

She yelped and spun backward through the archway.

Preuss grabbed Larry Bright and with McShane providing cover behind him half-pulled, half-carried Bright through the house and out the front door and across the porch and down the driveway to his Explorer.

Preuss threw Larry into the back seat.

McShane dove in beside him.

Preuss jumped behind the wheel and floored the Explorer backwards down the driveway, spraying gravel all the way out to the road.

57

"Are you hit?" Preuss shouted.

He turned his head and saw holes in McShane's raincoat.

"No," McShane said. "I'm wearing a Kevlar."

McShane was on an adrenaline high. Preuss could feel him vibrating in the back seat. This is what he lives for, Preuss thought: elemental combat between the forces of good and evil.

"What about him?" Preuss asked.

"I'm checking now."

McShane opened Larry Bright's jacket and tore Larry's shirt. McShane gave him a fast once-over. "Shoulder wound," he said. "Don't see anything else on the front."

He pulled Larry forward and saw another gunshot wound on his back. "Exit wound. Looks like a through-and-through. Didn't nick anything serious or he'd be bleeding out."

McShane pulled a first-aid kit out of his tote bag on the floor in the back. He pulled out a length of cotton gauze and bunched it up to stanch the bleeding.

"I'm dressing it," he said. "But he's going to need attention."

"I'll find the nearest hospital," Preuss said.

"No! Stay away from hospitals! They'll have to alert the police. We'll take him to my guy instead."

"What guy?"

"My guy in Hamtramck."

"Seriously? That's over an hour away."

"He'll be fine till then. I'm watching him."

"Yeah, because we wouldn't want the police involved in a multiple shooting with at least one fatality."

"Jesus, there you go again," McShane said. "Look, the cops'll take care of this without us just fine. How do you suppose these guys operate out in the open up here? They got protection, Preuss. That's why Johnson wasn't worried about the State Police. They're all part of it, man."

58

Larry Bright was too weak to stand by himself. Preuss helped him out of the Explorer. The back seat was dark and wet with blood.

Preuss and McShane walked him up to the porch of a frame house on a narrow street in Hamtramck (a few streets from where Grace Poole lived, Preuss noted). A squat bald Chinese man in a wrinkled white shirt stretching over a huge belly opened the door.

"Come in," he said.

Preuss and McShane eased Larry inside the house, which smelled of sandalwood incense. They got Larry settled in a wheelchair in the foyer inside the door.

McShane rattled off something in fast Chinese.

The Chinese man nodded. He pushed Larry in the wheelchair through a set of sliding pocket doors into a darkened room.

In the gloom, Preuss saw a woman waiting to take Larry further into the house.

"Wait here," the Chinese man said to Preuss and McShane, then slid the doors closed behind him.

McShane sat on an old wooden church pew in the foyer. Beside the pew, a long fish tank burbled on a stand and a dozen multicolored fish swam, without a care in the world.

"May's well have a seat," McShane said. "Might be a while."

"Who is this guy?"

"Name's Dr. Cho. He was head of the Department of Emergency Medicine in Changchun, China. Till he had to flee the country one night. Wound up here."

"And how do you know him?"

McShane gave Preuss a baleful glare, which by now Preuss could interpret as *You know better than to ask.*

Preuss and McShane had been in a scuffle outside a nightspot in Detroit the previous year. McShane took a bullet and afterwards insisted Preuss drive him here to get patched up instead of a hospital.

That time it had taken less than an hour for Dr. Cho to fix him up. This time, however, Dr. Cho didn't reappear for more than an hour and a half.

Dr. Cho motioned for McShane to come closer. They put their heads together and Dr. Cho explained something in rapid-fire Chinese.

When they were finished speaking, Dr. Cho gave Preuss a curt nod and returned to the room on the other side of the sliding doors.

"What was that all about?" Preuss asked.

"He said the guy we brought in is in bad shape. Cho fixed up the wounds without any problem. But he said the kid's suffering from malnutrition and appears to be in the throes of a full-blown psychotic episode. Wants to keep him here for a little while to stabilize him."

"And you said okay?"

"Of course. What good is he going to be in this condition? The better shape Cho gets him in, the more useful he'll be, no?"

"Our chief suspect is going to stay here, unguarded?"

"Preuss," McShane said, "you don't know Dr. Cho, right? I do. So trust me on this one. There's no way anybody's getting into this house."

"If you say so."

"I do. Now take me back to the gas station so I can go home and get out of these clothes. I hate the smell of blood."

59

Toby was sitting up in his reclining chair when Preuss got to his house. Propped up by pillows so he wouldn't fall over sideways, Toby was holding one of his toys in his stiff hands. It was a rabbit with long flexible arms and legs that he could get his stiff fingers around to hold. One of the nurses had given it to him for an Easter present a few years ago and it was one of his favorites.

"Hey, sweetheart," Preuss said. He leaned over and gave his son a noisy kiss on the side of his head.

Toby yelled. Seeing his son for the first time in what seemed like weeks, after the day he had, Preuss felt like yelling, too.

He sat on the side of the bed opposite Toby's chair and massaged his son's feet. Like his hands bent at the wrists, Toby's feet were bent inward at the ankles from his cerebral palsy.

"How the heck are you?" Preuss asked. "Did you forget you had a father?"

Toby gave him a broad crooked smile.

Preuss's heart melted.

After dropping McShane off at the Shell station, Preuss drove home and showered and changed. His clothes, like McShane's, were drenched in Larry Bright's blood. He stuffed them in a plastic bag and left them in the trash can in his garage.

Then he went to Toby/s. If ever he needed a Toby fix, it was tonight.

Melissa the aide told Preuss Toby was waiting for the bathroom to be free so he could have his bath. Preuss told him what his day had been like . . . a day that started at four in the morning in Grace Poole's bed—though Preuss left out this part when he narrated his day's events.

He also didn't mention coming under fire twice. He didn't know how much Toby understood, or if he even knew what a gun was, but Preuss always assumed Toby understood everything; he didn't want to upset his son by talking about how his life had been in danger this day not once but twice.

And how foolish he was, he thought now, sitting with his son, rubbing Toby's thin legs.

What would become of Toby if something happened to me, he thought. If some stupid derring-do went bad and Preuss was killed? His son would be left alone, with no one to care for him but strangers for the rest of his life.

The sorrow he kept at arm's length—over his wife, before and after she died; over Jason; over all the mistakes he had made in his life—it all now combined with his guilt over his own recklessness and came close to overwhelming him.

But being with Toby always calmed him and gave him a way to redress the sadness. And talking about his crazy day helped to put it in the past. For Toby, there was only the now, and for Preuss when he was with Toby only *now*—the time he was spending with his son—should matter.

Melissa stuck her head in the room. "Bathtub's free," she sang.

"I'll get him undressed," Preuss said.

"I'll run the water."

This was another part of being with Toby that Preuss loved, the comforting rituals of caring for his son: getting the Hoyer lift canvas sling underneath him, attaching it to the ceiling extension, hoisting Toby into the air (which Toby also enjoyed as he hung and swung by the hooks), getting him on the bed, unhooking the sling, undressing him, getting the mesh bath sling under him, reconnecting it to the ceiling tracks . . . all to give his son what he most enjoyed in the world, the full-body stimulation of a hot bath.

Once he got Toby into the tub in the large bathroom down the hall, Preuss scrubbed him and then let him soak, the whine of the Jacuzzi jets making Toby laugh and the force of them rocking him in the water. Watching his son enjoy his bath was almost as relaxing for Preuss as if he had taken the bath himself.

After a while, Toby gave one great shiver; he was starting to get cold. Preuss got him out of the bath and into his chair wrapped in his bathrobe, then back in bed. Melissa stepped in to get Toby dried off and lotioned, and into a fresh diaper and his pajamas.

Then the nurse came to give Toby his night meds and his evening fillup of his formula nourishment.

By the time Preuss tucked Toby in, his son was sound asleep.

Preuss put Judy Collins on the CD player, kissed the boy goodnight, and went home.

60

He stood at the counter in the kitchen, drinking a glass of water. The crack of the guns still rang in his head, and the acrid bite of the smells hung sharp in his nose. Now that he was home by himself, his stomach was roiling in the aftermath of the adrenaline rush.

He had been in a few gunfights earlier in his career with the Ferndale police, so this was not new to him. You don't think about the danger in the midst of the battle because the adrenaline is pumping hard; it's afterward, standing at the sink in the peace and quiet of your empty house, when you start to reflect on what happened, and how close you might have come to death.

And leaving your precious son all alone in the world.

He put the glass in the dishwasher and wandered around downstairs, turning off all the lights he'd turned on earlier. He sat on the sofa in his living room in the dark, a rhombus of light streaming in through the living room window from the streetlamp outside.

With his wife dead, his older son gone who knew where, and his younger son in a group home taken care of by people paid minimum wage to do it, he sat in the darkness and silence and felt the sounds in his head quiet as his loneliness closed in on him. He shut his eyes and let his head loll back on the sofa cushion with his arms outstretched. He focused on breathing for a few minutes, hoping to relax enough to sleep tonight.

But he couldn't. He kept hearing the gunfire. The sounds of the bullets thunking into the side of the truck he hid behind.

Seeing the bodies fall.

Feeling now the cold fear he would be one of them.

His phone was in the kitchen, where he had plugged it in to charge when he got home.

He went in and unplugged it and punched in Grace Poole's number.

"Hey," she answered. Her voice was husky and sleepwarm.

"Hey," he said. "Did I wake you?"

"Yeah."

"Sorry."

"S'all right. Glad you called."

"How are you?"

"Oh, don't ask. You?"

"You definitely don't want to ask."

"Bad day?"

"Uh-huh."

"Still working on Charlie Bright?"

"Yeah."

"How's it going?"

"Coming together."

"See, when you have a bad day, I'm guessing it's more than boring meetings with your faculty colleagues."

"I guess it is."

"It's more like, 'Drop the gun, Louie!'"

When Preuss didn't reply—it was too close to what McShane had said to Eddy Slovenic—she said, "Oh man. Maybe I don't want to know after all."

"No," he said, "I don't think you do. Not today, anyway."

"It didn't have anything to do with that thing up in Helmford, did it?"

At once he was alert.

"What thing?"

How did she know about that?

"I was at Suzy's having a drink after dinner," she said, "and there was a report on her TV. There was some kind of shootout at a house up there."

He said, "I haven't seen any news reports tonight." Not answering her question, but the truth.

"Yeah. What's weird is, I recognized the name of the guy who owns the house. He's a known white nationalist. That's what Charlie was working on when he died."

"What do you mean?"

"He was writing a book about white nationalists. I helped him with it. I got some data for him. And he showed me a couple of chapters."

"I thought he was retired."

"He was. But he was going to make this his last project."

Which turned out to be true, Preuss thought, in a way Bright never intended.

"What was he going to do?" he asked.

"Write a history of the white power movement in Michigan," she said. "He was going to go back to the era of the Ku Klux Klan and the Black Legion in the beginning of the twentieth century, and trace it up to the hate groups operating around the state today. In the excerpt I saw, he named names. Not just the members of the white nationalist hate groups, but he was also going to trace how they're spreading everywhere. He was going to identify people in police departments, in the military, in the state legislature, judges, journalists, evangelical ministers . . . He said they're making inroads everywhere."

Preuss thought about this in silence.

"He used to say it's like an octopus with tentacles throughout society," Grace went on. "He used to tell me, 'If we don't stop them now, we won't be able to stop them tomorrow.' That's why he was going to be specific about who's involved."

"Is there a backup copy of the manuscript anywhere?"

"No. Just on his computer."

Which was destroyed when he was killed, Preuss thought.

Then, to change the subject, she asked, "Is a day like today normal for you?"

"No. This was an untypical day in almost every respect."

"Glad to hear it. But sorry you had to live through it."

I'm not sorry I lived through it, he thought, considering the alternative. But he didn't say it out loud.

She sighed. He heard her bedclothes rustle. He had a sharp sense memory of how she smelled, her perfume and the tang of her sweat. The feel of her skin.

"Want to come over?" she asked.

"I do. But this isn't a good night."

"That's fine."

"Sorry."

"No, don't worry. I have to go to Chicago in the morning. I'm giving a paper at a conference. I'll be away for the weekend. I should get some sleep tonight anyway."

"Yeah. Me, too." If I can, he thought.

They were both silent. He could hear her breathing.

Then he said, "Last night was nice."

"It was. Nicest night in a while."

They were both silent again until she said, "Was it strange?"

He thought for a moment, then said, "Yeah. You're the first woman I've been with since my wife died. Was it strange for you?"

"Yeah. But maybe not the way you mean. I've been with lots of guys. After my husband died, I went a little crazy. But it was different with you."

He thought she seemed troubled by that fact—as if with their developing intimacy, she has been unfaithful to her husband's memory.

He felt something similar—that he was being unfaithful not to Jeanette's memory, but to the vow of unhappiness he had been living with since she died.

"You feel like you betrayed his memory?" he asked.

"Yeah. I do."

"That going to be a problem?"

"No," she said, but she waited a long time before saying it.

And she qualified it right away. "Maybe. Maybe it is."

Okay, he thought. Is this where the pull-back starts? Reel me in, push me away? The Janie Cahill Relationship Strategy.

Still, in the silence between them he felt the heaviness of her heart.

"All right," he said, "we'll talk more about this another time."

"Okay."

"I'll let you get back to sleep. I just wanted to hear your voice."

"I got to hear yours, too. We'll talk when I get back from Chicago."

"Deal."

They said goodnight and disconnected.

He went into the dining room, where his laptop sat on the table. He turned on the light and opened the computer and went to the *Detroit Free Press* website. The top story was "Fatal Shootout in Helmford."

A mistaken address in Helmford today left a tragic bloodbath in its wake.

The rest of the article contained nothing about Larry Bright, or Preuss or McShane. Or Kevin Johnson as a white nationalist. Instead, he read:

> *Helmford police say today's violence was the result of an attempted robbery gone wrong.*
> *"We believe the perpetrators got the address mixed up," said Helmford police chief John Morton. "The robbers meant to hit someone else's home."*

Preuss was relieved to read that Kevin Johnson wasn't dead, but was listed as serious but stable condition in St. Joseph Mercy Livingston Hospital.

The article portrayed him as a heroic homeowner fighting off the confused crooks to protect his home.

Preuss closed the laptop and returned to the sofa, where he stretched out and closed his eyes again. McShane was right. They're already covering it up.

Lying about what happened. Reframing the entire event. The white nationalist was now courageous.

Disgusted, he went upstairs, showered, and got into bed.

Instead of sleeping, however, he found himself replaying the waking nightmare that was his day.

Friday, March 8, 2013

61

Toby!

He jumped awake, his heart racing, and grabbed for his iPhone on the nightstand.

Not Toby's caretakers.

Unknown number.

McShane's raspy voice.

Saying, "Preuss, I talked to Cho. He wants us to come out and see the kid."

"What's the matter?"

"He didn't say. Just said to come."

"Want me to pick you up?"

"No need. I'm in your kitchen."

Preuss threw on Levis and a hoodie. Sure enough, Franklin McShane was sitting at the dining room table. He was looking through Preuss's laptop.

"What are you doing?" Preuss said.

"You leave your laptop here so anybody can walk in and steal your identity?"

"Like you, for instance?"

"Preuss, trust me, out of all the identities I'd want, yours isn't one of them. I'm checking your history. You read what they're saying about Helmford."

"Yeah," Preuss said. "You called it. The cover-up is already in place."

"Told you. These cockroaches are everywhere."

Preuss closed the laptop and took it away from McShane.

"You talk about government intrusion," Preuss said, "and you're the one snooping around."

"Hey," McShane said, "you left it open, you're asking for it. You think the NSA and the FBI aren't already watching you? They can get into your computer faster than you can."

"I don't want to hear it," Preuss said, and went in to pour a cup of the coffee McShane had already made.

"That's the problem with you people," McShane said. "You don't want to hear how the government's already infiltrated your lives. And once the fascists completely undermine our democratic institutions—and it won't be long—it's going to be worse than you ever thought possible."

It was true, Preuss didn't want to hear about it from McShane, and sure didn't want to get into this with him. McShane was one of those people whose minds can never be changed. Or even shaken in any way. They're convinced they're the smartest people in every room.

Though in this instance, Preuss had to admit McShane was probably right.

"Bring your coffee," McShane said. "Cho's waiting."

Dr. Cho led them through the sliding pocket doors and into the living room of the flat. In the daylight, Preuss saw it was a typical parlor in an 1920s home that led into a dining room with a coffered ceiling.

Cho pushed through a plastic curtain dividing the dining room from the back of the flat and they were in a medical suite. There were three ten-by-ten rooms, each of which was set up with a hospital bed and medical equipment.

Judging by the beeps and whirs Preuss heard, at least two of the rooms were in use.

In one, Larry Bright lay in bed on his side. His eyes were closed. An IV line attached to his arm snaked up to a machine that wheezed a rhythym from a Rolling Stones song.

Some kind of ventilator

Some kind of ventilator

The three men crowded into the small room.

"How's he doing?" Preuss asked, his voice low.

"Don't need to whisper," Cho said. "He asleep. Not wake up so easy."

"But how is he?"

"As you see, resting. I give him a sedative after I fix his wound. He start to rant and I thought he hurt himself. In my opinion, he need more care than I can give. Not set up for long-term psychiatric care. That is what he needs."

"What was he ranting about?" Preuss asked.

"Couldn't make sense of it. Let me ask my daughter. Yu Yan?"

A young Chinese woman came out of one of the other rooms. She was wearing a white lab coat with a stethoscope hanging from one of the side pockets. She inclined her head to Preuss and McShane and Cho spoke to her in Chinese.

She nodded. "Yes," she said to Preuss and McShane. "I was here when he was brought in. I heard what he was shouting about."

Her English was good, better than her father's though she still spoke with a heavy accent.

"Could you tell what he was saying?" Preuss asked.

"Mmm," she said, "it was very hard to understand. But I believe he was shouting about his father."

"Do you remember what he was saying?"

"Mmm, I thought he said something like, 'They killed my father. I saw them kill my father.'"

"That's what he said? He saw his father killed? Not *he* killed his father?"

"Mmm, no," Yu Yan said, "I'm quite certain he said he saw his father killed. And he was shouting, 'No! No! Don't! Don't!' Then he became very agitated and the sedative my father gave him started to take effect and he quieted down. Then he fell asleep."

"Sound like hallucination," Cho said.

"His father was killed a few weeks ago," Preuss said.

"Could still be hallucination, think he saw it happen," Cho said.

"Or if he did see," Yu Yan said, "that might have been enough to push him into this psychotic episode. On top of his malnutrition and other mental or emotional problems he was having, along with the stress of being homeless. He was having an episode last night."

"How long can you keep him here?" McShane asked.

"I keep him here for long time," Cho said, "but I say, not set up for psychiatric care. The sooner he get someplace for treatment, better for him."

"May I get back to my other patient?" Yu Yan asked.

Cho nodded and said something to her in Chinese. She responded in Chinese, then said goodbye to Preuss and McShane and returned to the back of the house.

Preuss stood looking at Larry Bright. His face in repose was peaceful compared to his distress in the other times Preuss had seen him.

Cho led them out of the room and back through the plastic strips to the dining room.

"How much is his care costing here?" Preuss asked Cho.

The doctor and McShane shared a glance.

"Don't worry about it," McShane said.

"What does that mean?"

"I take care of Cho's fees."

McShane glared at Preuss under the brim of his ballcap, daring him to ask how he was taking care of it.

One more thing about McShane that wasn't worth asking about.

Sitting in the Explorer, Preuss said, "We have to get this guy into a program someplace."

"I'll make some calls," McShane said. "Does he have any next of kin?"

"He does."

"Maybe they can help with the payment."

"Maybe."

Larry's closest relation was Ken Krempka.

"Then again," Preuss said, "maybe not."

62

Rhonda was on the phone when Preuss got in, explaining an invoice to a client. She raised a hand in greeting.

After dropping McShane off, Preuss had stopped at a Tim Horton's to pick up two bagels. He left one at her desk.

He settled into his office and brought his Bright case notes up to date. He remembered what William Warnock, the former police chief in Ferndale, said to him after a close call during the Kaufman investigation: "You're getting to be quite the action hero."

He heard Warnock's voice in his head again as he described the previous day's work.

Let's try to stop doing this, he told himself.

Rhonda stuck her head in his office. "Thanks for the bagel."

"My pleasure."

"I have a Detective Juhasz on the phone for you. He's from the Utica Police Department. Are you in?"

"I am."

He connected on the office line. "Albert."

"Hey Martin," Juhasz said. "How you doing?"

"Hanging in. What's up?"

"I had an employee of yours in here."

"Angie," Preuss said.

"Yup. She had a tale to tell."

"Okay," Preuss said. He braced for whatever Detective Albert Juhasz was going to tell him.

"Thing is," Juhasz said, "she broke the case for us."

"Excuse me?"

"You sound surprised."

Gobsmacked, more like.

"I am."

"Yeah, she came in with a story about seeing somebody dump what she thought was a body in a trash bag. And it turned out she *did* see this guy dump a body. We picked him up and he told us the whole story."

"Phil Ruhle?"

"Yeah. Your girl brought us what we needed. We went down to the creek site and found trace evidence to justify bringing him in. Once we told him what we knew, he crumpled right away."

"I'll be damned."

"Turns out this guy's an ex-priest. Nuts, eh? Has a compulsion for killing prostitutes. I guess it has something to do with his mother."

"Doesn't it always."

"No, I'm serious. A lot of these guys, they can't explain why they do what they do. But this guy seemed to know he had a hatred for women he just couldn't control. Very articulate about it, in fact."

"Just what you want in a priest."

"What triggered it, his mother died last year. And that seemed to free him up to follow his compulsions. So anyway, I wanted to let you know. And say thanks for sending your gal our way."

"Glad it helped."

"I owe you one, buddy."

They disconnected and Rhonda appeared in his doorway again

"Did you hear that?" he asked. He told her what Juhasz said

"Damn," was all she could say.

"Can you give her a call and let her know?" he asked.

"It'll make her day."

"Thanks, Rhonda."

It put a slightly different face on Angie Sturmer, he thought. He might have to revisit hiring her as a stringer.

He tried to turn his thoughts back to the Bright case, but couldn't get past what Juhasz said about Phil Ruhle and his compulsive hatred of women.

He put his head in his hands. He felt as if hatred were polluting the air everywhere. Hatred of women, hatred of Jews, hatred of blacks. Hatred of Arabs. Hatred of parents by children.

Hatred was one of the three poisons the Buddhist teacher, Roshi Ross, had talked about. Kindness and compassion were antidotes against it.

What were the other two poisons?

Ignorance and avarice.

Delusion and desire.

Versus wisdom and generosity.

How's that working out for us so far, Preuss thought.

He couldn't take sitting at his desk for another minute. He stood and told Rhonda he was going for a walk to clear his head.

"Are you okay?" she asked.

"I will be."

Outside at the far end of the parking lot the building management had placed a picnic table and two benches for workers to have their lunches in nice weather. It was too cold to come out now so no one was there.

Preuss sat and thought about hatred.

Specifically, a child's hatred for his father.

He returned to the question of who killed Charlie Bright.

Reg (and Emma, speaking of hatred) thought the employee at Wendy's did it. Preuss still doubted it.

Did Larry Bright do it? Preuss had first thought Larry Bright killed his father, and Ken Krempka put him up to it. But what Preuss had learned over the past few days threw doubt on that. Larry Bright might not have killed his father after all.

Preuss didn't think he had the wherewithal to pull off such a complicated and bloodthirsty act. Besides, what Yu Yan said he had been hollering would suggest he might have been there, but didn't do the job himself.

Then who did?

The next best suspect was Ken Krempka, the closet white nationalist who hated his Jewish stepfather. Krempka had a good alibi for the time of his stepfather's death. He was in charge of a large fundraising event; a hundred people could vouch for him.

But could they? Could there have been any time when Krempka might have snuck out and gone into Ferndale?

He went back to his office and searched through the piles on his desk for the program and DVD Krempka had given him.

He read through the program again, then put the DVD into the slot on his laptop to play it.

The opening credits said it was a production of the Woodbrooke Academy Media Center. It was a professional-looking creation, with high production values, good camerawork, and sophisticated editing. Not surprising, considering these girls would have had access to the latest and best equipment and the finest teachers.

Ken Krempka was present in almost every shot, from the introduction to the closing benediction. Assuming the medical examiner's estimate of Charles Bright's time of death was correct, there was no way Krempka could have killed his stepfather.

Even if the medical examiner had gotten it wrong by a few hours one way or the other, Krempka would still be out of the picture. Krempka said he was at school by seven in the morning and left at six in the evening, which would be easy to check. He wouldn't have had enough time to get to Ferndale, kill Charles Bright, and get back to school again.

Preuss went through the video one more time, going slower and faster in different spots as he did. There were lots of scenes of the crowd.

He studied the faces at the round tables filling the gymnasium. The guests were mostly white, grey-haired, and well-off, with the shine of money around them.

Which was what he would expect. The school was an exclusive upper-class girls' school in one of the wealthiest suburbs in the country.

And what are you going to learn from this, he asked himself as he watched it again. Ken Krempka couldn't have done the crime himself.

Could he have arranged for it? Sure, easily. Any number of thugs in the movement would have done the job on Charles Bright, and Preuss had evidence of Krempka's connection with white nationalists (though not the American Identity Brigade specifically).

Absent Krempka, Charlie also could have been a victim of the kill squad that Douglas the UC mentioned.

Yet the manner of Charles Bright's death was what was described on Krempka's posting on the neo-Nazi website. Krempka had to have some involvement.

In the video, the camera panned across two, then three, then four tables. Then the lights went down and a ten-minute video about the athletic program at Woodbrooke started. That video, too, had been produced by the Woodbrooke Academy Media Center.

Preuss paused the DVD and backed it up to the section that panned across the tables. He slowed down the playback to frame-by-frame and studied the faces.

He froze the image at one of the tables. Sitting there enjoying a cup of coffee was a woman he thought he recognized.

The more he looked, the more he realized it was her.

Ken Krempka's sister.

Gloria—formerly Cecille—Krempka.

63

Preuss zoomed in. The image blurred a bit, but the camera they used must have been a fine one because the image was still clear, even paused and enlarged. He was certain the woman at the table was Gloria Krempka. He recognized her weather-toughened face and the set of her jaw.

What was she doing there?

He examined the others sitting with her. She sat next to an empty chair, but he didn't recognize anyone else at the table.

Now he went back to the beginning of the program. He fast-forwarded and searched for her, and saw her again in another series of shots of the crowd. During one of the breaks between presentations, Preuss saw her standing talking with her brother Ken and several other men.

Definitely Gloria.

Preuss went forward at double-speed, now on the alert for her. When it came to the video on the athletes, he skipped ahead. He knew there wouldn't be any shots of the attendees while the video played.

In this way, he went through the entire three hours of the recording and saw her again several times later in the program.

Except after the athletes' video, the seat next to her was occupied by a bulky man with a bald head.

Preuss paused the playback and examined him.

He had seen this guy before.

He tried to remember if he had been one of the trio protecting Ruth Anne Krider, but he didn't think so.

He could have been the man Preuss had seen for a second when he spoke with Gloria Krempka at the dairy farm. Then he was wearing a bulky jacket and a watch cap, so Preuss couldn't tell if he was bald.

He guessed this was Hugo Zimmer from the build and the shape of his face. He was also deep in conversation with Gloria every time they were on camera in the video.

At one point, Preuss watched the man eat the dessert in front of him—a chocolate cake—then he ate Gloria's. Then he ate a piece that someone at the table had left uneaten.

Gloria had said her partner would eat only sweets if he had the chance.

So Hugo Zimmer was at the luncheon, too.

When had he slipped in?

Preuss watched the video through to the end, and Hugo Zimmer was present in all the final scenes. But he was not there during the first two-thirds of the program, Preuss was certain.

Ken Krempka had said the program started at eleven. Preuss checked the time code on the DVD, and tried to figure out what time Zimmer had slipped in, assuming a start around eleven.

Preuss calculated Zimmer would have taken his seat at roughly 1:30.

There were a thousand possible reasons for him to be there, and to be late.

Only one interested Preuss.

Driving from Ferndale to the Bloomfield Hills school took a half hour; Zimmer could have left Ferndale as late as one o'clock to make it to the school by 1:30.

More than enough time to kill Charles Bright within the ME's timeframe.

But why would he kill Bright?

Preuss searched for the file Sylvia Bloom had given him. Rhonda left it where she had found it when he asked her for it, under other files on Preuss's cluttered desk.

He found the page with the list of known associates of the American Identity Brigade. He went through them, starting at the end of the alphabet working toward the front.

And there was the name: Hugo Zimmer, address in North Lakeport.

Next to his entry, Zimmer was listed as Secretary of the Defense Force, American Identity Brigade, and a minister in the Christian Nation United movement.

If Gloria Krempka was a rabid anti-Semite, it made sense her partner was, too. She hated her stepfather enough to change her name and live with her aunt rather than live with her mother and her mother's Jewish husband. Would she have hated him enough after all these years to convince her partner to kill him?

Or would he have his own reasons for doing it?

He called Sylvia Bloom at the ADL.

She was in.

"Sylvia," he said, "it's Martin Preuss."

"Martin. How are you coming with your case?"

"A question came up and I'm hoping you can help me with it. Have you heard of the Christian Nation United movement?"

"Of course."

"What can you tell me about them?"

"Wow. They're from the nuttiest wing of the nut-job movement. They're a quasi-religious, blatantly anti-Semitic and racist organization. They believe white Europeans, not Jews, are the true descendants of the Lost Tribes of Israel. They believe Jews are Satan's spawn, literally. The editor of the *Dearborn Independent*, William J. Cameron, was an influential thinker in the group early on."

"That's Henry Ford's paper?"

"Right. The weekly put out by Ford in the twenties. At one time, it had a circulation of almost a million around the world. Ford's anti-Semitic ideas influenced Hitler through that paper. Hitler gave Ford Nazi Germany's highest decoration for foreigners, the Grand Cross of the German Eagle. Numerically, Christian Nation United are small now, but they've influenced a lot of white power ideologies. Why are you asking? Have you come up against them?"

"They've made an appearance in my case."

"Watch yourself, Martin. They're dangerous. They're *all* dangerous."

He thanked her and they disconnected.

So Hugo Zimmer bridged the American Identity Brigade and Christian Nation United. To know how to kill Charles Bright in the way Ken Krempka described it, he would have needed access to all the white nationalist hate sites on the web, including the one where his brother-in-law Ken Krempka described in detail how Jews and blacks should be killed.

Possibly Zimmer was a member of Krempka's terror squad. What did he call it?

Preuss searched through his case notes to find where he had seen the article by "Hans Goring."

American Identity Warriors. Was Zimmer part of that?

But the instructions on the web site were so precise, and Bright's body matched them so well.

Could Zimmer have written those articles himself?

Preuss had assumed Krempka was "Hans Goring," but maybe he wasn't . . . maybe Hugo Zimmer was.

He searched through the web sites to find the photo of Gloria Krempka and her brother in *VolksGuard*, the one where he thought he saw Ken identified as "Hans Goring."

In the photo, they were standing among a group of people. Next to Gloria was her brother Ken. The man on the other side of Gloria in the photo was the same man sitting with her in the Woodbrooke Academy video.

Hugo Zimmer.

Preuss reread the caption.

It wasn't clear if "Hans Goring" was on her left or right.

So he got it wrong. Ken Krempka wasn't "Hans Goring," as Preuss first assumed. Gloria's partner was.

If Hugo Zimmer wrote the article describing the technique of how to kill a minority, maybe he also killed Charles Bright to demonstrate it.

Even so, questions remained: why Bright? Why now? Why would Zimmer kill Charles Bright? What was the trigger?

Preuss read through the entire case file again.

On a hunch he went to the website of the *Flint Journal*, Flint's newspaper.

He spent a tedious hour searching through the archives for the previous year.

Then it jumped out at him.

He called McShane, who didn't answer. As usual. Preuss left a message and asked for a call back as soon as he got this.

He called Reg Trombley. That call went to voicemail as well.

Rhonda was at her desk. "I tried Angie, but she wasn't there," she said. "I left a message."

"Okay. Listen, I'm going up to North Lakeport."

"Where on earth is that?"

"Up near Port Huron. If you should hear from McShane or Reg Trombley, tell them this is where I'm going to be and I'm going to need their help."

He handed her a slip of paper with the address on it.

"Who's up there?" she asked.

"One of the white nationalists."

"And you're going there by yourself?"

"No, if either or both call back, tell them to meet me there."

"Martin, I wish you wouldn't do this."

"It'll be fine. I'm not going to do anything stupid."

"What if they don't call back?"

He said nothing in reply, but raised a hand in farewell.

That was a good question.

Preuss wasn't sure he had an answer.

Yet.

64

He exited the highway onto the road toward North Lakeport and pulled over. He tried calling McShane and Trombley again.

Again, neither answered.

And neither had called him back.

Preuss didn't need to debate with himself the wisdom of continuing on to the Zimmer Dairy Farm alone. There was nothing wise about it, he knew, especially after chastising himself about the danger of these kinds of solo heroics.

But—he argued with himself—he wasn't going to try to arrest Hugo; he no longer had that power. He just wanted to talk with him, to see if he could pin down the answers to some questions—so when he did take this to Trombley, he would have it all wrapped up for him.

And you're already out here, so . . .

He continued on to the farm.

He passed the laughing cow sign—which now seemed macabre rather than jaunty—and drove down the long entrance driveway. He stopped in the apron between the barn and the house. He heard the lowing of cows as he stepped out of the Explorer.

No one was waiting to greet him this time. He looked into the barn. The pungent smell of cattle. They all turned their heads to examine the strange human, then went back to their cow business of stomping and mooing. No one was with them.

He approached the door of the farmhouse and it swung open. Gloria Krempka came outside. She wore a layer of hoodies and hugged herself against the cold.

"You again," she said. "What are you doing here? I told you the last time, I got nothing more to say to you."

"I came to ask you a question, Gloria. I saw you in the video of the luncheon at Ken's school a few weeks ago."

"So?"

"What were you doing there?"

"You came all the way out here to ask me that?"

"You're not an alum of the school, are you?"

"No way."

"So what were you doing there?"

"If you must know, I was invited."

"By your brother?"

She nodded.

"What for?"

"The farm's making a big donation to the new gym. He asked me and Hugo to come as a guest."

"Why was Hugo late getting there?"

She huffed in exasperation. "I'm tired of talking to you. And I'm cold. Whyn't you get back in your car and get outta here?"

She turned away and opened the door to the house.

"I didn't come to talk with you anyway," he said. "I came to see Hugo."

"Hugo?" She turned back and watched him with suspicious eyes. "What for?"

"Is he here?"

"No."

"Do you know where he is?" Preuss edged closer.

"As a matter of fact, he's with the men's group from his church."

That made Preuss laugh out loud.

"The First Church of Jesus Christ Racist?" Preuss took another step toward her, unconvinced Hugo wasn't home.

Gloria reached back into the house and came out with a shotgun. She sighted down the barrel at him. "Hold it right there."

He stopped. "Planning to shoot me?"

"If you don't get off my property right now, I just might. And the law'd be on my side."

"If not the law, then the lawmen."

He heard a car barreling down the long driveway behind him. Expecting Hugo, he turned and was surprised to see instead a dark blue Honda Odyssey skid to a stop a few yards from him.

The driver's side door opened and Angie Sturmer came out and knelt behind the door pointing a Ruger Scout rifle out the open window at Gloria.

"Drop your weapon," Angie yelled.

Gloria looked at her as though wondering what planet she had just landed from.

Preuss did much the same thing.

"Who's *that?*" Gloria asked him.

"Reinforcements," he said.

"I got your back, Mr. Preuss," Angie called.

Gloria never moved the gun barrel away from Preuss. She resettled her feet.

"Then you can *both* get the hell off my property," she said. "I'll shoot you both for trespassing."

"Don't do it," Angie warned.

Preuss held a hand out to restrain her. Don't let this get out of hand, he silently pleaded with her.

"Gloria," Preuss said, "I know what happened between Hugo and your stepfather in Flint."

She lowered her weapon. "He wasn't my stepfather. He wasn't nothing to me."

"He was something, even if you don't want to admit it."

She hawked and spit on the ground. "That's what he was."

"Charles Bright didn't do a thing to you, Gloria. He loved your mother, and he would have loved you and Ken, if you'd given him a chance."

"Neither one of us wanted anything to do with that Jew bastard."

"Why? Because you hated what he was and stood for? Kindness? Decency? Compassion?"

"Decency? Last time I checked, they're mud people. They need to be *exterminated.*"

She raised her gun barrel as if she were going to exterminate Preuss.

"Don't do it," Angie yelled again.

"I want you off my property," Gloria said. "Now."

Another rumble of vehicles came down the long driveway.

"You wanted to talk to him," Gloria said, "here he is."

Three pickup trucks roared into the clearing where Preuss stood. The trucks pulled around Angie's Honda and surrounded Preuss.

Hugo Zimmer jumped out of the driver's seat in the lead pickup and then five others tumbled out of the other two trucks. They were all armed with AR-15s. Preuss recognized one of the men as Roger, the chubby school guard from Westland, Ruth Anne Krider's boyfriend.

Hugo took a moment to scope out the scene. His eye went from Preuss to Gloria to Angie and back to Preuss.

"What's all this?" he asked.

"They was just leaving," Gloria said.

But Preuss said, "I came to talk with you, Hugo."

"About what?"

"Larry Bright."

Hugo said nothing for a few moments. Then he said, "I heard what you did up in Helmford yesterday." He spoke so low Preuss had to strain to hear him. "You left a mess, they tell me."

"But I got what I came for."

"Not sure coming here was the best idea."

Preuss made a show of looking at all the guns pointing in his direction. As if on cue, a cold light rain began falling.

He decided on a gamble. "Our talk can wait. Larry's safe."

Hugo was silent.

"Like I said, safe. Tomorrow he'll go into a psychiatric program to bring him back from the state he's in. And when he comes out of it, he'll testify about what he saw."

"What's he think he saw?" Hugo couldn't help asking.

"He saw you kill Charlie Bright. And," Preuss added, "saw what you did to Charlie's book."

A look passed between Hugo and Gloria. Having honed his skills at interpreting body language with Toby, Preuss understood it at once. *How does he know about that?* their look said.

Hugo was silent for another moment. "Who's going to believe a whack-job like him?"

"Nobody, now," Preuss said. "That'll change once he's stabilized. He'll tell everybody everything. He's an eyewitness, Hugo. He saw it all."

"He dunno what he's talking about," Gloria put in.

"I think it was purely a matter of chance you ran into Charlie at that demo in Flint," Preuss said, "when you and your bully boys beat him up. Once you and Gloria figured out who he was, and found out what he was up to, you both saw it as your chance to unleash your hatred on him. For different reasons."

"You know what all this is, don't you?" Hugo said. "It's all made-up bullshit. I didn't even know the guy."

"Charlie brought Larry home the night before he died to give him a place to sleep. And the next day Larry saw or heard everything. I think in part that's what drove him over the edge. And once he comes back from the edge? You're toast."

At that, chubby Roger lost his composure. He came forward with his weapon on Preuss. "Say the word, Hugo," Roger said. He was trembling with anticipation at shooting Preuss.

Preuss saw some calculation going on behind Hugo's eyes.

"But Larry's safe for the time being," Preuss said. "I have him someplace safe."

"How about you get out of here before I goddamn shoot you myself?" Hugo said.

Preuss didn't move. Hugo broke the tense silence by firing into the air. The shot got the cows in the barn stamping and lowing in agitation.

"Next one's between your eyes," Hugo said.

"And the one after that's going between yours," Angie shouted.

Every gun pointed at her.

She didn't move.

Preuss raised his hands. "See you around, Hugo."

He turned and walked backwards to where Angie was still in her shooting position behind her car door.

He leaned down to her. "There's a McDonald's on the road to the expressway. Meet me there."

65

Angie was still trembling when she slid into the molded bench across from him. He handed her a Coke and took a sip from his iced tea.

"Thank you," she said.

"Thank *you*."

"Mr. Preuss, I tell you what, I thought we were both goners there."

"You hadn't been there, I might have been."

"Yeah, well, I had no idea I'd be walking into *that*."

"Don't take this the wrong way, because I was happy to see you," he said. "But what were you thinking, coming out here?!"

She took a deep drink of her pop. Her hands were still shaking, but not as much as when she first sat down.

"Rhonda called me," she said. "When I called her back, she goes, 'He's by himself on the way to meet some bad people.' I go, 'What's the address,' because I thought you might need backup."

"I appreciate that."

"Well, Rhonda was worried about you being out here all on your own. And those guys you called to ask for help never called back, so . . ."

"That was a gutsy thing to do. You could have gotten hurt."

"Yeah, well, I didn't know that beforehand."

"I figured Larry Bright was our get-out-alive card," Preuss said. "As much as Hugo wanted to kill me, he wouldn't as long as he didn't know where I had Larry stashed."

"Could have fooled me."

"You showed me something today, Angie."

She smiled. "Thank you, Mr. Preuss."

"Borrow your phone?"

She handed it to him and he took out his own phone, checked a number, and sent a text to it. He handed back her phone.

"What was that?" she asked.

"I just sent an anonymous text to Gloria, telling her the address where Larry Bright is."

"Why?"

"I want her to tell Hugo."

"Won't Hugo go after him there?"

"I hope so."

On the way back to Ferndale, he called Reg Trombley's cell. This time he got through.

"What's up?" Trombley asked.

"Reg. We need to meet."

"Martin," Trombley began.

"No," Preuss said. "Just listen."

66

Half past two in the morning. The neighborhood quiet. Mild for March, in the mid-30s. Here and there patches of snow left over from the previous day's fall. Where the ground showed, a hint of spring in the fumes rising from the damp, warming soil.

The only sound was a pickup cruising down the street, its tires sibilant on the road, still wet from the rain earlier in the day.

A few minutes later, the same truck cruised the street again, slowly this time.

Preuss's house was dark. From a window on the second floor, he watched the pickup make a U-turn at the corner and come back to park several houses down from him.

Two men got out of the truck and eased their doors closed. They slipped down the sidewalk and up the driveway to the rear of Preuss's house. They were big men, one tall, the other shorter and stouter with a belly Preuss recognized.

About time, he thought.

He crossed to look out the back window.

He had installed a motion detector light over the doorwall leading from the rear deck into the house. Both men stood dead still.

He saw one of them raise his hand, but no light went on.

Lucky break, they would think.

Earlier in the evening, Preuss had unscrewed the bulb.

The men stopped at the foot of Toby's ramp leading up to the deck. They examined the back of the house, where a frosted glass window glowed upstairs.

The two men crept up the ramp and paused. The taller one in a dark coat with a knit cap on his head tried to peer into the house. He would see the dining room that the doorwall opened to, and he would see the living room beyond, both dark. He would see through to the kitchen, where the light from the clock on the stove cast an underwater green glow into the room. He wouldn't spot anything else.

From above, Preuss watched the big man try the doorwall. The handle gave a quarter of an inch, then stopped.

He looked at the man next to him. From his vantage point above, Preuss watched as the second man withdrew something from his pocket and stepped up to the doorway. He inserted picks into the lock in the handle, and after a few moments there was a "click." He pulled at the handle and the doorwall slid open a few inches.

Both men waited, holding their breath, and listened for a tell-tale buzz of an alarm.

The big man came around the stouter man and opened the door enough for them both to slip through. Preuss heard the slow roll of the doorwall on its track.

They moved into the house. Upstairs Preuss heard no further noises, but sensed the slight disturbance in air pressure as the strangers slow-walked around.

One of the men opened the door to the basement to a creak of hinges.

The old wood of the steps squeaked as they bore a heavy weight halfway down the steps. Must be the big man. From halfway down the stairway, he would be able to see the entire basement and could tell it was empty.

He came back up the basement stairs and began the slow walk up to the second floor.

More creaking of steps as the shorter man followed.

The house went quiet as both figures paused at the top of the landing. The room with the light on was the bathroom. Three other doors were on the second floor. One door was open, one was closed, and one was ajar.

The intruders started up again. Both pulled handguns from their coats.

From a dark corner behind a curtain in the bedroom with the open door, Preuss watched it all.

The big man stuck his head in and satisfied himself in the light from the bathroom that this room was empty.

Then he pushed open the door that was ajar and stopped. A dim nightlight glowed from a socket.

He turned and nodded to the shorter man. He pointed a finger at the room with a closed door.

The shorter man crossed the hallway and eased open the closed door.

He stepped inside, eyes on a shape on the bed, and closed the door behind him.

A figure materialized out of the shadows inside the room and took him to the ground on his stomach with a foot on his back in one swift and silent move.

Angie Sturmer leaned down to whisper in Roger's ear, "Make a sound and I'll break your neck."

In the room with the nightlight, the big man stood for a moment, looking at the bed. It held a long shape curled up and facing the wall, covered by a blanket.

"So long, Larry," the big man murmured.

He held a suppressed Walther P22. He shot three times into the shape on the bed.

He moved into the room and aimed his gun at the spot where Larry's head would be. He fired twice more.

Hugo Zimmer was about to lean down to take a closer look when Preuss came into the room. Hugo stood straight when he heard footsteps behind him but Preuss slipped a wrist around Hugo's throat before he could turn and pushed him on the lower right side of his back and walked him backwards.

The move dropped Hugo on his ass.

Preuss flipped him on his belly as Reg Trombley came around him and stood on Hugo's gunhand and shoved the barrel of his own gun into the base of Hugo's skull.

"Freeze," he said. "Detective Trombley, Ferndale Police. Let go of the gun."

Hugo turned his head to sneer into the black man's face. "Or what?"

"Or I'll shoot you in the head," Trombley said.

"I don't think you will."

"You sure about that, Hugo? Bet your life on it?"

Preuss could almost hear Zimmer calculating the odds.

Trombley pressed the gun harder against Hugo's head. "Give me an excuse, motherfucker," Trombley said into Hugo's ear.

Zimmer released his weapon. Preuss swept it away.

Trombley cuffed Hugo's hands behind him.

Trombley and Preuss pulled him to his feet and Hugo looked at the shape in the blankets.

Trombley pulled the covers back.

"Pillows," Hugo said.

"Oldest trick in the book," Trombley said. "You white power guys aren't too bright, are you? Hugo Zimmer, I'm arresting you for the murder of Charles Bright."

As Trombley went through the caution, Preuss noticed Angie standing in the doorway watching the action with her mouth open and Roger's gun in a plastic evidence bag by her side.

"Wow," she said. "Just—wow."

In the other room, which was his bedroom, Preuss saw she had Roger on the floor, arms handcuffed behind his back and hogtied to his feet.

Preuss knelt down beside the furious restrained man. "Roger," he said. "Long time no see, man. How you doing?"

67

Angie left—after thanking Preuss for letting her take part—and Preuss walked Trombley to his Taurus parked on the next street.

"So Charles Bright had three children?" Trombley asked.

"One biological son, Larry, and two stepchildren, Ken Krempka and Gloria Krempka. Both white nationalists."

"We interviewed Krempka. Seemed like a slick customer,"

"At first I thought he'd gotten his brother Larry to kill their father," Preuss said. "Larry was in bad shape mentally, and I thought he was open to being manipulated by Krempka, who hated their stepfather. Charles Bright was killed in a ritualistic way described on a white nationalist web site, which I thought was written by Krempka. Then I realized the description wasn't from Ken, it was from Hugo Zimmer. I also realized Larry Bright didn't have the wherewithal to pull off something like his father's murder."

"But Hugo did," Trombley said.

"He did, and he had additional motives. Those papers that were burnt in Charlie's basement? They were a manuscript he was working on when he was killed. He was writing a book that was going to identify members of the white nationalist movements in Michigan, past and present."

"Where'd his information come from?"

"He must have had an informant. The book was going to reveal names of the white supremacists operating in Michigan. He was also going to name their fellow-travelers, the network of racists and anti-Semites who are seeding themselves in institutions across the state."

"For what? A race war?"

"As part of a larger civil war with the goal of establishing the country as an exclusively white Christian nation," Preuss said. "Hugo Zimmer and the rest of the movement didn't want those names exposed. It would have tipped their hand before they were ready."

They stopped at Trombley's car.

"I got word to Hugo I was holding Larry Bright here for the night," Preuss said, "and then he was going into a secure rehab program. I was counting on him wanting to act fast."

"Then he'd come looking for the one person who could name him as Charles Bright's killer," Trombley said.

"Yes," Preuss said.

"So where is Larry?"

"In a safe place. And he's on his way into a treatment program as soon as we find a bed for him."

"Man," Trombley said, "we made a mess of this one."

"You were on the right track. I kept running into people who told me you already talked to them. But Chrysler took the investigation and gave it to Emma Blalock too soon. You didn't have enough time to develop the case."

Trombley agreed.

"But now you know what the best part is?" Preuss asked. "You're going to bring in Charlie Bright's killer yourself."

Saturday, March 9, 2013

68

She didn't want to meet him anywhere near her home, so Preuss suggested the one place he was certain no one would know Ruth Anne Krider: the parking lot of the Stage Deli on Orchard Lake in the heavily Jewish suburb of West Bloomfield.

She pulled into a parking space down the row from him, and waited in her car for a long time. To see if she's been tailed, Preuss thought. She was smart.

When no other cars turned into the lot, the woman fast-walked down to Preuss's Explorer. She opened the passenger door and slipped in.

She did a double take when she saw Toby propped up with pillows in the back seat.

"Who's that?"

"My son," Preuss said.

"I thought you were coming by yourself."

"Toby won't bother you."

Ordinarily he wouldn't have taken Toby with him on anything work-related, but they had more stops to make and Preuss was certain Ruth Anne would not be a threat.

She gave Toby a long look, then turned in her seat and stared straight ahead. "What do you want?"

"It's over," Preuss said. "Charles Bright's killer is in custody."

"So I heard."

"It was Hugo Zimmer. But you knew that."

She kept staring straight ahead.

"I also wanted to tell you I know Charlie was writing a book about the white nationalist movement in Michigan. And I know who his source was."

She was silent.

"It was you," he said.

Then she sighed, whether in relief or distress he couldn't tell.

"I thought I was pretty convincing back at the high school," she said. "Telling you I didn't know the guy."

"We both knew that was more for Roger's benefit than mine. What Charlie was writing about, the level of detail, only somebody deep inside the movement would know. You were the only one who knew Bright who was also an insider."

She remained silent.

"But one thing I couldn't figure out," he said, "was how did Hugo and the American Identity Brigade learn Charlie was writing his book?"

She looked away, across the parking lot.

"Again," he said, "you were the only insider who could have known."

When she said nothing, he said, "Why would you tell them?"

"Dr. Bright was a good guy to me," she said at last. "I heard all this hatred toward Jews and blacks from my brother and all his groups my whole life. But Dr. Bright was the first Jewish person I ever sat down and talked to. And he was a nice man. He got me to think about what the Brigade was doing, and what I was doing to help them."

"That's when you started passing him information?"

"He told me he was writing a book and they were in it. I said I could help him. Except when I saw what Hugo and the others did to him in Flint, how they beat him so badly, I was so angry with them, I couldn't help myself. I told my brother what a stupid thing it was to hurt him because Charlie was writing a book about them all and they were just asking for trouble. I said they'd be sorry for what they'd done."

She was quiet for a long time.

"He was such a nice man," she said. "Everybody else at Wayne was pissed at me for putting up those posters. Not him. He talked to me. He was so kind. I haven't met many people like him."

And what you told your brother got that kind man killed, Preuss thought but did not say. There was no point in pointing it out; she knew it as well as he did.

So the trigger was the altercation between Hugo Zimmer and his thugs and Charlie Bright. If they hadn't beaten Charlie, Ruth Anne wouldn't have told Warren Cattrell about Charlie's book. The retired professor would be alive today.

"So what happens now?" she asked.

"With what?"

"With this. What you know."

"I've taken it as far as I'm going to. The case is over for me. Hugo's in custody. The Ferndale police will get a warrant for your brother's arrest. They'll probably bring Ken Krempka in to consider charges against him. Do you have copies of what you gave Charlie?"

"It wasn't on paper. It was all up here." She tapped her head.

"Why don't you write the book he was going to?"

"Gee, I dunno," she yelled, "maybe because I don't want to wind up like Charlie?"

Her outburst startled Toby, who had been listening quietly to all this. Now he said, "Ummmmm."

Preuss kept silent. He knew her outburst wasn't directed at him.

"The storm is coming, man," she said. "These guys are gaining strength by the day. There's going to come a time in the not-too-distant future when they're going to get enough political cover to come out of the shadows. In a few years, they're going to be marching in the streets."

"You can help make sure that doesn't happen."

She was silent. Finally she said, "I'll think about it."

He gave her a slip of paper with Sylvia Bloom's name and phone number.

"Call this woman," he said. "She'll know what to do with what you know about these guys."

She gave him another quick glance. "Anything else?"

He shook his head. "Take care of yourself, that's all."

She opened the car door and stepped out. Before closing it, she turned and said, "It's not me you should be worrying about, you know that, right?"

"What do you mean?"

She paused with the door half open. Then she opened it all the way and stuck her head back in the car.

"There's a kill list."

What the UC Douglas had talked about.

"I've heard of it," he said.

"It's real. A to-do list for the Brigade's terror squad. Charlie Bright was the first because of his book. But there are a dozen other names on it."

"Whose?"

"Newspaper editors. Reporters. Judges. Politicians. Other people who stand in their way. Maybe now you."

"Who's running it?"

"Hugo was. With him out of commission, the Identity Warriors are on pause. You stopped them for now. But somebody'll start them back up again when the time is right."

She closed the door and returned to her car.

He watched her drive away, then looked in the rearview mirror. In the back seat, Toby had been attending to their entire conversation.

"A kill list," Preuss said.

Toby gave a quiet and ominous hum.

"Toby, you took the words right out of my mouth."

Sam Rifkin and Lloyd Corrigan were waiting at a table inside the Stage Deli. He had asked to meet them there after he set his appointment with Ruth Anne. Preuss wheeled Toby over to where they were sitting. The clergymen stood to shake hands with Preuss, then gathered around Toby.

Who had fallen asleep between Preuss's car and the front door of the restaurant.

"My son, Toby," Preuss said. "He usually loves the commotion here, so he'll wake up in a bit."

"A very handsome young fellow," Rifkin said.

"Very," Corrigan agreed.

Preuss ordered coffee, then, after some talk about Toby and his problems, Preuss explained to his two clients how the Charles Bright investigation ended.

"Poor Charlie," Rifkin said. "No one should have to go through that."

"This'll all be in my final report," Preuss said. "I'll make sure you both get a copy. But I like to sit down with clients and explain things, see if you have any questions about what I found."

"Thank you, Mr. Preuss," Corrigan said. He reached out to shake Preuss's hand again. "Thank you for pursuing this to the end. Manny said you were the right man for the job."

"It was my pleasure to help," Preuss said.

"How d'you do it?" Rifkin asked. "How d'you manage to see what you see and not become jaded about humanity?"

"This guy," Preuss said. He patted his sleeping son on the knee. "He teaches me what's important. It's never money, or power, or personal influence."

"No," Rifkin said. He reached out and laid a hand on Toby's head, as though in blessing. Toby woke up with a snort. "These youngsters are special because of what they bring out in us."

The server came to take their order. Rifkin and Corrigan ordered breakfast, but Preuss said, "Nothing for me, thanks. We have to be in Royal Oak in an hour."

"Royal Oak!" Corrigan said with a wry smile. "Toby likes the hot spots, does he?"

"Lloyd," Preuss said, hoisting his cup for one last sip, "you have no idea."

69

Barton Park, behind the theatre building on Main Street. One of the dozens of small pocket green spaces dotting Royal Oak's urban and residential areas.

He made a U-turn and stopped in front. Sitting on benches under the roof of a gazebo in the center of the park were Grace Poole and the man Preuss knew as Rabbit.

At the sight of Preuss, Grace grinned and waved.

She came down to the car as he was getting the wheelchair out of the back. She wore a black mid-length leather coat and holey black tights where her skin showed through.

"Hey," she said.

"Hey. Doing okay?"

"Better now."

They hugged.

"And who's this young man?" she asked.

She peered into the back seat where Toby was buckled in. At the sound of a woman's voice, Toby—now wide awake—looked for her out of the corner of his eye and gave her one of his crooked grins.

"This is the famous Toby. My son."

"Hey handsome," she said. "I've heard a lot about you."

Toby gave her his flirtiest smile.

"He's heard a lot about you, too," Preuss said.

He set up Toby's chair and hoisted him into it, then lifted up the Red Wings poncho to attach the chest strap and seat belt.

Grace knelt down to Toby's eye level and said, "Your dad told me you were a sweetheart, but he didn't tell me you were so gorgeous. Look at those beautiful brown eyes. I think I'm in love."

Toby tried to focus on her, but his head wag made it hard.

When he made visual contact at last, Toby and Grace exchanged a long glance and then Grace kissed him on the side of his face. The same spot where Preuss himself always kissed him.

Toby wound up with a deep breath and exploded with a loud, long exclamation.

"You made a conquest," Preuss said.

"You speak Toby-ese?"

"Fluently. You're winning over the whole family."

"Need help with anything?"

"If you could grab that case in the back seat?"

Preuss pushed Toby up the hard incline to the ramp leading into the gazebo where Rabbit sat surrounded by his belongings.

"Hey," Rabbit said. "Who this little man?"

"My son Toby."

"Pleased to meet you, Toby," Rabbit said. He reached out and patted Toby's shoulder.

Toby looked for Rabbit but not with the same fervor as he had for Grace.

"Having an outing with your pops?" Rabbit asked Toby.

"He's non-verbal," Preuss said, "so he won't be able to answer."

"That's cool, that's cool," Rabbit said. "We on the same wavelength."

Grace came up behind Preuss carrying the long, flat rectangular case from the car. She gave it to Preuss and he handed it to Rabbit.

"For you," Preuss said.

"What's this?" Rabbit said.

"A gift."

Rabbit opened the case. Inside was a three-tone sunburst Fender Telecaster in a plush molded blue bed.

"Aw man," Rabbit said. "You not giving me this?!"

"I am."

"No, no. I can't accept this."

"Sure you can. It's one of mine. Plays great, but I never play it anymore. I figure you can make better use of it than I can."

Rabbit took his gloves off and picked up the guitar. He held it as though it were delicate. He examined it, sighting down the neck and running a hand over the finish on the back.

"There's other stuff in there, too," Preuss said. He opened the accessory compartment in the case and pulled out a pocket amplifier and a pair of earbuds, and a tiny battery-powered mini amp and cable.

"Thank you, Martin," Rabbit said. "Thank you thank you thank you."

"You're welcome."

"But . . . how'm I gonna hang onto this? This gone get stolen, just like the last one."

"It'll fit in your gig bag," Preuss said. "Pack your clothes around it and nobody'll know it's there."

Rabbit shook his head. He was speechless.

"Give it a try," Grace said. "Let's hear how it sounds."

Rabbit connected the guitar to the mini amp and gave it a quick tune. He turned up the volume on the amp and tossed out a series of slow blues riffs. He bent the high E string up and up and came back down the neck through bends and pull-offs and double-stops to modulate into the opening riff to "I Shot the Sheriff," and from there to a driving reggae version of the song.

Preuss could tell Rabbit was out of practice, but even with fingers stiff from the cold, the man had impressive chops. He would have been a phenomenal guitar player in his prime.

Toby, of course, loved hearing it.

Sitting next to him on the bench, Grace put an arm around Preuss's shoulder. "Finish your case?"

He nodded.

"Caught the bad guy?"

"Yup. Tell you about it later."

They listened to Rabbit play. They were cozy under the gazebo in the pocket park, but it was only temporary, Preuss knew—a respite before the coming storm, as Ruth Anne Krider had said.

That's fine, I'll take it, Preuss thought. Let's learn the lesson from Roshi Toby and be present in this moment.

This rich, eternal moment.

After another minute, Grace leaned into Preuss and put an arm around his shoulder.

"You're a good man, Martin Preuss," she said, and kissed him on the lips. Hers were soft and pillowy and tasted like coffee.

Then she bent toward Toby, sitting in front of them. "And you, my new friend," she told him, "are a chip off the old block."

She gave Toby an extended, noisy, elephant-pulling-its-foot-out-of-the-mud kiss on the side of his face.

Preuss said, "Sandwich kiss," and gave Toby the same kiss on the other side of his face.

A Toby sandwich.

Toby squealed in joy.

The sweetest sound in the world.

Acknowledgements

The characters in this book are entirely fictional, as are the white nationalist organizations mentioned in these pages. The white nationalist movement itself regrettably is not fictional, and as of this writing poses an increasing threat; for information on it, I am indebted to the Anti-Defamation League and the Southern Poverty Law Center, especially Hatewatch.

Warm thanks for their assistance and support in the preparation of this book go to Michael Kitchen, retired police chief of Ferndale, for his ideas about the direction of the book; Steven Patterson, for information on Buddhism, the staff at the Berkley Public Library, where much of this was written; Rich Carnahan of Publish Pros for his cover design artistry; Andrew Lark for his insightful comments on early versions; Karen F. Dimanche Davis for her keen editorial eye; and Virginia Lark Moyer for her editorial expertise.

As always, I thank my late grandson Jamie Kril, for providing the model for Toby and for the abiding spirit that infuses these pages; and my wife Suzanne Allen, whose love and support continue to sustain me.

Finally, my sincere appreciation goes out to the readers who have followed me over the course of this series. Your encouragement has meant more than you can know.

If you enjoyed this book, please consider posting a review on Amazon, Goodreads, or my website, www.donaldlevin.com.

About the Author

Donald Levin is an award-winning fiction writer and poet. Besides the seven Martin Preuss novels, he is the author of *The House of Grins* (Sewickley Press, 1992), a novel; two books of poetry, *In Praise of Old Photographs* (Little Poem Press, 2005) and *New Year's Tangerine* (Pudding House Press, 2007); *The Exile* (Poison Toe Press, 2020), a dystopian novella; and co-author of *Postcards from the Future: A Triptych on Humanity's End* (Whistlebox Press and Quitt and Quinn Publishers, 2019). He lives in Ferndale, Michigan.

To learn more about him, visit his website, www.donaldlevin.com, and follow him on Twitter @donald_levin and Instagram at donald_levin_author.

The Martin Preuss Mystery Series

CRIMES OF LOVE | BOOK 1

One cold November night, police detective Martin Preuss joins a frantic search for a seven-year-old girl with epilepsy who has disappeared from the streets of his suburban Detroit community. Unwilling to let go after the Oakland County Sheriff's Office takes the case from his city agency, he strikes out on his own, following leads across the entire metropolitan region. Probing deep into the anguished lives of all those who came into contact with the missing girl, Preuss must summon all his skills and resources to solve the many crimes of love he uncovers.

THE BAKER'S MEN | BOOK 2

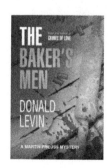

Easter, 2009. The nation is still reeling from the previous year's financial crisis. Ferndale Police detective Martin Preuss is spending a quiet evening with his son Toby when he's called out to investigate a savage after-hours shooting at a bakery in his suburban Detroit community. Was it a random burglary gone wrong? A cold-blooded execution linked to Detroit's drug trade? Most frightening of all, is there a terrorist connection with the Iraqi War vets who work at the store? Struggling with these questions, frustrated by the dizzying uncertainties of the case, and hindered by the treachery of his own colleagues who scheme against him Preuss is drawn into a whirlwind of greed, violence, and revenge that spans generations across metropolitan Detroit.

GUILT IN HIDING | BOOK 3

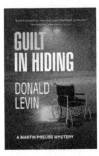

The third entry in the Martin Preuss mystery series finds Preuss called out to search for a van that has disappeared along with the woman who was driving and her passenger, a handicapped young man. Working through layer upon layer of secrets, Preuss exposes a multitude of contemporary crimes with roots in the twentieth century's darkest period. Complex, chilling, and compulsively readable, *Guilt in Hiding* finds Preuss investigating the most disturbing and unforgettable crimes of his career.

THE FORGOTTEN CHILD | BOOK 4

Newly retired from the Ferndale Police Department, Martin Preuss passes his days quietly with his beloved son Toby. When a friend asks him to look for a boy who disappeared forty years ago, the former investigator gradually becomes consumed with finding the forgotten child. Then ex-colleague Janey Cahill persuades him to help her locate the missing father of a troubled young girl. Juggling both cases, Preuss revisits the countercultural fervor of Detroit in the 1970s-and plunges into hidden worlds of guilty secrets and dark crimes that won't stay buried.

AN UNCERTAIN ACCOMPLICE | BOOK 5

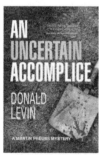

Twenty years have passed since Raymond Douglas went to prison for the kidnapping and murder of a local businessman's wife. Now Douglas's daughter has hired private investigator Martin Preuss to track down a previously unknown accomplice to the crime—who may or may not even exist. But no sooner does Preuss get involved than he finds himself entangled in two murders, a family whose wealth has bought them nothing but trouble, a body discarded in a dumpster, and a web of deceit stretching across metropolitan Detroit from the mega-rich suburbs to a hardscrabble trailer park.

COLD DARK LIES | BOOK 6

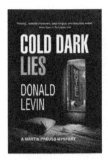

A young man takes a walk on the wild side and ends up clinging to life in a suburban Detroit motel. When private investigator Martin Preuss searches for the reason, he plunges into the young man's dark world of secrets and lies. Questions multiply: How is the young man involved with a missing prostitute? What's the link to a local rap mogul who moonlights as the city's main drug supplier? Why is a stone-cold killer out for revenge with Preuss in his cross-hairs? And—most upsetting of all—why is a local crime boss threatening Preuss's beloved handicapped son?

Made in the USA
Monee, IL
11 October 2020